# PILLOW TALK

Petra Flint and Arlo Savidge were teenage sweethearts in a chaste, old-fashioned way. They never really told each other how they felt. Now, years later, the dreamy and creative Petra is a jeweller by day who crafts beautiful, intricate pieces from precious metals and vibrant gemstones. But by night she is a sleepwalker, never fully able to rest.

Arlo is teaching an an eccentric boys' boarding school in Yorkshire. Like Petra, he carries with him something that makes it hard to sleep at night.

In a tiny ice-cream shop one rainy day, Arlo and Petra stand before each other once again. Is this their second chance? Isn't old gold as good as new? However, for love to blossom, they must finally put their pasts to bed. A past Petra can't quite remember. A past Arlo wants to forget.

# PILLOW TALK

Freya North

**WINDSOR**
**PARAGON**

First published 2007
by
HarperCollins
This Large Print edition published 2007
by
BBC Audiobooks Ltd by arrangement with
HarperCollins Publishers

Hardcover  ISBN: 978 1 405 61912 7
Softcover    ISBN: 978 1 405 61913 4

**British Library Cataloguing in Publication Data available**

Printed and bound in Great Britain by
Antony Rowe Ltd., Chippenham, Wiltshire

*In loving memory of my grandmothers,*
*Grandma Rennie and Grandma Net.*
*Never far from my thoughts*
*and always in my heart.*

By night, Love, tie your heart to mine, and the two together in their sleep will defeat the darkness

Pablo Neruda Love Sonnet LXXIX

# PROLOGUE

Something isn't quite right—I have a hunch about this. But I think I'll just tuck it into the back of my mind while I tuck my feet into my wellington boots. Now I'll open my front door and step out into the night.

I'm ready. Where is it I'm meant to be going? I can't quite remember. It'll come back to me in a moment. I'll just put one foot in front of the other and trust myself. I am turning left. If I am automatically taking this direction to Wherever, this must mean it is the right way to go.

Now where am I? I'm glad I'm wearing my gumboots. That was a good idea. I had to rummage for them as I can't remember when I last wore them. I can't remember when I last had a weekend away from the city. No one has ever whisked me away. Not that I've ever asked—that wouldn't be me. That's not to say I haven't daydreamed of it, though.

But enough of this mental meandering, I must walk on. This way. That way. I don't feel very comfortable. I'm rather cold and my feet feel—strange.

I'm hoping for the landmark to loom, to say to me that I've arrived at my destination. I know metaphysics would say that it's not the arriving but the journey that's the point—but I'm going to have to have a sit-down and a rethink if I don't get there soon. Perhaps I've gone the wrong way. I don't want to admit to myself that I don't really know the route because that would call into question the

1

destination which, actually, I can't remember at all. Well, I'll keep on walking this way. My feet are really sore. I'd love a bar of chocolate. I'm quite tired now. Sleepy, in fact. Something will jog my memory.

*     *     *

It was not Petra Flint's memory that was jogged. It was her slumber. By the police. She woke with a start and in a panic; for a split second she thought she was blind. Actually it was very dark and she was lying face down on the ground. Earthy, itchy ground, and wet.

'Are you OK?'

Petra lifted her head a little and glanced up: two police officers were looming over her. The sudden beam from a torch scorched her eye so she dropped her gaze and put her face back to the ground. She was wearing her nightshirt and her wellington boots, which were on the wrong feet, and she felt mortified. She also felt alarmingly cold. She spat. There was a tickle of grass and a crunch of soil in her mouth. The torch beam wavered. Shit. The police. She scrambled up, whacked by nausea as she did so. Disorientated, she still sensed an urgency to explain because it couldn't look good, to the police, that she'd been found sprawled on the ground in an oversized Snoopy T-shirt and wellies.

'Are you OK?' one officer asked, steadying Petra; the firm arm of the law surprisingly gentle at her elbow.

'Oh, I'm fine,' she told them, hoping to sound convincing but certain she sounded guilty. She looked around her. She recognized nothing. She didn't know where she was. A park. 'Where is this?' She caught the glance that passed between the officers. She just wanted to go home. Warm up. Tuck in tight for a better night's sleep. Better not ask any more questions then, better leave that to the police. Better still, give them answers before they even ask. 'My name is Petra Flint,' she said clearly, 'and I sleepwalk.'

*     *     *

Oh my God, my grandmother is dead. The shrill of the phone woke Rob with a start; his ailing grandmother his primary thought. He grabbed at his watch, noting it was almost three in the morning as he said hullo. He listened carefully, soon enough faintly amused by how he could be relieved it was just the police. Grandma is fine, Rob thought, though he wondered whether he'd now jinxed her life by anticipating her death.

'Yes—Petra Flint,' he said with the measured bemusement of a parent being called before their child's head teacher, 'Petra is my girlfriend. Yes, she is known to sleepwalk—though usually she takes measures to prevent this, keeps herself under lock and key. You found her *where*?'

He scrambled into some clothes muttering that Christ he was tired. As he found Petra's keys and snatched up his own from the mantelpiece, he wondered why somnambulists never managed to subconsciously take their keys when they took off into the night. On one sortie, Petra had filled her coat pockets with onions. On another she had taken the remote control from the television with

3

her, having first removed the batteries and placed them in a careful configuration on the kitchen table. In the ten months Rob had known Petra and on the many occasions she had sleepwalked, only a few times had she made it out into the night yet not once had she taken her keys. Or a penny. Or her phone. And, as he drove off towards Whetstone at the behest of the police, Rob decided that, in this age of mobile telecommunication, it was for sleepwalkers alone that phone boxes still existed, providing shelter and the reverse-charges call until someone arrived to take them home. This was, however, the first time he'd been called by the police.

Her sheepish expression could have been due as much to her Snoopy nightshirt as to the circumstance. Rob thought she looked rather cute, all forlorn and mortified. If he ignored the wellington boots and the dirt on her chin.

'Petra,' he said, raising an eyebrow towards the duty officer, 'what were you *thinking*?'

He always asks me that, Petra thought petulantly. And he never listens when I say I *don't* think, I don't *know*. Somewhere, in the deeper reaches of my subconscious state which I simply cannot access when I'm awake, I obviously thought that this was a very good idea at the time.

She shrugged. 'Do you have my keys?'

'Yes,' he said, 'come on.' He put his fleece jacket around her shoulders and bit his tongue against commenting on her wellington boots. They certainly weren't Pinder's, they weren't even imitations. These were old-fashioned: shapeless tubes of black rubber reaching the unflattering point midway up her bare calves. Tomorrow, he'd

4

see the funny side. Tonight he was tired and a little irritated.

'One day you'll get hurt, you know,' Rob warned her, before starting the car.

My feet really hurt right now, Petra thought, even though each boot was now on the correct foot. 'I'm sorry,' she said, pressing the side of her head hard against the car window, the judder at her temples convincing her she was truly awake, 'I can't remember a thing. I don't know where I was going.'

'So you always say,' Rob nodded. 'Do you mind if I don't come in?' he said, soon pulling up outside Petra's flat. 'I have clients from Japan first thing in the morning.'

'Sorry,' Petra shuffled, 'sorry.'

Rob looked at her, his exasperation softening a little. 'It's all right. It's fine,' he said.

'Goodnight, Petra—and lock your bloody bedroom door.'

# CHAPTER ONE

The first Wednesday in March was going to be a peculiar day for Petra Flint but it would take another seventeen years for her to consider how seminal it had been. Usually, school days were utterly dependable for their monotony, with daytime plotted and pieced into fifty-minute periods of quality education. The reputation of Dame Alexandra Johnson School for Girls and its high standing in the league tables was built on courteous, bright girls achieving fine exam results and entry into Oxbridge and the better Red Bricks. The school was sited in a residential street just off the Finchley Road, east of West Hampstead. It occupied four Victorian houses, somewhat haphazardly interconnected, whose period details sat surprisingly well with blackboards, Bunsen burners and the students' adventurous artwork. All members of staff were upright and eager, and it was as much the school's edict to impart a similar demeanour on the girls as to teach them the set curriculum. The headmistress, Miss Lorimar, was of indeterminate age, looked a little like an owl and could swoop down on misconduct or mess in an instant. She infused the girls and staff alike with a mixture of trepidation and respect. *Ad vitam Paramus*, she'd often proclaim, in morning assembly or just along the corridors, *Ad vitam Paramus*.

Petra liked school. Miss Lorimar had only ever had cause to bark praise at her. Petra wasn't staggeringly bright, nor was she tiresomely popular

7

but in keeping a naturally quiet and amicable profile, she was well liked by her teachers and classmates. She liked school because it provided respite from home. On her fourteenth birthday last year, she had been summonsed to Miss Lorimar's office.

'Sit.'

Petra had sat. She had sat in silence glancing at Miss Lorimar who was reading a letter with great interest.

'I see it is your birthday,' the headmistress had announced, 'and I see you are having a rotten time at home.' She brandished the piece of paper which Petra then recognized as coming from the pad of light blue Basildon Bond that was kept in the console drawer in the hallway at home. 'Your mother has disclosed the situation with your father.' Petra's gaze fell to her lap where she saw her fists were tightly clenched. 'I shall circulate this information in the staff room,' Miss Lorimar continued, as if referring to a case of nits. There was a pause during which Petra unfurled her fists and worried that her fingernails weren't regulation short. Miss Lorimar didn't seem interested in them. 'Happy birthday,' she said, her bluntness at odds with the sentiment. There was another pause. When Miss Lorimar next spoke, the steely edge to her voice had been replaced with an unexpected softness. 'Let school be your daytime haven, Miss Flint,' she said. 'You can be happy here. We will care for you.'

\*       \*       \*

And Petra was happy at Dame Alexandra Johnson

8

School for Girls and she did feel well cared for and now, a year on from her parents' divorce, home was no longer a place to trudge reluctantly back to.

*       *       *

That first Wednesday in March, double maths, first break and double English were blithely pushed aside as Miss Lorimar strode into the Lower Fifth classroom after assembly.

'I wanted to call it Task Force,' she bellowed and no one knew what she was talking about, 'but the governors thought it sounded too military.' She narrowed her eyes and huffed with consternation. Twenty-eight pairs of eyes concentrated on the dinks and notches in the old wooden desks. 'So we are calling it Pensioners' Link instead. One lunchtime each week, you will go in pairs and visit pensioners in the locale. You will do odd jobs, a little shopping and, most importantly, you will provide company.' She looked around the class. 'The elderly have started to become forgotten, even disposable, in our society,' she said darkly. 'It's an outrage! They are the cornerstones of our community and much is to be learned from them. You will sit and you will listen. Thank you, ladies.' A spontaneous hum from girls desperate to chatter erupted, though a withering look from Miss Lorimar soon silenced it. With a tilt of her head towards the classroom door, a group of people filed in. 'We welcome members of social services who will be your chaperones today. You will be back in time for final period before lunch—and the concert.'

The concert. Oh yes, the *gig*. Noble Savages, the

band made up from Sixth Formers at nearby Milton College Public School for Boys, were playing in the hall at lunch-break. What a strange day for a school day. Rather wonderful, too.

\*     \*     \*

Petra had been paired with Darcey Lewis and they'd been teamed with Mrs McNeil who was eighty-one years old and lived on her own in a flat in the mansion block above the shops near Finchley Road underground station.

'I didn't know people even lived here,' said Darcey.

'God you're a snob!' Petra said.

'I didn't mean it that way,' said Darcey ingenuously. 'I meant that I haven't ever bothered to look upwards beyond McDonald's or the newsagent or the sandwich shop.'

'It is pretty spectacular,' Petra agreed, as she and Darcey craned their necks and noted the surprisingly ornate brickwork and elegantly proportioned windows of the apartments sitting loftily above the parade of dog-eared shops.

'This is such a skive!' Darcey whispered as the lady from social services led them into the building. 'Missing double bloody maths to chat with an old biddy.' Darcey's glibness was soon set to rights by the dingy hallway and flight after flight of threadbare stairs. 'Why do you make someone so old live up here?' Darcey challenged social services.

'Mrs McNeil has lived here for twenty years,' was the reply. 'It is her home and she does not wish to move.'

10

The walls were stained with watermarks from some long-ago flood and from the scuff and trample of careless feet. The building smelt unpleasant: of carpet that had been damp, of overheated flats in need of airing, faint whispers of cigarette smoke, camphor, old-fashioned gas ovens, a cloying suggestion of soured milk. Mrs McNeil's front doorknob was secured with a thatch of Sellotape, the ends of which furled up yellow, all stickiness gone.

'She won't let us fix it,' the social services lady told the girls, as she rapped the flap of the letter-box instead.

'Bet she smells of wee,' Darcey whispered to Petra.

'Shut up,' Petra said.

Mrs McNeil did not smell of wee but of lavender cologne, and her apartment did not smell of sour milk or mothballs. It did smell of smoke but not cigarettes, something sweeter, something more refined. Cigarillos in cocktail colours, it soon transpired. She was a small but upright woman, with translucent crêpey skin and skeins of silver hair haphazardly swooped into a chignon of sorts. 'Hullo, young ladies,' her voice was a little creaky, but her accent was cultivated and the tone was confident, 'won't you come in?'

They shuffled after her, into the flat. Mrs McNeil's sitting room was cluttered but appeared relatively spruce for the apparent age and wear of her belongings and soft furnishings. A dark wood table and chairs with barley-twist legs jostled for floor space against a small sofa in waning olive green velvet with antimacassars slightly askew, a nest of tables that fitted together from coincidence

11

rather than original design, a tall ashtray from which a serpentine plume of smoke from a skinny pink cigarillo slicked into the air. On the walls, pictures of sun-drenched foreign climes hung crooked. Around the perimeter of the room, butting up against the tall skirting boards, piles and piles of books, all meticulously finishing at the same height. Petra thought they looked like sandbags, like a flood defence, as if they were protecting Mrs McNeil and keeping her safe within these walls. Or perhaps they kept mice out. Perhaps the tatty patterned carpet simply did not fit properly wall to wall. Petra looked around her; there just was not the room for enough shelving to house that many books. And the walls were for those paintings of somewhere hot and faraway.

At that moment, surrounded by decades of life and so much personal history, Petra deeply missed having grandparents of her own. She took Mrs McNeil's bony hand, with its calligraphy of veins and sinews and liver spots, in both of hers.

'It's a pleasure to meet you, Mrs McNeil,' she said, looking intently into the lady's watercolour-pale eyes. 'I'm Petra Flint.'

'You may call me Lillian, Petra Flint,' she said.

'Hullo, Lillian,' Darcey said slowly and loudly with unnecessary stooping. 'I'm Darcey Lewis.'

'*You*, dear, can call me Mrs McNeil,' Lillian said tartly.

And so began a friendship between Petra Flint and Lillian McNeil which, though it would last less than three years, was deep in its mutual fondness and, for Petra in particular, longstanding in its reach. On that first visit, while Darcey sat on the green velvet sofa and helped herself to ginger snaps, Petra asked Mrs McNeil if she would like her pictures straightened.

'I've never been abroad,' Petra said. 'Please will you tell me a little about them, as I straighten them?'

'Let's start here, in Tanzania,' Lillian said, peering up at a painting. 'I lived there forty years ago. I loved it. This is Mount Kilimanjaro at dawn. I sat beside the artist, under this baobab—or upside-down—tree as he painted.'

After that, whenever Petra visited, often twice or three times a week, the paintings she had previously righted were crooked again. Invariably one was more skewed than the others and that was the one that Lillian McNeil planned to talk about that day. Darcey rarely visited Mrs McNeil again. She swore Petra to secrecy, bunking off Pensioners' Link to meet her boyfriend for lunch at McDonald's instead.

From the tranquillity of Mrs McNeil's flat, Petra and Darcey walked straight into an overexcited buzz back at school. There was usually something going on in the school hall at lunch-times, but it was more likely to be drama or dance club or one of the classes practising a forthcoming assembly. In its hundred-year history, this was the first lunch-hour in which the school had been put at the disposal of five boys and their impressive array of rock-band paraphernalia. Miss Golding the music teacher, a sensitive creature for whom even Beethoven was a little too raucous, looked on in alarm as if fearing for the welfare of her piano and the girls' eardrums. While she backed herself away from the stage, her arms crossed and her eyebrows knitted, other members of staff bustled amongst

13

the girls trying to calm the general fidget and squawk of anticipation. It was only when Miss Lorimar introduced the members of the band that the students finally stood silent and still.

'These are *very* Noble Savages,' their headmistress quipped, tapping the shoulders of the singer and the drummer. 'First stop: Dame Alexandra Johnson's, next stop: *Top of the Pops*!' She made a sound unsettlingly close to a giggle before clapping energetically. The girls were too gobsmacked to even cringe let alone applaud. But before Miss Lorimar had quite left the stage, before Miss Golding had time to cover her ears, the Noble Savages launched into their first number and the varnished parquet of the hall resounded to the appreciative thumping of three hundred sensibly shod feet. Just a few bars in and each member of the band had a fan club as yelps of 'Oh my God, he's just so completely gorgeous,' filtered through the throng like a virus. 'I'm in love!' Petra's friends declared while she nodded and grinned and bopped along. 'God, I'm just *so* in love!'

*Nuclear no!* Arlo Savidge sang as Jonny Noble, on rhythm guitar, thrashed through powerful chords and Matt on drums hammered the point home.

> *Government you are meant*
> *to seek peace*
> *not govern mental.*
> *Time to go! Nuclear no!*

The girls went wild and the majority of them made a mental note to join CND at once. After thank-yous all round from the band, Jeremy skittled his fingers down the run of piano keys, took his hands right away for maximum drama and then crashed them back down in an echoing chord of ear-catching dissonance.

*Jailed for their thoughts*
*Caged for their beliefs*
*Imprisoned behind bars of bigotry*
*But still their spirits fly*
*Set them free*
*Set them free*
*We must*
*Set them free.*

The older girls were shaking their heads, while hormones and concern for political injustice sprang real tears to their eyes.

'Free Nelson Mandela,' Darcey said to Petra with a very grave nod.

Petra closed her eyes in silent supplication.

'Do you think the drummer would like to free me of my virginity?' Amy asked and her classmates snorted and laughed and gave her a hug.

'Do you think the one with the red-and-white guitar would like me in a big red bow and nothing else?' Alice asked.

'Shh!' Darcey hissed, beginning to sway. 'It's a slowy.'

'"Among the Flowers",' the singer announced, his eyes closed.

While gentle chords were softly strummed by Jonny, Arlo caressed the strings of his guitar. The sweetest melody wove its way through the crowd as 'Among the Flowers' floated like petals through

15

the hall. The harmonies seduced even Miss Golding who tipped her head and appraised the band with a timid smile. When Arlo began to sing, it was without the strident, Americanized preach of 'Set Them Free' and 'Nuclear No!'; instead it was deeper and pitch-perfect, wrought with emotion and, one felt, his true voice.

*I see her walking by herself*
*In a dream among the flowers*
*Won't she wake*
*Won't she wake*
*And see how I wait*
*See how I wait*
*For her*
*Is she walking all alone*
*Is she lonely in the flowers*
*Can I wake her and take her*
*Take her with me through the flowers*
*Out of her dream*
*And into mine*
*Out of her dream*
*And into mine.*

He sang with his eyes shut, his mouth so close to the microphone that occasionally his lips brushed right over its surface. Arlo only opened his eyes when the piano solo twinkled its romantic bridge between the verses. All eyes were on the band but the focus was on Arlo who had eyes for one girl alone.

Is he looking at me?

No, he's looking at me!

Fuck off, it's me he's looking at.

16

*        *        *

*It's me*, thought Petra, *he's looking straight at me. Aren't you. Hullo.*

*        *        *

'Out of her dream,' Arlo sang to Petra, 'and into mine.'


## CHAPTER TWO

The morning after Petra sleepwalked towards Whetstone was the morning she would hear again 'Among the Flowers' for the first time in seventeen years. But it wasn't the song that woke her, it was the telephone.

'Where are you? It's bloody Wednesday—it's your day to open up so I didn't bother to bring my keys. Your mobile is off. Bloody hell, Petra.'

She clocked the voice: Eric. She noted the time. She had overslept and she still felt exhausted.

'I can't get hold of Gina or Kitty,' Eric was wailing with a certain theatricality, 'and I've been waiting bloody *ages*.'

'I'll be right in, I had a bad night. I'll be there in an hour. Sorry.'

Petra flung back the duvet and stood up quickly which compounded the fuggy nausea of having been awoken with a jolt. Physically holding her head, and with her eyes half shut, she shuffled to the bathroom to take a shower. It stung. Glancing down, she saw that her right knee was badly

17

grazed. Carefully, she flannelled off the small sticky buds of blackened blood and bravely ran the shower cold over the freshly revealed abrasion. Scrubbing dirt from her fingernails, she observed a blade of grass whirl its way down the plughole. She gave a little shudder. She hated these hazy half-memories of the night before. She dried herself, dabbing gingerly at her knee, smoothing on Savlon and sticking a plaster lightly over the wound. Jeans felt too harsh so she pulled on a pair of old jogging bottoms, hurried into a sweatshirt and odd socks and shoved on the bashed-up trainers she favoured for work. But she had to clench her teeth and screw her eyes shut at a sudden scorch of soreness from her feet. Easing the shoes off, peeling her socks away, she inspected large blisters at each heel; one had burst and was red raw, the other bulged with fluid. If I cry now, Petra told herself, I won't make it into work at all. Bloody stupid sleepwalking—where was I going? What was I thinking?

She placed a pad of cotton wool on each heel, secured with Sellotape, slipped her feet into socks first stretched wide and then slid her feet into sandals. Sandals which she liked but which Rob referred to as 'German lezzy abominations'.

'If Rob could see me now,' she muttered, giving her reflection a cursory glance before heading for the studio. 'I hope he's OK.'

\*     \*     \*

Eric felt a little sorry for Petra when he spied her at a distance limping along Hatton Garden. He waved at her and she tried to pick up her pace. He

18

gestured the universal sign-language for 'Coffee?' to which she nodded and clutched her heart so he nipped into the café outside which he'd been loitering and as Petra reached him, a comforting cappuccino was placed in her hands.

'Sorry,' she said, 'and thanks.'

'You OK?' Eric asked, taking the studio keys from her as they walked in the direction of Leather Lane.

'Yes, I overslept,' Petra said.

'You know, socks and sandals are generally unforgivable in all but children,' Eric said with a superciliously raised eyebrow, 'but mismatched white socks and spoddy sandals are a breach of the public peace. Gina will wince in pain and Kitty won't let you hear the end of it.'

'*Spoddy sandals*?' It made Petra smile. 'Rob calls them my German Lesbian Things,' she confided, frowning guiltily at her Birkenstocks.

'I know a German lesbian or two,' Eric qualified, 'and let me tell you, I have never seen them wear socks with *those*. They are spoddy sandals. They're the summer equivalent of Nature Trek shoes. Without socks they are tolerable. But with socks they are indefensible.'

'I have the most terrible blisters,' Petra explained, as Eric unlocked the studio and they went about flicking on lights and hoicking up blinds.

'Have you been hiking up mountains since yesterday evening then?'

'You could say that,' Petra said quietly. 'I sleepwalked last night. Right out of the house. Almost a mile. In wellies.'

'Dear God,' Eric exclaimed. He took a long look

19

at her. 'What are we going to do with you?'

In the fifteen years he'd known her, since they were undergraduates in jewellery design at Central St Martins, he'd become familiar with her two very different morning faces. Her complexion soft and peachy after a good night's sleep or, as today, sallow and slightly haunted from the disturbance of somnambulism. When they had shared student digs, Eric had been the only one amongst the housemates not to laugh at her expense, never to tease her, always to believe it was entirely involuntary and an onerous affliction. What Petra doesn't know is that Eric used to wedge a chair outside her door and if it clattered he would wake and find her and gently guide her back to bed. He still brings in cuttings about the subject, buys Petra herbal preparations promising to rebalance the soul and promote uninterrupted sleep. He's tried to monitor when it happens most, or when the episodes are more extreme or when they happen least but so far his analysis has established no set pattern or reason.

'Rob rescued me,' Petra told him.

Eric pursed his lips to prevent himself from saying, Well, *that's* a contraction in terms.

'Actually, the police found me,' Petra clarified, 'and they called Rob.'

'The police,' Eric sighed but more because he had a bit of a thing about men in uniform.

'*Police?*' Gina exclaimed, having arrived at the studio just at that moment.

'Oh fuck, not the bastard police,' scowled Kitty, right behind Gina but hearing even less of the conversation.

'Stop picking up fag ends,' Eric said.

20

'But you *are* a fag,' Kitty snorted.

'And we *did* come in at the very end of what you were saying, darling,' said Gina.

Gina carefully put her cashmere cardigan on a coat-hanger before placing it on one of the coat hooks, hanging her butter-soft nubuck leather Mulberry bag beside it. She slinked her slender frame into a pristine white lab coat and swept her hair away from her face with a wide velvet hairband. Kitty meanwhile took off her black crocheted shrug and slung it over the back of a chair, kicked off her thumping great black boots with the integrated steel shin guards and clumped down into the old pair of black trainers she kept at the studio. It was only when she tied back the drapes of her dyed black hair that her eyes became visible, meticulously delineated by bold swipes of black eyeliner, shaded in with eye shadow the colour of bruising and emphasized by thick slicks of jet black mascara.

Jewellers Kitty Mulroney and Georgina Fanshaw-Smythe shared the space with Eric and Petra and over the years the four of them had formed a thriving community, each referring to the others as their Studio Three. They shared the overheads, divvied tools and equipment, pitched in for a compact kitchenette, divided the chores and dished out praise for each other's work and support for each other's lives too. Their studio occupied a section of the third floor of an old building on a narrow street running between Leather Lane and Hatton Garden. Though it was not a big space, toes were never trodden upon. But the true success of their working environment was due to their extreme differences on personal and

21

creative levels.

The variously pierced and tattooed Kitty, with her kohl-black make-up, dark pointy dress sense, and hair the colour and consistency of treacle, nevertheless made jewellery of painstaking delicacy and femininity; beautiful filigree pieces, two of which were on display at the Victoria and Albert museum. She sparred with Eric, trading insults and nicknames—though she had checked in advance if he'd mind her calling him 'Gayboy' and she was actually quite flattered when he retaliated with 'Jezebel'. She also had a gentle fascination with Gina whose vowels were as polished as her beautifully bobbed fair hair, whose tools were in the same perfect condition as her weekly manicure, whose domestic set-up appeared to be as neat and classy as the ending of a Jane Austen novel. In turn, Gina had nothing but awe and respect for the impecunious Goth from New Cross. She marvelled at Kitty's sullen darkness, her apparent self-sufficiency when it came to love, her brazenness when it came to sex, her creative nonchalance when it came to money—not to mention her fascinating ways with black leather, black everything.

'I'm two-a-penny in SW3,' Gina had once said, 'but you, Kitty, *you* are unique. *Exotique.*'

What was neither predictable nor dreary was Gina's work; large and chunky, fusing tribal design with modernist juts and twists.

'One thing you are *not* is predictable or dull,' Kitty protested. 'You have daughters called Harry and Henry—how much more rock-and-roll can you get?'

'But that's short for Harriet and Henrietta,'

22

Gina said.

'But *you* call them Harry and Henry and when people see you loading them into your Sloane Range Rover, that's what they hear.'

Eric Bartley, far more girly than any of the women, felt it his duty to cluck over them like a mother hen. He brought in cakes and treats and new-fangled organic tonics and was the one who made the tea most often, earning him the moniker 'Teas Maid'. If any of the women seemed below par, he'd give them a grave, sympathetic nod. He constantly sought their advice: from Clarins versus Clinique, to his frequent relationship dramas and what to cook that night; from his hair colour or his weight, to whether to buy *Grazia* or *Men's Health*. But when he was working on his strong, masculine, classic designs, he worked in utter silence, interspersing long periods of extreme concentration and productivity with bursts of manic chatter and scurrilous gossip.

\*       \*       \*

Today, all eyes are on Petra. She may have washed the grass from her hair and restored its long, glossy mahogany curls, her fingernails may now be clean and jogging pants hide the plaster on her knee, however it is not the odd white socks and Birkenstocks which betray her in an instant, it's her demeanour. Everyone is used to Petra being the quieter member of their tribe, but today she is exceptionally wan. It casts a pallid mantle over her already delicate features; darkened hollows compromising the rich hazelnut of her usually bright eyes. She's slim, but today she looks brittle.

23

Though her clothing rarely courts much attention, today she looks a mess.

'Are you all right, Petra darling?' Gina asks.

'Because you don't look it. You look crap,' says Kitty, 'if you don't mind me saying.'

'I had a bad night,' Petra tells them. 'I'm fine now. Just a bit tired.'

'Rob?' Gina mouths to Eric who shakes his head.

'Not Rob,' Petra hurries. 'Rob came to my rescue. I just went walkabout whilst I was asleep. You know me.'

'Right out of the house,' Eric whispers to the other two. 'She was walking to Whetstone.'

'I don't even know where Whetstone is,' Gina said, as if it was possibly as far flung as the Arctic. 'I thought you just tottered off to rearrange things in the kitchen, or bumped into the odd wall or door.'

'I do, usually,' Petra says.

'Do you have any history there?' Kitty asks darkly. 'In Whetstone? A past life? Or ancestors? Bad blood?'

Petra smiles and shakes her head.

'Then maybe you weren't so much walking, as being *led*?' Kitty suggests in a hush.

'I just walk,' Petra shrugs. 'I don't know where I was going, or why, because I can't remember. But the police found me and Rob came for me.'

'Did you hurt yourself?'

'Bashed, bruised and blistered,' Eric interjects, 'the poor lamb. Look at her footwear—that's necessity, not fashion.'

'I'm fine, I'm fine,' Petra says, suddenly tiring of the attention. 'I'm just knackered. And pissed off

24

with myself because I haven't actually left a building in my sleep for a good few months.'

'Not since the fire-escape incident?' Eric asks, with a sly wink.

'God,' Petra says, covering her face in horror.

'You escaped from fire?' Gina asks ingenuously.

'You were in Bermuda, Gina,' Kitty growls. 'Petra was staying at a hotel in the country for her friends' wedding.'

'And woke up freezing cold and stark naked on the fire escape,' Eric adds.

'And the only way back in was through the main entrance,' Kitty says.

'And of course she didn't think to take her room key,' says Eric.

Gina is flabbergasted. 'What were you wearing to Whetstone last night?' she hardly dares ask.

'Gumboots and an oversized Snoopy T-shirt,' Petra mumbles from behind her hands.

'Well, that's better than nothing,' Gina says kindly though the look from Kitty says that she begs to differ.

'There must be something in it,' Kitty says. 'Whetstone, the wellies—don't you think? Tarot will tell you. I have my cards with me—do you want me to read for you?'

'If sleep specialists can't tell me why I've sleepwalked since I was eight, then I'm not sure the answer lies in tarot,' Petra says. 'Not after nearly twenty-five years. Perhaps there's nothing in it anyway. Maybe my body is just restless. Or my brain just can't quite switch off. No one seems to know. It's just my—*thing*.'

'But the cards *will* know,' Kitty says darkly, fiddling with the hoop in her right nostril.

25

'Go on,' Eric says, 'let her read for you. You might discover you're to meet a tall, dark, handsome stranger.'

'But I have my tall, dark, handsome Rob,' Petra protests and raises her eyebrow defiantly at Eric who has already raised his at her.

Kitty shrugs. 'Another time, then. I need to get on with my cuff.' She unwraps from a soft cloth her current work in progress: delicate swirls and serpentines in white gold, like calligraphy in three dimensions, which she's designed to be worn around the upper arm.

'It's stunning,' Petra tells her.

'Thanks,' Kitty says shyly. 'I just wish I didn't owe my gem dealer so much—I really want those rubies for here, here, here and there.'

'Those earrings you made for Gallery Tom Foolery—they'll sell like hot cakes,' Gina says encouragingly.

'Hope so,' Kitty smiles and tucks herself in to her bench.

'Is it a Radio 2 day or a Classic FM day?' Eric procrastinates.

'Two.'

'Two.'

'Don't mind.'

And the group settles down to work. Kitty filing and filing in pursuit of perfection; lemel, or gold dust, gathering like specks of wishes glinting in the pigskin slung like a hammock, hanging over her lap from the curved inlet of her bench. Gina is scrutinizing turquoise and amber. Eric buffs and polishes two wedding rings he's just finished, his hair safely away from the spin of the machine in a girly topknot, his eyes protected by goggles.

26

Petra wonders what she actually has the energy to do. She has some out-work from Charlton Squire, the gallery owner and jeweller who takes a sizeable commission of her sales but who keeps her earnings a little more constant by giving her his own designs to make up. She sips tea. She is starting to feel more human. She sends Rob a text to say sorry bout last nite—ta 4 saving me! hope meeting v.g. luv u! p xxx

Spring sunshine filters through the dusty studio windows. Eric looks so comical and sweet. Kitty is stooped in concentration, the cuff sending out dazzles of light as the sun catches it. Gina is beating life into silver by beating the hell out of it, singing along to the radio between clouts from her hammer.

I like this song, Petra hums to herself. She analyses Charlton's design, sticking the papers to the wall in front of her. She chooses her tools. A sudden thunder of hammering from Gina drowns out the presenter's rambling and when Gina stops, the next song playing is one she doesn't know and therefore can't sing along to.

But Petra knows it.

Instantly, Petra is wide awake and utterly alert, transported back seventeen years, back to school, back to being fifteen. Back to that strange lunch-time after she'd first met Mrs McNeil, when she was serenaded across the packed school hall by a Sixth Former from Milton College. Arlo Savidge.

The song playing just now is 'Among the Flowers' and its exquisite melody and gentle lyrics drift out of the communal stereo straight into Petra's soul.

# CHAPTER THREE

But it's not Arlo's voice. At least, I don't think it is. In fact, I'm sure it isn't. His voice is still crystal clear in my memory—though I'm having to rack my brains to remember exactly what he looked like.

Arlo Savidge. I wonder whatever happened to Arlo Savidge. Who would know? I don't keep in touch with anyone from school and I never heard from or of him after I left. It wasn't unrequited love—because he never actually asked and so there was never anything I could actually answer and of course nothing ever really happened. But it *was* love, in its own gentle, quirky way. A love without a kiss, without a single touch, let alone a declaration. More pure, probably, than any physical relationship I've had. It was all so beautifully and yearningly unsaid. And yet we only knew each other for just under eighteen months.

I felt as though there was a spotlight on me, during that one song in that one lunch-time at school. As if Arlo had told an invisible lighting technician that there was a girl in the Lower Fifth, milling with her pals in the middle of the crowd and when I sing I'll be singing to her so can you shine a light and pick her out so she knows. So that she knows how I feel and so that she will feel special.

And his song was the light and I knew all right. I felt it. It was odd and I felt as though I didn't know where to look, as though I wanted desperately to look away but of course I couldn't because I was

28

transfixed. I do remember his eyes even though he was over there, up on the stage. It was only later that I knew what colour they were. Blue. Very very blue. His eyes were locked onto mine—even when he closed them with emotion, he'd open them straight into my gaze. He didn't glance away once, he didn't look at anyone else and I don't think I even blinked. And I do remember his lanky physique, his white school shirtsleeves rolled just above his elbows, the lovely strong forearms of his burgeoning masculinity. You could see his muscles delineate according to how passionately his played his guitar. He stood, legs slightly apart but relaxed, one foot tapping the rhythm, lips right against the mike. He had nice hair, I remember at the time thinking he had *cool* hair—in retrospect, it was nice and cool in that archetypically schoolboy way—just about within the school regulation side of Jim Morrison. Carefully unkempt curls and waves. Sandy rather than blond.

But it wasn't him as a package that I fancied. In fact, I didn't ever really fancy Arlo—I bypassed that stage and fell in quiet love. Fancy was too vulgar a reaction to being serenaded. I remember loving him in an instant because he was singing to me, because, somehow, he had written that song for me. And the magic between us must have come from him not knowing he'd written it for me until he saw me that day and me not knowing what it felt like to be at the centre of someone's world until just then. I think he felt that way too. But I don't know because he never said and I never asked.

*Is she walking all alone*
*Is she lonely in the flowers.*

29

But this voice, today, is not Arlo's. It's his song but it's not him. Though no doubt his voice will have changed over the intervening seventeen years, it won't have changed into this. It'll probably have just deepened a little, lost a slice of its purity, gained a little worldly gravel to its timbre.

Whatever happened to Arlo Savidge?

I remember feeling woozy, a little breathless, that lunch-time. It was so thrilling—me, a Lower Fifth Year, being the focus of a Sixth Former. It was, I suppose, the most romantic thing that anyone has ever done for me. Rob took me to Claridges for my thirty-second birthday in December, but that was ostentation, not romance; we'd only been together a few months. And he bought me a pen from Tiffany for Christmas and red roses on Valentine's Day. But all of that is relatively easy if you can afford it. Back then, Arlo only had pocket money yet he created something unique and beautiful and precious. And lasting.

I wonder if he has ever stopped to wonder, over the years, whether I've been walking all alone, whether I've been lonely in the flowers? Rob sent me flowers last month after that blazing row when he stood me up but when they were delivered I buried my nose in them and as I inhaled their heady scent I sobbed. I felt desperately alone in those flowers.

Things seem to be quite good at the moment. Or at least, they're getting better.

*     *     *

But just perhaps, just say things were better way back then. They say that our school years are the

30

best years of our lives. Do I agree? Is that true? Is it still too early to tell? But I think back to all I achieved, to the colourful mix of my schoolmates, to the eccentricities of my teachers. Have I ever been part of such an intense mêlée of uniqueness since? We had school uniform—yet though young and not quite formed, we all stood distinct. When I went to college, all we students shared an unofficial, interchangeable uniform of our own which made everyone blend and bland. Slouchy grouchy stressed and broke. I don't even know where Arlo went to university. Maybe he's a super rock god in America. Perhaps he jacked it all in and is an accountant. Maybe he's an impoverished musician in a garret in Clerkenwell. Or perhaps he's a middle-class husband with 2.4 kids. Perhaps the litheness and the curls are gone and he has a paunch and a bald patch. I don't know. But how beautiful that his music will always exist. What a legacy. It's on the radio. It's finishing.

'*That was Rox and a hit from five years ago, "Among the Flowers". Beautiful. And it's approaching midday so it's over to Annie for the news and weather.*'

Did you hear that? It was a hit five years ago. Where was I back then that I never heard it? Nowhere in particular. It just passed me by. How odd. Am I that square not to know what was top of the sodding pops five years ago? I *have* heard of Rox. But I didn't know they covered Arlo's song. I wonder how they came by it? Are there other bands out there covering his other tracks? Is he some hugely successful songwriter? Why am I even wondering about any of this? I saw him so rarely, if I think about it.

31

My school and Milton College used to join up for activities like choral society and pottery and drama club. I was never outgoing enough to go for drama club, and choral society was a bit naff, but I was very good at pottery. That summer term—the term after that lunch-time gig—I used to walk over to Milton College with Anna and Paula on Wednesday afternoons to do pottery. Some of the boys asked us if we'd come because we were good with our hands; I took it as a compliment and said yes—but Anna and Paula took it as a come-on and they were delighted and said things like, That's for us to know and you to find out, guys.

We *were* good with our hands, us three. Very good. Paula and Anna took to the wheel and threw gorgeous pots and bowls. I liked working more organically and constructed great big urns that were really glorified coil pots which I'd burnish and burnish and then scarify the sheened surface with these dense little marks like hieroglyphics. I spent hours on them. Because it was summer, Mr WhateverHisNameWas let me sit outside with my pots and my tools and that's when I saw Arlo again. He walked across the playground over to me, like a strolling troubadour, strumming and humming until we shared a great big grin. Then he sat a little way off, playing.

Every Wednesday afternoon after that, during that summer term, he'd somehow appear when I appeared, mostly with his guitar. He never sang 'Among the Flowers' for me again. Not from beginning to end. Not with the words. Every now and then he'd hum it and strum it but very delicately, slipping a few bars in between other melodies. We kept each other's company, those

Wednesday afternoons, though we didn't say much at all. I asked him what A levels he was doing. I can't remember now. He asked me how many O levels I was taking. Christ, how many did I take? Eight. And passed seven. He told me about some of the mad teachers at his school. I told him all about Mrs McNeil. And then I didn't really see him until the following spring because I chose print-making during the winter term. And though he'd've been swotting for A levels, he did find time most Wednesdays to find me. And we just picked up from where we'd left off.

'How's your little old lady?' he'd ask, when we were sitting not talking and not really working. I'd tell him some of the stories she told me, some of the funny little errands I ran for her. Once he covered his eyes and winced and I asked what was wrong and he said my halo was so shiny and bright it hurt his eyes and I chucked a little wet clod of terracotta clay at him and he laughed. Mostly though, we shared happy little interludes of chat in an otherwise quietly industrious atmosphere. I was engrossed in my terracotta urns and he was deep in thoughts of chords and riffs. Out in the playground, in the warmth of his final summer term at school. We'd sit together, though we were actually a couple of yards apart. We were certainly sitting together none the less, separate yet united in our little hive of creativity and tenderness every Wednesday afternoon.

And now I make jewellery. I wonder what Arlo does because he used to make music. And, for the first time in seventeen years, I've just heard the song he wrote for me. On national radio.

# CHAPTER FOUR

'Sir,' Nathan whined, '*sir*.' He'd been saying 'sir' for ages but Sir didn't seem to hear. Sir seemed a bit lost in thought, somewhat distracted by the bright spring morning ablaze outside. 'Sir! Mr Savidge! *Sir* Savidge.'

Nathan's teacher finally turned his attention to him, raised an eyebrow. 'I'm liking the "Sir Savidge" moniker, Nathan. In fact, class—you can all call me Sir Savidge from now on. OK?'

'Yes, sir. Savidge. Sir.'

'Nathan—what can I do for you?'

'Would you say that rhythm is the soul of music, sir?'

Arlo regarded his pupil, unable to keep an affectionate smile at bay. He remembered being just like Nathan. A keen fourteen-year-old, happy to study but also keen to add personal philosophy to the dry curriculum. God, what a gorgeous day it was. Warm too.

'I mean, Sir Savidge, sir,' Nathan said. 'Rhythm is the soul of music—wouldn't you say?' he repeated, dragging his teacher's gaze away from the view outside. 'But sir, if you put that kind of thing in your GCSE do you think the judges give you better marks?'

Judges. Sirs. Arlo changed his sigh into another smile and focused on the boy. 'I think the examiners would mark you higher if you said something along the lines of rhythm being the *lifeblood* of music, Nathan. Think of blood, all of you—how it pulses, how it pumps. If blood doesn't

34

pump—if it ceases to pulse around our bodies—what are we?'

The class was silent.

'Come on, guys, what are we?'

The class loved it when their teacher called them 'guys'.

'Fish?' offered Lars.

'*Fish*?' said his teacher.

'Fish are cold-blooded,' Lars muttered while the class began to snigger. 'Isn't that the same thing?'

'No no no,' Arlo said, thinking he ought to check it anyway with Mr Rose the biology teacher. 'I'm talking physically and metaphysically. Come on, guys, if our blood isn't being pumped then it's not pulsing around our body—then what are we?'

The boys gawped at him.

'We are dead!' he said.

There was a murmur, a gasp or two. Schoolboys love the word 'dead'.

'So, if rhythm is the lifeblood of music, it must mean it is at the *heart* of it. Music needs rhythm to breathe its life into the listener—don't you think?' There was silence as twenty-five pens scribbled away at exercise books, frantic to copy Sir's quote verbatim. Good old Lars with his fish, Arlo thought. But poor old Nathan—he'd been on the right track but with the wrong metaphor, just a little unscientific when it came to the particular anatomy of music. Arlo considered how, though the whole class was committing his improvement on Nathan's quote to memory, the GSCE examiners would no doubt put a red line through the lot. 'If it's not on the curriculum, it doesn't exist,' Arlo said under his breath though not so quietly that the eternally eager Finn right in front

35

of him didn't start to write that down too.

'Finn—you can't quote me on that.'

'Sorry, sir.'

Arlo glanced at the clock. Fifteen minutes till his charges swapped rhythm for the thwack of leather against willow. 'Mussorgsky and Marley,' he announced, browsing the CD shelves much to the boys' anticipation. 'They knew a thing or two about rhythm,' Arlo said, loading discs into the machine. He tapped the remote control against his lips. 'The Russian, Modest Petrovich Mussorgsky, died in 1881 and the Jamaican, Robert Nesta Marley, died in 1981. Listen to this.' He chose 'Pictures at an Exhibition' by the former and 'Get Up Stand Up' by the latter. The boys were entranced; toes tapped, rulers and pens bounced gently against the edges of the desks. They would gladly have relinquished cricket to listen to more but the bell went and Mr Savidge ejected the discs and released the class.

'Well done, guys,' he said. 'See you whenever.' And he took up his gazing out of the window.

*     *     *

From the empty classroom, Arlo looked out across the rolling manicured lawn to the plotted and pieced playing fields beyond. He considered that schoolboys in cricket whites at that distance were basically interchangeable with the sheep scattering the North York Moors beyond the school's grounds. They shared that peculiar characteristic of inactivity interrupted by sudden bouts of gleeful gambolling. But neither sheep nor cricket did much for Arlo. He was more of a dogs and tennis chap. Just then, he quite fancied a knock-around on court. He checked his timetable. He had a couple of hours until he taught the First Years but then only the odd half-hour during the rest of the day and no opportunity that evening because he was on prep duty. He gathered his papers and books into the worn leather satchel the boys often teased him about and wandered over towards the main building.

He came across Paul Glasper in the staff room, enjoying a cup of coffee with the illicit luxury of the *Sun* newspaper. 'It's today's,' Paul bragged.

'Who smuggled that in?' Arlo laughed.

'One of those blokes doing the electrics in Armstrong House,' Paul said.

'There's a waiting list for it,' came Nigel Garton's voice from behind a copy of the *Daily Telegraph* which better befitted his Head of Physics stature, 'and I'm next.'

'You lot are incorrigible,' said Miranda Oates, enjoying a digestive biscuit and a copy of *Heat* magazine. Arlo flicked his finger against it. Miranda peered up at him. 'There's more world news in this than in *that*,' she said, tossing her head in the direction of Paul and the *Sun*. 'This is essential reading,' she smiled. 'It helps me keep my finger on the zeitgeist. It helps me understand my students.'

'Bollocks!' came Nigel's voice from behind the *Telegraph*, while Paul asked Miranda if he could have a flip through the magazine once she'd finished.

'Only an English teacher could use "zeitgeist" in such a context,' Arlo laughed, spooning instant coffee granules into a relatively clean mug.

'Anyone for tennis? Paul? Fancy a knock-about?'

'I'm busy,' said Paul, shaking the *Sun* and snapping it open again.

'Dickhead,' Arlo laughed. 'Nige? Come on, a quick game, set and match? You slaughtered me last week.'

'And I'd love to slaughter you again, but I'm nipping into Stokesley for a haircut.'

'You look gorgeous, Mr Garton,' Arlo teased, 'for a physics teacher.'

'I've got a date,' Nigel said.

'I'll come,' said Miranda.

'No, you won't,' Nigel said, 'much as a threesome is on my wish list. But I try not to bed my colleagues.'

'Not with you, prat,' she said, 'with *you*, Arlo— I'll have a knock-up with you.'

'Ooh er, missy,' murmured Paul, who obviously wasn't as engrossed in the *Sun* as the others thought.

Arlo gave her a glancing smile and made much of checking his watch. 'Actually, on second thoughts, I think I'll go into Stokesley with Nige and get my hair cut too.'

'You haven't got any bloody hair, Arlo,' Paul piped up again.

'I have more than you,' said Arlo, running the palm of his hand lightly over the fuzz of his crop. 'This is long, for me. I can practically do a comb-over on my receded parts.'

'Do you have a date too?' Paul asked.

Arlo baulked.

'Well, you're not joining me,' Nigel protested.

Paul caught the look on Miranda's face that said, I'll be your date Arlo, before she buried her head in *Heat* when she sensed she'd been noticed.

'Miranda's got a demon serve,' Paul told Arlo.

'Another time,' Arlo told her. 'I'll come into Stokesley with you, Nige.'

\*       \*       \*

They belted along an empty road, lush flat fields to the left soon giving way to the sparser grazing on the moors rising and rolling away.

'Daft, isn't it,' Arlo remarked. 'We're the teachers but I feel like I'm bunking off.'

'You need to get out more,' Nigel teased.

'Probably,' Arlo conceded. 'It's just so easy to not leave the school grounds now. When I first joined, I was exploring the region at every opportunity—rarely stayed in unless I was on duty. Now, four years on, I go out for a haircut, or to the pub once a week for precisely three pints and a scotch, and that's about it.'

'It's cyclical,' Nigel said. 'I went through that. But I've been there two years longer than you and I'm telling you, I now plan my next outing hourly.'

'Who's your date?' Arlo asked.

'She's called Jennifer,' said Nigel. 'I met her in Great Ayton last weekend. She was in front of me in the ice-cream queue at Suggitts.'

'You sad old git,' Arlo laughed, 'spending your free time hanging out at ice-cream shops waiting for totty.'

'Sod off,' Nigel said. 'She's a lawyer. She was with some cycling group and they'd stopped off at Suggitts. You know how they do. All those Sunday riders.'

'Well,' Arlo said thoughtfully, 'good luck.'

'Haven't had a shag in months,' Nigel muttered. He looked at Arlo though he knew the answer. 'You?'

'Nope,' Arlo said, assuming Nigel knew it was actually years but didn't dare comment.

'Miranda Oates would have you,' Nigel told him.

'I don't mix work and pleasure,' Arlo said.

'All work and no play . . . as they say,' Nigel warned him, pulling into a parking bay and putting a permit on his dashboard.

'She isn't my type,' Arlo said.

'Who is, then?' Nigel asked as they walked towards the barbers. 'In all the time I've known you, I haven't a clue who your *type* is.'

'It's not that simple,' said Arlo, relieved that they'd arrived.

\*      \*      \*

Half an hour later, they were back in the car, Nigel's short black hair slicked this way and that with product-assisted trendy nonchalance. Arlo's hair was cropped even closer to his head, the style coming more from the fine shape of his skull, his smooth forehead, the slight but neat receding of his hairline. 'I can't believe they charge me twelve quid for what was essentially a couple of minutes with mini horse clippers.'

'Mine was twelve quid too—and I had a blow-dry and a load of styling goop,' Nigel laughed.

'And you look lovely, darling,' Arlo said drily. 'It'll be your lucky night.' Nigel swerved as he turned to wink at Arlo, before tootling more cautiously through Stokesley and back out into the countryside.

'It's a nice enough spring day—but this is a wee bit optimistic,' Arlo commented, as 'Summer in the City' played on the radio. Both he and Nigel knew they would have to tolerate the usual squalls and sudden chills of April before they could move truly to spring, let alone nearer to summer.

'What exactly is a "loving spoonful", I've always wondered,' mused Nigel. 'I think it might be a type of cake. Or a wedding spoon like those Welsh love spoons. Or perhaps a feed-the-poor charity?'

'Stop philosophising and step on it, will you,' Arlo said. 'We'll miss last lunch at this rate.'

'My hunger is for Jenn,' Nigel growled lustily.

'You prick,' Arlo laughed. 'Come on, I'm starving.'

They drove along, commenting on the Radio 2 playlist, humming and occasionally singing out loud. Nigel started some lengthy anecdote about a previous girlfriend and a curry when suddenly Arlo wasn't listening at all because 'Among the Flowers' was playing on the radio. The lyrics more chantingly familiar to him than the words to the Lord's Prayer. The melody the theme tune to his life.

'Do you remember this one?' said Nigel, turning up the volume and tra-la-ing to the closing bars. 'Awesome song.'

'I wrote it,' Arlo said quietly.

Nigel laughed. 'And I wrote "Jumping Jack Flash".'

Arlo didn't respond. What was the point? The song, so much a part of his life, was nevertheless part of a past life so different and distant to that which he currently led.

Now 'Mr Tambourine Man' was playing.

'And I wrote this one, too,' Nigel said, singing along dreadfully. 'Hang on, this isn't Bob Dylan.'

'It's the Byrds,' Arlo said patiently. 'Dylan wrote it. The Byrds adapted the lyrics and added a twelve-string guitar lead and I did write the one before.'

' "The One Before"?'

'No—the previous song. "Among the Flowers".'

'Sure you did,' said Nigel, busy zooming up the school's majestic driveway, whacking over the speed ramps, hurtling into the car park with a lively skid along the meticulously raked gravel. He switched off the engine.

'I did,' said Arlo.

'You need to get out more, Savidge,' said Nigel, 'you really do.'

\*     \*     \*

Arlo's Year Eight thought pretty much the same thing that afternoon. But they weren't complaining. He hadn't said a thing to them all lesson, just looked at them queerly, while Beethoven filled the room. The 5th piano concerto. 'The Emperor'. And however much Arlo loved the music, just then he couldn't hear a note. And however much he loved his job, though he stood in front of his desk with his eyes trained on the twenty-two boys before him, he didn't much notice them at all. He was somewhere else entirely and, for a few moments, he didn't want to be there at all—horribly ensconced in five years ago. So he flung himself back further still. And was charmed to arrive back at half his lifetime ago, when he was seventeen and in the Lower Sixth at school and

42

had written the song he still considers his best.

\*       \*       \*

'Among the Flowers'. In terms of subject matter, the seventeen-year-old Arlo had risked derision by his schoolmates but the melody he had created was so sublime that it immediately excused the unmitigated romance of the lyric. He wasn't really aware of the starting point. Usually, the songs he wrote for his band were inspired by his fiery teenage response to political injustice worldwide and his middle-class upbringing. But 'Among the Flowers' was utterly at odds with 'Soweto Sweat' and 'Not Quiet on the Western Front' and 'Life under Cardboard'—all of which had swiftly become veritable anthems at Milton College. Perhaps studying *Tess of the D'Urbervilles* for A level English had been a subliminal source. He'd fallen a little bit in love with Tess, had seen her through Angel's eyes, when she walks through the juicy grass and floating pollen of the garden at Talbothays, drawn by Angel's harp but conscious of neither time nor space, her skirts gathering cuckoo-spittle as she meanders through the dazzling polychrome of flowering weeds. But ultimately, Arlo's Flower Girl was wholly mythical. She embodied the woman he was aspiring to hold as his own one day. He thought that if he could create his ideal, set his wish list to the six strings of his guitar, perhaps he could lure her to him, perhaps he'd give her life.

His then girlfriend was lovely enough but she didn't inspire him to write. He'd lost his virginity to the girlfriend before that one and she'd made him

43

horny as hell but love hadn't come into it. Love was out there, of that he was sure, but even at seventeen Arlo trusted the logic of time and, for the time being, he embraced (rather physically) the fact that schoolgirls were to be very nice stepping stones towards the real thing. Arlo assumed, quite sensibly, that his teenage years should be about amorous fumblings and sticky sex. He had a feeling that university would probably provide more adventurous fornication and a serious relationship or two. And he imagined that his walk through the flowers to the love of his lifetime would probably be taken in his late twenties.

What he was not expecting, at the age of seventeen and on the day his band had been invited to play a lunch-time set at the nearby private girls' school, was to come across his flower girl in bud. He had no idea that a fifteen-year-old girl would so completely embody the fantasy he eulogized in 'Among the Flowers'. But having sung about Soweto to a sea of bouncing schoolgirls, having had them clap their hands above their heads to 'Nuclear No' and chant the chorus of 'Set Them Free', he launched into the melodious and ethereal 'Among the Flowers'. And there, from the sway and the smiles of one hundred and fifty pubescent schoolgirls, on that first Wednesday in March seventeen years ago, Arlo Savidge had caught sight of Petra Flint and realized in an instant that he'd written the song solely for her.

\*　　　\*　　　\*

Arlo quite liked evening prep. More than seeming an after-hours affliction cutting into his evening, it

44

was a quiet and useful hour and a half when none of the boys pestered him, concentrating their energies instead on finishing their homework so they could make the most of their free time before bed. Usually, Arlo used prep to do his marking or planning, or he'd write to his mother, perhaps check his bank statements; sometimes he just read a book, other times he simply sat and thought of nothing, occasionally he sat and thought about quite a lot. Tonight was one of those times.

'What is it, Troy? No, you don't—you can borrow my pen instead.'

Hearing 'Among the Flowers' on the radio at lunch-time had sounded odder to Arlo than when Rox had first released it five years previously. It seemed so totally out of context that he should be listening to it, on Radio 2, in the middle of North Yorkshire, as he returned to his teaching job having just had a haircut. He didn't blame Nigel for not believing him. It wouldn't cross Nigel's mind that he was telling the truth. Why should it? Who has songs published and played on national radio, yet teaches music at a boys' private boarding school in North Yorkshire? For Nigel it had just been typical banter; they were at it all the time after all, the staff. A little like grown-up schoolboys themselves; mercilessly teasing each other, taking the piss, saying daft things, catching each other out.

'Lars—give Nathan back his calculator, please. Come on, guys.'

Was it self-indulgent, Arlo wondered, to have one's own song on one's mind? Was it an insult to Bob Dylan—for Arlo, the greatest songwriter of all time—that all afternoon he had so easily forsaken

45

'Mr Tambourine Man' to mentally play his own ditty, penned at seventeen years of age, over and over again instead? Similarly, that he'd utterly blanked Beethoven? The version of 'Among the Flowers' on a loop in his head was most certainly his own, not the version covered by Rox. He didn't mind their interpretation—and it brought welcome royalties each year. He didn't much care for Rox's subjugation of the acoustic emphasis he'd intended in favour of soft sentimental rock, but he could see why their record label would have encouraged it. Much more *Top of the Pops*—as indeed it had been five years ago. And his version, the way he conceived it, wrote it, had only ever sung it, was in all probability a bit introspectively adolescent. Not commercial enough. Not slick enough. It occurred to Arlo that he hadn't actually sung it in years. He'd written other stuff since. Not that he sang that much either. And though he knew 'Among the Flowers' off by heart he doubted he'd ever sing it out loud again. It was tainted now, charred.

But it was different when he wrote it, over a decade before Rox took it. He liked who he'd been back then. The keenness, the naivety, the energy and optimism for the future: for Life, for the mystery of Love.

*    *    *

Petra Flint.

Blimey.

Now there's someone he hadn't thought about for a while.

Arlo glanced around the class as if he'd just spoken out loud, but the boys had their heads down.

'Finn, stop chewing your shirtsleeve.'

When Rox had first released the song and had nodded their shaggy locks and generally postured in a deep and meaningful way on *Top of the Pops*, Arlo had briefly wondered about Petra, whether she was watching, whether she'd heard the song, remembered it, remembered him. But there had been so much else on his mind five years ago, he hadn't had the capacity to dwell on it.

He thought about her now, though. In evening prep. Petra Flint. His unwitting muse and the prettiest girl he'd seen back then; the personification of the song's subject matter who came into his focus out of nowhere the day that the Noble Savages had performed at her school. Whatever happened to Petra Flint?

'Nathan, flick one more ink pellet at Troy and you'll forfeit your next exeat.'

Petra Flint is probably an artist or a housewife, Arlo decided, bringing himself back to the present sharply. And here he was, aged thirty-four, sitting in an oak-panelled study room in a school that was over three hundred years old, presiding over twenty teenage boys who were battling with their homework and tiredness and boredom and their need to be just boys. He looked at them. They looked like a bunch of scraggly terriers who could well do with a noisy belt around the playing fields. He tried to see himself through their eyes. One of the slightly more cool teachers, he reckoned with some satisfaction: his small gold hoop earring, his excitingly varied taste in music, his occasional swearing, the fact that he had a tattoo on his upper arm which the boys had glimpsed but never seen in

47

full, the fact that he called the boys 'guys', that he told them, when they asked him, that yes he had done certain drugs at certain times in his life. They'd never asked him about sex, though. They reserved that topic as a dare—preferring to cloak their queries with faked innocence and pose them to female members of staff instead. The cheeky buggers. Or perhaps they didn't ask him because he didn't give out that vibe. You can ask Mr Sir Savidge about music and drugs and tattoos because he knows about all that stuff. But don't ask him about sex because he doesn't have sex any more.

And if ever they should ask him, what would he say then? That he was celibate from personal choice? And that had been the case for five years? Was that the line he'd spin to Miranda Oates if she kept up her attention? Arlo thought about Miranda Oates with her shapely rear, her nice tits, her penchant for dark lipstick and bare legs, her obvious interest in him. And he wondered if it wasn't just a bit sad, perhaps a little worrying, that he was thinking of inventive ways to fob her off when once he would quite happily have shagged her, gamely dated her even.

'That's the end of that,' he said, suddenly out loud, and the boys took it to mean the end of prep and scarpered from the room a full five minutes early.

# CHAPTER FIVE

Despite the mercy dash to Whetstone in the small hours, Rob's meeting with the Japanese had gone well. Petra was very tired after the previous night's sortie and though most of all she craved an early night, she'd phoned Rob and offered to cook at either her place or his. He suggested she join him in town. Getting ready, she asked herself a couple of times why she was doing something she didn't want to do, why didn't she just slob around at home and eat finger food in front of *Location Location Location*. But she answered herself sharply—her relationship with Rob was just ten months old and there was no time for complacency. Furthermore, Rob seldom invited her to socialize with his work people, though he frequently did. So she should be honoured, she told herself. And she shouldn't let bloody sleep, or lack of it, dictate her life. She stood in her bedroom in a bath towel and wondered what she could wear that was appropriate for a night on the town with Rob and his cohorts, but would be comfortable. Her grazed knee was still too raw to go plasterless and her blistered heels necessitated backless shoes. But not my Birkenstocks, Petra thought, not on Rob's big night—he'd be appalled. She decided to wear her slippers because they didn't look too much like slippers; indeed, people wore a similar style as shoes. A pair of slip-on flat mules in a type of glorified plastic netting decorated with sequins and beads. She'd have to wear socks or tights because she couldn't very well have her heels on display, with plasters or without. She hated anything drawing attention to herself. Just then, for a moment, she hated herself more for sleepwalking.

'If I didn't bloody sleepwalk, I could be tottering about in strappy heels. Not that I own a pair,' she muttered to herself, slouching in front of the mirror. 'Pop socks and slippers. For Christ's sake.' In the event, her cropped black trousers covered the offending top of the pop socks, and a plain black camisole teamed with a cardigan lightly decorated with beads gave her look a cohesion that pleasantly surprised her. Concealer helped with the bags under her eyes and mascara widened them beyond their weary proportions. On the tube, she congratulated her inventiveness: no one gave her a second look or even registered her choice of footwear.

*       *       *

'And here is Petra,' Rob announced as she approached his table at a busy Soho bar, 'and—dear God—she's wearing her slippers.'

Though she stood while everyone remained seated, she felt small and mortified. Two of Rob's male colleagues glanced down at Petra's feet in fascination, a couple of his female colleagues analysed them with pity, whilst circling their own beautiful footwear.

'Blisters!' Petra shrugged, making a lively joke of it.

'They're cute,' one of the girls said lamely.

'Watch out that none of these louts tread on your tootsies,' slurred the other.

'How are you, babe?' Rob asked, pulling Petra towards him for a boozy kiss, his hand lingering over her buttocks.

'Fine, fine,' Petra said, aware that one of the other men was entranced by Rob's hand on her bottom. There were no spare chairs.

'You get the next round, darling,' Rob said, 'and you can perch on my knee.'

'*You* get the drinks in, Rob, you wanker,' said the woman who had defined Petra's slippers as cute. 'Here, your bum is quite small, cop a pew with me.' And she shuffled to the edge of her chair, making room for Petra.

'Thanks,' said Petra. 'I'm Petra.'

'I know,' she said. 'I'm Laura. I work with Rob. We all do—we're toasting ourselves because the Japs love us.'

'Cheers,' said Petra, though she had no glass to raise.

'Get the girl a drink!' Laura told Rob who flung his hands up in defeat and made his way to the bar.

'Oh dear,' Petra said, trying to look fondly after him, 'he looks slightly the worse for wear.'

'All the blokes do, they are all worse for wear,' the other girl leant across and said, 'whereas we girls are just pleasantly pissed.'

Petra wondered whether to toast this fact, but not having a drink enabled her to just nod and grin while the other women drained their champagne flutes. She didn't much care for champagne, or wine bars. She preferred vodka and tonic in friendly pubs. This place was heaving yet echoey and she wasn't sure whether she liked the milieu, a noisy rabble of suited men and highly well-heeled women bragging and flirting; money mingling with

51

cigarette smoke and arrogant laughter. She felt intimidated and that irritated her. However, when Rob returned with a bottle of champagne but also a vodka and tonic for Petra, she reprimanded herself not to be so provincial and judgemental.

She sipped her vodka and grinned awkwardly while Rob and his colleagues talked about stuff she didn't understand and people she didn't know. She found herself making mental notes: pay bills, speak to her bank, ring her father—her mother too. It had been ages since she'd spoken to either, let alone seen them. She'd try and arrange to visit one on Saturday, the other on Sunday. She'd take Rob along. Over the last ten months, her mother had met him only a couple of times and her father just the once. She glanced over at Rob, a slight sheen to his face from euphoria and the effort of the day, his voice loud and fast from alcohol and high spirits. He looked nice in a suit, she thought, and wasn't it good to see him in his element, holding court amongst colleagues, reeling off extravagant anecdotes and technical data from the working day just gone. Just then, Petra felt a wave of resentment towards Eric and Kitty and Gina who were not particularly subtle about their doubts over Rob. Particularly Eric. And Kitty. Gina slightly less so.

And yet look how Rob's lot include me, Petra thought to herself—Laura and the other girl asking all about our relationship, that bloke with the wet patch on his shirt asking me about diamond merchants, that other one buying me another vodka and tonic. If Rob hadn't been stressed out and moody that day he visited the studio, perhaps my lot would be more

52

accommodating. And I probably haven't helped—taking into the studio my daft insecurities and niggles. They're very quick to criticize, my Studio Three. I bet they wouldn't say my slippers are cute.

Petra tried desperately to stifle a yawn.

'Are we keeping you up?' one of the men teased her.

'You do look a little tired,' Laura commented.

'She was up half the night,' Rob said.

'Phnar phnar,' one of his colleagues nudged him.

'Not likely,' Rob laughed. 'My girlfriend gets up to all sorts of shenanigans at night—but it's nothing to do with me.'

'I sometimes sleepwalk,' Petra mumbled in, hoping to curtail details.

'Yesterday—Christ, the early hours of this morning,' Rob was saying, 'I get a call from the police asking me do I know a Petra Flint, does she have wellingtons and a Snoopy T-shirt and is there any way she could have walked towards Whetstone whilst asleep.'

'You're joking,' Laura said, the focus of her pity directed at Rob which disappointed Petra.

'Appalling,' Petra said quickly. 'Hence the slippers—from my blisters.'

'Mind you, at least she was clothed,' Rob said, raising his glass at Petra and winking.

Oh God, don't, Rob, please.

But Rob was bolstered by Bollinger and he had a captive audience and he quite liked the power of being a raconteur.

'When I took her to meet my folks down in Hampshire, she walked into their bedroom, switched on their light, opened their cupboard

53

doors, had a rummage around and then walked out again.'

'Rob—'

But Rob paused for dramatic effect only. 'Starkers!' he told the table. 'I don't know who it was worse for—Petra, or my parents.'

Petra hid her head in her hands.

'Do you really not realize a *thing*?' the other girl asked, slightly accusatorily. Petra shook her head without raising her face.

'Why don't you go to bed wearing something—just in case?' Laura asked her.

'I do,' Petra said, 'especially when I'm staying away from home. I put on layers and layers before I go to bed. I don't know why I take them off—I don't know why I take off.'

'Can't you take a sleeping pill or something? It could be dangerous.'

'So could taking sleeping pills,' Petra said. 'I've seen specialists, had tests. No one knows why I do it or how to stop me.'

'I can't believe she walked into your parents' room naked,' Laura said to Rob, and Petra would rather she'd said it to her.

'I don't mean to,' Petra said, trying to look imploringly at Rob who didn't seem to feel her gaze. 'I don't like it.'

'Petra will kill me for this one—apparently, before I met her, she actually got into bed with complete strangers.'

'Oh my God—did you have sex with them?'

'Of course not,' Petra said crossly. 'I was staying at a place in the country for my friend's thirtieth birthday. I didn't know the house and I think I was getting flu anyway. But yes, I walked in my sleep

54

into another bedroom and got into bed with a couple.'

'What did they do?'

'Tried to get me out,' Petra said. 'I only stayed for a few minutes anyway and then I went out of my own accord.'

'Out?'

'Into the grounds of the house,' Petra explained, 'but someone was having a spliff outside and they led me back.'

'They must've thought it was damn good skunk,' one of the men laughed.

Petra shrugged. 'I know it sounds funny and crazy—but it's not. Believe me.'

'It's a liability,' Rob said. 'That's why I'd like to say that I'm particularly proud of the deal we did today, chaps—because I was up half the night in Whetstone bloody police station.'

Everyone raised their glasses to Rob, and Petra suddenly wondered whether it would have been entirely her fault if he hadn't closed the deal with the Japanese. Poor Rob, she thought, I am a liability. So she raised her glass highest of all. And though she was desperate to go home and snuggle up with him for an early night, she stuck it out at the bar because she felt he deserved it.

\*       \*       \*

Later, much later, they took a cab back to Rob's flat in Islington. Petra was beyond exhausted but woozy with vodka too. When she sobered up, she would think how it was not particularly logical to be mad at Rob for humiliating her yet also to want to impress him, seduce him, enamour him of her—

55

so that perhaps he wouldn't do it again. When she sobered up, no doubt she would wonder why on earth she hadn't just said, Rob, you sod, please shut up—it's private and you're embarrassing me. But she was a little drunk and her heels throbbed and she'd knocked her knee on the side of Rob's chair and it was the same chair she'd once wet in her sleep. And suddenly she loved him for having not humiliated her by revealing that episode to his colleagues. And foremost in her conscience was that she'd pissed Rob off the night before and so now she ought to make it up to him because she didn't like upsetting people and she didn't like arguments and she didn't like conflict and she wanted to remind Rob that there was more to her than Snoopy T-shirts and calls from the police. And it would be so very nice if this relationship could last beyond a year.

Before he had time to pour himself a whisky, Petra was behind him, encircling her arms around him. She kissed him between his shoulder blades, huffing hot breath through his shirt while she travelled her hands down his stomach and unzipped his trousers.

'What's all this?' he murmured though he took her hand and thrust it down his boxers. He turned and kissed her hungrily. He tasted slightly rancid, of too much beer and champagne on top of a liquid lunch, but Petra told herself to block it out. She kissed him back thoughtfully, taking care to skip her tongue around his mouth, her teeth grazing his lips. She looked into his eyes which were a little bloodshot but no doubt hers were too. She didn't really like his face so much when he was drunk—it was what Eric would term 'leery' and Eric had seen

Rob pissed once before. But leery was fine for now because sex was on the agenda. He squeezed her breasts and bucked his groin against hers. She swept her hand downwards and thrilled at the feel of his erection holding the fine wool of his suit trousers aloft. He fumbled with his belt and pushed his trousers and underpants down. His hands at her shoulders urged Petra to squat down though she stifled the wince of pain as her knee objected.

'Suck my cock,' he panted and Petra obliged, though she didn't need his hands guiding her head and she wished he wouldn't because it made her gag. 'God, I'm horny,' he murmured, pulling her up to standing, which again sent waves of pain through her knee as it was straightened. 'Got to fuck you now,' he said, groping and pulling her trousers as he backed her towards the sofa. His desire for her was what turned Petra on most about Rob. He could be arrogant, he could be moody. They hadn't that much in common, really. He wasn't what she'd term tender, which was a quality she rated, and he was attentive really because he could afford to be—flowers and gifts and nice dinners in upmarket restaurants. But he was very good at sex, and it was obvious that he thought Petra was very good at sex. He liked sex a lot and he liked lots of it and it flattered Petra that she appeared to turn him on so much and it was a thrill for her to take credit for his libido and his satisfaction.

So he fucked her rudely and quickly on his sofa and she thought to herself that, though her knee was being scuffled painfully against the fabric because he was taking her from behind, if they had been in missionary then both her sore heels would have suffered anyway. So it was OK. It was good, wasn't it, as he humped into her, his hand between her legs fiddling around for her clitoris. As he came, his mouth was at her ear and his gasps and groaning turned her on more than his cock or his hands and she moved herself urgently so that she came too.

They lay in a post-orgasmic, drunken slump.

'Nice fuck,' Rob said at length, easing himself off her. 'Petra,' he said sternly, *'pop socks?'*

'You weren't meant to see,' she said with a coy smile, 'but you were in a rush to have me.'

He raised his eyebrow and shook his head. 'Sometimes I think of you as so refreshingly quirky—but sometimes I think you're just odd. Come on, girl. Bed-time. And dear God, don't go walkabout tonight.' He locked his front door and locked the key in his briefcase which had a combination code Petra didn't know.

*       *       *

But she did walk. A couple of hours after they'd fallen asleep she'd left the bed and walked into the wall where she thought there was a doorway as she assumed she was at her flat.

'For fuck's sake,' Rob said, not that Petra could hear him. He found her in his sitting room, standing stock-still. He turned her shoulders and gave her a little shove every few steps.

'Petra, I can't be doing with this.' She looked at him directly, her eyes vacant though she spoke at him.

'I know what you mean,' she said flatly.

58

'I doubt it,' Rob said back though he knew they weren't conversing.

'But I wouldn't agree with you about Gordon Brown.'

She made to turn back to the sitting room but he steered her to the bedroom and she lay down without a murmur.

'Sorry, babe,' he said, 'but I'm fucking knackered.' And he took a tie from his cupboard, binding it around her wrist and securing it to the bedpost.

## CHAPTER SIX

Petra's knee healed faster than the blisters so she continued to wear her Birkenstock sandals with socks to the studio all week, and still had to wear her pop socks and slippers when she saw Rob a couple of evenings later. I'm wearing pop socks again, she advised him, so if you want to do unmentionably rude things to me, can you give me warning so I can take them off first. Rob had called her a little hussy—much to her delight. And in the event, she left her socks on and they had sex energetically while he slapped her buttocks and called her a naughty naughty girl. When she woke the next morning, though her buttocks felt decidedly tingly it was her left wrist which felt really sore and when she looked at it, it was red; scorched like a burn. She showed it to Rob who'd said, Don't you remember me pinning you down as I rogered you senseless? However Petra couldn't remember, precisely. But the sex had been kinky and mostly in the dark and perhaps all that spanking had distracted her, so maybe he had. As she showered, she did quietly consider how, as good as they were at sex, it would be nice if she and Rob could be a little better at the bits in between. But she quickly washed away the notion that, quite possibly, it was beyond Rob's natural personality to loll about chatting idly, or to hold hands whilst walking, or to make love rather than always fuck.

\*     \*     \*

'Petra, what have you done to your wrist?' Gina asked her in the studio.

Petra pulled her sleeve down but gave Gina and Kitty and Eric a saucy lick of her lips. 'Rob's a bit of a tiger,' she giggled, sashaying out to the toilet.

'He's a bit of a prat,' Eric said dryly when Petra was out of earshot.

'He's a lot of a prat,' Gina defined.

'I don't like it,' Kitty said darkly. 'Petra is naturally gentle—physically and emotionally. I'm sorry, but I don't like to think of someone being rough with her.'

'She can look after herself,' Eric snapped because actually he wished he'd come out with Kitty's insight.

'No, Eric. *I* can look after myself,' Kitty said. 'Petra was born someone to be made love to—I'm someone born to fuck.'

Gina giggled. 'Kitty, you are outrageous. You're putting me off my work.'

Kitty shrugged, her skeins of blue-black hair snaking around her shoulders like a latter-day Medusa. 'Sorry, Gina,' she said, 'but I do have

60

authority to speak. I've had more sex with more people than all the hyphens in the double-barrelled surnames in your street.'

Gina giggled again. 'Rob *is* a prat—but it's not for us to say so. Anyway, Petra is very fond of him. And she's really set on making this relationship last.'

'Even if it doesn't necessarily work,' Eric sighed. 'Christ.'

'True,' said Kitty, 'but if I think he's hurting her, then no one's bloody gagging me. Silence has no place in the shadow of violence.'

Both Eric and Gina quietly hoped that this was the end of the matter and that Petra would not come into work with marks on her again. Neither of them fancied Rob's chances against Kitty.

\*　　　\*　　　\*

'I'm taking Charlton's piece back to him,' Petra announced when she came in again. She showed them the ankh pendant she had fashioned out of gold according to Charlton's precise design; Celtic ornament enlivening the surface. 'Does anybody want anything?'

'Can you pop into Bellore for me?' Gina asked. 'They phoned to say my turquoise is in—it's all paid for.'

'And I need some 4mm setting strip,' said Kitty. 'Can you lay out for me and I'll pay you back?'

'Anything else? Eric?'

'Oh go on, twist my arm—I'll have a cappuccino,' Eric said. 'But better make it a skinny one—my belt was tight this morning. Do you think I've gained weight?'

61

Petra raised her eyes at Kitty and Gina and left them to deal with Eric's neuroses while she went about her errands.

*       *       *

On one side only of Hatton Garden there is a line of trees which bow subtly towards the kerb like some kind of benign, eco-friendly security grille. It is on this side, about halfway down, that Charlton Squire has the original of his two jewellery galleries. The other, opened last year, is off New Bond Street in the West End. Like Electrum in South Molton Street, Charlton Squire Gallery is revered as a hotbed boutique of cutting-edge talent. However, there's a price to pay for such innovation in precious metals and gems and designs and it's high; the pieces for sale are marketed meticulously as luxury goods for those who can afford them. There's also a price to pay by the jewellers whom Charlton chooses to exhibit at his gallery and that is hefty commission charges. However, to exhibit at Charlton Squire means access to wealthy clients and occasional exposure in the pages of *Vogue* and *Vanity Fair*.

'It's a six and two threes,' Petra had justified when she told the others at the studio that Charlton had selected her work.

'It's a rip-off,' said Eric.

'Your nose is just out of joint because Charlton didn't select you,' Gina chided.

'More like Eric's dick is out of joint because Charlton turned down his crown jewels,' Kitty said.

'I didn't offer him my body,' Eric objected, 'only my work. I don't fancy him anyway—he's not my

62

type. He's too big and swarthy and I don't like his accent.'

'You Southern poof,' Kitty teased him.

'Charlton Squire sounds like the love child of Jimmy Nail and Molly Sugden,' Eric said. 'I only understand every other word.'

'You snob,' said Kitty.

'And he looks like their love child too,' Eric said.

'You bitch,' said Kitty. 'Meow.'

*       *       *

Charlton Squire did not look like the love child of Jimmy Nail and Molly Sugden, in fact he looked quite unlike anybody. He certainly did not resemble either parent; his mother a whippet-wizened Yorkshire lass, his father a solid Geordie. At nearing six foot five and eighteen stone, Charlton looked more like an oversized cliché, alarmingly like a tribute act for the leather-clad chap from the Village People; a look which hadn't gone down well in his home town of Stokesley but had gone down a storm when he hit the gay scene in London twenty years ago. He'd ditched the thick moustache in his forties and had more recently relaxed the tightness of the top-to-toe leather and the amount of chest on public view. But he still came across as textbook gay and he used it to his advantage, whatever the sexuality of his clients. He'd charm the straight ones, flirt with the gay ones and inhibit anyone pursuing a discount by wielding his weight alongside with a winsome expression of abject hurt if they dared ask.

Though Charlton Squire's own designs were coveted worldwide, his secondary skill was as a

63

scout. He could swoop down on promising talents and quickly appropriate them as his protégés, as if their genius was of his making and that he alone was responsible for tapping into their potential. Though ruthlessly ambitious, he liked to exude an air of benevolent altruism and eagerly promoted himself as a philanthropic patron and mentor. He still loved designing jewellery but he also loved the showmanship of owning his galleries. He had neither the time nor the inclination to physically make up his own pieces any more and so as well as having bench-workers in the workshop behind the gallery in Hatton Garden, he also sent out his designs to skilled jewellers he trusted. Petra Flint being one of them. She didn't mind. She didn't find it demeaning and it didn't take her away from her own designs; she used her out-work from Charlton as a way of keeping her current account healthy and honing her dexterity as a jeweller—something she believed could always be more and more finely tuned.

*     *     *

What Petra loved most about Hatton Garden was its history and its honesty. It wasn't as chic or salubrious as the West End but there was a definite sense of it being the genuine hub of her industry. The retailers in Knightsbridge, in Regent Street, lower New Bond Street and South Molton Street were simply trading the wares which could be mostly traced back to the Hatton Garden area anyway. She knew some young jewellers who had studios in Hackney, in Kensal Rise, but though she paid a little more for the privilege of renting studio

64

space in London's true jewellery quarter, it was money well spent for the buzz and the impetus it gave her. She loved the naffness of some of the shops; the lack of pretension of window displays haphazard on faded flower paper or frayed velvet boxes or cracked plastic cushions; she enjoyed the delusions of grandeur of others—from the geographically schizophrenic Beverley Hills London to the blingtastic Go for Gold with its windows stuffed full of solid gold chains thick enough to hoist anchor. She liked the way that the modern and ultra-chic could coexist quite happily with the old-fashioned and low key. R. Holt, with its frontage resembling a hardware store in need of a dust nevertheless nodded proudly at Nicholas James opposite, all uber-hip and with a minimalist take on window design. Cool Diamonds believed in the lure of its name alone in lieu of any window display while Petra's personal favourite, A. R. Ullman, was endearingly Dickensian in the higgledy-piggledy jam-packedness of its diminutive shopfront. As she walked to Charlton's, she browsed; said hullo to familiar faces, detoured via the Wyndham Centre to enquire about reflexology for sleep disorders. Kitty, Gina and Eric had sent her there for her birthday last December, booking her a crystal healing with chakra balancing session. She'd felt well and truly stoned afterwards.

When she was buzzed in at the Charlton Squire Gallery, the eponymous owner, in all his enormous campness, was locked in discussion with a young Hasidic Jew whom Petra recognized as Yitzhak Levy, from a family of renowned diamond dealers. Charlton stood a head and shoulders taller than Yitzhak and compared with the latter's paleness,

Charlton looked positively orange. But whatever Yitzhak lacked in physical stature, his magnificent hat and beautifully tonged sideburn ringlets gave him gravitas. From Charlton's leather trousers and contour-skimming silken shirt the colour of midnight, to Yitzhak's eighteenth-century Polish dignitary's dress, the men epitomized the theatricality, the tolerance, the unique and unchanged trading mores of Hatton Garden. Petra knew what would happen next. There'd be gesticulations, perhaps some banging of fists and the throwing up of arms and then shrugs and nodding and handshakes. The diamond merchant dug into his overcoat pocket and produced the stone which Charlton exchanged for a wad of banknotes. More handshaking. *Shalom. Kol tov.* Deal done for the day. The men turned and noted Petra. Charlton swaggered over, cupped her face in his hands and kissed her forehead. Yitzhak nodded amiably enough but kept physical space at a premium.

'He buys my diamonds,' Yitzhak shrugged, 'but none of his good money will buy your tanzanite, hey, Miss Flint?'

Petra shook her head vehemently.

'And if I give you top dollar for it—will you trade with me?'

Petra shook her head again and shrugged. 'It's not for sale, Mr Levy.'

'It's only for keeping in a cotton hanky under her mattress,' Charlton said, exasperated, 'isn't that right, Pet?' He often called her Pet, it being a common endearment in the North-East as much as a convenient diminutive of her name.

'I've brought your pendant back,' Petra said,

because her tanzanite was not for sale, not even for discussion.

'May I?' Yitzhak asked and Charlton handed the piece to him. 'Very nice,' he said. 'A bit heathen for my liking. You ever thought of designing a nice Star of David range, Mr Squire?'

'Most my clients are *goyim*,' Charlton bantered back, the Yiddish for 'non-Jew' coming as easily as a second language.

Yitzhak shrugged. 'If you make them—they will sell.'

Charlton nodded. 'You're probably right. Now bugger off and flog your diamonds elsewhere.'

The men laughed and shook hands again. Yitzhak nodded at Petra and left.

Charlton scrutinized her work in silence. He compared it in minute detail with his design and analysed the craftsmanship under a loupe.

'Excellent,' he said at length. 'Do you want cash or have it as a credit against commission?'

'Has any of my stuff sold?' Petra asked him though she could see her work displayed beautifully in a well-lit cabinet.

'Not this week, Pet.'

'I'd better have the cash then, if that's all right with you.'

'Planning to go crazy at the weekend?'

'Hardly,' Petra said. 'I'm off to see my parents.'

'Are you taking the boyfriend?'

'I am,' she said proudly.

'He'll be down on bended knee in front of your pa, Pet.'

'Don't be daft,' Petra said, though privately she thrilled to the notion.

# CHAPTER SEVEN

'Hullo?'

'Dad?'

'Hullo?'

'It's Petra.'

'Petra. Hullo. How are you?'

'I'm fine. And you? I was thinking about popping in tomorrow.'

'Tomorrow?'

'Yes—is that OK? About elevenish?'

'Oh. Elevenish isn't very good as Joanna has ballet. How about after lunch?'

'After lunch? Or what about lunch-timeish?'

'After lunch is better. If it's all the same to you.'

'Oh. OK. After lunch, then. See you tomorrow. And Dad? I'm bringing Rob.'

'Rob?'

'My boyfriend—you met him before Christmas.'

'Investment chappy?'

'Yes. It's going really well.'

'Well, we'll see you both tomorrow then.'

\*　　　\*　　　\*

Rob couldn't think of anything he'd like to do less with his Saturday than go on a day-trip to Watford to visit Petra's father. And he certainly wasn't going to give over his Sunday to journey out to Kent to visit Petra's mother. He'd rather visit his own parents in Hampshire, and that was saying something. His week had been long, mostly lucrative but exhausting. He fancied having a weekend left to his own devices. Certainly not to be wasted by being paraded in front of Petra's parents. Why was she so keen to do that anyway? It wasn't as if she was particularly close to them. Rob knew he could make it up to her by begging her forgiveness and promising that he'd have theatre tickets awaiting her return on Saturday evening, and the finest sushi in London when she came back on Sunday. Bloody work, he said. Bloody boring, he said. He didn't say that visiting her parents was hard work and boring.

*      *      *

On the Metropolitan Line to Watford, Petra fought a losing battle against nostalgia. It was always the same and on each occasion, only as she felt her spirits start to sap would she remember how she always asked herself why was she making this trip—uninvited yet feeling duty bound? She knew she'd leave deflated and reflective. She could be snuggled up with her boyfriend instead, if only he was a bit more into snuggling. Or she could be out shopping then. She could be cleaning her flat or curled up with a book. She could be having a nice, easy day.

The journey to Watford was relatively short but it was long enough for her to let the train window, against which she rested her head, judder memories and thoughts from the safe and private place she usually kept them. She always felt positive in advance about visiting one parent or the other, but as the destination neared so did a sense of trepidation and the hunch that on her homeward journey she would question why she

69

made the trip in the first place. Petra envied people whose parents continued to live in the old family home, enabling them to return to the cornerstone of their childhood each time they visited. No matter how far away that home might be, by definition it would be an easy journey to make. But Petra's childhood home had been sold when she was fourteen and her parents had divorced. She and her mother had moved into a flat nearby and her father had moved away.

Petra gently played her fingertips over her lap as if in silent piano practice; in fact she was totting up the years. It occurred to her that John Flint had lived in his current house in Watford with his new family for the past fifteen years. In the same house. Which meant he'd been there a year longer than all the time he'd spent at home with Petra. Psychologically though, he'd moved out of that house long before his bags were packed and his current house was much more his home than theirs had ever been.

She looked out of the window, glimpsing cars at a standstill. John had offered to buy her a car for her twenty-fifth birthday, but she'd sensed he'd hoped she'd decline because at the same time he'd made much of Joanna's school fees and there being another baby on the way.

There'd been another since then. Something good had come out of the split between her parents and that was half-siblings for Petra. Joanna and Eliza and Bruce. She peeled back the cellophane on a bland-looking sandwich. It was hard not to feel hurt that she hadn't been invited for lunch. But Joanna had ballet and no doubt big families were on tight timetables at weekends to cram everything in. Including visits from the daughter, the stepdaughter, the half-sister.

Christ, I've just realized Joanna is the same age as I was when Dad left.

*     *     *

'Petra!' Eliza flung herself at Petra's waist while Bruce tried to squeeze in between their bodies.

'What a welcome,' Petra told them, noting Joanna slunk around the banister. 'Hi Joanna, I'm loving your haircut. How was ballet?'

'Jo,' said Joanna. 'I like being called Jo now.'

'Sorry,' Petra said. 'Jo suits you.'

'I'm giving up ballet—I'm just going to do modern and tap.'

'Wow,' said Petra.

The teenager approached and helped her half-sister peel Bruce and Eliza off her limbs.

'Did you brung us things?' Bruce asked.

'Yeah! Presents!' Eliza shrieked. Petra noted that even Joanna now had an expectant twinkle in her eye.

'Let the poor woman in, you lot!' It was Mary. Petra's father's wife. From the start, Petra had somehow seemed old enough, self-contained enough and simply didn't visit often enough for her to appear remotely in need of a stepmother. So Mary and Petra's relationship bypassed that aspect. To Petra, Mary was her father's wife. To Mary, Petra was John's daughter. They both referred to him as John. They liked each other well enough.

They kissed. 'John is out—he should be back soon. I'm just doing an online supermarket order.

Kids—show Petra in.'

'She's brung us stuff,' Bruce said cheerily, poking Petra's bag as Eliza dragged her through to the sitting room.

Mary paused and Petra could see her assessing the subtlest way to do her familiar disappearing act. 'Petra, do you mind holding court—then I can just finish off on the computer?' And Mary wafted off muttering that she couldn't believe she didn't have time to go to a real supermarket these days.

An hour later, she reappeared. 'Where on earth is John?' she said. 'I'll phone him. Back in a sec.' But soon enough, Petra could see her in the back garden, pruning half-heartedly before sitting down to sip from a mug.

Half an hour later, John arrived back.

'Daddy!' clamoured his two youngest children, rushing forward. Joanna glanced up momentarily from her teen magazine.

'Hi, Dad,' said Petra, with an awkward half-wave, hanging back. She was always surprised at how grey her father's hair was; in between visits it automatically restored itself in her mind's eye to the darker thatch she remembered best. It had definitely thinned more too, even since her last visit before Christmas. Today he also appeared smaller around the shoulders yet more slumpy around the waist.

'Hullo, Petra,' he said, craning forward to kiss her cheek while Bruce and Eliza clambered around him like chimps on a trunk. 'Sorry I'm late—you know how these things drag on.' But Petra didn't know, because she didn't know where he'd been or what the things were that he usually did on a Saturday in early April. 'You look well, darling.

72

How long can you stay?'

Petra looked at her watch. 'Oh,' she said, 'about another hour, really. Rob's taking me to the theatre tonight.'

'Rob?'

'My boyfriend.'

'The investment chappy?'

'Yes. Him.'

'You must bring him along next time you visit,' John said.

'OK,' said Petra, wondering just now if she'd bother to visit before Christmas and wondering, very quietly, if she'd still be with Rob then anyway.

'How's work?'

'Great, thanks.'

'And everything else?'

'Yes, everything's fine, Dad, thanks.'

'Where's Mum?' John asked and it was instinctively on the tip of Petra's tongue to say, Still down in Kent actually I'm visiting her tomorrow—before she realized that he was asking the question of his other children.

'Online,' Joanna said, with a roll of her eyes.

'Mummy,' Eliza called.

'She's in the garden,' Petra told him. And off he went, followed at intervals of a minute or two by his children. Petra brought up the rear.

'Isn't it lovely to see Petra, everyone,' John announced. 'Shame you have to go so soon. Next time, come for longer.'

'And bring your boyfriend,' Jo said.

'OK,' said Petra, 'I will do.' And it dawned on her that though she could stay until she physically needed to leave to catch a train, her visit had probably run its course already. 'I suppose I'd

73

better make tracks, now.'

'Well, it's lovely to see you,' Mary said.

'Don't be a stranger,' John added. 'Come on, I'll run you to the station.'

'It's not necessary,' Petra told him. And John then said, 'well, OK then, if you're sure,' at the same time as Petra said, 'But a lift would be great, thanks,' and there was a momentary stalemate during which they laughed awkwardly and wondered how to backtrack.

'Come on, the least I can do is run you to the station,' John said.

'Don't dilly-dally,' Mary warned him. 'I've been run off my feet all day.'

John spread his palm to signify five minutes.

'Bye, everyone,' Petra said and the smaller children hugged her and bemoaned her leaving while Jo said, 'See you,' with the nonchalance characteristic of her age.

*  *  *

'Great to see you,' John said as he pulled up outside the station. 'You look very well, darling.'

'Thanks, Dad,' said Petra.

'Are you OK for money?' he asked, twisting to locate his wallet in his back pocket.

'I'm fine, Dad,' said Petra. 'Thanks.'

'Well, here,' he said, passing over a twenty-pound note. 'It's not much these days—but you can buy your chappy an ice cream in the interval at the theatre tonight.'

*  *  *

Petra felt almost euphoric as the train pulled away.

*He remembered that Rob is taking me to the theatre tonight!*

But the feeling soon disintegrated into the familiar sense of deflation. She rested her forehead so that it banged lightly against the window.

*I am never an unwelcome guest in my father's house, but I am always an uninvited one.* She felt close to tears and resolved not to arrange another visit until Christmas-time.

*　　　*　　　*

Petra's mother now collected chickens with much the same passion as she'd collected shoes when Petra started at Dame Alexandra Johnson School for Girls. When the letter arrived announcing that Petra had a place and a bursary too, Melinda Flint had taken her daughter into town in a taxi and told her to choose anything within reason at John Lewis. Petra had chosen a thick pad of cartridge paper, bound beautifully, and a Rotring draughtsman pen. Her mother had then spent ages in the shoe department, finally deciding on a pair of slingbacks in vivid scarlet suede. 'Don't tell your father,' Melinda had said, swooping down on a packet of cotton handkerchiefs monogrammed with a delicately embroidered P. Petra wondered how on earth her father could take offence to cotton handkerchiefs with her initial on them. Until she realized that her mother was referring to the shoes.

The only time John passed comment on her mother's shoes was in the heat of an argument.

75

And there were plenty. Shoes and arguments.

On a bright Sunday morning, Petra alighted from the train at East Malling, waited for a taxi and then asked the driver to stop so she could buy some milk.

'My mother is into soya milk,' she explained, 'and I don't like it.'

The soya-milk phase had lasted far longer than the red-shoe phase which came to an abrupt end when John left. She'd thrown the shoes out. Dumped them in a bin bag along with any items of his he'd left. She'd then eschewed anything as lively as red shoes in favour of elegant dressing so dark and demure it was almost funereal. However, when John and Mary had moved into the house in Watford to prepare for Joanna's birth two years later, Melinda had reverted to her maiden name of Cotton and, Petra assumed, the dress sense of her premarital days too. She forsook the nicely cut suits in sober colours to go with the flow. And everything was soon free flowing and colourful, from her hair to her long skirts to the yoga poses she did in the corner of the sitting room while Petra tried to watch *Blue Peter.*

When I finished school, Petra liked to explain, it wasn't me who left home, but my mother. As soon as Petra's place at Central St Martins was guaranteed, her mother left London.

Melinda lived first in a yurt near Ludlow for a few months, then she tinkered with communal living in Devon. She tried Portsmouth with a boyfriend called Peter and she stayed a while in Lincoln with a boyfriend called Roger. She settled on chickens and Kent a few years ago and is now more settled than Petra has ever known her to be.

So self-sufficient, in fact, that she seldom has the need or the nous to phone her daughter for a chat, let alone to arrange to see her.

*       *       *

Today, it seems, Melinda is not in.

Petra wonders how long to give her mother. She half-heartedly rings the doorbell again and phones the number, hearing the phone ringing inside the cottage. She puts the bag with the milk in the shade and tries to see over the unruly hedge. She can hear clucking, as if the chickens are muttering under their breath that all the doorbell and phone ringing is an imposition on a quiet Sunday morning. She feels irritated. She doesn't have a number for a local taxi firm and the cottage is not walking distance to any shops that might. She now feels relieved that Rob is not here. How pissed off would he be! He already refers to Melinda as Hippy Chick-en. She stomps around the cottage and peers into an old Renault she is sure cannot be her mother's. Her mother hates cars. Last time, she reeled off a load of incendiary facts about emissions and the ozone to Rob when they had turned up in his Mercedes before Christmas. The memory enables Petra to feel again relieved that Rob isn't here with her today.

After half an hour, and on the verge of drinking some milk straight from the carton, Petra can hear voices and over the stile on the other side of the lane, her mother and another woman appear.

'Yoo-hoo!' Melinda calls, as if Petra has just arrived and not spotted her.

The other woman waves.

77

'We've been for a lovely walk,' her mother tells her, 'hours and hours. Isn't it a joy to be in flip-flops in April! Lovely to see you, darling. Come on in. Oh Christ, look at this, Tinks, my daughter has brought her own milk with her!'

*      *      *

Each time Petra visits her mother, she is surprised and a little alarmed by how much stuff can be crammed into such a small space. By contrast, the chickens live in a stylish and spacious way, in designer coops bought at great expense.

'There must be thirty birds in your back garden,' Petra remarks, her head bobbing as she vies for a view from the kitchen window not obliterated by wine bottles with candles stuck in them or pelargoniums growing up from the sills meeting the spider plants clambering down from macramé hanging pots at the ceiling.

'Twenty-six,' Melinda corrects her, 'but two bantams are joining us next week. You'll come and collect them with me, won't you, Tinks.'

There is silence.

Melinda and Petra look around but though the cottage is crowded with belongings, there is certainly no one else there.

'She must have gone,' Melinda says airily. 'Well, the cacti can have her tea. I insist you try rice milk, Petra. I've changed from soya.'

They take their tea out into the back and the chickens squawk their irritation but soon settle down into a sort of muttering indifference.

'Rob says hi,' Petra says.

'Tell him I say hi and Have you sold your horrid

78

car, Rob,' Melinda says and she starts giggling.

'Mum,' Petra objects quietly.

'He's too businessy for you, Petra,' Melinda says. 'You need someone more—I don't know—less Mercedesy.'

'Don't be so judgemental,' Petra says. 'You hardly know him.'

'I'm not being judgemental,' Melinda says. 'I'm just making an observation. How long have you been with him?'

'Coming up for ten months.'

'There,' Melinda says. 'Obviously you know him better than I—but there again, perhaps I know you better than he.'

Petra wants to say, You hardly know me at all, Mum—we rarely speak and I hardly see you. 'Don't talk in riddles,' she says instead. And though she wants to defend Rob, she decides to leave it at that. Because, annoying as it is, her mum is a little bit right. Rob is businessy. He is Mercedesy. But Petra thinks it's up to her to decide whether he's too much so.

Petra is starting to feel tired and irritable. I just want a normal cup of tea and a sensible chat.

'Yoo-hoo!' It's Tinks, suddenly appearing from inside the house.

'I thought you'd buggered off!' Melinda says and the two women fall about laughing.

Petra bites her lip, not sure if she'd like to swear, cry or just yell.

'I have to go, Mum,' she says. 'Rob has tickets for—a thing.'

'You've only just arrived,' her mother protests.

'Actually, I arrived two hours ago,' Petra says, 'but you weren't here.'

79

'Oh come now, darling,' her mother says abruptly, 'you can hardly blame me for going for a stroll on a beautiful day like today. It's April! Flip-flop time! Goodness me, you Londoners, you youngsters, you're always in an insane rush, obsessing with schedules and timetables. Anyway, you can't go just yet, I need to collect some eggs for you.'

*     *     *

As Petra headed home, with the eggs and also the milk that her mother would not allow in her fridge, she thought about the period when her mother was slightly more staid and her father a little less dowdy. She must have been about eight or nine. But what was clearer than recollections of how they looked at that stage, what was more vivid than memories of family outings to the zoo back then, or those supper-times with Ambrosia Creamed Rice for pudding, was that this was precisely the period when Petra had first started sleepwalking.

## CHAPTER EIGHT

Petra had made much of not going into work the following day. She curled up under the duvet in Rob's bed that Monday morning and tried to entice him to stay with her.

'Play hooky?' she asked playfully.

'Why?' he said.

'Don't go into work,' she said.

'Why not?' he said.

'Stay right here and play with me!' Petra said. Rob hadn't asked why she wasn't going into work. 'I feel a bit low,' she told him, as if he had, 'after the weekend. My parents. You know. It's difficult.' Rob didn't ask why specifically.

He sat on the edge of his bed and traced the pinky beige aureole of her nipple thoughtfully, as if weighing up the merits and consequences of her offer to stay at home, but then he tweaked her nose between his fingers and slapped her buttocks as if she was a puppy. 'I have to go to work,' he told her, 'and you should too. It's not healthy to play hooky.' And with that, he swept back the duvet and flicked cold water at Petra from the glass beside the bed. She giggled and shrieked and writhed about the bed.

'I'm working late tonight,' Rob told her, ignoring her nakedness which quite hurt her feelings. 'And I'm away overnight tomorrow. I'll give you a call later in the week.'

'It's your birthday on Friday,' Petra said.

'Whoopee doo,' said Rob.

'You can't wake up alone on your birthday,' Petra said, though she remembered she'd done precisely that last December.

'You girls and bloody birthdays,' Rob said under his breath, procrastinating over which tie to wear.

'You realize you need never come back to an empty bed after a long hard day's work,' Petra said, making much of her coy expression though her heart was thudding as she let slip what was on the tip of her tongue. 'That is—if we lived together.'

Rob looked at her blankly. 'Those are the times when I need my space the most,' he said.

She cringed, not at the bluntness of his response

81

but at what suddenly seemed the misfired audacity of her proposal. She sat herself up and fiddled with winding her watch. Rob's expression softened. 'We'll go out Friday night and you can celebrate my birthday for me in whichever way you choose,' he said. He ran her hair through his fingers. 'It's a bit soon, for me, to be talking about cohabiting and whatever.'

Petra nodded. 'Sorry,' she said.

'You've got keys, haven't you—remember to double-lock when you go.'

*     *     *

Petra cursed modern technology for its failings. Emails and text messaging and phone calls were all very well for shrinking the world in an amicable web of global communication but the truth was that her oldest, closest friend lived abroad and though the phone was marvellous in making a mockery of vast oceans and time zones, what Petra wanted most just then was simply a cappuccino in Lucy's actual company. Feeling a little sorry for herself, she made one from the coffee machine in Rob's kitchen. Sitting at his breakfast bar, calculating the time differences with Hong Kong, she decided to send a help! ☹ text message. If she was lucky, Lucy would be back from the school run.

She waited; toyed with the idea of phoning too but decided against it—her mobile phone bill was large enough and realistically this wasn't an emergency, it was just her feeling a little down. She finished her coffee. Her phone remained blank. She took a shower. Still there was no reply. There

82

wasn't anything worth watching on daytime TV. And there was no food in Rob's fridge. Just champagne, which irritated her. He's a bit of a cliché, my boyfriend, she thought and wondered fleetingly how much else would get on her nerves if they did move in together. There now seemed little point in playing hooky; Rob had gone into work and her best friend was apparently oblivious to her cry for help. There was nothing to do but leave Rob's flat and head for Hatton Garden.

\*       \*       \*

'Good weekend?' Eric asked.

'Ish,' Petra said with a shrug.

'Rob?' Eric asked, expectantly.

'Parents,' Petra said.

'How's Mother Hen?' Kitty teased, but carefully.

'Barking mad,' said Petra.

'Does her hair still look like alfalfa?' Kitty asked, because she loved this previous description of Petra's.

It raised a smile. Petra nodded. 'You'll have to visit with me one day, Kitty,' she said.

'Your mother would love that,' Kitty said. 'One look at me and her hens will be laying eggs for their life.'

'The thing is, my mother *would* love that,' said Petra.

'Did Rob chauffeur you about?' Eric asked.

'Well, he would've,' Petra said, 'but he had loads of work to do.' Though she'd said it airily, there was uncharitable silence from her workmates. 'It's his birthday on Friday.' Gina, Kitty and Eric nodded but returned to their work. 'I'm going to surprise him,' Petra said, 'but I don't know how just yet.' Quietly, she paused to consider how hard she worked at choreographing this relationship without truly knowing whether Rob was much good at dancing to her tune. Their musical tastes were another thing that actually (along with a taste for champagne) they did not share.

*      *      *

Petra sketched. Recently she'd spent a lot of her studio time sketching. Sketching or doing out-work for Charlton. Though he had a selection of her pieces for sale, realistically, until funds came in, she couldn't really justify purchasing the gold or the gems for her new designs. In fact, she just couldn't afford it at the moment. She had a tab at Bellore, the suppliers to the trade, but Petra didn't like letting that run too high. For the time being, she would just have to be content making up her designs in copper or steel wire for future pieces in precious metal. Perhaps if Charlton or one of her private clients liked them, they'd commission the real thing. But Petra wasn't a saleswoman and the thought of contacting a previous client with a direct pitch for business appalled her.

'I'll do it for you,' Eric had offered.

'But they spent one thousand pounds on that crocheted gold necklace with the aquamarine only six months ago.'

'So you suggest matching earrings,' Eric had shrugged.

'I don't know, Eric,' Petra had said. 'It seems a bit mercenary.'

'Oh, for God's sake, Petra,' Eric said. 'It's your bloody job, woman.'

'Don't swear at her,' Kitty growled from the background.

'My friend Sophia is turning forty this year,' Gina said helpfully. 'I could ask her hubby if he wanted to splash out on a gorgeous Petra Flint something-or-other. They've got buckets of cash and a penchant for the finer things in life.'

'But surely you should be pushing him to splash out on a gorgeous Gina Fanshaw-Smythe?' Petra said.

'My stuff is way too chunky and vulgar for Sophia,' Gina had replied ingenuously. 'She's very refined, is Sophia. Your style is perfect.'

\*       \*       \*

As Petra sketched that Monday morning, working on curlicues and arabesques and serpentines, she recalled Gina's compliment and it gave her a boost. Perhaps if she showed Gina a couple of her designs it would prompt her to mention Sophia again and maybe this time Petra might just say, Oh, OK then, if you think her husband might like to see my work, by all means show him. She worked again on an idea that had been nestling in her mind and her sketchbook for some time. She took coloured pencils and slicked mentions of gold over her soft pencil lines. Then she took a blue pencil and a violet one and worked the hues over each other. The design was for a necklace. Fine rose-gold belcher from the back of the neck slinking just over the trapezius where it then met an undulating line of solid rose gold sitting sinuously along the

85

clavicle. From the centre of this, a gemstone. Tanzanite. Something sizeable, 4 carat or so. Balanced by two smaller tanzanites, a carat each, uniting the junctions between the gold chain and the solid gold.

She stood up, stretched, looked out of the window to the hubbub of Leather Lane. It's busy this morning, for a Monday morning, she thought until Eric suddenly announced, 'Lunch-time!' and she looked at her watch and marvelled how the hours had rattled by while she had been so silently absorbed in her work. She felt quite triumphant, stimulated, productive. And very hungry. Gina was still engrossed in hammering a silver bangle and Kitty appeared to have left the studio. Petra decided to leave her sketch-book open and accompany Eric to the sandwich shop.

When they returned, Kitty and Gina were poring over Petra's designs.

'It's stunning,' Kitty said. 'Classic but contemporary, delicate but strong.'

Petra looked at Gina expectantly. 'You're a clever bunny,' Gina said. And Petra said, Do you think so, thank you, thanks a lot. But she couldn't bring herself to mention Sophia's fabulously rich husband.

'Don't let Charlton see it,' Eric said. 'He'll copy it, the sod.'

'That wouldn't be your tanzanite, would it?' Gina asked.

Eric looked at Petra's drawing. 'Her tanzanite is twice the size.' He squinted at the sketch. 'Three times the size.'

'Bring it in again one day,' Gina said, 'so we can all have a jolly good ogle.'

Petra hadn't been home since before the weekend. She'd gone directly from Watford and later Kent to Rob's place and stayed over both nights. She'd rented her flat for just under two years. Recently she had renewed the lease. She'd asked Rob's advice a couple of months ago, hoping that he'd say, Move in with me, babe. But his advice had been solidly financial. He pointed out that she couldn't afford the down payment for a suitable flat in an area she liked and, with it still being a seller's market, she may as well continue to rent for the time being.

Her flat was small and fairly sweet. The lounge could take a gateleg table and three folding chairs as well as a sofa; it also had a fireplace with coal-effect fire and alcoves with shelving to either side, stripped floors and sash windows. The bedroom accommodated a double bed and the narrow church pew which Petra had bought as a student and had taken from bedroom to bedroom ever since. As there was only a clothes rail, a small, narrow chest of drawers and no cupboard, the pew's surface was invaluable. The bathroom had no window, just a noisy Vent-Axia but, bizarrely for the lack of space, a bidet too. Her upstairs neighbours were the landlords and they were a friendly if heavy-footed family.

Today, she came home to a note from them saying, 'There's a leak!!! We've had it fixed. Hope nothing of yours is affected??? Insurance will cover if so!!' Petra looked around the sitting room and suddenly noticed the yellowed bulge at the far end

87

of the ceiling and the beige fingers of damp clawing their way down the wall; her paperbacks on the shelf directly beneath were puffed swollen and soggy but they appeared to be the only casualty. In fact, Petra found herself more distressed by the state of her fridge—that her milk had gone off and that the KitKats she thought she still had were not there. She was going to slump down to sulk, then she thought she'd stomp off to the corner shop, but then she noticed the flashing of her answerphone.

'It's me! I've just done the school run! Where *are* you? Phone me and I'll call you straight back.'

It was Lucy. Or, rather, it had been Lucy, phoning from Hong Kong. Hours and hours ago. It was now gone six and over the seas and far away Lucy would be fast asleep. In fact, it was already Tuesday for her. If Petra waited until eleven, she'd catch Lucy at breakfast.

*       *       *

The conversation started as it always did: with brief marvelling at the clarity of the phone line and how much time had passed since they last spoke.

'I miss you,' Petra said. 'What are you having for breakfast?'

'Fruit salad,' Lucy laughed. 'Miss you too. I did phone yesterday. What's up?'

'Well, I feel OK now—because I had a productive day at the studio. But I woke up feeling crap—because I used up my weekend visiting my parents.'

'It's not Christmas,' Lucy said.

'I know.'

'I thought we'd decided you'd only visit at Christmas?'

'I know. I don't know why I did it, really.'

'How were they?'

Petra paused. 'They're both always so preoccupied. I just feel inconsequential.'

'You are far from it,' Lucy said, almost sternly.

'Thank you,' Petra said. She paused because she wanted Lucy to continue.

'You're the strongest person I know,' Lucy said. 'All your achievements are your own. God, it's not as if your parents gave you a leg-up, a foot in the door or even a pat on the back. You've always managed to stride out by yourself. And look at your success.' She said it with triumph. 'Does that help?' she added.

'Ish,' said Petra.

'Don't let them upset you,' Lucy said, 'because of course they don't mean to. They're not bad people—they're just, well, crap parents.'

Petra paused.

'You don't really need them,' Lucy said.

'But sometimes I want them,' Petra said.

'Everyone needs a sense of family,' Lucy said, 'in every sense of the word. You don't quite have that and that's tough. How are you sleeping?'

'Not good,' Petra said. 'I've been waking up knackered. I think I must be sleepwalking a lot.'

'How is Rob?' Lucy asked.

Petra paused. She was acutely aware that she never paused when Eric or Gina or Kitty asked the question. She always jumped to his defence; blowing his trumpet and singing his praises. But with her oldest friend, such exaggeration was pointless. Honesty though, required greater effort.

89

'Fine.'

'Fine?'

'Ish,' Petra qualified.

'I don't like the sound of "ish",' said Lucy, wishing she was in the UK, wishing she knew Rob better because her first impression of him hadn't painted her a particularly pleasing picture.

'I'm not quite sure where I stand and I feel I should after ten months,' Petra said. 'After all, I've made it my mission to ensure that he wants for nothing from me. Sex. Support. Affection. Space.'

'You give,' Lucy defined, 'but what do you get? Does he actually warrant all the effort you bestow?'

'I wish he'd ask me to be with him—you know, move in, or something,' Petra said, pointedly ignoring Lucy's question. 'I wish he'd just ask. I'd like to feel that he loves me enough to at least ask.'

On the other side of the Pacific, Lucy had closed her eyes and frowned. Love shouldn't be such an effort. But she didn't think love was the point—she suspected it was self-esteem. Petra will stick with Rob, Lucy thought, because Petra loathes the thought of splitting up. Petra wants to feel loved regardless of whether the object of her affection is actually worthy of hers.

'It's his birthday on Friday,' Petra said, aware of Lucy's silence and changing tack because of it. 'I won't see him until then. He's too busy. He says.'

'Will you be going out to celebrate?' Lucy asked, her tone of voice light. If she couldn't physically be there to pick up the pieces, then she couldn't very well dish out the home truths.

'Yes. Somewhere in town, I guess. He hasn't decided. He's not really into birthdays.'

90

'Don't take that personally,' Lucy said.

'I've bought him a leather document case. Cost a bomb. And I might let myself into his flat beforehand,' Petra told her. 'You know—prepare it for later.'

'What, balloons and banners?'

'And rose petals!' Petra enthused, missing Lucy's sarcasm.

'He's a lucky boy,' said Lucy and she really meant it.

'Thanks, Luce,' Petra said.

'Call me,' Lucy said, with a touch of urgency, 'whenever. Seriously. Any time.'

# CHAPTER NINE

Perhaps Rob's mobile was on silent. But he'd said he'd be working late, so Petra wondered why on earth she was trying to distract him with phone calls anyway.

'Oh well,' she said, 'may as well go to bed.' But first she went from room to room, collecting her damaged paperbacks which had been splayed over the radiators all evening to dry. She took them all into the sitting room. In drying, they had fanned themselves out, some almost 360 degrees, like drab versions of Christmas paper lanterns which take form when folded in on themselves. She scouted the room for heavy items to place on them. Some she put into piles, placing chair legs on top. Her Tony Parsons paperbacks she lay side by side underneath the television set and she set her John Irving collection upright, against the skirting board, wedging the sofa against them.

There were still another sixteen paperbacks remaining, fanned out like Elizabethan ruffs, but all the heavy items in the sitting room had been put to good use. Petra checked her mobile. It was still blank. Gathering the books, she took them into her bedroom and laid them in a shambolic pile on the pew while she upturned her mattress and jostled it off the bed frame and up against the wall.

On her bed base, she put Barbara Trapido shoulder to shoulder with Nick Hornby and was just about to add Hilary Mantel to make an interesting threesome when she was distracted. Near the head of the bed and over to one side was a black velvet pouch with a thin gold silken cord. Petra leant across Nick Hornby, nudging Barbara Trapido out of the way as she did so, and took the pouch. She didn't open it; initially she just brushed the velvet against her cheek, her lips, as she sat cross-legged on the edge of the bed.

After a while, she slipped out the knot in the cord and eased open the neck of the pouch. With a little shake, she tipped out the contents. A white cotton handkerchief wrapped carefully around something hard. As she began, slowly, to unfurl the handkerchief, taking time to trace the embroidered 'P', she was about to detour in her mind's eye back to the John Lewis department store, to shopping with her mother, to the time when her mother bought her this handkerchief, a time when her mother wore glamorous red shoes and didn't have alfalfa for hair—but Petra pulled herself back from that memory because there was somewhere else she'd rather be. The handkerchief was now open and there, glinting and breathtakingly beautiful, lay Petra's tanzanite. The size and gloss of a peeled lychee: 39.43 carats of it, beautifully worked into a stunning pear cut with a dazzling array of light-reflecting facets. Internally flawless; brilliantly blue with a seductive wink of violet too.

On her bed, she cupped her hand as a cradle for the gem. It felt warm and rock-solidly reassuring to hold while she travelled back seventeen years, back to the day she first heard about tanzanite.

\*     \*     \*

'Mrs McNeil?' Petra called through the letter-box.

93

'Lillian? Hullo? It's me, it's Petra.'

The door opened less than ajar. 'So it is,' said Lillian McNeil. 'Come on in, dear.' And she opened the door precisely wide enough for Petra to sidle her slim, fifteen-year-old body through sideways.

'Oh, Mrs McNeil,' Petra said softly, sadly, raising her hand gently to the bruising around the lady's right eye. 'It looks worse today than the day before yesterday.'

Mrs McNeil swept at the air as if her black eye looked far worse than it felt. 'The good news is they caught the little scamps.'

'Lock them up and throw the key away,' Petra said angrily.

'There was only a few bob in my purse. And my watch was cheap as chips—it just looked fancy. And my eye—well, I fell, you see. That part was just bad luck. They didn't actually touch me at all.'

'I'd quite like to swear now.'

'Absolutely not. Swearing does not become you, Petra Flint.'

'I'm just so *angry*.'

'Let it pass, Petra. If I have—you must.'

'Well, I bought you something—Walnut Whips. I bought you a packet of milk ones and look, new plain ones too.'

Lillian's eyes sparkled rather than watered now. 'You'll have to help me eat them.'

'OK! Oh, and I brought you this. I took it out on my library card.' She handed Mrs McNeil an audio-cassette of *Pride and Prejudice*. 'I thought— if your eye was sore. I thought—if you didn't feel like reading. I know how you love your books.'

'Bless you, little Miss Flint.'

94

Petra shrugged off the compliment. 'Let's eat the Walnut Whips,' she said and she let Mrs McNeil choose between the plain and milk chocolate packets. 'Shall I make tea, too?'

'No, dear,' Lillian said, 'I'll do that. Young people just don't have the knack.'

'We're not taught properly,' Petra agreed. 'Before I met you, I'd never seen loose tea, just bags.'

While Mrs McNeil was pottering and clattering around the kitchenette, Petra browsed the room. She'd been visiting Mrs McNeil for nearly two terms. In fact, the summer holidays had just started, but it didn't occur to Petra not to visit. It might be the school holidays but it wasn't as if she was going on a family holiday this year. That in itself would be a contradiction in terms. It couldn't be much of a holiday if there wasn't much of a family. And anyway, there was something really nice about visiting out of school hours and not having the time restraints of double maths or netball or pottery at Milton College to rush away for. And, though there had been the unpleasant incident with Mrs McNeil's bag at the bus stop the previous week, Petra would have visited Mrs McNeil today anyway: she was her companion, not her duty.

That room. That lovely room; walls awash with art of all description, surfaces heaving under the breadth of possessions accrued over decades, even the floor space reduced by that veritable library of diverse tomes. How many times had Petra been in this room? And there was still so much to look at. She loved all the trinkets and keepsakes from a history of visits to a wealth of countries and cultures; the antithesis of just the two statement pieces of Lladro that her parents had bought to embellish the mantelpiece, one of which had gone to Watford with her father. Most of all Petra loved Mrs McNeil's pictures, some of which were prints, others originals in oil or watercolour or pastel or charcoal; some representative, others abstract, some framed, others tacked up with drawing pins. She was lost in thought, gazing at a vibrant oil painting, when Lillian came in with the tea.

'Mrs McNeil,' Petra said slowly, not turning around, still transfixed by the painting, 'I've just got it!'

'You shouldn't use the word "got", you know,' said Lillian, 'or "get". It's lazy.'

'I mean, I've just figured it out!' Petra qualified, her eyes still on the painting. Slowly, she turned, her face flushed with excitement. She walked across the room, towards Lillian and went to the watercolour of Kilimanjaro which hung by the front door and which she'd admired on her first visit. 'This is Mount Kilimanjaro,' she said, then walked over to the colourful abstract in oils which had so mesmerized her. 'And this is, too!'

Lillian McNeil regarded her, steadily but expressionless. It didn't matter to Petra.

'All these times I've been here, in your home, I thought this painting was just a gorgeous colourful explosion of colours and shapes. You know, *abstract art*. I thought maybe it *symbolized* fire and light and atmosphere—a bit like Joseph Mallord William Turner who we've been doing in art.' Petra stared at the picture. 'But I didn't realize it was real,' she whispered. 'Hang on—I've lost it!' She fell silent. 'Here!' She traced her finger over the coloured shapes to denote the form. 'It's real, isn't it—it's Kilimanjaro. But to me, it looks like Kilimanjaro is on fire!'

'It is,' Lillian said softly, a little sadly. She paused. Then she straightened herself and smiled. 'That painting was done over twenty-five years ago, Petra, and it appears you and I—and one other, who is no longer with us—are the only people to recognize its true subject matter. Most people think it's a colourful pastiche of Clyfford Still.'

'Who?'

'You'll learn. In art.'

'But it isn't.'

'No, it isn't. It's by Hector McNeil. My late husband. He painted that. He painted it for me. We loved Tanzania. We lived there, happily, with Kili as our magnificent backdrop. More than a backdrop. That mountain was our everything.'

Instinctively, Petra went over to the chair in which she always sat and nodded gratefully as Lillian poured the tea. She placed the cup and saucer carefully on her knee and sipped daintily. She was sure such manners were the outcome of taking one's tea in a bone-china cup and saucer. At home, there were only clunky Denby mugs.

'Is the fire real or abstract?' Petra asked. 'Did the mountain really catch fire, when you were there?'

Lillian poured tea for herself, settled into her chair. 'Legend has it that a great fire struck the mountain and that is what Hector's painting celebrates. Fire needn't necessarily destroy, Petra dear. Fire can reveal. Fire can create. Fire was the reason we came to be in Tanzania.'

Though Petra meant to sip, in her excitement it turned into a slurp. 'Sorry,' she said.

'Actually, the story starts a fair few years before the fire, Petra,' Lillian began, '585 million years ago to be precise, when the continents collided in the pan-African event and caused a geological phenomenon. There, you can knock your geography teacher for six when you go back to school.'

'What was the phenomenon?'

'A most beautiful and rare gemstone was born.'

Petra's glance ricocheted from the watercolour of Kilimanjaro by the door, to the vibrant oil of the mountain on fire across the room.

'Have you heard of the Masai?' Lillian asked her.

'Of course,' said Petra, 'we did them in geography last term. We watched a video and our teacher brought in real Masai beads. I wore the bangle all lesson.'

'A Masai legend tells of how a lightning bolt struck Kilimanjaro, setting the mountain ablaze and creating a magic fire in the sky. When the flames died down, glistening amongst the ash were stones of the most amazing array of blues: royal blue, midnight blue, indigo, periwinkle, lavender, blue-violet, violet-blue, pure violet. You see, the conditions had to be right those millions of years ago for the gem to be born and then, many millennia later, conditions had to be right for its existence to be revealed.'

'Wow,' said Petra. 'Is it a sort of diamond then?'

'It's actually a thousand times rarer than a diamond, Petra. And that's a fact.'

'Sapphire?'

'No—it is the colour sapphire wishes it could be.'

'What is it?'

'It is tanzanite.'

'Tanzanite?' The word was lovely on the tongue.

'And in just a few decades or so, there will be no more tanzanite. At all. It will be gone.'

'Gone? For ever? Why?'

'Because the only place in the whole world where it exists is a three-mile zone in the foothills of Kilimanjaro—the Umba Valley, the area outside Arusha in the Merelani Hills.'

\*　　　\*　　　\*

Petra looks up from her lap to the wall opposite her bed where the abstract oil painting of Kilimanjaro ablaze hangs. She smiles, a little sadly. Dear dear Lillian McNeil. Petra takes the tanzanite and lays it between her index and middle fingers. Even in the dim of her bedroom in the middle of the night, the stone resounds with colour and hue; deep brilliant blue one way, glimpses of vivid violet the other. She can hear Mrs McNeil's voice, as clear as if she is sitting beside her, alive still.

'A Masai warrior I knew told me that if you look into the heart of tanzanite and see through to its soul, you see the colour of Kilimanjaro through the morning haze—which no paint, no pigment can replicate.'

\*　　　\*　　　\*

Petra looks at her clock, surprised to see it is

99

almost two in the morning. She looks at her tanzanite. Soon enough, there will be no more tanzanite. Anywhere in the world. Diamonds are for ever, tanzanite is not. And she keeps hers under her mattress. She humps the mattress on top of all the paperbacks. She checks her mobile phone. The screen is still blank. Poor old Rob. What a thing to have to work so late.

## CHAPTER TEN

'Are you going to tell?'

Paul Glasper forsook the history A level essays he had settled down to mark, to pose the question to Miranda Oates in an excitable whisper, as if it was the juiciest secret to hit the school.

'What? Tell what?' asked Nigel Garton as he came into the staff room, as bleary-eyed as the pupils to whom he'd just taught double physics.

'Who?' Arlo Savidge asked, a step behind him. 'Tell what who when?'

Paul held his hands up. 'It's not for me to say,' he said with a slow and obvious wink to Miranda who rolled her eyes and flicked him a 'V' with her fingers.

Miranda shrugged. 'I'm going for a job interview.'

'A job?' said Nigel. 'What sort of job?'

'A teaching job, of course.'

'But you already have a teaching job,' said Nigel.

Miranda shrugged. 'Head of English.'

'You're Head of English here, aren't you?' Arlo said.

'Yes, but I don't want to base my entire career here at Roseberry Hall. Unlike you two.'

She looked at them while they looked at each other, baffled.

'Don't know why not,' Nigel muttered, a little affronted.

'It's easy to forget that there's life outside Roseberry Hall,' Miranda said.

'But isn't the sense of belonging, of community, the point, surely?' said Arlo.

'You sound like the school's prospectus,' Miranda said. 'Anyway, how about "Good luck, Miss Oates"?'

'Good luck, Miss Oates,' Nigel said flatly.

'Good luck,' said Arlo, 'of course good luck. But you'd be sorely missed if you left.'

Paul noticed how a sparkle enlivened Miranda's eyes, that the smile she shot over to Arlo was laced with a glance of hope.

\*       \*       \*

Roseberry Hall was not a large school in terms of population, but in terms of acreage it was vast. The estate was contained, yet also heralded, by the original fine stone wall, something of a rarity in the hedge-bound locality. It was some eight feet high, crowned every few yards by a small decorative turret echoing those which were a feature of the Hall itself. From a distance and depending on the time of year, ramblers walking the Norse Lyke Wake Walk could look down on the Roseberry Hall estate in its entirety; from that perspective, the buildings and grounds and the wall running the entire perimeter resembled a well-constructed sandcastle complex. The eighteenth-century Hall itself, with its turrets and thick-silled casement windows and magnificent arched doorway, managed to be imposing in its grandeur without being intimidating. The founder of the school, Radcliff Lawrence Esq., a wealthy philanthropist whose special interests were education and architecture and the consequences of the one on the other, was sensitive to the effect that entering through that portal could have on a schoolboy. Lawrence believed that a school's job was to teach by nurturing, not by fear. A child will not want to learn in a building he is intimidated to enter; but if the building inspires awe then the passage to the classroom will be an eager one. Lawrence's ethos has lasted as well as the buildings themselves and to this day, despite the school being called Roseberry Hall Public School for Boys, the pupils themselves continue to be known as Radcliff Lawrencers.

It wasn't a league-topping school in terms of academic excellence but in terms of producing well-mannered, bright and confident boys, it was exemplary. Everyone who worked there and every parent who paid handsomely for a son to be educated there, understood this to be the higher point. Roseberry Hall wasn't about bullying astronomical grades out of the boys nor was it about saturating Oxford and Cambridge universities with alumni. Rather, the school was about *not* forcing a child to learn but inspiring them to want to listen. David Pinder, headmaster for over two decades, would reiterate in every speech he gave—to the boys, the parents, the governors, his staff—'Manners Maketh Man: our

102

pupils join us as boys and leave us as fine young men, fully equipped to deal with the world at large.' It was a proclamation that could be repeated by rote—by parents, pupils, governors and the staff alike. As if carrying Radcliff Lawrence's torch, Mr Pinder, with his jolly demeanour and ebullient commitment to the school, instilled in everyone connected with Roseberry Hall his belief that the school occupied an important and enviable niche within the British public boarding-school system. For the staff and the three hundred and fifty boys from the ages of eleven to eighteen, no one could doubt that the school also occupied a privileged niche of English countryside. Tucked safely and scenically into genteel grassland at the foot of the North York Moors, the school was positioned twenty minutes from stunning coastal scenery yet just a short journey to many of the most picturesque villages in the area. The lie of the land was perfect for sports: manicured pitches within the school's grounds opening out to serious cycling and running country. It was as if Roseberry Hall sat in state, receiving the varied gifts of the region. Depending on the weather conditions, even the plumes and fugs of effluence, the occasional colossal flares from the monstrous ICI works stretching for miles like a space-age city outside Middlesbrough, were considered to add drama and aesthetic intrigue to the big skies above the school.

The demarcation of work and rest was another of Radcliff Lawrence's philosophies, thus schooling was contained in either the main Hall itself or in the newer science block built sympathetically from local stone with a more modern take on the turret emblem. The boys were lodged in five accommodation houses with sizeable apartments for the housemaster or mistress and their families, and lesser apartments for their deputies. The rest of the staff were scattered through the grounds, either in annexes, or in quirky little turreted follies just large enough to comprise a living room, kitchenette, small bedroom and compact shower room. Miranda Oates had a folly. Paul Glasper was deputy housemaster of Armstrong House. Nigel Garton's rooms were part of the pavilion on the sports field. Arlo had a folly. Steven Hunter, the art teacher, lived above the decidedly grand boat-house. David Pinder resided in the headmaster's house, an ornate turreted cottage that looked a little like a cake. After prep each evening, the Hall was shut, as if it was as important for the building to have a rest from the scamper and flurry of school-time as it was for the community to have a break from school. If the staff wanted a place other than their private quarters to spend their evenings, they used the Old Buttery, a self-contained building whose atmosphere was part staff room, part den. It was a healthy mix of shabby old leather suites and a huge plasma screen; Cook's home-made cakes and the staff's lethal home-brew. The evening of Miranda Oates's interview, fortunately a Friday night, the Old Buttery was heaving with her colleagues glad of the excuse to test Barrel number 4 which had been fermenting since the New Year.

'How did it go?'

'Pretty damned well—if I say so myself.'

'When will you know?'

'By half term.'

'Have you told Pinder?'

'He'll take it personally, you know.'

'Bet he cajoles you into staying.'

'Go on, Oatcake, stay!'

'Look, I haven't got the bloody job yet!'

'Christ, this stuff is good.'

'Bet your new school won't have beer this brilliant.'

'Bet it bloody will, Nige. Anyway, will you all just quit! You'll jinx me.'

'Where's Arlo?'

'He said he'd be along.'

'Speak of the devil.'

\*　　\*　　\*

Arlo arrived with a bag of tortilla chips and an affable smile to bat away the taunts and jests from colleagues already well under the influence of Barrel number 4.

'He loves to make his entrance, does our Mr Savidge.'

'And lo! He comes bearing gifts of frankincense, mirth and Doritos.'

'Shit—I left the frankincense behind. But here—Doritos.'

'Look at you, all primped and preened and perfumed. Anyone'd think you were on the pull, Savidge.'

'Thanks, Glasper—you know I've always had a bit of a thing for you.'

\*　　\*　　\*

Arlo held the pint glass up to the light, observing

the cloudy liquid the colour of burnt caramel, the head on the beer not so much a creamy foam as a rather unnerving beige spume. 'Barrel number 4, hey?' He tasted it. He was never really sure if, objectively, their communal efforts at home-brewing created a great-tasting beer, nor whether, penny for pint, the financial savings were worth forsaking the excellent beer of the local pubs. But really the pleasure was in the process—the anticipation of when they would be drinking their carefully nurtured product—and ultimately the beer's status was lauded before a drop had been tasted.

'Hey, Miranda,' said Arlo, 'how did it go this evening—did you get the job?'

\*       \*       \*

Later, much later, with Barrel number 4 running dry, the Doritos all gone and Cook's cake nothing but crumbs on the floor, the staff congregating in the Buttery began to bid each other goodnight; envy from those who had to be on duty for Saturday morning school or sports fixtures, relief from those who didn't. Barrel number 4 had both emboldened Miranda and loosened Arlo. With the prospect of a new job, a getaway clause, she could afford to take liberties with her current position.

'Walk me home,' she nudged Arlo.

'I can practically see your front door from here!'

'I'm pissed. Give me a piggy-back. Go on.'

'God almighty, woman, come on then.'

To depleted cheers and a drunken nudge-wink from Paul, Arlo set off from the Buttery with Miranda humped against his back. It felt weird, to him, to have such close physical contact in such a prosaic manner. But for Miranda it felt wonderful to be against the body she desired; even if her legs were being pressed slightly too tightly against his sides. She tried to cross her ankles tantalizingly close to his groin but the effects of Barrel number 4, or perhaps Arlo's stride, made this awkward. She could, though, let her lips linger enticingly close to his neck.

'Thank you, kind sir,' she said, her mouth just catching the back of his left ear.

'My pleasure, milady,' Arlo said, wondering whether it was the beer that made her feel heavier than he'd expected, or whether he simply wasn't as brawny as he used to be. 'Here we are.'

'Down, boy!'

'Easy there. Well, goodnight, Miss Oates.'

'Arlo—come in?'

Her features—illuminated becomingly by the poetry of moonlight and the effect of home-brew. His body—feeling suddenly chilled by not having her against him.

'Me come in?'

'Yes. Just for a mo'. I wanted to—show you something.'

\*       \*       \*

Arlo glances around her room looking for what it is she might show him. Those old sepia photographs of a relative, perhaps? The two goldfish in a tank with a small fake skull as their playground? The painting on the wall, not a very good one, of Roseberry Topping? Please don't let it be her own artwork. The ethnic rug that looks slightly greasy? Not that ugly old clock. The half-bottle of blue-label vodka, perhaps?

*      *      *

No, Arlo. None of those. None of my things. I just want to show you that I really really fancy you.

*      *      *

Fuck. She's kissing me.

*      *      *

Kiss me back. Why don't you kiss me back?

*      *      *

'It's late, Miranda. I really must go.'
  'No, you don't. You really can stay.'

*      *      *

Why are you shaking your head? Christ, I'm a sure thing, Arlo. And last time I checked I was a pretty attractive package. And I'll probably be leaving the sodding school anyway so I don't even come with any strings attached.

*      *      *

'I have to go, Miranda.'
  'Well, that's a shame.'
  'It is late.'
  'Sure, Arlo, it's late.'

108

'Yes, very late. But sleep well, Miranda. Sweet dreams.'

'You could stay?'

'No. I'd better go.'

## CHAPTER ELEVEN

'It's one minute past midnight,' Petra says to the sleepy silence of her flat. 'It's Friday. It's officially his birthday now.'

She sends him a happy-birthday text message and waits a long ten minutes for no reply.

She is not to know yet that the day Rob turns thirty-five will be the day that her life will change. And even then, it will take some time before she will see that the change is for the better. For now, though, she goes to sleep. Drifts off, dreamlessly, with sixteen paperbacks and almost 40 carats of tanzanite under her mattress. She doesn't sleepwalk and she wakes feeling rested and excited about the day ahead.

\*        \*        \*

'You look chipper,' Eric said to Petra who had bounded into the studio with cappuccino for everyone, and doughnuts too.

'It's Rob's birthday today.'

'You're not expecting us lot to sing, are you?' said Kitty, pointing her safety-back needle file at Petra. 'Don't stick your tongue out at me.'

Petra laughed and stuck out her tongue again. Then, with eyes asparkle, she drew the velvet pouch from her bag. 'Look.'

'Sweet Jesus, she's brought in her tanzanite,' said Eric, feigning a faint.

Gina, Kitty and Eric crowded round. The upper side of Petra's hand was outstretched and steady. Placed over the line between her index and middle finger, the tanzanite dazzled. The other jewellers had seen it before but still they stared, momentarily speechless, as if seeing it for the first time. Gently, Kitty took Petra's wrist and moved it so that the gem's kaleidoscopic colours shot out according to the axis.

'I know I should be most impressed by the size of it, the cut, that it's perfect and flawless,' Kitty said, 'but what gets me is the *colour*. I've never seen colour like it.'

'Colours,' Eric quantified and for once Kitty didn't chip back at him.

'Trichroic—I love that word,' Gina said, holding out her own hand onto which Petra carefully placed the stone.

'Part of tanzanite's great allure is that it is trichroic,' said Petra, 'that it actually radiates a *different* colour from each of its axes. It's not a trick of the light. Those different colours exist, simultaneously. Look through it this way—how vivid is this blue? Now look that way—'

'As dreamy-violet as Elizabeth Taylor's eyes.'

'God, you're so gay, Eric.'

'Sod off, Kitty. It's as if a violet-blue flame burns at the heart of the stone.'

Gina had gone very quiet, mesmerized by the tanzanite nestling on her fingers. 'And you won't sell it? You really won't sell it?'

Petra shook her head.

110

'Thought not—and still no clearer what to do with it?'

Petra gazed at the stone. 'I have ideas—but I don't know yet what this stone wants to be.'

'It would make one huge fuck-off ring,' Kitty laughed.

'Isn't tanzanite too soft for rings?' Eric asked.

'That's a bit of a myth really,' Petra said. 'I mean, tanzanite is nowhere near as hard as diamonds—but it's still a 6–7 on the Mohs scale so it's hardly soft.'

'Shaun Leane produced some stunning rings with tanzanite.'

'But I don't know if my tanzanite wants to be a ring. I feel it should be seen in the round. Somehow.'

Gina passed the stone to Kitty who smiled and smiled, a warm gentleness washing over her face as she gazed into the depths of the stone. 'It seems to go on for ever,' she said.

'I think it was of its time to leave the pavilion at the base open, not finish it to a precise ridge or point—possibly because they didn't have the cutting technology in the 1960s that they have nowadays. But in all other respects, the proportions of the cut are near perfect.'

Kitty admired the flat table at the topmost part of the stone, then the crown facets, the girdle, the pavilion.

'My go,' said Eric, who held it up to the natural light, moving it between finger and thumb so that colour and light and energy shot out. He draped the velvet pouch over an upturned plastic cup and balanced the tanzanite on top. 'If that's not the ultimate touchstone of inspiration for us all today,

111

then what is!'

And they set to work. Every now and then looking up intentionally or otherwise to catch sight of the rare profound blueness, the flashes of violet, the sparkle and the beauty. The gem seemed to hum, to have a resonance that flowed into the room and touched the tools, charging the jewellers' hands as they worked.

'The thing is, even when you've made it up into something—will you actually be able to sell it then?'

'It depends if I win the lottery in the meantime,' said Petra.

\*     \*     \*

Mid-afternoon, Petra announced that she was sloping off. 'And the tanzanite is coming with me.'

'Spoilsport,' pouted Eric.

'Don't stick your tongue out at Petra,' Kitty barked.

'I'm taking it straight back to my bedroom. Then I'm going to nip round to Rob's flat before I meet him in town this evening. You know—scatter rose petals, put champagne on ice, a silk blindfold on fresh sheets.' Though she said it lightly, Petra's Studio Three could see how earnest she was.

'He doesn't deserve you,' Gina said, so kindly that Petra heard it only as a compliment. And though Kitty made vomiting gestures, she did so with a soft wink.

'Well, have a lovely time,' Eric smiled but with a sly barb to his voice. 'You can thrill us with the details when we see you on Monday morning.'

Petals. Can one actually buy petals or must I demolish entire flower heads? Do roses have a season? How far will the petals from a dozen roses stretch? Perhaps I ought to buy two dozen. And will they still be fresh and fragrant by late tonight or might they wilt and discolour? How can I prevent that? Perhaps I should ask the florist for the tricks of the trade. A florist or a wedding specialist. Or a romantic novelist. Oh shut up, me.

Champagne. I don't really know much about champagne because I don't really like it. But Rob does. Isn't Bollinger a bit clichéd? Bolly this, bolly that? I could buy pink champagne to colour-coordinate with the rose petals but Rob probably won't notice that. And perhaps pink champagne is naff. Look at the choice, even here in my local offy. I can't pronounce that one—but fortunately I can reach it. It's pretty expensive so it must be good.

I'll take my Diptyque candle—and some matches—and I'll light it as soon as we're through the front door. Chocolates! Hand-made truffles! There's that shop in Islington—it's walking distance from Rob's. I'll go there on my way to his.

What else what else what else.

Does Rob have a bucket?

Music! I can't work his iPod so I'd better set up a CD and then all I'll have to do is press Play when we get back later.

Play indeed. This is fun! I hope he'll love it. I hope it touches him. I hope he'll really love me for it.

But maybe this is all a bit over the top. Perhaps it'll irritate him. Perhaps it's not his thing at all,

113

though it's very me. Maybe I should just go and meet him in Soho as arranged and not bother with all of this.

*     *     *

But just before six o'clock Petra arrives at Rob's flat, laden with all the things she can think of, all the things she can just about afford, and a couple of things she can't really afford, to make his birthday unforgettable. To ensure his birthday goes with a bang. To guarantee this will be a memorable day in their relationship. She's proud of herself and excited. And she's just let herself into Rob's flat.

Something is wrong. Instinctively, Petra knows that something is very wrong. She surveys the scene fast. Everything looks almost as it should. But only *almost*. Because there are *two* pairs of shoes that have been kicked off near the sofa and only one set belongs to Rob. And Petra allows herself just a moment to think that it would be fine, it really truly would be fine, if perhaps those spike heels were actually his too and simply exposed a secret cross-dressing proclivity. That it would be all right. Funny, even.

However, in those heightened milliseconds of being able to circumnavigate the entire scene of her imminent destruction, Petra knows that her straw-clutchingly pathetic notion is far from the truth. Somewhere in Rob's flat is the naked truth—possibly the butt-naked truth—but Petra doesn't want to go looking. She sits down on Rob's sofa and does not look at the shoes. She concentrates on holding tight to the flowers and

114

the chocolates and the champagne and the tin-foil which she was going to wrap around the bucket to cool the champagne. She's holding on as tight as she can while she sits there waiting to be found.

*       *       *

Rob saunters through, whistling, and stops abruptly and says, Fucking hell, Petra, what are you doing here? And Petra stands up and says, I was going to give you the best birthday ever. And then Laura walks in—Rob's workmate, the nice one, the one who was kind to Petra that night in town quite recently. And the thing is, it's not as if they're naked. So maybe they were in Rob's bedroom because Laura wanted to see, just wanted to see— his built-in wardrobe. Or his ensuite walk-in shower. Something like that. Because Petra heard the shower going. Because perhaps Laura has— just bought a flat. Or something. Innocent as you like. Because they have their clothes on. And it's six o'clock on a Friday. And Rob's meeting Petra in town, for his birthday, in an hour's time. But all this reasonable blamelessness lasts just a split second.

Their hair is damp. And, at the very moment that Petra clocks Laura's bare feet, Laura says, Oh God, Petra! Oh shit! It's not what it seems! It's just—you know! And in a glance Petra can see that Rob's expression is telling Laura to shut up, shut the fuck up.

'Rob?'

'Petra—I can explain.'

'Go on then.'

But he can't very well explain with Laura there

115

so Laura says, Oops! I'd better go. And once she's gone, Rob looks at his girlfriend of ten months and he shrugs.

'I didn't mean to hurt you, Petra,' he says. 'Honestly. It's nothing serious.'

'Nothing serious? The thing is, Rob, I don't know if you're referring to me—or her.'

'Her!' Rob says too quickly. 'We just got pissed at lunch-time—you know what it's like.'

But Petra doesn't because Rob inhabits a world so different from hers.

'It was stupid. It didn't mean anything. It doesn't matter.'

But it matters very much to Petra. It means everything to her. And she feels very very stupid. And rather sick. She drops all the things she's been holding onto so tightly, all the accoutrements for a stupid bloody happy sodding birthday. And she bolts from Rob's flat and out into the lively thrum of Upper Street, Islington, which is buzzing on a Friday evening as people start to celebrate the end of the working week and all the fun of the weekend ahead of them.

## CHAPTER TWELVE

What is she going to do?

What can she do with this information?

What is she going to do with her night, with her weekend, with her life, with her tomorrow?

Who can she turn to right now? No one should have to weather a trauma like this alone.

116

Petra Flint may be a romantic but she's also fairly sensible. She would quite like to throw up in the middle of Islington but she breathes slowly and methodically instead, to calm herself and quell the nausea. She could easily collapse into sobs at the bus stop but she bites down on her lip and decides to hail a taxi. What price the security of home?

And quickly, please. I know it's rush-hour but if you could drive like the clappers I'd be grateful.

Train to catch, love?

No. I just want to be home.

Well, it'll be sticky up the Archway, love, but it'll ease out after that.

Sticky up the Archway. Sticky up the arch way. Stick it up yer archway. To Petra, just then, it sounds bizarrely vaudevillian and she is taunted by an image of a sticky sweaty Rob pushing up into Laura.

*       *       *

Petra is home.

The solitude and safety of her own space render obsolete the composure she maintained so brilliantly in Islington and in the taxi. She closes her front door and presses her back hard against it. Then she doubles over, clutching her stomach. She drops to her knees and cries, No no no, hammering her knuckles against the carpet. She curls herself onto the floor just inside the door even though she's within arm's reach of the sofa. She can't cry properly and it is painful. The sobs are caught like sharp obstructions in her throat and she can no more swallow them down than she can wail them up. Her tears try to itch and ooze their way past aching eyeballs as if her tear-ducts are constipated. She is light-headed but the pit of her stomach is leaden. Her brain is having difficulty computing all the immutable information and her heart hurts. It simply hurts. From a situation so sordid, comes pain so pure. It's all unfathomable.

*      *      *

She woke up pleased to find herself still on the floor near the door, because such a trauma could well have had her sleepwalking way past Whetstone. Common sense told her not to mope and not to be alone and the hands of her watch said that, at just turned tomorrow, it would be breakfast-time again in Hong Kong.

'Luce?'

'Stay right there—I'll phone you straight back.'

*      *      *

The beauty of your oldest, closest friend is that, in a crisis, she has no compulsion to do anything other than come to your rescue. She puts her life on hold as she steps into your shoes to fight your corner for you. Because she can feel your pain, so she can take just a little bit of it away. She won't mince her words or indulge you, she'll talk to you straight and tell it how it is. But she'll also intersperse her constructive help to there-there you like a mother. In Petra's case, in lieu of her mother. And she'll carefully lay the foundations of her advice on a soft bed of much-needed sympathy.

118

So Lucy listened and gasped and squeezed her handset tight as if it was Petra's hand or Rob's sodding neck. She was livid and distressed and frustrated by the distance that separated them. She was outraged and felt Petra's pain as keenly as if it was her own. After Lucy had done listening because Petra was done talking, she soothed her with utter sympathy and a genuine croak to her own voice. Encouraging Petra to use the phone call to sob all she wanted, Lucy willed her affection and her support to traverse the Pacific or bounce off the telecommunication satellite or whichever route was the quickest to go down the phone and into Petra's soul. And only then did Lucy take charge of the situation and of her friend's immediate future.

'This will *not* damage you, Petra, because the problem is his and not yours. It's your opportunity to wrest your life back from the hold he had over you. You are allowed to hate him. You can enjoy it. Then you might well pity him. And soon enough— I promise you—you simply won't think of him at all. If you find yourself missing him, ask yourself what it is you miss.'

'But I worked so hard at loving him.'

'You worked *too* hard at loving him for too little return.'

'But he didn't love me.'

'You are right—but that's his shortcoming, not your failure.'

'I tried so hard.'

'It is not your fault. He probably does love you in his own half-baked way. Love means different things to different people. It's the centre of your world—but it's on the periphery of his. But he'll probably make a play to get you back.'

119

'Do you really think so?'

'You shouldn't be sounding hopeful—you should be sounding horrified. You are better off in the long run. Please believe me. If he comes crawling and begging and dripping with diamonds please say no.'

'It's all right for you, Luce. You're married and sorted. I'm on my own.'

'Better to be on your own than settling for so little. You shouldn't be with Rob to make yourself feel better, because I'm telling you, Rob did not love you as you should be loved. And he won't miraculously change. You know what I think, Petra, I think deep down you were never sure about his feelings for you and that's why you tried so hard. God, it was like a full-time job—the effort you bestowed. You worked so hard at being a sexpot, a wifey, a fascinating person, an amazing girlfriend.'

'What more could I have done? Why wasn't that enough?'

'You are trying to measure yourself against how much affection you could inspire in him. That's why you're feeling so wretched—because you are judging yourself on how little he loved you. All you expected in return was respect, affection and fidelity—none of which he gave you. But you listen up, Petra—he didn't *not* love you because you're unlovable, my darling. He's emotionally imbecilic. You must not take this personally.'

'How can I not?'

'I know. I know. At this stage, that's impossible. Answer me this, though. If he came round right now and asked you to marry him, would you say yes?'

'Yes! I would! I would say yes yes yes!'

'Petra, if he came round right now and asked you to marry him *tomorrow*, would you say yes?'

The line went silent.

'Petra?'

'I . . .'

'Would you? Would you marry Rob tomorrow? I'll come over—I'll go to the airport right now. Will you marry him tomorrow? Marry him tomorrow and for ever?'

Silence.

'Petra?'

'I wouldn't marry him tomorrow. Not tomorrow. No.'

'Good girl. You will see that actually, it's nothing to do with the love, or lack of, that he had for you. Ultimately, you'll see that you didn't really love him enough to be with him for good anyway. The more you doubt someone's love for you, the harder you work at trying to secure it. It's bizarre. Perhaps you set out to see if you could be the one for him without stopping to truly consider whether he was the one for you?'

'Oh, Luce.'

'He's not worth your tears, my darling. And the person worthy of you won't make you cry like this. I promise. Phone Eric first thing because you'll feel very unsure again when you wake up. So phone him. OK?'

'OK.'

'And Petra?' Lucy paused. 'You're beautiful and gorgeous and it would be wrong to settle for anyone less than a man who adores you.'

'OK.'

'And Petra? Double-lock your door tonight.

Hide the key in the coffee jar right now and put the coffee jar at the back of your cupboard and balance something like a shoe on top of the cupboard door so it will clonk you if you open it. Go on. Just in case. You know how trauma can set you off.'

'OK. But I wish you were here, Luce, *really* here. Round the corner, like you used to be.'

'We'll be back later in the year. We'll be back for good in a couple of years' time.'

'OK. But please don't hang up yet.'

\*           \*           \*

Petra didn't sleepwalk, she didn't have nightmares, she didn't even dream. She slept without knowing she slept; hours of uninterrupted nothingness making time pass, giving the brain a rest, allowing the heart to beat a little more calmly. And when she awoke, she was momentarily tricked by the charm of those first gentle minutes of reverie, by sunlight seeping in through the gap in the curtains promising a fair spring day. It was only when her slumbery focus sharpened to settle on the strange sight of her Birkenstock sandal perched on top of her ajar cupboard door, that she recalled what had caused her to sleep to such numb depths.
*Sandals.*
  *Cupboard.*
    *Coffee jar.*
      *Door keys.*
        *Sleepwalk.*
          *Lucy.*
            *Rob.*
              *Birthday.*

122

*And Laura.*

*And not me.*

Her spirits tumbled with the thudding realization of the horrible truth. She closed her eyes though she knew it was pointless—there would be no sleep while her heart was busy beating double time and the cogs of her brain were in overdrive. And closing her eyes didn't stop her tears and it didn't prevent her from staring straight into the bare facts of the situation.

Yet looking around her room, she suddenly hated every inch of it. She hated the trickery of the sunshine. It was all a lie. It wasn't a nice spring day at all. How could it be. She was waking up very alone, and for Petra that was a terrible place to be. A whole day—more, an entire weekend—stretched ahead of her as one long enervating slog.

*I've spent my adult life avoiding weekends on my own.*

Petra stumbled from bed and hurried to phone Eric.

'He's been shagging someone else.'

'I'll bring wine I'll bring fags I'll bring chocolate I'll bring scented candles I'll bring *Jerry Maguire* I'll bring my Eve Lom stuff and give you a facial that'll make the world seem all right again. I'll bring all this stuff with me—and much much more. I'll be over at lunch-time.'

Petra clung to the phone and loved Eric very much just then.

\*        \*        \*

He brought a carpet picnic fit for a queen.

'I haven't heard a word from him,' Petra said

123

quietly, having eaten her fill.

'He was shagging someone else! There is no explanation!' Eric protested. 'You deserve so much more. It's shitty and it hurts—but it's for the best. He was no good for you, the tosser. I never much liked him. None of us did. He's not your type—and you're not his.'

Petra ruminated over this. 'But why didn't you say something sooner?'

'We did try but you were so full of how much you loved him. Note—*you* loved *him*. You were very happy to love him, too. You wouldn't have heard me. Anyway, you wouldn't have listened.'

'He didn't love me,' said Petra, her strength rapidly sapping. 'I tried so hard.'

'Love should never be such a one-sided effort. Anyway, do you know what I think? I think he's a sad fat fuck, that's what. He probably did love you in his own way, to his own inadequate limit.'

'That's what Lucy says.'

'Petra, much better to have your propensity for great love—big generous sexy caring love—than his limit for only so much lukewarm love. You'll be able to bestow it on a very lucky chap—and next time, it'll be reciprocated.'

'I don't want to be alone. I don't want to be on my own.'

'That's why you worked so hard on Rob. Not because he was worth it but because you didn't want to be on your own.'

\*       \*       \*

Early evening, a text message bleeped through to her phone and in the instant she prayed it would be

124

from Rob, Eric prayed it would be from Lucy. Petra's prayer, it seemed, was heard first.

u ok? I can xplain!! plus jamais!! promise!! xxx

'Christ,' Eric muttered, 'if ever there was a time to go easy on exclamation marks.' But he felt bad when he saw how his cynicism, however reasonable, had swiftly stripped the hope and joy from Petra's face.

'Three kisses, Eric—he never usually does kisses at all.'

Eric decided not to comment but to give Petra a look instead which said, I've known you for over fifteen years—will you please just trust me.

'But maybe it's only now that he realizes that he does really love me,' Petra said, 'and he's come to his senses.'

Eric gave Petra the look again. He thought how if Kitty was here she'd be yelling at Petra and physically shaking her. Or if Rob were here then yelling at him and physically shaking him too. But harder.

'Are you going to forgive him?' Eric asked, feigning nonchalance by laying out his jars of Eve Lom facial products like a chef preparing to cook up a treat.

'I read somewhere that we all make mistakes but it's how we make amends that defines us.'

'Petra, it's easy enough to think, Ooh, desolate text message! Ooh, three Xs. But are you intending to forgive a man who didn't bother with kisses until now—and, more to the point, who's been fucking someone else behind your back but claims it's readily explainable?'

'You're not helping, Eric—and anyway, who says he was pathologically unfaithful? It was just the

125

once. It was his birthday. He was a bit pissed. He never meant for me to walk in.'

'And that makes it OK? Petra, why are you defending him? He hasn't been nice enough to you—from the start. Please use this as an opportunity to walk away. Please. You're too good for him. He doesn't suit you.'

Oh God, won't you just take your Eve Lom lotions and potions and sod off. Petra went quiet, not because the sense of Eric's sentiment struck home, nor because he was slathering a thick, aromatic gloop on her face. She was really tired of talking, tired of trying to think, she didn't have the energy to know what she ought to do next but she just wanted to be allowed to make up her own mind as to whether Rob was as much of a sod as those who loved her best decreed him to be. It was a strange thing: desperate not to be alone yet suddenly wanting to be all by herself.

So, when Eric suggested they crack open the wine and watch *Jerry Maguire*, Petra told him that actually she'd rather go to bed because she was exhausted. Before he left her flat, he checked all the windows were locked and then hid her keys, texting her the next morning to tell her under which cushion they could be found.

## CHAPTER THIRTEEN

She may think she's all alone, she may bemoan the fact that her best friend lives abroad and that Eric's facial didn't really help much at all, but although a little self-pity can be constructively

126

cathartic in times of crisis, if it lasts too long it becomes destructively self-indulgent. Sunday morning finds Petra very quiet. The sunshine is tauntingly brilliant, Rob has re-sent his text message to her and she feels she needs someone to tell her what to do next. Kitty has left the sweetest message about a friend of a friend who does voodoo and though Gina has sent a text inviting her to supper in SW3, Petra suspects neither approach is what she needs just now. She could catch Lucy, she could phone Eric again but they wouldn't have any new answers for her. They'd be happy to hear from her, they'd be pleased to be there for her, they would sweetly say the same things they said yesterday and they wouldn't mind her repeating herself and crying afresh, but until Petra gives them her thoughts, they can't really shed any new light on her situation.

She goes back into her bedroom and gets back into bed, sliding her hand under the mattress for her tanzanite, her touchstone, perhaps today her crystal ball. She tries to lose herself in its mesmeric colours and facets but she sees only its pure beauty which lifts her spirits but gives her no answers. What it does do, though, is transport her back in her mind's eye to peaceful afternoons spent in the company of this tanzanite's original owner. What succour was to be found with Lillian McNeil.

*    *    *

Petra at just-turned sixteen. Having a tough old time of it at home and a crap time at school because mocks loomed after half term and she hated maths and didn't understand why it was compulsory at O level when she felt sure she'd fail anyway. Plus, she wasn't picked for the first or second netball teams and she'd rather not play at all than be a reserve. And her dad has gone away on his second honeymoon and her mum needed to sort her head out so she's gone to a Tibetan centre in Scotland.

'Bizarrely, the climate and the soil in Tibet are similar to areas of Scotland and they share many indigenous plants and herbs,' Lillian McNeil said carefully because she had yet to ascertain who was looking after the child.

'Oh. Did you ever live there? In Tibet or in areas of Scotland?'

'I am Scottish but I haven't been back for years—and I've never been to Tibet.'

'Oh.'

'How is your revision going, Petra?'

'Well, I revise hard at the stuff I find easy—at the expense of the stuff I find hard.'

'I'm sure your mother will be helping you?'

'She's in Scotland.'

'Silly me. You did say. Well, who do you have to test your French vocab instead?'

'Well, you could, if you like. I could bring a list along next visit? Shall I come back tomorrow?'

'Yes, do—but I mean, I'm sure whoever's house-sitting could help you with maths this evening?'

And from Petra's embarrassed smile, Lillian McNeil had her answer: the child was alone.

'When is your mother back?'

'When her head is sorted, she said.'

The elderly lady and the schoolgirl looked at each other, aware that the dynamic had swung completely. The point of Pensioner's Link was that

Petra could pass on any concerns from or for Mrs McNeil. Just then, her pensioner was wondering whom she could contact on Petra's behalf.

'Please don't tell,' Petra pre-empted. 'Please.'

Mrs McNeil lowered her voice. 'Do you have money and food?'

Petra nodded and Lillian thought, What on earth is the value of money and food when there's no parent to nourish the child?

'My mum said it was a credit to me that she felt she could go.'

'If you have a sleeping bag, you are welcome to stay with me, Petra.'

'Oh, I'm fine. Thank you. If anything, I get more revision done without my mum doing her chanting or getting me to henna her hair.'

'And you feel safe?'

'Oh yes.'

'And not too lonely?'

'Oh no.'

'Well, do come and visit me tomorrow. I'd like that. Will you buy me a quarter of ground coffee from Carwardines in Swiss Cottage—my usual? And bring some French vocab with you.'

'I will. I'll come in the morning.'

'And stay for lunch.'

'Thank you.'

\*     \*     \*

You always knew what to do, Mrs McNeil, you knew what I needed. When I came in that following day with that bump on my head and a bruised elbow because I must have sleepwalked into a wall, you had a bottle of distilled witch hazel

129

and you dabbed it on and it worked. You also had a little chore for me, every day during that half term, and that worked too. And when my mum came back, magically there were no more chores. You knew what to do because you knew about everything. From Tibet to Tanzania. From French vocab to witch hazel. You had a remedy for any situation. You were wise and kind and sensible. What would you say to me today? If you were here? What would you have me do?

*      *      *

'I would say, Petra, my dear, you ought to have a jolly good look at yourself in the mirror. Don't give yourself a talking-to. Just stand and see yourself from the inside out, from beyond the reddened surface of your cried-out eyes.'

I'm looking, I'm looking and I look like shit. I feel ten times worse than I look.

'If you think of Rob, do you glow? What does the thought of him do to your eyes?'

I'm looking. I'm thinking. I'm seeing how my eyes dull down and I look anxious.

'A man should release your sparkle, not deflate your bounce.'

I'm very good at putting on a brave face.

'From necessity. That's nothing to be proud of. It's a little sad.'

I don't want to be alone.

'None of us does. You want to believe in happy-ever-after.'

What's wrong with that?

'Nothing at all. But you have to be happy with the person involved for the concept to be

130

workable.'

Do you think he's as wrong for me as Lucy and my Studio Three seem to think?

'Only you can know that. And there's no point kidding yourself. No point at all. It'll take you further away from happy-ever-after and that would be a daft place to end up.'

# CHAPTER FOURTEEN

Petra doesn't inform Rob that she's on her way. He never goes out on a Sunday morning anyway. He wears boxer shorts and his old university rugby shirt until lunch-time and drinks a lot of strong coffee. He sprawls around with all the papers spread about and Radio 4 as background sound. Petra could never get him to change his schedule no matter how appealing her suggestions: a trip to the farmer's market off Marylebone High Street, a visit to the Huguenot house in Folgate Street, a day out at Hampton Court, a picnic on Hampstead Heath as a change from his de rigueur brunch at the same crowded Islington brasserie. Today, this finally irks her. Sitting on the top deck of an empty bus, Petra really resents Rob and it feels quite liberating. Ten months' worth of Sundays when she hasn't had her say. Just before her stop, she briskly scoops up her hair into a pony-tail. The natural twists and tumbles of her hair give a lively bounce every time she moves her head.

But it seems she can't take her empowerment with her as she disembarks the bus. By the time she's jaywalked across Upper Street, she's taunting herself that she's probably five minutes away from coming across Rob in flagrante again. She can almost hear him at it. The sod. The domineering, controlling, adulterous sod who's been telling her what to do with her Sundays while he does what he wants behind her back. And she's within a stone's throw of finally being able to tell him what he can do with his bloody Sundays.

Every corner she turns, a new mood sweeps over her. Anger. Reluctance. Trepidation. Foreboding. Only when she finally turns into his street do the negative but determined feelings subside, replaced outside the front door to his building with rushes of adrenalin carrying surges of hope and delusion. She releases her pony-tail and hides behind a screen of ringlets.

*      *      *

She has keys but she daren't use them so she rings the bell and wonders if he's in or out. A moment's wait feels like an hour.

He must be out. So I think I'll just go.

Oh God, he's in. So I think I'll just go.

*      *      *

He looks tired and wan, which is a good sign, isn't it—he's suffering, he's atoning, he does love me after all.

'Babe,' he says, his voice hoarse; he opens the door wide but they stand still, on either side of the threshold, worlds apart. He shrugs. Petra waits. Their eyes dart across each other's faces for reasons and answers and who's going to speak first

132

and say what.

'Tell me I was sleepwalking,' Petra whispers, locking in on eye contact like a torpedo to its target. 'I was only sleepwalking, wasn't I?'

Rob looks pained and says nothing and won't meet Petra's gaze and she can't misread this so now she has her answer.

'Wake me up?' she says in a meek, final bid. And she wonders whether to hit him, to see if he's real—and if he is real, she'll really want to hit him again.

But Rob has walked into his flat and she shuffles in after him. His flat is really tidy, apart from the surface detritus of the Sunday papers. Petra was hoping for a hovel; that he'd have turned his world upside down in his remorse, in his search for life-changing answers. Actually, his life is personified by this flat. Swank and gadgets and gloss and a little mess on the surface that can be dumped at the end of the day. He stands, turned away from her, clasping his hands behind his head as if he's trying to stretch away the stress of it all. She can't see his face, she can't read his expression. She can only guess. And it's that which decides her. Without even seeing his face she realizes she'll always guess wrong with Rob. She wants him to be wearing an expression of torment and repentance. However, when he turns around he just looks harassed. But though he looks like shit and though it hits her in the gut, she is able to force herself to see that there's no love in his eyes for her.

'Coffee?'

'No.'

'Anything?'

'Nothing.'

He pinches the bridge of his nose. It's something that he does when he's hassled. Petra has seen him do it often; when the Japs are giving him gyp or when dealing with the Yanks is a total wank. He pinches his nose when something or someone is getting right on his bloody nerves.

'I wasn't sleepwalking, was I?'

Rob shakes his head and regards her blankly, his gaze so level it hurts her all the more. 'I know I can tell you that Laura is no big deal—that we're just fuck-buddies. But you won't get it, Petra. We're too different, you and me. I like living as I do. It's a shame you have a problem with it.'

Is he actually implying that this is Petra's failing?

Petra is desperate for something to say. But while she is silently mulling soliloquies, her instinct takes over and suddenly she hears her voice and it's strong and cutting and it's out in the open, loud and clear, slashing across the detachment on Rob's face.

'Actually, I only came for my bucket and my tin foil, you total cunt.'

\*        \*        \*

And as she walks purposefully away from Rob, strides from his flat and out into Islington, she doesn't know whether to sob or giggle, only she's all cried out and she can't quite summon the energy to laugh just yet. But she does know how proud everyone who loves her will be when she tells them what she did and what she said. They'll make her repeat her final *coup de grâce* again and again. They'll shriek with laughter and punch the

134

air and hug her close. And they will all give her special dispensation for using the 'C' word. They'll think she's a star, they'll know she's going to be just fine. They'll know that great times are her due. But it'll take a while before she nods and says I know that too.

## CHAPTER FIFTEEN

On any given night there are 26,000 people sleepwalking in the United Kingdom. A child will walk in on her parents' dinner party and hold an engaging conversation of total gibberish before tottering off. A grown man in Sheffield will eat gravy granules and take a block of butter back to bed with him. A businesswoman will wake up to find soil under her fingernails and twigs in her bed. A fifteen-year-old girl will wake up in her nightie on top of a crane in east London and her story will make it into the newspapers.

Some somnambulists will shuffle around their homes mistaking the kitchen chair for the toilet seat. Some will take the pictures from the walls or ornaments from window sills and pile them up. Some will rummage through their wardrobes and quite willingly explain that they're looking for Tony Blair or Madonna or the Queen. Some will take off all their night-clothes, others will get fully dressed ten times over. Some will leave their homes: one or two will climb out of a window and make it onto a roof, one or two may even get into their cars and drive off. Some will sleepwalk vividly through a building that they are actually not in and will consequently be in danger of harming themselves.

Petra was one of those.

She thought she was at home.

Not home as in her rented flat in North Finchley.

Not home as in the student digs in Camberwell which she shared for four years with Eric.

Not the flat she lived in with her mum in West Hampstead once her dad had decamped to Watford.

Not Mrs McNeil's cramped quarters.

But through her childhood home. This is where Petra sleepwalked. The 1930s detached house in the outer reaches of Cricklewood, the house with the bay window and the part-glazed porch leading to the red front door. The house with the kitchen with the serving hatch into the dining room and the archway going from the dining room into the lounge. The fancy fireplace with marble surround and polished brass grate purely for display. Magnolia walls above the dado and restrained Anaglypta one shade darker below. The large cheese plant whose leaves were given a weekly wipe, on its own fancy stand next to the coat rack. Parquet in the hallway. 80/20 wool mix everywhere else. Brass stair treads that were a bugger to keep gleaming. On the first floor, the bedrooms off the corridor. Petra's little room overlooking the neighbours' garden. Then the spare room. The family bathroom. Finally, surveying the driveway and the Rover, her parents' room.

Go in. No, don't. Back up. The spare room. What's going on in there? Go in, no don't, go in, no don't. The door's ajar. What is *that*? Who *is*

136

that? What are you *doing*? Why are you doing *that*? Turn and run. Run back to your room. Quickly. Don't let anyone know you're awake. Your bedroom door is open and you can dive into your bed. Quickly, just hide under the duvet and scrunch your eyes tight shut. Quick! Before anyone sees you, before anyone notices that you saw what you saw.

But you can't do this if you are Petra at thirty-two who hasn't lived in that house for over half her life. You can't do this if you are Petra who now lives in a rented flat in North Finchley. You can't do this because there isn't a door just there. There's a wall. If you try and run through that open door in Cricklewood, you find that you run hard into the wall in North Finchley. So hard that you'll actually knock yourself out and you'll wake up with hair encrusted with blood and a cracking headache. You'll have to go to Barnet General and wait four hours in A&E for butterfly stitches.

As Petra did.


## CHAPTER SIXTEEN

'Jesus Christ, Petra. What happened? Did you sleepwalk *again*?'

'I'm OK, Eric. It's just a bump. Stop making a fuss.'

'Oh yes, you're just fine and dandy for someone with stitches in her head and a right shiner over her left eye.'

'Kitty—'

'And you're limping.'

'Gina—'

Petra, they say together, this is not good. We're worried. It's been two weeks of this.

'It's always worse at times like this.'

'Do you want me to stay with you for a couple of nights?'

'Thanks, Eric—but no.'

'How about I come? I'll bring a bundle of sage to burn—it's very cleansing. We'll do a release ritual.'

'It's tempting, Kitty. But not just yet.'

'Darling, I have bags of room—in fact, I have rooms and rooms. I'll pad out one for you, I'll put duvets on the walls and lock the door.'

'Gina, you're really kind and I am so tired. But if I can't sleep on my own, where can I sleep?'

'At mine,' says Charlton Squire. Despite his bulk, he's been standing unseen at the back of the studio for a few minutes. 'You can sleep at mine.'

They all look up at him, towering in black butter-soft leather, a silk shirt expensively crinkled, blackout sunglasses, hair coifed camply like Tintin. They've heard all about Charlton Squire's house. It's in Holland Park and very grand, apparently. Ten years ago, when he was at the height of his flamboyance, he used to host parties there. The stuff of legend: Bacchanalian romps with a jaw-dropping guest list of louche celebrities.

'Not in London,' Charlton qualifies, 'in North Yorkshire. I have a place there. A cottage. It's not really a cottage, really, it's single storey.'

'Bungalow?' Eric asks, unable to prevent it sounding snide.

'Converted eighteenth-century stone stables,' Charlton says, not bothering with eye contact.

138

'I meant—good—no *stairs* to fall down,' Eric backtracks meekly because no one in the jewellery industry ought to rankle Charlton Squire. 'Petra once fell down the stairs when she sleepwalked at a friend's house and lost her hearing for over a month.'

'No stairs,' says Charlton.

'I've offered to pad out one of my spare rooms,' Gina says.

'And I've suggested a sage-clearing at her flat,' says Kitty.

Petra hears them all. Their well-meaning concern as they compete with each other's suggestions. Suddenly she thinks how they're exacerbating her headache too. She wonders if taking time off work and time away from London might not be a very good idea.

'Really? Could I?'

They all look at her.

'Of course,' says Charlton. 'The keys are at the gallery. Pick them up whenever you like—there's also some money for you, two of your necklaces sold. You can work there too, if you feel like it— there's a shed at the back of the garden with a bench and a skin and some tools. It's where I started out. It's a happy place, Pet.'


# CHAPTER SEVENTEEN

'Boys. Boys. Come on, guys—I need your eyes and ears for just a couple more minutes, then you can bugger off for Easter.'

Like dogs in a fidget to be free from their leads

139

as soon as the park is in sight, so Arlo's restless class could practically taste their Easter eggs and their three-week respite from school.

'Homework,' Arlo called out above the din. 'You have your projects to tide you over and I want all of you to bring back music that you feel sums you up. OK? Nathan, if your parents have a copy of "Mad Dog" by Deep Purple, I suggest you bring in that.'

'Mr Savidge, sir?'

'Yes, Lars.'

'If we do it, will you do it too?'

'Pardon?'

'Bring in music that sums *you* up.'

'"Boy Named Sue!"' came a voice from the back.

'Who was that? Was that you, Troy?'

The class fell silent and Troy looked appalled. Mr Savidge milked it for a few moments.

'Ten out of bloody ten for knowing your Johnny Cash,' Arlo marvelled which made the boy audibly sigh with relief.

'Are you going home, sir?'

'Home's pretty much here for me.'

The uniform expressions of the class told Arlo they thought him mad and sad.

'But I'll be popping down to London to visit my mum.'

Madder and sadder.

'And perhaps go to some gigs.'

Wow. Cool.

'Now bugger off. And have a good Easter.'

*     *     *

The parents had been charmed, the boys waved off, the dorms and rooms had been double-checked. Staff sunbathed on the cricket pitch, chatting about anything other than school; Nige and Arlo played tennis and relished swearing out loud at each other. On the gravel, Cook set up a trestle table laden with left-overs. 'I'm off,' she said, giving a roll of bin liners pride of place in the centre of the table. Headmaster Pinder bustled about, looking behind radiators and under benches, checking padlocks and windows, turning a blind eye to his staff in a state of undress on the cricket pitch and a deaf ear to the ripe insults ricocheting around the tennis court. They all convened, fully dressed and polite, for his headmaster's debrief and demob a couple of hours later. After that, the few staff not leaving that day rolled into Great Broughton for a nice relaxed pint.

Now, late evening, they were back, packing for their recess, tidying their quarters, ready to journey home, up and down the country. Arlo, who wasn't going anywhere for a few days and would be going for only a few days at that, meandered from colleague to colleague. Need a hand? No, ta, just taking a few bits and pieces home. Actually, you could bung in my washing for me. Sure, no problem. Oh, and could you keep an eye out for anything that looks like a credit-card bill. Sure, no problem. You're a sad fuck, Arlo—a couple of days with your mum and the rest of the hols up here? Yeah, well. Why don't you go away? I might. Yeah, right.

With all his colleagues preoccupied, the lights on in their follies speckling the school grounds like giant fireflies, Arlo sauntered over towards the main building, wondering if anyone had done as Cook requested and cleared up. But as he approached, he saw that the trestle table was still up, a little litter lying about, the bin bags ignored. He was quietly wrestling with a rustle of black plastic, trying to find which end had the opening, his mouth full of broken biscuits, when he clocked Miranda watching his every move from her perch on the stone steps a few yards away.

'Hullo,' she said, raising her hand then letting it drop as if it was heavy.

Arlo made a vaguely salutatory noise through a muffle of crumbs.

'How many men does it take to open a bin bag,' Miranda asked drily, rising to her feet and walking over to him. 'Answer: none. Men are genetically incapable of opening bin bags.' She took it off him, placed it between the palms of her hands, gave a single swift rub and one vigorous shake to open the bag fully. 'Ta da. Not just a pretty face.'

Arlo, finding it difficult to swallow the biscuits with his mouth now utterly dry, gave her a round of applause instead.

'I'm a bit drunk,' she said.

Arlo coughed.

'Christ, it may not be ladylike but it's not that shocking, is it?' she asked, while giving him hearty thumps between the shoulder blades. To her, his back felt lovely through his cotton T-shirt and she turned her slaps into strokes and pretended she was drunker than she was so that she could change her strokes into a caress.

Arlo straightened stiffly and backed away. 'I must tidy up. Cook said so.'

'God, you're weird.'

Arlo didn't know whether to be relieved or affronted by the remark.

'Aren't you going to wish me luck?' Miranda said, all coy. 'I'll hear about that job any day.'

'Good luck,' Arlo said. 'Do you still want it?'

He regretted the double meaning immediately but Miranda enhanced her drunkenness to jump on it. 'Oh yes, Arlo, I want it.'

'Well, I hope you get it.'

'Can I have a good-luck kiss? Please, sir?'

Arlo made to kiss her on the cheek. Miranda was ready for him. She turned her face quickly and their lips met. Before he could pull away, she'd flicked her tongue over his lips and cupped her hand over the groin of his jeans, arching her back so that her breasts pushed against his chest.

'Miranda—'

And he pulled away.

And she stood there and thought, How dare he.

'Miranda,' he said again but she interrupted him before he could back it up with any explanation.

'Yeah yeah. Miranda Miranda, it's late, you're drunk, we're at school, it's a Thursday, it's not a full moon, it's still Lent. Christ, Arlo—I don't want marriage and babies, I just want a shag.'

But Arlo was already walking away, across the lawns, to be swallowed by the dark Yorkshire night now illuminated only here and there by the lights still on in just a couple of the follies.

# CHAPTER EIGHTEEN

It was dusk when Petra arrived in Stokesley and found the Old Stables. The first thing she did was check the security; the windows and doors—how they locked and how well they locked. This was a procedure she undertook in every place she visited; not to keep potential intruders out, rather to keep herself in. Only when she'd noted that the door was locked by two different keys and two bolts in opposing directions, that the windows were secured by thin metal rods which needed a specific Allen-type key and a lot of turning to be removed, did she divest herself of her rucksack, sit down and take stock of her surroundings.

If she'd been shown photographs of the place, and a list of people to whom it might belong, she would never have picked Charlton Squire. In utter contrast to the edgy chic of his gallery and totally contradicting his own blatantly camp leather-and-silk urban gayness, the Old Stables was almost monastic in its simplicity but all the more homely for it. Charlton had knocked four stone stables into one space, keeping some features like the cobblestone flooring and one old iron hay rack while imaginatively adding others. The front door opened straight into the sizeable living area and Petra almost wished it was winter so that she could have a fire in the stone fireplace which was positioned in the centre of the room and subdivided the space into living and dining areas. Off the dining area, in a little modern lean-to that blended subtly, was the small kitchen with an original loose-box door out to the garden. Off the living area to the other side, in another quiet modern extension, was a cosy double bedroom and surprisingly luxuriously appointed bathroom.

Everywhere the walls had been painted a chalky white, allowing the shape of the stone to butt through, adding texture and hue. The cobblestone floor was made more practical by a homogeneous assortment of woollen rugs; an old leather tub chair was softened by a sheepskin; and an old tapestry sofa was made more welcoming by a variety of plump cushions. Window sills presented local finds—antique glass bottles, interesting pebbles, esoteric books by local poets and artists.

Nothing was over-styled, it was neither rustically twee nor rurally ascetic. Sympathetic and sensitive was how Petra thought she might describe the place to Lucy or Eric or the others. And hadn't Charlton been sympathetic and sensitive to Petra too, in handing her the keys? The Old Stables was quiet and sturdy, unpretentious and obviously loved. For someone so publicly theatrical as Charlton to allow essentially an employee access to his more private and perhaps truer self was a compliment indeed. Petra was touched and she felt at home.

Though she purposely didn't hunt around for the window-lock key, and though she hid the door key under one of the rugs and hauled the tub chair on top of it, she actually slept the whole night through for the first time in a long while.

When she woke, she lay in bed listening to birdsong. It sounded vivid and close by and despite the fact that she was in a single-storey building in a little town sitting at the foot of the Cleveland Hills,

145

she felt higher up than hitherto she'd been. She'd spent most of the previous day travelling, arriving in a place further north than she'd ever travelled. She visualized her journey as a small dotted line heading steeply up a map of the country. Consequently, she had the sense of having travelled uphill all the way from King's Cross. As if the further north you went, the higher your place of arrival. Way down at the bottom of Petra's hill, she imagined the South in general, almost out of sight. It made her think of Mrs McNeil's tales of Scotland, how herbs and plants of a similar genus to those found in Tibet grew there. She sensed those herbs and Mrs McNeil's Scotland simply further north up this great hill, that she was closer to them than she was to the weeds eking out a living between the paving slabs of Finchley.

'Look where I am,' she said quietly, as if to Mrs McNeil. 'Look at me.' She felt peculiarly triumphant. Big bloody deal, she could faintly hear Rob say but she shook her head to dislodge his voice and thought to herself that actually this *was* a big deal, to up sticks and leave and travel up, up and away, to have herself totally to herself.

She reached for her mobile phone; the signal was scant and it was with some satisfaction that she turned the thing off. It wasn't as if London seemed simply downhill; the city felt so far away as to be in another country altogether.

\*       \*       \*

As she took a shower, Petra wondered. Was this all it took? Has a quick injection of North Yorkshire vaccinated me against heartache? If I were to pack

146

up and go back down south again, right now, would all be right as rain? Perhaps. Perhaps. So perhaps I'll treat myself to a long overdue holiday before I go. They say a little TLC goes a long way—but maybe you have to go a long way first to find it.

After breakfast, when she ventured out across the small walled garden and checked out the compact but well-equipped studio, Petra knew she wouldn't be putting a time limit on her stay. Initially she'd thought in terms of running away to convalesce, of fleeing from London and escaping the spectre of Rob. Now she was actually here, feeling rested already, feeling herself unwind, she decided to skip the melodrama and simply see her stay in terms of a working holiday perfectly timed.

*　　　*　　　*

The market town of Stokesley surprised Petra in its elegance. She hadn't really noticed much on arriving the previous evening; the Old Stables had been the sum of her focus. Now, on a bright and mild Wednesday morning, Petra ventured out and swiftly let go of her preconceptions of rugged types with whippets, of ee-by-gum, of quaint rustic cottages with smoking chimneys and all manner of parochial cartoonery in general. Located in the lie of the Cleveland Hills and the North York Moors National Park, Stokesley sat proud and sedate, boasting fine Regency and Georgian buildings either in rosy brickwork with pale pointing or else rendered in subtle heritage colours. A bustling wide high street, partly cobbled, with buildings in the middle too, open spaces either end, and the River Leven flowing just behind the main street.

But what pleased Petra from the start—more than the revelation that she could get a decent cappuccino—was that Stokesley was a big enough place for her not to be stared at, yet small enough to preserve a quality of community spirit. People, it seemed, had the time of day for each other. Quite literally, in Petra's case. Out and about on the high street to establish her bearings and pick up some shopping, she regularly asked the time because she was heartened by the little conversations which ensued—from the teenagers hanging outside the Co-op to the pensioners pottering about. Ten to, five past, quarter past, twenty-five past ten you say? Is it really ten to eleven? Thank you. Oh, another thing—where would I find a chemist? A place to buy light bulbs? A bus timetable? Is there a bookshop? A public library? Yes, I'm new around here. Well, more of a working holiday, really. London, actually. No, I don't drive, I came by train. Sorry—I forgot to ask, is there a bike shop in town? There's a bike at the place I'm staying, you see, but it's set up for a big bloke.

The bike shop assistants winced and tutted at the state of Charlton's bike and shook their heads gravely when Petra asked them to lower the saddle to fit her. They told her to push it back home and come and hire one of their bikes. Half an hour later, she was happily cycling back to the Old Stables with a clutch of photocopies of local rides and a free sports bottle; a bag of groceries, light bulbs and the local paper swinging from the handlebars.

\*       \*       \*

Though it was fun for a couple of days to make like a tourist and pore over guidebooks and maps, tasting the unusual place names and genning up on local history while planning excursions, Petra was also keen to set herself up as an honorary local. After learning certain routes off by heart, she was soon pedalling off as if she'd ridden the roads her whole life; a nonchalant smile hiding the fact that her lungs throbbed from the limited fitness she'd maintained in London. Another good reason to stay on, she thought. Within a week, she was softening her Southern accent, dropping the 'r' from words like 'ask' and 'fast' and 'laugh', and she even dared ditch the occasional 'g' from the endin' of certain words, especially when she was goin' cyclin'.

Great Ayton, to the east of Stokesley, quickly became one of her favourite routes and Captain Cook was soon her local hero. She visited the museum dedicated to him in the old school he attended, she walked up to Easby Moor and ate her sandwiches by the monument to him, returning to Great Ayton by the obelisk of stones from Australia marking the site of his childhood cottage. But perhaps the best thing Petra discovered in Great Ayton was a small, old-fashioned sweetshop and café, Suggitts, whose eponymous ice cream, whether taken away in a traditional sugar cornet or eaten at one of the Formica tables, was irresistible. Before she rode off home, she'd treat herself to a quarter of some childhood confectionery or other—pear drops, sherbet lemons, chocolate bonbons, liquorice comfits—all of which were invariably infused with the nostalgic taste of paper bag by the time she arrived back at the Old Stables.

149

One morning, Petra decided to cycle south for a couple of miles, to visit Great Broughton, but soon after ran into the escarpment glowering above her and meekly decided to return to Stokesley for an afternoon in the studio and a lot of muttering to herself about improving her fitness. The next ride she did was to the north, on the old Nunthorpe Road, the landscape not so dramatic and the flatter farmland towards Middlesbrough gentler on her tired legs. Revitalized, she cycled west from Stokesley the following day to the village of Carlton and, with prior warning from her guidebooks, she only cycled the first part of Carlton Bank, sitting by the ponds and looking out over Cleveland while she had her packed lunch. She pushed her bike up the rest of the climb, a strenuous slog demanding gritted teeth and determination and rewarded by the wide open plateau of the bank itself. She stood there, holding her handlebars as if they were her best friend's hands, wiping the sweat from her face, her heart pounding, a satisfying ache in her legs. She propped her bike by the Lord Stones café which appeared to be hewn from the rock, and made her way out onto the bank. It was flat and high, carpeted with closely cropped downy grass. Overhead, gliders silently swooshed like great colourful benevolent birds and she felt that if she belted to the edge of the bank and took a huge leap off the edge, she'd join them. Far below, the arable patchwork land of the Cleveland plains; the vista stretching all the way to industrial Teeside. All around, greater than she'd ever known, a vast sky virtually cloudless, a lively breeze whispering excitedly that summer wasn't far off.

Petra lay on her back with her eyes closed, her heart rate settling. The air smelt so fragrantly clean and, as she inhaled deeply through her nose and exhaled fully through her mouth, she felt herself let go of any vestige of angst that still lingered. She could have drifted off for a nap, it was so tempting, but instead she sat herself up, ready to face a few home truths head on while her sight was filled with the beauty of the landscape. It was as if only in a place so high and uncompromised, with air so clean, could she finally look back over recent events with the clarity of hindsight.

*       *       *

It wasn't pain that I felt when I came across Rob and Laura. It was mortification.

It wasn't heartbreak really, it was humiliation.

My heart isn't actually broken—it was mostly my pride that took a pounding.

I suppose that what I felt for Rob wasn't love at all, it was need.

I thought I needed to be in a relationship.

I wanted to believe that I could inspire him to love me.

For a while I judged myself on that.

Daft cow that I am.

Was it a good thing or bad overall? Probably bad.

Was it a waste of ten months? No, not really.

Am I damaged by it? No, I am not.

I suffered more of a knock when I physically sleepwalked into my wall, than the emotional knock from my relationship with Rob coming to

151

such an undignified end.

I think I can finally see some providence in the situation. I wouldn't be here, today, would I? Up on Carlton Bank on a glorious day with the Old Stables all cosy and awaiting me.

I'm OK.

I'm lucky, really.

I feel well.

I'm going to have an ice cream.

I called him a cunt. I never use that word! I rarely go stronger than 'sod'.

And actually, Rob was just a bit of an oaf, really.

We were not a match made in heaven—but neither have I gone through hell. His moral code conflicted vastly with my own. Fuck-buddies—I don't ever want to be someone's fuck-buddy. Not for me at all. I'm a romantic. And that's nothing to justify or defend—it's something to be proud of.

This place is so beautiful. The world feels really pretty good from up here.

It's Good Friday the day after tomorrow. So tomorrow I'll pop into Great Ayton and treat myself to an enormous Easter egg from Suggitts.

\*     \*     \*

Which was precisely what Arlo Savidge was thinking.

He doesn't much care for chocolate, though.

He's planning to go to Suggitts tomorrow to buy an enormous Easter egg for his mother. Because then he's off down to London to visit her.

152

# CHAPTER NINETEEN

Arlo looked around his room. There wasn't much he'd be taking on his trip south. Unlike some of his less seasoned colleagues, Arlo had happily adapted to the confines of his living space and was not remotely bothered by the fact that his life had to fit the distinctive dimensions of the folly. Because of its nooks and alcoves and obtuse angles, life was easier if one didn't try to make the space fit one's belongings. Fortunately for Arlo, beloved possessions such as his guitars seemed to back nicely into corners as if the room had been custom designed for such a teacher. In fact, apart from his guitars—and he had four of them—Arlo had few personal effects, though what he did own he had in startling quantities. Racks of vinyl in 7 and 12 and even 10 inches, towers of CDs. It meant that there was no wall space for pictures or clocks or mirrors but as Arlo was neither vain, nor bothered by the passing of time, this was no sacrifice. However, he did need to take *something* home to show his mum, it would be important to her. He decided to take his students' work because therein lay the proof of a worthwhile and successful career. He travelled light. His bashed-up old canvas shoulder bag contained a change of clothes, a clutch of exercise books, his iPod and room enough left for an Easter egg.

He had the loan of a car from a colleague who was spending the long Easter weekend in Amsterdam, on the proviso that Arlo chauffeured him to and from the airport. And Arlo had said yes, he accepted the terms and conditions, as long as they could detour via Suggitts so he could buy his mother a very large Easter egg.

It was raining but the rain didn't seem to come from the sky at all. It wasn't falling downwards from above. It built its momentum from the moors and appeared to travel crossways in great swathes of wringing-wet mist, sweeping and tumbling across the land like wafts of wet gauze, drenching everything in its path.

'Want anything?' Arlo asked, parking the car and thinking himself an idiot for wearing only a T-shirt. 'Sherbet Dip Dab? A quarter of boiled sweets for the plane? Some genuine Yorkshire toffee to endear yourself to the Dutch? Lemfizz? Dolly Mixture? Tom Thumb drops?'

'Will you just fuck off and hurry up, Savidge.'

Arlo shrugged. 'I don't share,' he said, 'and I intend to spend a fair whack in Suggitts today.'

'Savidge, you're a prat. Hurry up.'

Leaving the car, Arlo thrust his hands deep into his pockets—as if, by hunching his shoulders up and looking down at his feet as he ran, he'd somehow get less wet. Not a chance. Once inside the shop, little rivulets dripped off him into puddles, as if he was a shaken umbrella.

'Nice day for it!' he said cheerily at large.

'Lovely,' said the shopkeeper, hoping he wouldn't touch anything with a paper wrapper.

'Got any Easter eggs?' he asked, terribly solemn so that she didn't know whether he was being funny, facetious, blind or just dumb. She tipped her head in the direction of the impressive display. Then she caught the eye of her solitary café customer dawdling over a cup of tea on the other side of the premises and they raised their eyebrows at Arlo's expense.

The door opened and another drowned rat squelched in.

'Wow! It's *mad* out there!'

'And I thought you were just a fair-weather rider,' the shopkeeper said warmly. 'Hullo, pet, you're wet.'

Arlo chuckled without turning around. He did love the local humour, their ability to state the obvious in such a deadpan way. Their humour remained dry whatever the weather.

'Easter eggs!' Arlo heard the wet pet declare and a few footsteps later she was standing by his side.

And there they stood, their arms almost touching as they perused the seasonal chocolate in the little shop area to the left of the cash desk and café. They didn't look at each other—what was the point, it was raining, everyone looks the same when they're that wet. There was something cheering about being the only two people mad enough to get that wet for the sake of chocolate. But it was the serendipity of both reaching for the one huge Lindt chocolate bunny at exactly the same time which made them turn and regard each other.

*      *      *

And he doesn't have the lovely mop of Bob Dylan hair he had seventeen years ago. In fact, he seems generally smaller. But his dimple is still there and his eyes haven't changed and nor have his forearms. Today they glisten with rain as he passes the bunny over to her. Seventeen years ago they were sheened with sweat as he played 'Among the Flowers' for her. And Petra knows it's Arlo.

And she doesn't have the bouncy bob she had when she was fifteen and it doesn't matter that her hair corkscrews off her head in sodden spiralling rats' tails apparently made of treacle—he'd know that face anywhere. Those great big brown eyes and that little retroussé nose. And the fact that she seems to be wearing a tent doesn't fool him. And when he sees that it's a man's cagoule, that doesn't bother him either. For Arlo, not even revolting pea-green Gore-Tex can hide the fact that it's Petra Flint under there.

\*       \*       \*

'Petra?'
  'Arlo?'

\*       \*       \*

Just then it doesn't seem crazy or weird or even amazing that they should meet like this, right here, after all this time, in an old-fashioned sweetshop on a God-forsaken day in North Yorkshire. For a perfect moment it makes sense completely.

## CHAPTER TWENTY

'Petra Flint? Petra Petra Flint. No *way*! What are you—'
  'I know! But Arlo, I mean how—'

'You look amazing—you look the same. But very wet.'

'You too—just the same.'

'But bald as well as wet.'

'You're not bald—you're—you're. Just not as hirsute as you were when you were a teenager.'

'I—what are you—?'

'I'm thirty-two.'

'No—I meant—'

'Oh! Oh I—you know.'

'I can't believe it.'

'No—nor me.'

(Some time later, after Petra and Arlo had left Suggitts, the shopkeeper would remark to the customer still dawdling over the cup of tea, Did you see them? Those two—grinning away at each other like soppy idiots? Sopping idiots more like, the customer would add, finishing his tea with a Ta-ta, see you tomorrow.)

'It's been—Christ—it must be seventeen years?'

'Yes.'

'Last time I saw you was half my life ago, Petra.'

'Over half my life ago, Arlo.'

'That car horn is for me. I have to go. He won't stop honking until I'm in the car. Can I give you a lift? It's raining.'

'It's pouring. I have a bike.'

'Do you live here?'

'Not really—but sort of.'

'I'm going to London. Today. Now. As you can hear from all that honking.'

'I live there too. Sort of.'

'I live here. How long a tenancy is a "sort-of"?'

'I don't know.'

'Will it stretch till I'm back? After Easter?'

157

'I think so. I don't know. I haven't thought.'
'Please be here.'
'OK.'
'Petra Flint.'
'But how will I find you, Arlo?'
'I'll find you.'

\*      \*      \*

And, under a barrage of irritated car horns, Arlo backed out of the shop without taking his eyes off Petra. And, though he could lip-read his colleague masticating a stream of expletives, hammering on the car window and mouthing, Come-fucking-*on*, Arlo needed a moment to raise his face to the sky.

If I believed in God, I'd say the rain falling on my face feels like the fingertips of angels playing out a tune.

\*      \*      \*

For the first time in years, Arlo wanted to write a song. Lyrics and notes surged around his body like the flow of blood, cascading from his brain to his soul, rooting him to the spot while the lot was transcribed to his memory.

'Savidge—what the *fuck*?' his colleague was yelling out of the car window, a newspaper held over his head.

Arlo wanted to say, Drive yourself to the flaming airport, I need to write a song. And he wanted to make a phone call and say, Sorry, Mum, I just can't come home today. I need to stay here—and make sure I don't lose her for another seventeen years.

'Savidge!'

The song was safely sealed in his thoughts. It was a gift he didn't give much thought to these days—the ability to create an entire composition in seconds and commit it to memory in a moment. He couldn't afford to acknowledge it—if he did, he'd have to question his teaching career; a career that had kept him occupied, solvent and safe these past years.

He didn't care if he looked like an idiot but he felt like a latter-day Gene Kelly, singing in the rain, as he jogged to the car with a lightness of step not even he remembered having.

'Sorry,' he said with a beatific smile which unnerved his colleague into silence, 'just sorting my life out.'

'In *Suggitts*?'

'It's as good a place as any.'

It's OK, Arlo thought to himself. I can do the airport. I can do London, I could even do another seventeen years if I had to. Because she'll always be there. She'll be there for me to find. In a crowd of schoolgirls. In a sweetshop in North Yorkshire. In the sunshine. In the rain. Among the flowers.

\*       \*       \*

The shopkeeper stared at the door while Petra gazed at the small puddle which was all that was left of Arlo. She didn't want anyone to step in it.

'He left without paying for his Easter egg—the soft lad,' the shopkeeper remarked to his puddle. 'Ah well, I know where he lives.'

Petra suddenly realized she was hugging the chocolate bunny in the crook of her arm as if it

159

were a soft toy.

'I'll pay for his,' Petra said, 'and mine.'

'All this equality—it's not right, pet. Romance should be old-fashioned,' the shopkeeper teased. 'He's not what you'd call *the Milk Tray Man*, is he.'

'I don't like Milk Tray.'

'Just as well. He's not much of a Sir Walter Raleigh either—look at that puddle.'

'Well, James Cook's my hero, he was a far superior explorer,' Petra said primly. 'Now, what do I owe you—for both?'

'Six pound for yours, ten for his. Sixteen pound, pet.'

Petra paused before she left. 'I haven't seen him for seventeen years. And now he's buggered off down to London.'

'Well, did he not say he'll be back?' the shopkeeper said, reddening at the disclosure of her eavesdropping.

'He said he'll find me—but I don't know how. We didn't swap numbers—we just talked about, I don't know, each other's *hair*.'

'Well, if Captain Cook could find Australia, then I'm sure that lad'll find you.'

## CHAPTER TWENTY-ONE

'Darling!'

'Happy Easter, Mum.'

'It's huge.'

'I stole it.'

'You what?'

'I walked out of the shop without paying.'

'Good God, darling.'

'They know me there.'

'For shoplifting?'

'No, not for shoplifting, Mother. I just had a moment. I'll settle up next week.'

'I don't think I ought to eat stolen goods, darling.'

'Bollocks, Mum. It's finest Swiss chocolate. You enjoy it.'

'Do you talk to your students with that mouth?'

'No, but I kiss my mum with it. Hullo, Mum. It's good to see you.'

\*     \*     \*

Arlo wrapped his arms around his mother and gave her a long hug. It never ceased to surprise him that he was a head and shoulders taller than she. Though his upbringing had been liberal, lenient and laid back, the demarcation of parent/child had never been compromised. So, though Arlo had been allowed to say 'bollocks' and 'bugger' and 'bloody Nora' at home, to him his mum was his mum and he was her child and it always felt funny that he was grown-up enough to see over the top of her head.

'Go and unpack and check all your Action Men are where you left them,' his mother said brusquely and Arlo knew he wasn't to comment on the tears in her eyes.

'I haven't really got anything to unpack—your Easter egg took up all the room.'

'Arlo, you're dreadful. I'm going to make a pot of tea.'

When she came back into the lounge, with tea

for two on a tray, Arlo was revisiting all the family photos on the mantelpiece. She loved to see him do this; it was his little routine whenever he came back, saying a silent hullo to his family through the years. Hullo, Grandma. Hullo, Mum and baby Arlo. Hullo, Arlo aged six with the orange Space Hopper and terrible haircut. Hullo, Dad. And hullo, Dad and Arlo flying kites, hair and flares flapping cheerfully in some summer breeze thirty years ago. Hullo, Mum and Dad on your silver wedding anniversary. Hullo, Dad the Christmas before you died.

'Ten years—next year,' his mother said quietly, knowing instinctively that her son was thinking the same thing.

'I know,' Arlo said, 'good old Dad.'

'You always called him "good old Dad".'

'I know—it used to wind him up.'

'Not really.'

'I know.'

She poured the tea and they drank, wistful smiles easing the loaded absence of father and husband.

'Mind you, it used to really wind *me* up when you'd call me Mum*my*, good and loud in public. Especially as you were in your twenties at the time. I'm glad you've outgrown that, Arlo.'

'That was to even the score for the period when you wanted me to call you Esther.'

'You were a teenager,' she shrugged. 'I thought you'd like to.'

'You were a dippy hippy,' Arlo laughed. 'You still are, a bit. I was the only one amongst my friends who never had to sneak joss sticks up to his bedroom.'

162

'You never even had to buy your own.'

'Yeah, who needed pocket money when your parents let you have all the joss sticks you wanted, Esther,' Arlo teased.

'Can't stand the smell of them now,' Esther confided.

'Me neither.'

'I have quite a thing for expensive scented candles, though.'

'So I can detect,' said Arlo, thinking that the house smelt particularly fragrant and feminine and it was such a comforting and lovely ambience after weeks of eau de boys, photocopiers, floor polish, games kits and home-brew.

'Take one back with you,' she said. 'Every occasion I've visited, I've noted that your folly smells of moss and stone.'

'It's made of moss and stone.'

'Not on the inside. Mind you, I'm sure I have a Jo Malone candle that is called Moss or something.'

'Mum, if I start burning scented candles I'll get a reputation for being even more of a poof than they already think I am.'

'Darling—you know it wouldn't matter to me if you were.'

'Bloody Nora, Mother!' Arlo declared. 'Where's that come from?'

Esther looked mortified, though Arlo hadn't really taken offence. It had been such an Esther thing to say. Like when she'd told him she didn't mind if he wanted to be Jewish when he spent part of his gap year on a kibbutz. I think you have to be born to a Jewish mother, Arlo had told her. Well, I'll look into it myself, if you like, she'd told him.

'I just meant—' Esther said. 'Oh, I don't know what I meant. Here, let's crack this Easter egg.'

'What you meant,' Arlo said, having sucked thoughtfully on a full mouthful of divine chocolate, 'was, How's my love life?'

His mother feigned her mouth being too full to respond.

Arlo shrugged. 'It's difficult, Mum. After Helen. It's still difficult.'

'It's gone five years, darling.'

'But I flicked off that particular switch, I de-sensitized myself to the merits of romantic love. I can live without it. Quite happily, actually.'

Esther's eyes welled. 'But that's so sad. You're so good at it. You are your father's son—and look how happy we were.'

His mother was the one person for whom Arlo's shrugs didn't work.

'You need to let Helen go, darling,' she said abruptly. 'It wasn't your fault.'

'That's easier said than done, Mum.'

'Letting go of Helen—or believing it wasn't your fault.'

'You're right—it's over five years ago. Nothing left to talk about.'

'But something to think about.'

'What if I *have* met someone?' Arlo said quietly, more to steer the direction of the conversation away from Helen and events of five years ago.

Esther let the information hang. 'Who?' she asked gently.

Arlo thought of Petra. In his mind's eye he didn't see the vision of the drowned Ophelia who'd dripped back into his life that morning. He saw Petra at fifteen, wrestling with a big clay pot in the

164

playground of his school. Wearing Dunlop Green Flash and her summer uniform. Ringlets crying out to be pinged. Cheeky smile. Nice knees. 'A schoolgirl,' he said vaguely.

'A *school*girl?' His mother's frown knitted her brow in such a way that she suddenly looked older than her age, as she might look in another decade.

'Someone I knew from when I was at school,' Arlo quickly explained. 'Someone I haven't seen or even thought of, really, for years and years.'

'And you met again?'

'This morning.'

Esther observed softness mingling with trepidation in her son's expression. 'How amazing,' she said.

'It is,' Arlo said, 'but I won't say more. I don't want to tempt fate.'

'You won't be tempting fate if you believe in it,' Esther said. 'If one has hope, one has the power to fulfil it.'

\*       \*       \*

Arlo lies in bed, the single bed that's always been his, and he's glad to be home. In retrospect, today was a mad day; it was all a bit weird, really. Not so much the fact that he bumped into Petra Flint in Suggitts, Great Ayton, having not seen her for seventeen years. But more, the feelings—strong, soaring, unequivocal—that seeing her has incited.

And Arlo feels a bit pissed off, actually. Because he was getting on fine in life without thoughts of love. And now his mind is whirring with them. And his mind's eye is playing a slide show on a loop, of Petra now, Petra then, Petra today, Petra

165

seventeen years ago. A drop of rain coursing down her face like a tear, this morning. Oh, to kiss it away. Dunlop Green Flash and a short summer uniform. Her legs. Her skin. The swell of unseen but imagined breasts demurely hidden by school shirts or a man's pea-green cagoule.

Arlo's hand goes to his cock, straining with pent-up spunk which he wanks away in seconds. He's been celibate, by choice, for five years, which isn't to say that he hasn't been aroused, hasn't masturbated; but for five years he's been satisfied with pneumatic anonymous fantasy women rather than anyone known to him.

He lies in the dark in his childhood bed, holding the duvet aloft while he wonders if there are any tissues. He laughs when he remembers how fastidiously prepared he was as a teenager for masturbation in this very room. Tissues. Magazines. Brilliant hiding places. Twice-, thrice-nightly eruptions of unharnessed pubescent lust. The noiseless route to the bathroom. Silent comings and goings.

Twisting, he flicks on his bedside light. There are no tissues in sight. He tiptoes fast to the bathroom, knowing which creaking boards to avoid, and cleans himself. He regards the jars of his mother's lotions and potions. This is something new, just as her penchant for expensive scented candles is new. He remembers when he was young watching her massage a little olive oil into her face, her neck. How she'd smile at him and dab a little on his nose. Good old Mum.

He's back in bed and he feels exhausted. His back is nagging. He's not used to driving such a distance. Nearly six hours from Ayton to London

166

via Durham Tees Valley Airport. But he can't get to sleep. Which is baffling because a wank is usually a good sedative.

And though he's spent, he can't stop thinking about her, seeing her.

What are you doing now, Petra? This precise moment in time? Are you in bed too? I feel I know the exact scent of your skin. But how the fuck can I? I've never got that close to you. Is this what love at first sight does, then? Imprints all your secrets, all of you, into me, in an instant?

Shut up, soft lad.

\*         \*         \*

It can't be love at first sight because that would negate how I felt for her years ago. And I did love her then. At a distance. Gently. I remember.

But if I loved her then, where's she been all these years?

*Where've you been all my life?*

Stop it, idiot.

\*         \*         \*

Is it love at second sight, then? Is that as good?

How will I know?

How can I find out?

Do I dare?

# CHAPTER TWENTY-TWO

A drawback of a converted stone stables is the cobbled flooring. It would be a crime to cover it up but it makes positioning of furniture problematic, if not precarious. The wobble factor requires specific alignment of items, with minimal room for manoeuvre in their placing. Then there's the chill factor: fitted carpets would be anathema, however if areas of the floor aren't covered by rugs then a year-round coldness travels up through the soles of the feet deep into the bones. If you're a sleepwalker, though, you would be safer without the rugs. You are at greater danger sleepwalking inside such an abode than if you opened the door and wandered out into Stokesley. Out in the town, the only threat you might come across would be the stares and sniggers from the kids loitering outside the Spar. Inside the Old Stables, however, your bare feet follow the undulations of the cobbles thus your toes can slide under a ruck in the rug, tripping you up and sending you down hard and fast; your hip catching the arm of the leather chair, your head whacking down on the stone slab of the fireplace. The pain will be so great that your subconscious tells you it's better to stay asleep than wake up. What would you do anyway—call a cab to take you to A&E at the James Cook University Hospital in Middlesbrough and explain that bumping into your first love had set you off crashing into furniture and fireplace?

Heart and hearth, in Petra's case, was not a homely combination.

*       *       *

It was the cold that awoke Petra just before dawn, when it's not quite light but nor is it night-dark; a wearisome time too early for waking up but too late to restore satisfying sleep. Petra scrambled up, which made her head spin. When that stopped, she noted that her jaw really throbbed. Gingerly she took her hand to her chin. The side of her face felt fat. Shivering and a little unsteady, she went to the bathroom to search for paracetamol and look at the damage. She had acquired a rather unbecoming jowl on the left side of her face though she couldn't quite tell if it was purple with bruising or with cold. Certainly, her lips had a bluish tinge.

'Arlo can't see me like this,' she told herself and was then simultaneously cheered but troubled that this should be her first thought.

'Bloody Charlton,' she muttered, scrabbling around in his bathroom cabinet. 'Why can't he have something simple like paracetamol?'

But more than the discomfort of being so cold and sore was the disappointment of having sleepwalked in the first place. She was really, really vexed by this. She'd been so high, so happy, all day yesterday; with thoughts of Arlo and the serendipity of it all. Now, she lay in bed, desperate to sleep; concentrating on relaxing her body, not scrunching her eyes tight shut. She took the duvet from the bed and went back into the sitting room, glowering at the small but significant lift of the rug, like a little mouse hole, that had caused her to trip. Swaddling herself, she nestled into the sofa and

169

tried to settle while night seeped away into day.

'Think nice thoughts,' she told herself—which was what Eric always used to say to her, instead of sweet dreams, when they house-shared. She imagined herself regaling Eric and Kitty and Gina with an embellished version of how she had come across Arlo, embroidering it into a windswept tale of Brontë magnitude.

And did he take you in his arms and kiss you? she could hear Eric ask with a swoon.

And what would she say? What could she say?

No, she'd have to say, we didn't touch. We were too wet. Too surprised.

But what did he say? Gina, ever the pragmatist, would no doubt ask.

Well, he said I looked just the same.

And then what? Kitty would probe.

He said he'll find me!

How? Kitty again.

I don't know.

Find you? What tosh. How can he? Does the ice-cream lady know where you're staying?

No.

Did you tell him?

No.

Did you even say Stokesley?

I can't remember.

Well, I'm sorry for deflating your bubble of romantic delusion, but even if he wanted to find you, he couldn't. And if he wanted to see you, he'd have asked for a number or something. And if he wanted you, he'd have bloody well kissed you seventeen years ago. Popped your cherry way back then. Been your boyf. Your first love. Christ.

Easy, Kitty.

'I know I know I know,' Petra said out loud, covering her ears as if her Studio Three were actually there.

'I know,' she said quietly. And then she did precisely what she would have done, had she been in the studio. She turned away from them, stopped listening, and concentrated on working.

Still cloaked in the duvet, Petra shuffled across the small garden to the workshop at the back. The birds seemed to sing louder as she went, as if protesting at her presence at a time when the garden should be theirs. Clear off and leave us to our early worms!

'Dew,' Petra said, crouching to the grass, transfixed. 'I'm never up early enough for dew. I don't see dew in London.' To her eyes, the buds of dew which clung to the undersides of blades of grass, rested on the veins of leaves, hung in stillness from twigs, seemed to be made of something heavier than water, a viscosity keeping them so perfectly round. Petra stood up; the air felt gauzy and as she looked around she noted a vaporous quality, more than a mist, more like a mild sea fret. Thank God I'm awake at this time, she thought, as she eased open the studio door and sat down, cocooned in the duvet, the thrill of wanting to get working swelling like a wave inside her.

This wasn't going to be a tanzanite moment. This was a time for something simple, something vernacular—something inspired by the North-East, for what it had brought her, what she had seen.

'Dew. And land that climbs and rolls and drops away. Khaki and slate and lilac. Air—up on the

171

hills it's so fresh you can taste it, here in the garden right now you can *see* it. Ice cream and chocolate and sweets. The river Leven at Ayton rushing over the weir. The Leven behind me, tiptoeing through town. Hills ahead. And moors. Rain licking down my face yesterday. Raindrops, like translucent pearls, on Arlo's forearms.'

With creative energy flowing and charging her brain, Petra was at once warm enough to be done with the duvet. She started to sketch though her design was already set in her mind's eye and before long she was working with copper, crocheting with fine wire and looping in tiny clear beads here and there. Copper as an economical preliminary for the finished work to be executed in white gold perhaps. Earrings, she thought. Long, sensuous, danglies. White gold with moonstone.

Suddenly it was late lunch-time. Petra looked at her work, slipping it over her fingers from hand to hand like a child with a pet hamster. She was delighted; the slink and flow was organic, the beads placed perfectly, just like dew buds glinting on stems against gauzy air, like the tiny flowers finding their footing on the moors.

'Do you know something? You're fine as you are. Copper is just right because the colour will change just like the landscape. And you're not going to be earrings, you need to trickle, not swing. You're going to be a rather gorgeous hair grip. And I'm going to have you.'

There were plenty of places to buy simple kirby-grips in Stokesley but it was only when she found everywhere closed that Petra remembered it was Good Friday. She had so fancied a cheese-and-onion pastry but she returned to the Old Stables,

172

empty-handed and alone. Just the chocolate Easter bunny for company and she bit off his head without pause for thought.

'He owes me ten pounds,' Petra said and it was the first time she'd thought of Arlo since the early hours. You bloody owe me ten pounds, she said again, softly this time and with the coy smile she'd use if he was here in front of her. If only he was. She didn't really want her money back, she just wanted to be able to ask him for it. It could provide the purpose, the excuse, to see him again. Otherwise, what could she say? With a day's distance from their encounter and a full morning's work behind her, she felt shy and a little detached. What would she say if she saw him again? Could she really be brazen enough to smile and flirt and say, Oi you, where's my ten quid?

She drifted off into fanciful imaginings of what could have happened the day before had they only had more time. If he hadn't been rushing off, if the rain had stopped. They could have walked a while, perhaps all the way up Roseberry Topping, the odd hill which looked from some angles like a child's drawing of a wave. They could have sat there and marvelled at both the view and the happenstance. And what would they have said? Every now and then I've thought of you. Always fondly. With a sense of regret that we didn't— That we never— That we didn't even ever kiss. Like this. Kiss like this.

Petra opened her eyes. She was still in the living room at the Old Stables, on her own with a headless chocolate rabbit lying decimated on her lap in his gold-foil coat. She didn't doubt that she'd probably always been a little in love with Arlo. Or the idea of him, at least. She hadn't seen him all that often, after all. Just when it was pottery, when he wasn't revising. But it was such a vivid time. He'd been in her life at one of her most vulnerable periods; when her parents split up and school work moved up a gear and Mrs McNeil, beautiful Lillian McNeil, was her extracurricular teacher of life, love and death.

But that was seventeen years ago. And it wasn't fate or Cupid that had brought Arlo to Suggitts yesterday. It was just a crazy coincidence. One Petra should perhaps marvel at for a moment and then let that moment pass. Because it wouldn't be realistic to imagine how they could possibly get it together. She lives in London, he lives up here. What has he done and where has he been these seventeen years? He's probably married with kids—that was probably his wife honking the horn of a nice MPV. And even if he isn't spoken for, however would he find her again? It was just something to say. It was a silly thing to say. He didn't mean it—how could he? In the age of mobile phones, who on earth offers to find someone else on wits alone? Who did he think he was, some Heathcliff type who'd tramp the moors bellowing Petra! Petra! and sweep her off her feet in the centre of Stokesley to carry her over the threshold of some picture-perfect cottage?

'Anyway, if I've learned anything from the Rob debacle, it's my tendency to fall in love with an idea; to let unrealistic daydreams falsely colour and distort reality. And my time here will change from being days in which I work productively and feel myself flourish—to hours dragging by with me wondering if he'll turn up. Hoping. Waiting.

Imagining. Romanticizing. It's daft.'

*     *     *

And so, straight after the bank holiday, first thing on the Tuesday, she headed south by rail.

At much the same time, Arlo belted back north, a day early, his internal compass buffed up and ready, primed to home in on Petra Flint.

## CHAPTER TWENTY-THREE

The lie of the land appeared to create an appropriate backdrop to Petra's mood. With the expansive romance of the moors, of the changing light and fast-paced weather, Petra could indulge her feelings of melancholy and drama. The roll and swoop of the moors, the rush and plummet of my heart. By the time she'd been trundled along the Great North-Eastern Railway network and deposited at King's Cross station to be then shunted up the Northern Line to Woodside Park station, just one more automaton with an Oyster card, she simply felt flat. And her flat, when she arrived, felt dull. Being in the basement, the presence of the family upstairs, their footfalls and furniture, for the first time felt oppressive to Petra. As if she was some caryatid, holding them up, or at least having to prevent them from compressing her. Her living space was small anyway, but she felt further diminished by it; envisaging an aerial view of herself where she was just another inconsequential speck of a person living in

175

cramped rented accommodation in a huge city.

Not taking into account the garden and the workshop, the Stables itself hadn't been much bigger than her flat. But Stokesley for Petra, though smaller than North Finchley, seemed to have the capacity to let its inhabitants breathe, according them their individuality, accommodating their sense of space. Slumping down into the sofa, she closed her eyes and banished the voice that asked her if she wasn't being a little too melodramatic—about her reasons for leaving North Yorkshire so abruptly as well as her ambivalence to her home city. A vivid recollection of Mrs McNeil, however, brought her to task.

'Home isn't necessarily where the heart is, Petra,' she remembered her saying. 'You have to put your heart into the place that you call home. That's how I made Tanzania work for me when we moved there. And that's how I established an affection for London when we arrived here from Tanzania.'

Petra wandered into her bedroom and took a pensive look at the watercolour of Kilimanjaro, next to Hector McNeil's abstract oil, both of which Mrs McNeil had bequeathed her. 'Didn't you also tell me a part of your heart would be for ever with this mountain?'

And she could hear Mrs McNeil answer her back, she could see again the wry smile arising from the lady's superior worldliness and wisdom. 'And when are you going to tell me that you left a little of your heart in North Yorkshire?'

'You'll say I'm daft.'

'I'll say no such thing. I only ask if you ensured that it was placed carefully before you belted back

176

here.'

Petra decided not to answer. Not to talk to the dead. Or to their pictures. She made herself a cup of camomile tea and decided not to phone Lucy or Eric as she'd intended. No more questions, thank you very much. Not when there were no answers to be had, anyway.

*       *       *

'Petra!' Gina and Kitty said in unison.

'Ee by gum,' said Eric. 'Hey up, lass.'

Kitty gave Eric a withering raise of her eyebrows before smiling at Petra. 'You're back.'

'I am,' said Petra, preparing to bat the volley of questions on the tips of the tongues of her Studio Three.

'How was it?'

'It was great.'

'Did you do much work?'

'Loads.'

'What's Charlton's place like?'

'Glorious.'

'And the surroundings?'

'Glorious too.'

'Nice people?'

'Lovely.'

'How did you sleep?'

'Pretty well.'

'What's with your jaw?'

'I fell.'

'Asleep?'

'Yes, you could say that I fell, asleep.'

'Very droll. Do you feel better about—you know—stuff?'

'Yes, I feel fine. Absolutely fine.'

'Did you make friends?'

'I didn't really fraternize.'

'Was a fortnight long enough?'

'Oh God, yes,' said Petra. 'It was great. Country air. Peace and quiet. But you know me, I'm a Londoner, born and bred. It's great to be back.'

\*     \*     \*

She fooled them for a week. Charlton Squire too.

No one who'd borrowed the Old Stables had ever returned the keys by plonking them on the glass top of one of his display cabinets. Usually, they were wrapped up with purple prose and tied with ribbons of gratitude; long thank-you notes extolling the accommodation, the area, the generosity of the host. Invariably, a bouquet or a bottle of champagne accompanied their return. But Petra sauntered in and put the keys down as if they opened nothing more than the stationery cupboard out the back.

'Thanks, Charlton,' she said. 'It was great. Must dash.'

\*     \*     \*

'There's something up with that girl,' Eric colluded with Gina and Kitty later that week when Petra had popped out to Bellore for some solder. 'I can't put my finger on it.'

'She's spending an inordinate amount of time gazing out of the window,' Gina said.

'But she's not sharing the view,' said Kitty. 'If she catches you watching her, she quickly returns

178

to her work as if she'd only looked up for a second or so.'

'I've asked, Are you OK? a couple of times,' said Gina, 'and she just says, Oh yes, I'm fine, with a breezy smile.'

'Perhaps she just doesn't want us all snooping and hovering,' said Kitty.

'Whatever—something is amiss,' Eric said. 'I know her better than you, remember.'

Gina turned her back on them. It amused her how Kitty and Eric competed over Petra. 'Do you think something happened up there?' she said as if the North was a wild and mystical place.

'Who can say?' Kitty said darkly.

'She'd have told *me*,' Eric differed, 'by now.'

\*     \*     \*

But Petra gave nothing away. She arrived in the mornings insouciant, often with cappuccinos all round. She spent long days working industriously. She took great interest in the works of her Studio Three but gave little away of her own project, preferring instead to work covertly, her arm across her sketchbook like a schoolgirl preventing classmates from copying. She spent hours at a time crocheting copper wire into strange, formless configurations, or else she was pressing sheets of it with other materials through the rolling mill to experiment with different textures. The mesh bags from washing tablets, fibrous plastic scourers, scraps of netting, popped bubble wrap, knots of wire—they all went through the mill with the copper, over and again; Petra seemingly engrossed both in the process and the results.

179

She'd been back a week when an opportunity arose for Eric to take a closer look.

'Where's Petra, Gina?'

'Post office.'

'What are you doing, Eric?'

'I'm intrigued, Kitty.'

'That's her sketchbook—you oughtn't. You know that.'

But Eric had already started to flip through the pages. 'I'm not spying,' he said quietly, after a while. 'I'm just taking a quick peek behind the façade.'

Kitty and Gina regarded each other but stayed put.

After a while, Eric looked over to them with a quizzical smile. 'It's all bollocks.'

'What is?'

'Everything! It's all been bollocks,' he said. 'What she's told us—and all this.' He held Petra's sketchpad up high and fanned through the pages.

'Define "bollocks",' Kitty challenged him.

Eric seemed amused. 'Well, it's not bollocks in that these are rather commendable sketches. But they have nothing to do with her vocation. These aren't preparatory drawings for future designs. Nor do they have anything to do with all the wire knitting and rolling-mill stuff—which in themselves are bollocks too.'

'Some friend you are,' Kitty said.

'She's been filling her days, my dears,' he chuckled softly, 'filling her days with stuff that has nothing to do with work or with London. Look.' He fanned the book again.

The women walked over and quietly examined the sketches.

'See,' said Eric, 'her mind is elsewhere. Her mind is not on work. It's not in London. Not in the here and now. Her mind is full of Yorkshire and so is her sketchbook.'

Pages and pages of Petra's book were filled with charming drawings of rural landscapes and river bends and sheep, little vignettes in pencil crammed with affection and rustic detail. There were sketches of ducks diving, of a bicycle propped against a tree-trunk, of cottages, of rickety gates and tumbling paths; there was a page filled entirely with cartoon ice-cream cones.

Kitty picked up some of the warped pieces of copper, indented with the imprints of the bits of junk Petra had run through the press. 'I have to agree with you, Eric.'

'It's not just her mind that's in Yorkshire,' Gina said at length, 'I'd say it's her heart.'

\*       \*       \*

By the following week, Petra suddenly couldn't sit still long enough to draw a lamb, let alone a flock, and she was far too fidgety for work at the rolling mill to be anything other than downright dangerous. She kept nipping out of the studio only to return empty-handed. She responded to direct questions with vague, incomplete answers. She frowned a lot. She was late into the studio and the first to leave.

Charlton crossed paths with her as she meandered along Greville Street.

'Hullo, Pet, you'll save my old bones those flights of stairs to yours. Can you take on some work for me? God, you look dreadful.'

181

'Thank you.'

'You can?'

'Can what?'

'Out-work? It's not big—but it's fiddly.'

'Oh. I don't know. I'm so busy with my own stuff.'

'Stuff?'

'Yes, stuff.'

'Sounds exciting.'

'Not really.'

'Are you all right, Pet?'

'Yes. Of course. Just fine.'

\*          \*          \*

And then, on the Wednesday night, Petra had a dream so compelling it kept her glued to her bed and gave her a sleep so deep that when she awoke she lay for a few minutes desperately trying to assess what was real and what was fantasy and hoping beyond hope that a substantial part of the latter might somehow have made it into the former.

She sat at her bench all morning, drumming her fingers distractedly against the skin while she gazed at nothing in particular in the middle distance. She didn't touch her tools or her sketches and she was immune to the concerned glances being directed her way from her colleagues.

It was Gina who approached her though Eric was soon at her heels, Kitty shoulder to shoulder with him. They were forming an arrowhead, homing in on her, and she looked up, alarmed. It was Gina who laid her arm gently around her shoulders. She didn't say anything but bestowed

182

upon Petra a skilled look of maternal affection and concern which she'd perfected over the years with her own family to elicit honesty and details.

'It's so silly,' Petra started. 'Really stupid. I'm angry with myself for being so stupid. But I can't seem to shake it off.'

'Shake what off?'

'I had a dream. Last night. And the dream has turned into a feeling. This idiotic feeling. I know that the feeling is so far-fetched it's almost laughable. And that's what's making me more miserable. I know it, but I can't help feeling it.'

'Feeling what?'

Petra opened her mouth and then closed it and her change of tack was visible long before she spoke. 'Do you believe in fate?'

'Yes,' Kitty whispered.

'I'd like to,' said Eric, looping his shoulder in front of Gina's.

'Not really,' said Gina.

'Oh,' said Petra.

'Why?' Gina asked.

Petra shrugged. 'It's just so stupid.'

'So you keep saying,' said Eric. 'Talk to me.'

'I dreamt about someone. It was someone I saw when I was in North Yorkshire. Someone I once knew,' she said. 'I hadn't seen him for seventeen years and then one rainy day just before Easter, in a tiny sweetshop in the wilds of Yorkshire, I bump into him—literally.'

'From city wanker to sweetshop owner,' Kitty marvelled. 'Marry this one, Petra.'

'He doesn't own the sweetshop, I don't even know what he does do,' Petra said and she glowered at herself. 'We didn't say much. We

183

didn't say that much, really, seventeen sodding years ago.'

'But you can't stop thinking about him and now you're dreaming about him and you wonder if fate put him your way and whether you should return north and give destiny a helping hand?' Eric's eyes sparkled.

'See how stupid it is?' Petra chided herself while nodding at Eric.

'Yes, it's fate. It's fate dressed as Cupid,' Kitty said. 'I'd say get the first train back there and personally hand Cupid the arrows from his quiver.'

Kitty's Studio Three gawped at the unmitigated romanticism spewing from the dark-burgundy lipsticked mouth of the variously pierced, multi-tattooed black-clad Goth in their midst.

'But Kitty,' said Petra, 'I couldn't tell Cupid in which direction to take aim. I haven't a clue where Arlo is.'

'Arlo?' said Gina.

'It means "manly",' cooed Eric.

'What *was* said?' Kitty asked her.

'He said he'd find me,' Petra said. 'God knows how. He doesn't know where I live either. That's what I mean when I say it's all so stupid. And pointless. And if it's stupid and pointless why can't I keep him from my mind?'

'Because it has the makings of a fairy tale,' said Kitty a little sadly, 'and fairy tales don't happen in real life.'

Petra shrugged. 'Exactly,' she said.

# CHAPTER TWENTY-FOUR

Arlo returned to Roseberry Hall. Not even in his wildest dreams had he envisaged Petra running in slow motion down the drive and into his arms, yet in reality it was still a shock to find he had only the grunting Walley Brothers for company. These grizzled old men, the longest-serving members of staff, spoke little and smelt a lot, mooching about the grounds as they did checking fencing, killing rabbits and removing fox dung. They'd grunt if they were feeling cordial, more usually they made a sound closer to a growl. No one liked them. Even the most mischievous boys steered clear. Even Headmaster Pinder privately considered there to be truth in the rumour that the Walley Brothers made personal use of the fox shit they removed, so odoriferous and generally repellent were they. No one was entirely sure of their Christian names but their lack of redeeming features, such as personalities in general, saw them only ever referred to as Mr Walley and Mr Walley. However, the playing fields never had a trace of fox dung and the fences were always orderly and as the Walleys' arrival at the school had predated Headmaster Pinder's by at least a decade, their jobs were safe.

Returning to school a good few days before the staff were due to filter back, Arlo swiftly decided Trappist solitude was preferable to any level of contact with the Walley brothers so he took to his folly and wondered whether he was slightly deluded to have come back early at all. He'd forsaken his lovely mum's home-cooking and the opportunity to spend time with a couple of his childhood friends, to belt back north on a whim. Late that night, while he waited in vain for sleep, he started to feel increasingly foolish for returning in such a hurry on what now seemed such a ludicrous premise. He decided he'd allocate himself two days to meander around the environs. If she's here I'll find her, he told himself, and if she isn't, I won't. Two days, and then life must return to how it was.

*      *      *

He window-shopped for the first time in his life; in Guisborough, Yarm and Stokesley, looking not at the merchandise but at the passers-by reflected in the windows. He lingered over a latte at Chapter's Deli—and soon after, over a pot of tea at the School House café, glancing nonchalantly at the clientele while trying to eavesdrop for clues. He went for a haircut and casually asked the stylist had she seen Petra? Petra who? Petra Flint—she's probably one of your clients, you know.

He dropped her name into conversation once or twice when he went for an early pint at the Blackwell Ox in Carlton, in a manner which suggested, Petra Flint? You know Petra! but none of the locals seemed to.

In Great Ayton the following day, Arlo procrastinated over precisely when to go into Suggitts so he went for a hike, pacing up Easby Moor, telling himself that he was marvelling at the view rather than scrutinizing it for someone who would barely register on such a vast panorama unless she was standing alongside him. He even

186

looked to his left, to his right. Over his shoulder. But he was most certainly on his own.

'I'm a stupid fuck,' he chided as he stomped back down to the village.

He bought a chocolate bar from Suggitts and made small talk with the sales assistant.

'Oh well, I'd better get going. Thanks for this. Take care now. Looks like it's brightening. No, the boys don't come back until Sunday. I'm just catching up on my marking, my lessons—making good use of the peace and quiet. Bye now.'

'Goodbye, pet.'

Arlo hovered in the doorway, his mouth full of Mars Bar. He gulped it down and turned back. The proprietor thought he looked as though he was going to choke. He cleared his throat a number of times and patted himself on the chest. He was about to turn away again but stopped himself.

'That girl—in the rain. Do you remember? Just before Easter.'

'The lass who paid for your Easter egg?'

'Yes.'

'What of her?'

'I don't know,' he said honestly. 'I don't know. Has she been back?'

'For your money?'

'Or maybe she's just been back here anyway?'

'She's not, I'm afraid. But all the Easter chocolates are reduced now, though they've still got a way on their best-before. But you could leave your money with me.'

'So she will be back then, you think?'

'She was in practically daily. Though I can't say I've seen her since.'

'Since when?'

'Since the rain, pet.'

'Her name is Petra.'

'That's nice.'

'If you see her—'

'—I'll tell her you wish to settle your debt.'

*     *     *

That night, staring at the cracks in the bedroom ceiling because closing his eyes had not brought him closer to sleep, Arlo found it hard not to feel deflated. It was hard to turn a blind eye to the taunt of images of Petra which alternated with memories of Helen in his mind. Arlo had constantly rationalized that what happened all those years ago with Helen had induced the celibacy he'd maintained ever since. He'd flicked off the switch which controlled thoughts of love, that switch which turned on desire; he'd unplugged it from his core, removed the fuse and hurled it away. And hadn't his life been all the more straightforward for it. Much better. Preferable.

Now, suddenly, after one incident with a chocolate rabbit and a furtive wank in his childhood bed, there were those unmistakable stirrings in his soul and his body surged again. He wanted to see her, hear her, touch her, taste her. He wanted to feel her hair, test how soft her cheeks were against his lips, see how her body might fit and fold into his; he wanted to scoop up her dizzy hair and gaze at the nape of her neck. And he wanted his body to be felt, he wanted her hand to slip round the back of his neck, her other hand to be laid against his chest; he wanted her lips to reach up to his, he wanted to sense how she'd

188

stand on tiptoes in the process.

But he hadn't found Petra and he didn't know where else to look and he thought himself a stupid fuck for even trying. Window bloody shopping. Pot after pot of sodding tea. Scouring the landscape. Grilling sweetshop owners.

It wasn't going to happen.

So why couldn't he just think, Oh well, what the hell, and forget her? Go back to the calm and surety of feeling that he simply didn't give a damn when it came to love and lust and all that life-consuming panoply.

And why couldn't he just go to bloody sleep? Look at the time, for God's sake.

*      *      *

When a knock at his door followed by a rapping on his windows awoke Arlo the next morning, his first thought was Petra, his second thought was the Walley Brothers. He checked what he was wearing—a T-shirt and boxer shorts—and assessed this would do for either. The thought that it might be Miranda with croissants and fresh orange juice hadn't entered his mind.

'Morning, sleepyhead,' Miranda said.

'Miranda?' said Arlo.

'Are you going to invite me in?' she said. 'I come bearing gifts.'

But she was already in. And Arlo really noticed that one of her gifts, alongside the croissants and orange juice, was her comely figure. Today displayed under a tight T-shirt that was just a little too short for the jeans she was wearing. Glimpses of flat toned midriff. It was as if, previously, he'd seen her only in monochrome, behind some sort of haze. Arlo felt suddenly ravenous.

'Is anyone else around?' she asked.

'Just you, me and the Walleys,' Arlo said and she wrinkled her nose with disdain.

'Well, I haven't enough to go around,' she said, 'so it would be rude to invite them in.' She walked through to his kitchenette and started busying herself opening cupboards and drawers though Arlo would have been quite happy to have swigged the juice from the carton and dabbed up any croissant crumbs from his lap. 'How was your Easter?' she asked, though she didn't wait for a reply. 'I'm taking that job. I've come back early to see David Pinder. Though he can't entice me to stay. It's an amazing opportunity—a feather in my cap. I'd be mad not to take it. So, this is my last term.' She turned. Two glasses balancing on two plates. Kitchen roll under her arm. Belly button pecking out under her T-shirt. Arlo speechless.

'Earth to Arlo,' she laughed. 'Are you awake?'

With one hand on his hip, Arlo ran the palm of the other over his closely cropped hair, down to his neck while he rotated his head gently, side to side, as if stiff from sleeping awkwardly. 'Yeah,' he said, 'I'm awake.'

'Come,' she said, all sparky, 'let's eat.' And she led the way back through to his lounge. And he followed her bottom all the way. And she was turned away from him, bending to place the plates on the coffee table. Now she was straightening to open the carton of juice. Bending again, to lay out the croissants. Black knickers. Arlo could see the tip of a tattoo in the small of her back. No idea of what it was. Whatever it was it was delineated further down, nearer her bum. She bent again, to pour.

'Juice?'

And Arlo was up behind her, the soft flimsy cotton of his boxer shorts providing no modesty for his cock grown hard. He pressed against her, her denim against his straining flesh. He slipped his hands down her sides, caressing the undulation of her waist. His hands going around to the front, the buckle of her belt, the soft strip of skin between jeans and top, the sexy little groove of her belly button. Tight white cotton stretched over fantastic tits. Nape of her neck. He put his lips there and at that moment she turned to him and his wet lips swept over her jaw, her cheek, to her open mouth where her tongue awaited him, lively and moist.

Her hands were fast and nosy, feeling every inch of him but spending just seconds before moving on; as if quickly confirming items on an order she'd placed long ago. Arlo was more leisurely, he just wanted to enjoy the sensation of the weight and warmth of a female form in his hands again. He was more than happy to linger; one hand squeezing her buttock, the other fondling her breast. Then going beyond her jeans to those black knickers, easing his fingers down between elastic and flesh. The crack of her arse. He was fit to explode.

She pulled away, looking wild and triumphant. With her tongue caught seductively between her teeth she wriggled from her T-shirt, snapped away her belt and ripped down the zip of her jeans. A simple white bra. Lacy black knickers. The best of both worlds, for Arlo. He took off his T-shirt, his cock now gamely protruding through the fly of his

191

boxers. She lay back on his sofa and with one movement he pulled down her jeans and her knickers with them. She grinned lasciviously and spread her legs.

It was like being at a smorgasbord having not eaten for a month. Where do you start? What do you choose as your first taste? Do you stop and assess all that's on offer, work from left to right, top to bottom? Go for a little cunnilingus for hors d'oeuvres, a full-on fuck for main course and a blow-job for pudding before an orgasm with the petits fours? Do you think with your dick, or dive on in head first? Kneeling over Miranda, Arlo dipped down to suck her nipples, moving his mouth to hers while his fingers delved between her legs to find her sex wet and yielding. Pushing her legs open with his, he eased his cock up deep inside her. The exquisite sensation, which he'd chosen to renounce for so long, was so intense that it registered on his face as pleasure-pain. It was like his first time. It was better than his first time, because he knew what was coming. He bucked and twisted and humped and thrusted and she groaned and panted and told him to fuck her harder.

'Christ.'

'It's OK—I'm on the pill. Come.'

As the spunk pelted out of him, he heard himself cry out. A hollow yell of relief. Five years. In a flurry of spurts, five years of abstinence and deeply buried thirst were quenched. Miranda was licking at his eyelashes to have him open his eyes, but he kept them scrunched shut. It wasn't her face he wanted to see. And he wasn't conjuring Petra's either; he couldn't, not in this situation. He had to keep his eyes tight shut so he could block out the sight of Helen. She was the last woman he'd slept with. When his heartbeat regulated and his breathing evened and his cock was limp, he levered himself away from Miranda. He focused on her nose as he smiled at her and then he went to the bathroom, buried his face in a towel and silently wept.

## CHAPTER TWENTY-FIVE

The general consensus was that Petra should return to North Yorkshire, for whatever reason and with whatever end result. Lucy had sent text messages hourly from Hong Kong saying:

  go! Lx
    u gone yet? Lx
      r u there? Lx
        is he there? Lx
          have u found him? L.

Gina who, in her sensible Chelsea way, felt that too much romanticized whimsy was not good for a person, was nevertheless most forthright about Petra returning. 'Even if just to see how he looks when he's dry, darling. For goodness' sake go—have some fun, get it out of your system, then come back and crack on.' After all, Petra had hardly lifted a tool since her return.

Eric's attitude differed. While he agreed with Gina that a fling might do Petra the power of good, he was less concerned with Arlo turning out to be some cad, than he was with Petra's sudden love affair with this far-off place.

'It's all very well falling for somebody—people

are generally a movable feast,' he told her over a baked potato and vegetable chilli at their favourite café in Leather Lane, 'but being seduced by the bucolic charms of a foreign country you hardly know is far more dangerous.'

'It's only Yorkshire!' Petra laughed, fanning her mouth. 'You don't need jabs and a passport to go there, you know.'

'Well, it would suit me if your fancy was tickled by someone closer to home,' Eric shrugged.

Petra shrugged back.

'It might all go horribly wrong,' Eric said, 'and you'll be miles away.'

'I'm a big girl now, Eric,' Petra said. 'It's time to look after myself.'

*       *       *

Kitty was busy organizing her work for a small display in the National Theatre foyer and Petra came back from lunch to find her flailing around the studio looking alarmingly like Morticia Addams.

'Petra!' she said. 'You're not busy. Can you anneal for me? I've so much to do.'

'No problem. What do you want?' Petra said, donning goggles and sitting at the flame.

'This piece, that one—and this part here on this one. Where's Eric?'

'Being moody.'

'Why?'

'Because he's worried I'm going to emigrate. To Yorkshire. Drama queen.'

Kitty laughed.

'Everyone's    confronting    me    with    their

twopence-worth of advice,' Petra said. 'Thank God you're too busy to talk.'

Kitty laughed again and Petra watched her face soften. 'Well, for what it's worth—and I think it's worth more than tuppence—my vibe says you *should* go. Even if nothing happens—even if you don't find him, never see him again in your life—I feel you should at least go. Allow your future every chance to unfold.'

They worked quietly. Kitty wrapping black velvet around a cardboard toilet tube to make a display unit for her bangles; Petra at the burner, annealing silver for her.

'You sound like someone I know,' Petra said.

'Who?'

'Someone I knew,' Petra corrected.

'Who?'

'A lady called Mrs McNeil. The pensioner I used to visit when I was at school—I've told you about her.'

'The tanzanite lady?'

'Yes. Amongst many, many other things.'

'When did she die?'

'God—let me see. Sixteen years ago.'

Kitty came up close to Petra. 'I'm very receptive to voices from the other side, Petra. You know what I mean when I say *the other side*.' Kitty regarded her gravely. Petra nodded, hoping she wore a sincere expression, despite the goggles, despite little belief in psychic power. '*They* make themselves heard, Petra. It's about contact, about shrinking the current world, about expanding life and constricting time.'

Petra was a little lost by the theory but seduced by Kitty's conviction nonetheless.

'What would she say?' Kitty asked her. 'Mrs McNeil?' She answered before Petra had a chance to think about it. 'She'd tell you to go, wouldn't she? She'd say the journey in itself would be worth it.'

Petra watched Kitty whirling around the studio like a pantomime witch. And she thought, She's right, that's just the sort of thing Mrs McNeil would have said. And then Petra thought to herself that she loved Kitty. When had this woman ceased to be just someone with whom she simply shared studio space and the bills? And Gina too, for that matter. And Eric, of course Eric. Her Studio Three: colleagues yes, but friends too. Firm and fast.

*     *     *

The journey in itself will be worth it.

The phrase became Petra's mantra on the crammed tube home.

In her flat, she chanted the sentence under her breath as she tidied the place and went from room to room to check if she was imagining a smell of gas. Petra glanced at Mrs McNeil's paintings of Kilimanjaro. Her voice, not heard for sixteen years, was still so vivid to Petra that she decided quite categorically that it couldn't have been taken on by Kitty. It was, however, a kind idea of Kitty's. And Petra was happy to think that they spoke as one, Kitty and Mrs McNeil. Kindred spirits—that would do.

*The journey itself will be worth it.* I bet that's what you told yourself when your husband took you to Tanzania in the 1960s. And if I asked you what I should do—about this Arlo business—you'd tell me the journey in itself *will* be worth it. So I will go. I'll give it a go.

*     *     *

It was Thursday: a week and a half after Petra's return from Yorkshire. The day after Arlo and Miranda had sex. The day of Kitty's display at the National. The day when Petra booked a train ticket to Northallerton for the following day, despite not knowing whether or not Charlton would let her stay at the Old Stables again. This time, her trip wouldn't hinge on his generosity. She was going. She'd find somewhere. Wasn't there a local noticeboard outside the Spar in Stokesley? The little tourist cabin at Great Ayton?

And suddenly, like details drifting back from a dream, or specifics recalled long after a trauma, Petra is transported away from her bench in the studio and straight back into the little shop in Great Ayton; Easter on its way, rain hurling outside, Arlo inside, Petra cradling a chocolate rabbit in her arms. And the shopkeeper is laughing and staring at the puddle Arlo has left in her shop and she is saying, *He left without paying for his Easter egg—the soft lad. Ah well, I know where he lives.*

*     *     *

Petra was too fidgety, too preoccupied to work and after an hour doing nothing at her bench but replay the woman's words, she raced to Hatton Garden, to the Charlton Squire Gallery hoping to

197

find him there.

He was.

Petra was breathless.

At first, Charlton was irritated—he had a wealthy client perusing the platinum collection, who required his most subtle but persuasive attention.

'Can I stay at your place again?' Petra said, tugging at his satin shirtsleeve for attention. 'From tomorrow? For a while, perhaps? Please?'

'This one!' the wealthy client declared, jabbing at the display case before flouncing over to a leather chair by the desk.

Charlton glanced swiftly from the opulent sapphire-and-platinum ring to Petra. Caught between a rock and a hard place, he thought to himself.

'Can I stay at the Old Stables? Please? I'm in love.'

Everyone falls in love with the Old Stables, Charlton thought as he swished over to the display cabinet, unlocked it with a tiny key and plucked up the ring. He glanced at the price of the ring as he took it over to the client. Sixteen thousand pounds. Lovely.

'Of course you can, Pet,' he hissed at Petra. 'Now pipe down—I'm serving.'

*　　　*　　　*

Petra returned home late that evening, having gone to the National Theatre with Eric and Gina to support Kitty. Gina had given them a lift in the back of her Range Rover where Eric and Petra had played like kids with the electric windows and the seat-back DVDs and the pop-out drinks holders; exasperating Gina to the extent that she jumped a red light and was flashed by a camera.

Initially, the three of them worried that Kitty's works looked frustratingly inconsequential in the echoey and capacious foyer. But then they saw how all who approached the cases were transfixed; the sumptuous filigree, the delicacy of design and the brightness of the precious metals radiating irresistible allure. Within a couple of hours, there were more red dots than not against Kitty's collection.

'I'm going to make that journey tomorrow,' Petra told her, giving her a hug. 'I'll see you whenever.'

Kitty kissed her smack on the lips. 'Bon voyage, girlfriend.'

*      *      *

Petra's answering machine was flashing. She thought it might be Lucy following up the text message Petra had sent about train tickets and fate and fingers-crossed Pxxxxx. But there was only one message and it wasn't long distance. It was from Kent and it was from her mother.

'Petra? Is that you? I think this is your number. Well, it's the last one I have for you. I'm coming to London! I need somewhere to stay. Can I stay at yours? I mean, I'd love to see you! Of course I would! And so I thought it would be fun to stay with you!'

But I'm meant to be going to Yorkshire, Mum.

*      *      *

Glum, Petra sat and stewed. It was nearly midnight when she dialled her mother.

'Mum?'

'Yes?'

'It's Petra.'

(She wondered why her mother never quite recognized the voice of her only child saying, *Mum?*)

'Petra! Did you get my message? Was that your number?'

'I did. It is. So you're coming to London?'

'I am! Tomorrow—oh! today. There's a hemp workshop in Hackney.'

'North Finchley is miles away from Hackney.'

'It's a damn sight nearer than Kent. My train arrives at fourish. Just leave the keys somewhere if you'll be still at work.'

'It would be nice to see you, Mum,' Petra said slowly.

'Oh yes—I'm looking forward to seeing you too, I'm sure there'll be time,' her mother rushed. 'It's been ages! I'll bring my own milk.'

'I won't be here, Mum. I'm going to Yorkshire first thing tomorrow.'

'Oh?'

'Yes.'

'Oh. I see.' There was a pause. 'Well, would you mind if I stayed at yours anyway? Do you have a cat that needs feeding, or plants which need watering?'

'No, I don't. But you can stay, Mum, if you like. I don't mind. Upstairs have my spare keys.'

'Thanks, Petra! I'll put some eggs in your fridge for you.'

200

'But I might stay in Yorkshire a while.'

'Oh, the eggs'll be good for at least three weeks. Well, thanks again, darling. I'll leave it all spick and span.'

Petra doubted it. But then she thought to herself that she'd rather not be in her flat when her mother overran it for the weekend. Then she thought how that was rather sad. However, she made herself consider how her mother hadn't asked a single thing about her—not how she was, nor even why she was going to Yorkshire. Had she forgotten that her daughter was allergic to cats? And Petra thought actually, all of that was far sadder.

## CHAPTER TWENTY-SIX

Arlo kept busy. And if he wasn't actually busy, he made sure he looked as though he was. He'd been most preoccupied the previous day, dashing across the playing field to the main hall, or hurrying back to his folly, or racing off to his classroom, or rushing over to the Buttery for meals, hands stuffed deep into his pockets, shoulders hunched, head down as if it were raining—which it wasn't. Yesterday had been a beautiful, balmy day when drifts of summer filtered through the spring air. Yesterday had been a relaxed day for all the teachers except Arlo. No meetings, no duties, no pupils; a light and liberated hinterland between one school term and the next. Time to linger with a lager over lunch, to loll the afternoon away chatting casually, have a knock-about on the tennis courts and be at liberty to yell, 'That was *out*, you fucker.' But not Arlo. He was far too busy working hard to appear as though he was working hard; his main objective being to avoid Miranda. Because he feared that, if she got to him, he'd have her. And he didn't like that feeling. He preferred it when it had been easy to abstain, when celibacy was a way of life, when his mind wasn't playing on one track and his body wasn't straining out and heating up. A day after having sex with Miranda, he loathed himself for thinking with his dick instead of about the consequences and he blamed her for rocking the status quo he'd carefully instilled in his life.

Rocking the status quo.

Status bloody Quo! It gave him an idea for a lesson. GCSE group. Genius. He strode over to his classroom to prepare.

Luckily for Arlo, there was little time for anything extracurricular today. Lager was off the menu, the tennis courts were out of bounds and swearing was strictly off limits; the staff had a packed day of meetings and memos. Even the odd few minutes of snatched chat was done in covert whispers, in much the same way as the pupils themselves communicated when they hurried from lesson to lesson.

Tonight was Formal Dinner, an institution held at the start of each term on the Friday evening before the pupils returned. Staff wore their scholars' gowns, drank from a heavily engraved Loving Cup and were addressed by Headmaster Pinder, partly in Latin. It was a black-tie affair, fine frocks for female staff. Miranda was having trouble with her zip and, eschewing help which was closer to hand, she snuck across the grounds, high heels in her hands, and knocked on Arlo's door.

He looked a little scared, which she thought rather endearing.

'I'm having trouble with my dress,' she said. 'Can you fiddle with my zip?'

'I'm,' Arlo began, 'just doing—stuff. Ask—you know.'

But she walked past him with a coquettish smirk, turned away from him, cocked her hips and held her hair above her neck. 'Just fiddle,' she said.

She couldn't see Arlo's discomfort written all over his face, but she could hear him sigh which she read as a breath of desire, rather than the unease which was closer to the truth. With a wriggle and a twist, she made the dress drop down a little and gape a lot. 'Fiddle!' she whispered.

Arlo was in his dress shirt and trousers but had been hunting for his bow-tie and any socks which were black, even if they weren't a pair, when Miranda arrived. He glanced at his watch: half an hour until they were expected. His gaze was lured over to the swoop of Miranda's shapely back, the rich crêpe of her midnight-blue dress accentuating the softness of her flesh as it clung to the curves not already revealed. Arlo knew that he had an erection but he refused to look at it; mind over matter, ignore it and it will go away. It's only a zip. It's only a woman. Don't look at her bare legs, her toenails glossy and red. Don't look at the high heels in her hands. Do up the zip. It's only a zip. She's not asking you to lace her into a basque or hook her bra strap. Zips were invented to expedite the closing of clothes. What's gone down can come up again. Zippity doo dah. Whistle.

He whistled, a jolly, inane, childlike tune made

up on the spot. He took the fob of the zip and it glided upwards, fast and smooth, a layer of dark blue fabric covering up Miranda's flesh. The zip stuck a few inches from the top and Arlo felt enormously relieved. In an instant, he believed that Miranda really hadn't come to him to seduce him, but only because her dratted zip was stuck and she was hardly likely to ask the ever-lecherous Glasper, whose folly was nearer to hers.

'Bugger,' she said, putting her hands behind her neck to try and shift the zip.

'Hang on,' said Arlo. They tugged fruitlessly. 'I know,' he said and he ran the zip down again, and up. And down again and up. Her back, the dip of her waist, the curve of her hips, the contours of her bottom; her bra strap on the middle clasp, a small brown mole on her left shoulder blade. But no need to whistle. No need to think of other things. It's only a zip. Run it down, zoom it up. There, see! All done.

'Thanks, Arlo,' she said. 'See you over there.' And she said it with a wink. Or perhaps it was just something in her eye.

He was late. Where was that sodding bow-tie? Blue socks would have to do.

*     *     *

A heady scent permeated the proceedings in the great hall. It was a wonderful and warming mix of roast beef and a gravy thick and rich, of beeswax and wine, of old wood polished to maximum sheen and warmed aromatically by the candelabras. Arlo had always felt the scene could be straight from Dickens. It was tradition on such evenings not to use first names so the Messrs Savidge, Garton, Glasper and Hunter bantered across the table to one another like doubles at table tennis, ducking and bobbing every now and then when the vast fruit platter obscured their view. Down the table, meanwhile, Miss Oates retrieved the odd stray comment as if it were a wayward ping-pong ball, tossing it back gamely and mostly in Mr Savidge's direction.

Headmaster Pinder's address was long and theatrical and the parts in Latin were understood more from his inflection and delivery than for precise translation. One didn't applaud at Formal Dinner, one tapped the edge of the table with a small flat spoon laid precisely for this purpose alone.

'And on to our notices,' the headmaster said. 'We have taken delivery of a new minibus, the cleaning of which will fall to pupils serving detention. I'd like to keep it sparkling so be liberal with your disciplining of the young fellows. Now, I know it's summer term but it is term-time for another ten weeks and Cook has lovingly tended a crop of peppermint which is for her culinary requirements, not for the jugs of staff Pimm's. News from the maths department: Mr Bierer and his wife have been honing their multiplication skills and are expecting twins in November—our congratulations to you both. We welcome Mrs Goborne as the new librarian. And sadly, we prepare to say goodbye to Miss Oates who will leave us at the end of the year for a prestigious head-of-department position at Cheltenham. Will you please ensure she goes with a bang.'

The double entendre breezed through the great

hall like a Mexican wave which wafted right over Headmaster Pinder's head. A few minutes later, official proceedings ended and the staff were invited to avail themselves of brandy and other liqueurs. Arlo loved brandy; it had been his father's favourite tipple and memories of a thimbleful being passed his way on special occasions remained vivid. Brandy always made him feel warm, a little nostalgic; happy.

'You're pissed,' Miss Oates whispered to Mr Savidge as she sashayed past him.

'Am not!' Mr Savidge protested a little too loudly and he wasn't too pissed to take this as his cue to call it a night and slip away.

He strolled back to his folly through the school grounds which, under the influence of good food and fine liquor, seemed to be cloaked in a velvety silence and lit theatrically by the moon. He spent a while gazing up at the moon, wondering whether it was its phase or the brandy that made it seem just not quite round. The stars were amazing, even if the alcohol had scattered a few more through the sky for good measure. Arlo was struck with the idea for a lesson, a lesson at midnight to focus on the inspiration of the moon, the stars, the night, the darkness for composers past and present.

'A little *Eine Kleine Nachtmusik*,' he said, stumbling and righting himself. ' "Starry Starry Nights"—a bit of schmaltz never goes amiss. And I can balance it with "The Whole of the Moon" because all boys need Waterboys. "Lucy in the Sky with Diamonds"—they'll love the LSD connection. And "Blue Moon". The sublime Billie Holiday.'

He began to whistle the iconic tune. His good strong whistle picking out the phrases of having no dream in his heart, no love of his own.

And as he neared his folly, a soft voice filtered out from the shadows, singing the words to his tune.

Miranda.

'Mr Savidge,' she said.

'Hi,' said Arlo, with an unnecessary little wave for emphasis.

'My zip is caught,' she said.

'Oh,' he said. 'Again?'

'Will you do the honours?' she said. 'Again?'

'Sure,' he said, opening up the folly, trying to whistle Holst. 'That's one for the boys to . . .'

'Pardon?'

'Just thinking about lessons.'

'Not my zip?'

'Sorry?'

'My zip, Arlo.'

She didn't take off her heels and in them, she was pretty much his height which he found both mildly unnerving and titillating. She turned from him and scooped her hair up. Arlo jiggled the zip down with ease. 'There you go, Miss Oates.'

She turned to him and he tried to focus on her level gaze. 'But Mr Savidge,' she said, 'are you not going to ensure I go out with a bang? Headmaster's orders—I'd hate you to lose your job for failing to comply.'

He tried to focus on her words and her wit. 'I'm drunk,' he said.

'Not too drunk,' she told him, stroking her finger up and down his flies as she flitted her lips across his. He didn't feel his zip go down and then he kidded himself that he didn't realize his trousers were down too. But he couldn't deny the feeling of his cock springing up, nor could he ignore a cool slim hand encircling it.

'Shit,' he said, closing his eyes. He felt dizzy from drink, so opened them. And got an eyeful of Miranda squatting down, about to take his cock in her mouth. He told himself to pull away after a few sucks. Then he told himself, What the hell it was only a blow-job and ignored memories of his twenties when even a simple blow-job had made life complicated. He attempted to say, Stop, but couldn't find his voice and soon enough the hot moist feeling of her mouth encircling the precise point of his pleasure emptied his mind as it emptied his balls.

As soon as he'd come, he prayed that she'd go. For Arlo, it was a feeling similar to a takeaway curry or a porn film. As soon as he'd had his fill, he didn't want to see any more of it in front of him.

'I—'

'See you tomorrow, big boy,' Miranda said. 'And tomorrow, it's *my* go.'

\*       \*       \*

The boys piled back, most armed with leftover Easter eggs. It was the first time Arlo had thought of Petra in days.

I owe her ten quid.

My almost Easter bunny.

And then he told himself that all chocolate has a sell-by date, that Easter eggs are seasonal, that Easter had been and gone and Petra with it.

And he told himself it had been just one of those strange, strange things, that's all, that day in Suggitts before Easter.

208

However, another strange thing had happened in Suggitts, or so it seemed to the proprietor. That lass came back—the one who had visited almost daily up until Easter. She popped up again, came in for a single cone and a quarter of liquorice toffee. And she dithered and dallied long after she'd paid. And finally she came out with it.

'I don't know if you remember—just before Good Friday, when it was chucking it down with rain? When I came in and bought a chocolate rabbit and it was pouring outside, really hammering down? And a chap came in and he stood by me and I don't know if I told you but I knew him years ago? And I paid for his chocolate—do you remember? Because you said, well you said, actually you called him a soft lad for forgetting to pay. Well, the thing is, you also said that you knew where he lived.'

'Yes, pet?'

'Do you? Do you know where he lives?'

'I do, love.'

'Please—could you tell me?'

'He lives at the school—the posh one. Roseberry Hall. He's a teacher. Been there years. That'll do you, pet?'

## CHAPTER TWENTY-SEVEN

'*Monday Monday*,' Arlo sang to his class, '*so good to me.*' And he meant it. Summer term and the living seemed easy. It was a pleasure to be standing there again, perusing their eager little faces, holding court, doing what he felt he did best. 'And talking of Mamas and Papas, I hope you all had a great Easter with your families.'

Nathan's arm shot up, the full stretch of which pulled the right side of his shirt clean out of his trousers.

'Yes, Nathan?'

'Mamas and Papas—I get it, sir! They also did a song called "California Dreaming", didn't they!'

Arlo smiled. 'Very good, Nathan, but it's an absent "g". *Dreamin'*. Can you sing it?' Nathan had a go. 'Good stuff. And it's certainly one occasion when I'm happy for you to rank the Mamas and Papas higher than the Boomtown Rats who didn't much like Mondays at all.' This went straight over the boys' heads but they were used to Mr Savidge's tangential and slightly obscure musical references. In fact, most of his pupils stored such information carefully, regurgitating at a later date to enhance their personal hipness.

Excited chatter filtered up from outside where Miss Oates was leading her Year Nine class to a patch of lawn. They flopped down and opened their poetry books. Arlo and his class were momentarily distracted.

'Sir?'

'Lars?'

'Can we do that, sir? Have a class outside? You know, maybe listen to the music of birdsong and the rhythm of the trees and stuff?'

'I can offer you one better than that,' Arlo said. 'Next week, we'll have our class outside at *midnight.*'

210

A murmur of approval travelled the desks.

'Or at least, once it's dark. I was thinking about it over the Easter break. The night—the moon, the stars, darkness and dreams—has inspired musicians over the centuries. It seems only right to consider such pieces during the hours which they sought to exemplify.'

The boys looked flushed.

'Anyway, tear your attention away from Miss Oates's alfresco teaching, steer your minds away from thoughts of midnight, and wipe from your ears the polite harmonies of mid-sixties San Francisco. Forget about darkness. You lot are coming on a psychedelic trip with me.'

He stopped and wondered the best way to continue. He had responsibilities. 'Drugs are bloody bad for you, gentlemen. Just say no!' he announced. 'But I have to say, they certainly added unique layers to the musical swirls of the late 1960s. Psychedelia.' And with that he spun around and pressed Play on the stereo. 'All aboard Jefferson Airplane,' he said and the boys were soon a little lost but pleasantly surprised by 'Somebody to Love' and 'White Rabbit'.

'Well, this next song wasn't so much written on drugs, it was actually written on the loo. The songwriter took to the toilet for some peace and quiet from his wife and this was the result.'

Arlo scoured the CD shelves. Then remembered he'd taken the disc to his folly over the weekend when he was preparing the lesson. The song was essential, the boys had to hear it. In the corner of the class, a guitar was propped. He clicked his fingers and pointed at it and Troy rushed to fetch it. For his students, such impromptu performances were the highlight of lessons with Mr Savidge. Arlo tuned the instrument quietly, then gently slapped the palm of his hand down over the strings to silence them, cleared his throat and seemed to look right through the class. Gently, his fingers appeared to tickle the strings, eliciting a melody, feminine and pretty. Suddenly, he crashed through it, strumming chords hard, his foot and often his hand too beating out the rhythm.

*When I look up to the skies*
*I see your eyes a funny kind of yellow*

Despite the boys hearing the song played only acoustically on a single guitar, Arlo's passionate delivery gave them 'Pictures of Matchstick Men' perfectly. He sang the song the whole way through, the boys tapping their toes, nodding their heads, loving the lesson.

When he finished, the applause the class gave him was matched from outside. Arlo glanced. Miranda and her class.

'Written on the loo, finished in the lounge,' Arlo announced, turning his back to the window. He felt high but suddenly tired.

'Who's it by?' Troy asked, as Arlo handed him the guitar.

'If you guess, you can have the rest of the lesson free.'

Even if they could have guessed, the boys didn't much want the rest of the lesson free. They'd prefer to listen to Mr Savidge play. His lessons were so cool you could almost forget it was school.

'Jefferson Whatsit?'

'Someone from Woodstock?'

'No, Lars. The song came from an album whose title itself typifies the psychedelic vibe of the late 1960s. "Picturesque Matchstickable Messages from the Status Quo".'

The boys looked bewildered. 'But my *dad* has Status Quo stuff,' Troy said with a slight frown, 'and it doesn't sound anything like that. He plays air guitar to it with his legs spread like he's doing the splits. Sometimes Mum has to help him stand properly afterwards.'

Mr Savidge had met Troy's father on occasion. He couldn't quite compute this new image of him. 'Well, long before they were rocking all over the world in their top-to-toe denim, they did "Pictures of Matchstick Men".'

'Play us something else!'

Arlo looked through the CDs and made his choice.

The boys listened. It was a lovely song, in a dreamy, woozy kind of way; enhanced by lyrics which spoke of castles and kings and porpoises laughing goodbye, goodbye.

'Who is it? Anyone?'

'Beatles?'

Arlo tutted. 'If you have to wonder whether something is by the Beatles, then it very probably isn't.'

'Give us a clue.'

Troy handed his teacher the guitar. Arlo played a little of 'I'm a Believer'.

'The *Monkees*?'

'Well done, Nathan—you can scoot. Off you go.'

'Could I just choose a song instead, sir?'

Arlo was taken aback and touched. He shrugged

and turned to the CDs.

'No, sir,' said Nathan. 'I mean, *you* do the music.'

But Arlo suddenly didn't want to play, or at least, not in front of an audience so he touched his throat and shrugged at his class. Then he caught sight of the spine of a CD and thought how he could have saved himself the performance in the first place.

'Ozzy Osbourne thought "Pictures of Matchstick Men" was good enough to cover. And so did these guys. Listen out for how violin replaces the guitar lead throughout.' Arlo set the CD playing and cranked the volume up. The melody, now familiar to the boys, belted around the classroom in a more wry and raucous way.

The class grinned.

'Who's that?'

'That, Nathan, is the rather wonderfully named American indie group Camper Van Beethoven. You might want to look out Bongwater's version of the "Porpoise Song" too—I have it somewhere, if anyone wants to borrow it. Now go—lesson finished three minutes ago. Mr Glasper will be waiting.'

The boys left the classroom, a certain rhythmic bounce to their step.

*     *     *

'I preferred your version,' Miranda said, coming into the emptied classroom and closing the door.

'Shouldn't eavesdrop,' Arlo said, re-alphabetizing a few stray CDs.

'I have a free period now.' She was perched on

214

the edge of his desk, swinging her leg so that the toe of her shoe just grazed Arlo's calf.

'I don't.' A stupid thing to say, because he did and she knew it.

'You do.' See.

A wave of resentment swept over Arlo, as if Miranda was knowingly undermining him; mining under every block of the barrier he'd built around himself over the last five years, furtively picking holes in the mesh of his carefully constructed safety net. It's not her fault, he told himself, I should be flattered.

'Miranda,' he began. He backed away and scratched his head.

'You look like a nervous schoolboy, Arlo,' she said and he could see by the sudden brave dullness to her eyes that she'd guessed. Instead of making him feel that this made things easier for him, it made him feel all the more wretched.

'Look, there's a lot you don't understand about me,' Arlo said.

'So, show me the whole picture.'

'I can't really. It's just something that happened. Something that changed me. Something that showed me that none of this,' and he waved his hand dismissively between the two of them, 'none of this is worth it.'

'Arlo, we're stuck here together, in this beautifully manicured but slightly claustrophobic institution, for ten more weeks. It's summer term—why don't we just have a little fun? I don't want anything more. I don't want you for your mind or your musical intellect—I'm happy enough with a fuck-buddy.'

Arlo regarded her for a loaded moment. 'But

215

you see, I love what you find claustrophobic. This is my home. I've made it that way. I like my metaphorical furniture just the way it is. I prefer celibacy to fucking buddies. I don't want to get involved—on any level. I'm sorry. It's just the way I am.'

'You're weird,' Miranda muttered.

'Maybe so,' Arlo shrugged, 'but I'm happy being weird.'

'You were hardly miserable when I sucked your dick and swallowed.'

Arlo looked shamefaced. 'I'm sorry,' he said again. Why was she still lingering? His free period was dwindling. Say something. 'Look, if I did want to be involved with someone, then you'd be absolutely the person I'd choose. Honestly. You're great, you're gorgeous. But all I want is the status quo I'd previously attained. It's nothing personal. I like my life this way. It's who I've become—which is better than what I was.'

'What the fuck happened to you, Arlo, to make you this way?'

'The worst thing in the world,' he said, 'but I'm paying the price.'


## CHAPTER TWENTY-EIGHT

Yesterday, Petra had spent the rest of the day hiding in the studio, pretending to work. During the evening, she pored over Charlton's various maps; staring at the precise position of Roseberry Hall School as if hoping to elicit secret signs, as if the harder she focused on the Ordnance Survey map, the more she might be able to activate some kind of psychic CCTV imagery. She knew it was far-fetched but she justified that it was probably what Kitty might suggest so she did it anyway. She didn't dare take the sensible, direct route straight to the school gates, as Gina would probably advise. She did not even take to her bike and simply cycle past the place, though today was a perfect Sunday for a gentle ride and the school was only three or four miles away. Instead, she pegged off in the opposite direction with a baseball cap pulled down low. She said to herself that it was only a matter of time before she and Arlo would meet, therefore she'd give herself all the time in the world to await such a preordained occasion. Charlton permitting.

It was perfect ice-cream weather but she didn't dare go back to Great Ayton for fear of bumping into Arlo. She justified that the day she actually felt like bumping into him would be the day when at last they would meet. Fate. It had to be fate. So, in the opposite direction, she picked at her packed lunch, sitting amongst early bluebells on a steep slope off the Great Broughton road. She hoped Arlo was indeed having an ice cream today. Because, if she had summoned the courage to ask in the shop after him, perhaps he would ask after her too. Or even if he didn't ask, perhaps he'd be told. And then Petra thought that perhaps she ought to go to the shop tomorrow to make it clear that should he come in, should he ask, or should he not ask but come in anyway, then he could be informed. Oh, and please tell him it's not about the money.

*   *   *

This visit, Petra had kept her phone on and was bolstered by the encouraging messages texted to her from Hatton Garden and Hong Kong. Her mother left her a message apologizing for flooding the kitchen but hoping she liked the hemp hand cream. Charlton left a message telling her to expect a courier, some time on Monday, with two small pieces of his work for her to finish.

Sorry, Arlo, she said to herself, can't track you down tomorrow either. I have to wait in for a delivery.

*     *     *

She hadn't sleepwalked so far, which she read as a very positive sign. But there again, she hadn't really slept much at all since arriving, which she told herself was quite daft really.

## CHAPTER TWENTY-NINE

By Tuesday lunch-time, Petra could kid herself no longer; her timidity was starting to get on her own nerves and she was having difficulty justifying further vacillations. She hadn't come all this way to do pieces of out-work for Charlton, or to take in the fresh country air, or to look at bluebells for inspiration (despite them providing an idea for a necklace in gold and enamel). She'd come up to Yorkshire to see Arlo. And she now knew where he lived, where he worked. So she wouldn't have to wander the moors hoping to be found. Yet, though he'd been within spitting distance of her for the last four days, she'd doggedly set her sights in the opposite direction.

Now, though, she felt focused. She stuck with the baseball cap, reasoning that it would keep the sun out of her eyes. She dispensed with the idea of taking a packed lunch and merely slowing down past Roseberry Hall en route to a nice place for a picnic, because she acknowledged she felt too fizzed to eat anyway. Though she had no intention of actually being seen, she still eschewed a T-shirt for her favourite Whistles top because, as Mrs McNeil had told her on many occasions, feeling good about looking good helps you feel good full stop.

She cycled through Stokesley and out onto the old Thirsk road, following it for a couple of miles before forking left at a large navy blue sign with gold lettering which somehow she'd never noticed before. *Roseberry Hall Public School for Boys*. It was here—behind this vast stretch of stone wall. Because of the insistent uphill gradient, she had to maintain a certain riding pace or the bike would wobble and the slog seem harder. At first, she assumed this was a minor road off which the school was placed. But every few yards smaller blue and gold signs sprang from the grass announcing *Slow!* Or *10mph*. Or *Hump*. Or *Ramp*. Humps and ramps felt the same on a bike, Petra thought to herself. It was then that she noticed large iron gates ahead, stretching across the road, held by heavy stone jambs crowned with fancy turrets. This wasn't a road, this was a private drive. She thought of her old school, fashioned out of three houses crammed into a domestic side-street. She remembered

219

Arlo's school, Victorian purpose-built with an impressive approach and abundant playing courts at the back but still compacted into a limited acreage. But both schools were essentially urban and their scale was subjected to the restrictions of space and the compromised greenery of city life. She'd never seen anything like the grandeur of Roseberry Hall Public School for Boys. In fact, she couldn't actually see the school buildings themselves. The rolling grounds obscured them from view and the majestic gates barred entry.

What about the intercom, Petra? *All visitors please ring.*

\*　　\*　　\*

She lay the bike down and hovered by the buzzer, standing on tiptoe, craning her neck, moving from one side of the drive to the other. Considered pressing the button. Thought about it a lot. But she didn't. Because she couldn't see a thing, she convinced herself he probably wasn't in anyway. Come back again later. Or tomorrow. Or ring first to make an appointment. Or perhaps write.

Or wander the moors, waiting to be found.

Or go back to London and that's the end of it.

\*　　\*　　\*

After an afternoon spent skulking in the studio doing Charlton's work, Petra comforted herself with a fish-and-chip supper, doused in salt, non-brewed condiment and ketchup; eaten from her lap, straight off the paper. It bolstered her spirits and she decided to take advantage of two more

220

hours of daylight and go for a nice cycle ride to work off her dinner. As she set off, she noticed a dark smear on the thigh of her jeans and realized it was ketchup which had seeped through the chip paper. It wasn't worth changing. It was only a recce. It wasn't as if she was heading out to meet anyone. If she had been, she'd have taken off her scruffy work top and done something about her hair which was currently spewing around her shoulders like a gorgon in need of a shower. Locks falling over her face in dusty brown misshapen coils—like telephone wire that has been pulled too much. Twists and turns—as if her hair could no more decide which direction to travel than she herself could.

*     *     *

Which way shall I go?

North, south, east or west?

The Helmsley road is nice. It was quiet this afternoon.

Oh! Will you look where I am!

*     *     *

Those sodding great gates.

*     *     *

And Petra starts to laugh because somehow, earlier that afternoon, she hadn't noticed how the gates span only the tarmac drive itself, restricting impromptu access by unannounced vehicles. Unannounced visitors on foot, especially those like

Petra wearing sturdy walking boots, are free to clamber the grassy bank flanking the driveway. There's no sign to say they can't. There's no dedicated buzzer to press to ask if they can. So she leaves her bike and clambers upwards and her breath is quite taken away as she looks down on the school sitting regally on its verdant carpet. The scale is astonishing. It's beautiful. Look at the *space*. Lights on in some windows, not in others, creating an extravagant silhouette. It's like a private world, Petra muses, one of privilege and peace. The scale of the place—against which she would only be seen as a tiny speck were she noticed at all—emboldens her to explore further. This is a very different type of grass. It's posh velvet lawn, she thinks, as she bends to brush her hands over the surface. She's surprised to see rabbits dink and dart a few yards ahead of her, as if surely they are far too common to be allowed here. She doesn't like the thought of rabbit droppings soiling the immaculate surface.

Look! Schoolboys. The scurry and scamp of pupils exiting the large hall and dispersing to smaller buildings. Probably just had their supper, now it's off to prep before pillow fights in their dorms. What do the teachers do now? Do they disappear into town for a swift pint or two? Stokesley? Maybe they have their own bar, somewhere to relax. Or perhaps they have to supervise letter-writing to mummies and daddies before doing the rounds calling, Lights out!

The architecture looks so beautiful. Especially in this light. Petra has to get closer. Look at those funny little angular stone buildings dotted here and there, lights on in some, off in others. Fancy

222

little outbuildings. Little follies.

The sound of a voice, male and stern, bellowing, Pipe down, Arladale!

No boy can be called Arladale, surely, Petra wonders. Perhaps it's a surname—oh, but surely they don't call children by their surnames in the twenty-first century, do they?

Well, if you get much closer, Petra, you'll be able to ask.

*     *     *

Footsteps behind her. She freezes. She's trespassing. She'll be given a detention. Or, worse, expelled from school before she's even got there. Someone behind her. She's helpless not to turn her head a fraction though she keeps her eyes focused straight ahead. The someone stops. A short, low chuckle. Clears his throat. She knows that voice. He knows that profile.

*     *     *

'Hullo,' says Arlo. 'Are you lost?'

*     *     *

'No,' says Petra Flint. 'Just waiting to be found.'


## CHAPTER THIRTY

Arlo lay on his bed, fully clothed, staring at the ceiling. It was a view he knew very well, its hairline

223

cracks, wisps of cobweb and uneven paintwork frequently providing interest for his eyes to scrutinize and his mind to mull over when sleep eluded him. As if sheep for him to count were dotted up there. But just then, it provided a clean, flat screen of non-distracting nothingness against which he could play over and again in his mind's eye what had just happened.

Petra Flint, once again at his school. Not in uniform, but in scruffy clothes. Not as a schoolgirl, but as a woman. And himself no Sixth Former; a master now. How grown-up does that sound! How pompous! Seventeen years. A long time. Yet the hindsight of that seventeen years' distance shows him how vivid she was to him back then. Despite only seeing her sporadically during term-time alone, seventeen years ago. But that was the magic of schooldays—its potency truly apparent only in retrospect? It was something he tried to impress on his pupils, however intangible it must seem to them at this point in time.

'You think one day is much the same as the next, gentlemen, that your school years are one long drag of homework and exams, rules and restrictions. But take it from an old git like me— when you look back on your schooldays, you'll see them as perhaps the most perfect period of your life, when friendships are made with no complexity and community is at its most nurturing and, believe it or not, at its least judgemental. And the world at large is wide open and welcoming.'

Yes, Mr Savidge. No, Mr Savidge. You get on our nerves a bit, when you drone on about the good old days, Mr Savidge. Can't you play us the Sex Pistols instead, Mr Savidge? And waffle on

224

about agitprop and the libertines of punk rock and the godfather of them all, Mozart?

*      *      *

Though there was much of interest on Arlo's bedroom ceiling tonight, far more fascinating was what he clenched tightly in his fist, resting this hand directly over his heart. He unfurled his fingers, unfolded the paper and regarded the eleven numbers.

How Petra had laughed when he told her he didn't have a mobile phone.

And how he'd grinned back when she'd asked how he'd be calling her then.

'Bell's conventional apparatus,' he'd said. And she'd looked all confused until he said, Land-line, Petra, land-line. Alexander Graham Bell and all that. I'll phone you from the land-line.

Promise that you will?

I promise.

Or shall I phone you tonight anyway, to say I'm back safely? What's your number? Your land-line?

I don't actually know.

You don't *know*?

Nope. Not off by heart. I have it written down somewhere.

Arlo!

Amazing, isn't it, this strange fossilized being that I've become.

Then she had paused and shuffled and had said, I think time has preserved you rather well, Arlo.

Thank you, Petra. Failing light is kind. It's almost dark. You should go.

Will you phone me, then, to check I'm back

225

safely? From your land-line?

I will.

*       *       *

Arlo looked at the clock. She should be back by now.

*       *       *

Petra felt sick with anticipation. She'd been nervous enough cycling back with only the feeble flicker from the dynamo light on the bike. Now, back at the Old Stables, she was suddenly anxious that Arlo might not call. She walked around with her handset, twisting it this way and that, raising or lowering it, seeing where the signal was strongest. Lucy had sent a text asking for any news but Petra didn't want to jinx the situation by responding just yet. Over and again, she replayed every moment of the encounter with Arlo, breaking off at regular intervals to check her phone's signal, to double-check she didn't have it on silent.

God, how unfit he must think me to be, not to have phoned me by now!

*       *       *

How long had their interlude lasted? Half an hour or so. He'd escorted her back to her bike; his hand at her elbow, her shoulder blade, her waist; away from the conurbation of fancy stonework, over the velvet grass, back along the drive to a small wooded area to the left of the gates. They rested their backs against the wall.

'You look so well, Petra. All grown up but just the same.'

'I'm glad it's getting dark because there's ketchup on my jeans and this is my work shirt. And I'm sorry about my hair. It has a life of its own.'

'At least you have hair! Are you working around here?'

'Sort of.'

'What did you grow up to be, Miss Flint? A potter?'

'A jeweller.'

'Wow.'

'And you teach, Arlo?'

'Yes, I love it.'

'Your music?'

'I teach music.'

'That's how we met. Through your music.'

'That's how we met. And how we came to know each other better—remember me playing for you, while you did pottery class in the summer term? How we'd sit and chat too?'

'Of course I do. Do you remember the first time, though, at my school in the spring?'

'Vividly.'

'I remember the song, Arlo. "Among The Flowers".'

'I'm flattered.'

'But I heard it not so long ago too—on the radio. Only it wasn't you.'

'I know.'

And he'd looked a little pensive. And she wanted to know why but didn't feel she could ask just then.

'Another time, Petra,' he'd said, anticipating. And he'd smiled, a little sadly, and tucked a

227

squiggle of her hair behind her ear. And for a split second they both wondered whether they were on the cusp of their very first kiss.

Yet there seemed no rush.

The only urgency was the failing light.

So that was when they had talked about telephones and he had told her to go.

She prepared to pedal away. He held the handlebars steady. His ran his index finger gently over the swoops and peaks of her knuckles.

'I did look for you, Petra,' he told her. 'I didn't really know where to start. I assumed you'd gone.'

'I had.'

'But you're back now. For how long?'

'I don't know, really.'

'Stay awhile.'

'OK.'

\*         \*         \*

Arlo looks at her number and he looks at the clock and he thinks, She might well be taken aback that I haven't yet phoned. We parted a couple of hours ago.

But what am I going to say?

And what is this going to start?

And what am I thinking—starting something at all?

\*         \*         \*

And Petra is looking at her phone and she's thinking, Why doesn't he ring? If he doesn't ring tonight, I'm leaving tomorrow.

228

*　　　*　　　*

'Hullo, Miss Flint.'

'Hullo, Arlo.'

'Get back OK?'

'Yes, no problem.'

'Good. Sorry I didn't phone earlier. I was marking.'

'Oh, don't you worry about that—I've been busy faffing around anyway.'

Pause. Fill it!

'How mad is all of this, Petra?'

'We could just look on it as a perfectly simple twist of fate.'

'I like that idea.'

'Well, that's what I'll do.'

'Me too, then.'

'That way, when we next see each other, we can just pick up where we left off and not worry about marvelling about serendipity and happenstance.'

'And kismet and karma.'

'Exactly!'

'How long has it been?'

'Two hours, Arlo. And seventeen years.'

'How about we start from now. Or, rather, how about tomorrow night? Can I take you out for supper?'

'Yes, please.'

'What else do you like, apart from chips and ketchup?'

'There's the Thai in Stokesley—do you know it?'

'Of course. I've lived here for four years.'

'I haven't been—but it always looks buzzing.'

'It's great. Let's go there. Let's meet there at

seven thirty. Tomorrow.'
  'It's a date.'
  Pause. Fill it!
  'Goodnight, Petra. See you tomorrow.'
  'Night, Arlo.'

*       *       *

He felt moved by the thought of Petra, on her own, passing the Thai but settling for chips. If only he'd known. If only he'd known earlier that she was here. If he had known earlier, where would they be by now? Further down the road? He shuddered. He wasn't worried about the path of true love running steep, he was worried about the terrible places it could lead to. He'd been there once before. Hadn't he decided that it was a journey he wouldn't be taking again?

*       *       *

Petra was euphoric. The date itself—and it was a date, wasn't it—and also the way it had come about. She praised herself to the hilt. For her composure. For keeping her voice nice and steady when all the time her fingertips had whitened from the pressure of gripping her phone so hard. Her heart racketing away while she managed to sound calm and collected. Her soul soaring with the blessings of karma and kismet. Her conscience trying to be heard above the din.
  Calm down.
  Calm down.
  You'll see him tomorrow.

*       *       *

However will I sleep?

## CHAPTER THIRTY-ONE

Arlo was not in the habit of lying but over the years he'd become adept at being evasive with the truth. So when Miranda asked him where he was going, he simply said Stokesley and left it at that. When Nigel asked if he wanted to join him and Jenn for a drink—they were now quite a couple—Arlo thought first to ask where they were meeting and when Nige said Chapters Deli he breathed a silent sigh of relief and declined. The Thai was round the corner from that bar and set back a little. And once Nige was installed at Chapters, he tended to stay there for the duration.

'Want a lift?' Nigel asked.

'Thanks but no—I'm just going to nip in on my bike.'

Arlo's colleagues assumed he was popping in to the Co-op. That's where one usually nipped in to Stokesley by bike. And Arlo decided not to put them straight. It was true—he was going to nip in. However, he was intending not to nip out again until much later that evening. But he hadn't been asked about that. So he wasn't going to elaborate.

*       *       *

Petra had sent out one communal text, the detailing of which would satisfy each of the

231

recipients. She was going on a date 2nite. V xited! Pxxx

Eric and Kitty fired back messages of encouragement.

u've waited 17 yrs, don't rush it 2nite, Lucy texted, wear manky pants!!! ;-)

Petra thought how comforting it was that though her friends were spread over continents and time zones, it was as if they were gathered in one supportive little posse, rooting for her.

The power of text messaging, she mused as she left the house. Can't believe Arlo hasn't discovered it. Bless him.

She went the long way around, walking along Levenside, by the river and the houses, instead of crossing directly to the High Street. She needed time to make her footsteps match her consciously slow breathing, or vice versa, she wasn't sure. But she walked slowly and breathed carefully and when she caught her reflection in the front windows of the houses, she liked what she saw and arrived at the restaurant excited but steady.

The restaurant was crowded but Petra spied Arlo sitting at a table, sipping a beer.

'Miss Flint,' he said, standing.

'Mr Savidge,' she said, sitting.

They bumbled over pleasantries and been-here-longs and come-here-oftens before immersing themselves in the menu to reassert their composure.

'I like your hair like that,' Arlo said after a thoughtful sip of beer.

'I like yours like *that*,' Petra said. 'I remember it all locks and curls and young Bob Dylan—but this way suits you too.'

'We're very Dandy Warhols,' Arlo said. Petra looked puzzled. He sang softly, '*I really love your hairdo, yeah, I'm glad you like mine too, see we're looking pretty cool.*' But he had to sing the chorus before she clicked and they duetted, '*And I like you yeah I like you,*' and they laughed and tucked into the prawn crackers. 'The thing is,' Arlo said, terribly seriously, 'once my hair started receding, it was a question of shave it all short—or grow a long bit to comb over.'

Petra looked momentarily horrified.

Arlo winked at her and she flicked a crumb of cracker at him in mock consternation.

'You look like What's-his-name,' she said.

'Bruce Willis?' Arlo asked. 'Quite a flattering trichological journey, really, from young Bob Dylan to mature Bruce Willis.'

Petra laughed. 'I meant that bloke off *Location Location Location.*'

'Good God, from the heights of Hollywood to flats in bloody Cricklewood?' Arlo protested.

'I have a bit of a crush on him, actually. Phil Thingy,' Petra said to her plate. 'So there.'

She looked up. Arlo had reddened a little. It made her grin. He shrugged. They took synchronized sips of their drinks and then laughed and chinked glasses. Petra Flipping Flint, he said. Arlo Sodding Savidge, she said. And they laughed again. Of course she felt nervous—but with excitement rather than unease because actually, he was easy to be with, easy to talk to. She wasn't having to prepare interesting conversation-starters. She wasn't having to formulate the manner, or the words, with which to respond. Compared to those ten stilted months with Rob, this first evening with

233

Arlo was natural. And fun.

They both wanted to ask each other everything, to hear the lot—the questions amassing from the seventeen-year hiatus, the marvelling that had filled their minds since they bumped into each other a month ago. Chit-chat was one thing, but to open their hearts for viewing and lay their souls out for inspection was another. What if I don't like what I hear? What if he-she doesn't like what I say? The food came to their rescue and tasted delicious after all those school dinners or takeaways. Discussing their dishes and sharing forkfuls provided the perfect foil to their awkwardness.

'Better than chips,' Arlo said.

'I do like my chips though,' Petra said.

'Well, let's do chips next time, then,' Arlo said. Immediately aware of his forwardness, his hand shot up, like one of his pupils', and he asked for the bill.

'OK,' Petra said slowly, arranging stray grains of rice into a pattern on the table.

'OK what?'

'OK to chips—next time.'

'Oh. Good.'

'Do you want a coffee—you know, a quick coffee, before you go?'

'Oh—I've asked for the bill.'

'I know. I mean—at mine.'

They looked at each other. Petra willing herself to give no glint to her eye; Arlo scouring her face for a glimpse of such a glint.

'Or tea,' she said.

'Coffee would be great,' said Arlo.

Again, Petra chose the more circuitous way back to the Old Stables for all the same reasons that she'd walked this route earlier. Arlo was pleased, because it took them away from Chapters Deli and the possibility, however slim, of Nigel looking out of the window at precisely that moment. Just because it was lovely walking by Petra's side, his bike clicketting satisfyingly as he pushed it, didn't mean he wanted to be seen just yet.

Under the archway and through to the Old Stables.

'I never knew this was here,' said Arlo.

'Nor did I,' said Petra. 'A couple of months ago, I'd never even been this far *north*.'

Milk? Sugar?

Just black, please.

'Nice place,' said Arlo. 'How did you come by it?'

'It belongs to Charlton Squire.'

'Who? Sounds straight from the pages of a Brontë novel.'

'Hardly. He was named after Bobby and Jack. He's a famous jeweller who sometimes I work for and he has a gallery where I sell some of my pieces. He owns this place. He's from around here.'

Arlo thought for a split second. Well, it had to be asked. 'Is he your boyfriend?'

'He's gay,' Petra said, pleased to have been

235

asked. Now ask me if I have a boyfriend, then I can say no.

'Do you have a boyfriend?'

'No.'

As she sipped coffee, she begged herself to enquire if he had a girlfriend but she dreaded an affirmative answer and left the question unasked.

'Do you want to see the studio?' Petra suggested because there's only so much gazing into coffee cups that two people can do. She led Arlo through the dark garden.

'Is this yours?' Arlo asked, putting down his mug and picking up some copper Petra had been working on.

'Yes, it's a rough. I plan to do it in white gold when I can afford the material.'

'It's beautiful.' Arlo looked at it intently, turning it this way and that. 'I remember watching you with your pots—great thunking things they were, and you so tiny.'

Petra's turn to redden. She sipped loudly at her coffee, now gaggingly cold.

As they stood there, the workbench still between them like some benign chaperone, the time gap seeming to diminish with every new moment, a natural ease increasing, they shared a glance. They liked what they saw and what they saw was transmuted into a feeling. The comfort of strangers who somehow know each other so well. In a glance, so much could be said.

'Will our past be enough?' Petra whispered, her eyes drawn to his.

'I think it's a really good foundation,' Arlo whispered back, dismissing the negativity he'd felt last night as a senseless by-product of insomnia.

236

Slowly, she reached out to him; her arm, her hand, her fingers—like a swan unfurling its neck. They touched fingertips before interlocking their hands. The contact, the affection; a connection that made communication easy.

'I wonder why we never—' Arlo stopped.

'I've been wondering about that,' Petra said.

'I suppose logistics played its part,' Arlo mused. 'I traipsed in to school from Potters Bar—did you know that?'

Petra cast her mind back. Reluctantly, she had to shake her head. However much she felt she knew about Arlo, or remembered from seventeen years ago, she had to acknowledge there was much she might have forgotten or not known about at all.

'Maybe that's why—you know—you and me, we never.' He paused and shrugged. Petra nodded, felt bolstered again. 'But there again, do you remember how people *not* in the same school year seemed either much younger or way older?' Arlo smiled wistfully. 'And it's different nowadays—schoolkids can flirt by email and text. They have their own phones for privacy and independence. They're much more savvy than we ever were. Ours was a time of "Mum? Can I use the phone?" and having to sit on the hall stairs with our hand cupped over the receiver. Perhaps if I'd lived nearer to you, we'd have bumped into each other out of school time—it would have been easier to have arranged to meet.'

'I met you at perhaps the loneliest time in my life,' Petra said, hoping she was reminding him, rather than imparting new information. 'My parents had split up. My dad had moved away, remarried. My mum and I moved and moved again.'

'I think I remember you telling me,' Arlo said slowly. He thought for a moment. 'I do remember that someone died. I remember that day. You, sitting on the iron fire escape at my school, sobbing—clunks of unworked clay in your lap. I had my guitar and I played to your heaving shoulders for a while. "Among the Flowers", of course. But I distinctly remember playing "Cat's in the Cradle". Acoustically, it's such a perfect melody, but actually, it's an incredibly sad song— daft bastard me for choosing it. I had played for you quite often but I just couldn't lure you around that time. So I slung my guitar behind my back and I came up to you and I put my arm around your little shoulders. Do you remember? And I kissed the top of your head.'

Reaching across the workbench again, Arlo gave Petra's hand a squeeze. 'I kissed the top of your head. Do you remember?' He took the palm of his hand to her cheek and she laid her face into his touch. 'It was the only time I ever kissed you,' he said.

*     *     *

If Miss Lorimar ever came into a lesson and spoke privately to the teacher, the girls knew something of magnitude had befallen one of them. On Wednesday 12 May of Petra's O levels year, Miss Lorimar came in halfway through the second part of Petra's double English lesson. Twenty minutes before lunch-break. Mrs Balcombe, the English teacher and Petra's favourite, nodded at the headmistress and tried desperately hard not to focus her one swift glance at anyone particular in her class. But, for a crucial split second, Petra could feel Mrs Balcombe's eyes hone in on her.

'Petra,' Miss Lorimar said, omitting her surname for increased tenderness, 'will you come with me, please?'

But I'm meant to be visiting Mrs McNeil at lunch-time, Petra thought as she followed her headmistress along corridors and down stairs. I bought her a triple pack of Walnut Whips. I hate to be late.

'Sit down, dear,' Miss Lorimar said and instead of taking her own place in the grand swivel chair behind her large leather-topped desk, she sat in one of the matching blue leatherette chairs in front of it and motioned for Petra to sit at the other. These chairs were low and placed in the lie of the headmistress's desk; they inspired awe in parents who sat in them and a degree of terror in girls ever summoned here. That day, though, with Miss Lorimar in one and Petra in the other, it all felt rather genial.

Petra wondered if she was about to be congratulated. Perhaps she'd won something—she'd sent a poem in to the *Guardian* and the same one to the *Hampstead & Highgate Express*. More likely, it was something to do with her parents. Again. She waited, a little sullenly.

'Petra.' Miss Lorimar's voice carried no indication of a prize. 'I have some very sad news. Very very sad news.'

As Miss Lorimar paused, Petra tried to guess but her heartbeat was a distraction. Guess. Guess. What. Who.

'Lillian McNeil passed away last night, Petra. I'm so sorry. I know how much you meant to each other.'

Petra sat in shock and disbelief and as the desolation crept in, she felt her already small world shrink a little more. It was as if a layer had been peeled away. A layer that had been of the finest cashmere, one which had wrapped her in warmth and protection. She felt raw and desperately cold. She was shivering. 'Mrs McNeil?'

'Yes, dear. Peacefully. Last night.'

I sleepwalked last night. Mum complained this morning—she has too much on her mind to be picking me up from crumpled heaps on the kitchen floor as well, or so she said.

Suddenly Petra had a feeling, desperate but sincere, that if she kept talking, kept asking questions, different information might transpire.

'She died last night?'

'Very peacefully.'

'Where?'

'On her way to hospital.'

'Hospital? She'd never been in hospital. Is there anyone at her flat?'

'No. I don't think so.'

'Should I go anyway, do you think? As arranged?'

'No.'

'No?'

'Petra dear,' and Petra could tell that her headmistress believed it would be a whole lot easier if the child just broke down and cried. 'I'm afraid that we have to let social services take over now. I know how well you looked after her, but officially she was in their care, you see.'

'She looked after me too,' Petra protested, 'and I know best just how she liked everything to be.'

And then Miss Lorimar put her hand out over Petra's wrist with the same stilted tenderness she'd displayed when talking to Petra of her parents two years before. 'You'll remember her your whole life.'

'I don't know what to do.' Petra had to mouth this because a punch of tears sat in a fist at her throat.

'Would you like to go home?' Miss Lorrimar had asked but Petra's expression told her sharply that this was the last place she could go to for comfort.

'I'm going to make you a nice cup of tea and you can drink it here and sit quietly for as long as you like.'

When Miss Lorimar left the room, Petra buried her head in her hands and cried so completely from the depths of her heart that no sound came out at all.

How Petra had loved Wednesdays, especially during the summer term. Double English with Mrs Balcombe, a longer lunch period visiting Mrs McNeil, then pottery class at Milton College all afternoon invariably enlivened by Arlo's company. She'd been working on a tall coil pot for Mrs McNeil. An umbrella stand onto which she'd incised Africanesque motifs, drawing on designs collected from books, from looking around Mrs McNeil's flat, from her own imagination. She'd be calling it an umbrella stand when it was finished, though really it was for Mrs McNeil's sticks. Mrs McNeil loathed her walking sticks, decrying them, A necessity I could damn well do without. Mrs McNeil had taught Petra what a contradiction in terms was.

Miss Lorimar's cup of tea had been comforting to hold though Petra hadn't taken a sip. And now it was well and truly lunch-time because she could hear the stampede along the corridor, slowing right down past Miss Lorimar's office before picking up pace with chatter increasing too. Petra didn't much feel like the company of her contemporaries. Nor did she want Miss Lorimar glancing at her every few minutes. She just wanted to go to Mrs McNeil's. That's what Wednesdays were all about. This one in particular. And she'd take the Walnut Whips. And then she'd finish the umbrella stand. And she'd never ever forget her.

\*       \*       \*

Petra climbed the stairs; her breathing laboured, the air heavy as if an invisible smog of sadness infused it. She reached Mrs McNeil's door, breathless. That sad old doorknob held against the wood by the yellowing web of ancient Sellotape. She stopped for a moment and wondered what to do. Then she thought back to Mrs Balcombe's class from which she'd been called away. The metaphysical poets. Donne's vehemence that death was not such a big deal at all, really.

*For those whom thou think'st thou dost overthrow,*
*Die not*

So Petra knocked for Mrs McNeil. Her usual pattern of raps. And then she flapped the letter-box too. Mistakes can be made. Miracles do

242

happen.

Mrs McNeil! she whispered. Mrs McNeil? It's me. It's Petra. It's just Petra. It's only me.

She looked through the letter-box, catching sight of corners of furniture. All seemed peaceful and ordinary. She posted the Walnut Whips through. Mrs McNeil, she crouched and called. Are you there? But only the faint scent of cigarillos and lavender whispered back at her.

No one here, Petra. No one here at all.

And Petra squatted down onto her heels, tucking herself into the door jamb, and at last she cried. The loss of Mrs McNeil. The loss of their friendship. The loss of Wednesdays being the best day of the week.

But it's only me. It's only Petra. It's only me.

\*   \*   \*

'I don't remember you kissing me, though,' Petra tells Arlo, her eyes damp from recalling the saddest day of her life. 'I don't really remember pottery at your school that afternoon.'

'I do,' says Arlo.

And holding her hand and stroking her cheek is no longer enough for him.

So he leans across the workbench, right across it. And he kisses the top of Petra's head. And Petra thinks, I'll never forget this kiss, this is the kiss that will last.

And Arlo is keeping his mouth there. And Petra is tipping her head back slowly, raising her face. She sees his chin. His lips, parted. His nose. His eyes. I know you, she thinks to herself, I know you off by heart. So she doesn't need to look to see.

243

Arlo isn't a dream, or a fantasy. He appears to be very real. She can feel him. She can close her eyes now—as he himself is doing—and their first shared kiss, a slow and gentle brushing of lips, speaks far more than they can possibly say just now.

And Petra thinks to herself how Mrs McNeil would most certainly approve.


## CHAPTER THIRTY-TWO

What do you do when the kiss you didn't know you'd been waiting so long for, comes to its natural end?

If you are Petra Flint, you assess in an instant that the pause for breath concludes a period you now see as having been Part I.

As you stand and look at each other, you feel flushed and euphoric because it's all being mirrored back at you. They feel as you feel. See, it's written all over their face and their eyes gleam with your reflection. You are right at each other's core. It's overwhelming and it sends a charge through your body like electricity or hot blood. So you cup your hands around each other's heads and pull that lovely face to yours and this time, your tongue tips dart about and the romance, the chasteness of Part I slides sensuously into the desire and instantaneity of Part II. Part I was then. Part II is now.

Part III weds love, lust and friendship, weaves them into a gossamer safety net that enables life to seem easy. Part III is a design for life which flows into for ever. How many people are lucky enough to make it to Part III?

*     *     *

It was all very well loving the idea of meeting up again after all these years. Of getting together with the person with whom they'd sort of been in love with all that time ago. But actually for the past to make sense of the present and head towards a future, Petra and Arlo had to like each other as they are now. And, on a baser but no less essential level, they also needed to fancy each other rotten. With their second kiss they hurtled into Part II; soon enough too hungry for each other for necking in the workshop with all those sharp instruments and the surprisingly chill air of an early June night and the solid workbench with its scatter of works in progress coming between them.

Petra pulled away and backed up towards the door. Arlo came around the bench and pressed her up against the wall. He sank his mouth into hers, his tongue searching out every answer from every clue her tongue gave him. Their hands were clasped together. Their bodies rocked instinctively against each other, the physical friction enhanced by their clothing adding fervour to their anticipation of what would happen when they took it off. For Petra, sensing Arlo's erection as he pressed against her transformed him from the almost deified figure of her memory into a man beside himself with lust for her right now. A man she wanted to feel inside her, whom she wanted to surround with her desire. She forgot Lucy's advice. She forgot about her manky knickers.

And Arlo dismissed the merits of celibacy and

245

ignored the complication of Miranda and even shelved the terrible legacy of Helen without a second thought. In his arms was Petra. In his mouth too. And his body ached to be closer still, straining to flood her with all he was feeling.

'Come on,' she whispered, her lips touching his as she spoke.

She led the way across the small darkened garden, her arm behind her keeping his hand enmeshed with hers. Suddenly he pulled her to a stop, came up behind her, both his hands on her breasts, his mouth working its way along her neck as if he was sucking up the most ambrosial taste from her skin. She turned to him and again they kissed; her hands now emboldened, sweeping their way over his back, his arms, over the satisfying stiffness in his trousers.

'Come on,' she whispered again.

*       *       *

But, after the chill of the workshop and the darkness of the garden, the Old Stables was just a little too bright, a little too warm and the route through the kitchen, over the cobbles of the living area to the bedroom, a little too detailed, taking a little too long.

Side by side, their hands touching lightly, Petra and Arlo stood in the doorway to the bedroom observing the bed. She'd stripped it earlier and had forgotten to remake it. It seemed to dominate the room. The mattress an optical swirl of peach damask, a large label prosaically proclaiming the orthopaedic qualities, calico-wrapped pocket springs and 100% lambswool stuffing. A jumble of linen in the corner of the room, like mountain scenery in a school play. Petra's two or three changes of clothes in a scatter on the floor. An empty packet of jelly babies on the bedside table. A paperback novel lying open and face down, its pages furling, its cover a little creased, like a fallen bird or butterfly.

This room was categorically not ready for two people ready to make love.

This room offered a private glimpse of Petra, one which she didn't mind Arlo seeing, and he soaked up the details.

Honesty was the only way to progress. She turned to him. 'I have to tell you, I am wearing manky pants too.' She shrugged. 'As a precaution—not to get carried away.'

He looked at her, looked around the room, absorbed the reasons and began to smile. He nodded, slipped his arm affectionately around her shoulder, kissed her forehead, squeezed her close. 'But do you own a pair of nice knickers?' he asked.

'I do,' Petra said. 'Quite a few, actually.'

'Will you wear them next time—and make the bed up too?'

Petra sparkled as she looked at him. 'Is that the same "next time" as when we're going out for chips?'

'The very same,' said Arlo.


CHAPTER THIRTY-THREE

Over the next two days, Petra regularly felt relieved not to be a teenager again. It was a given

247

that, after seventeen years apart, Arlo and Petra were entitled to make up for lost time. Now in their thirties, they didn't have to abide by the strict laws of those earlier years of playing hard to get, nor subscribe to rules of when to phone, who was to phone whom and in what tone of voice. In fact, Arlo phoned Petra frequently; in between lessons, before breakfast, last thing at night. They chatted blithely, they weathered awkward silences, they enjoyed a giggle and a tease. Yet the beginning of their relationship was also chaste in much the same way as it would have been had they been teenagers—they hadn't slept together on their first date, clothing had even come between them and Base Two. In addition, they did much of their initial courting via the phone—and during such calls, they bemoaned how bloody school was keeping them apart. Play rehearsals one night (Arlo had written a rousing score to accompany the Sixth Form production of *All Quiet on the Western Front*), evening prep the next, not to mention the inconvenience of Saturday morning school.

Petra used the time apart to her advantage. She felt energized and worked productively; calling Charlton to request more time and more work. There was an Internet office from which she could send jpegs of works in progress and sketches of future projects down to London—for advice and approval from her Studio Three, as well as emails and jpegs to tout for pre-emptive commissions from previous clients or Charlton himself. Her semi-precious hair slides were proving a hit. She ordered seed pearls and amethyst, silver and gold plus various essential gubbings from Bellore online.

She knew her new postcode off by heart. She ended any correspondence to Charlton, 'Are you sure you're happy for me to continue up here?' and yet she signed all her missives to her Studio Three, 'Do you miss me?' As if seeking permission from Charlton to stay while also hoping to reassure herself that if she did stay she wouldn't be forgotten by those she also missed. And miss them she did, though in herself she was no longer lonely.

On the Saturday morning, with an image in her mind of Arlo teaching a class in a rousingly *Dead Poets Society* manner, Petra locked up the workshop, cleaned the Old Stables and procrastinated only momentarily over what to do with the bedroom before putting clean sheets on the bed and adjusting the wooden Venetian blinds so that a gentle light and maximum privacy was afforded without it seeming that she was actively preparing the room for sex. She went to the Deli and bought a selection of Mediterranean dishes and rustic bread. Saturday papers. A pint of milk. She bought what she hoped was a decent wine from the Co-op and treated herself to nice paper napkins from the lovely homewares shop at the top end of the town. She couldn't resist a cheap and cheerful bunch of tulips.

She thought how, back in Rob days, she'd prepare for those dates in an exhaustingly thorough way—but the motivation had been diametrically opposite. She did things to please Rob and for optimum effect, hoping to entice that man to want her. Now, she had no ulterior motive—Arlo himself was worth it. It was like that kiss. Kissing Arlo like that had made her realize how, with Rob, her kisses had been carefully conducted for cause and effect. She used to kiss Rob hoping to inspire him to think, Wow I have to have her, I'd be mad to leave. Every flick of her tongue, each ounce of pressure from her lips, every coy nip from her teeth had been carefully calibrated for maximum effect. So much so that she rarely had the time to enjoy being kissed herself. Previously, Petra had judged herself by the degree to which she could inspire desire, and had deludedly equated it with love. She had wanted to be a magnet and, in as much as opposites do attract, she'd achieved that with Rob. But the achievement had been empty. What had been the point of pursuing such an opposite?

Arlo, though, wasn't an opposite. And kissing him had been a shared thing, bubbling with mutual desire. They hadn't had to think about what to do, or what to do next. They'd kissed each other like that because they really, really liked each other. Amazing how genuine affection can incite such sizzling lust. Two sides of the same coin and one of such worth. It's all one and the same and it's effortless and intense because it's so uncomplicated.

*     *     *

As Petra waited, she toyed with sending various text messages; south to London, east to Hong Kong. Perhaps even sneaking in a short phone call—the perfect time to catch Lucy. But she sought no advice today. If she did make a call, it would only be to share how excited she felt, how much she was looking forward to the hours ahead.

And then she thought that actually she'd quite like to sit still, by herself, and really savour the feeling.

Footsteps crunching their way from the pavement, through the archway and to the front door. A lively rap on the knocker. A beaming smile greeting her which she bounced straight back to him.

'Chips, milady,' Arlo said, holding a paper bag aloft, through which the warm heady drench of salt and vinegar steamed out.

We'll have the fancy food for supper then, Petra thought to herself. 'Yum,' she said. 'Come on in.'

So they sat together on the tapestry sofa, their thighs touching, the paper lain over their knees, the chips mounded high, and they tucked in.

'I like the crunchy ones,' Petra explained as she helped herself to the little pile Arlo had rejected.

'I like them blonde,' Arlo said, picking at the pale soft chips Petra had put to one side. Then he added, 'We're like Jack Spratt and his wife, you and me.'

'I hope it's only chips you like blonde,' Petra said and she twisted a lock of her hair between her salty fingers.

'I brought a bottle of peroxide with me—I thought we'd do your hair after lunch,' he said, deadpan, causing Petra to baulk for a millisecond before he nudged her and they laughed and they didn't want any more chips, crunchy or blonde, they just wanted to kiss.

\*       \*       \*

They tumbled into Charlton's sofa, limbs interlocking. He rolled her on top of him and she

251

licked at his lips. Salty. Vinegar. Warm. He filled his nostrils with the scent of her hair which flowed over his face in soft serpentines. He scooped it up, tugged it into a pony-tail, admired the sweep of her neck and took his lips there. Then he looked deeply into her eyes, his own a little glazed.

'What's the state of your knickers today, Miss Flint?' he asked.

Petra made much about thinking hard and the longer she thought, the harder she could feel him become. 'Well,' she said at length, 'I do believe they are black.' She kissed him. 'And rather minuscule.' He kissed her back.

'Right, I see,' he said in what she perceived to be his teacher's voice. 'Well, come along then.'

And laughing, they walked easily to the bedroom.

*     *     *

The surge of affection they felt for one another right then was rooted in the long period of time they'd known each other. It had germinated seventeen years ago and had continued to grow each time they chanced to think of one another over the intervening years. It had then burst from bud when they came across each other, wet and bedraggled and a blast from the past at Easter, and since then it had blossomed and grown lush. It was the longevity which had helped pave the way to this Saturday, this walk to the bedroom, this delight at the freshly made bed, this urgency to communicate physically as thoroughly as they could.

This is the woman from the girl I really rather loved when I was seventeen.

This is the man from the boy who serenaded me, who I loved quietly, when I was fifteen.

This is the first time they'll have seen each other naked. Something new. Something hitherto clothed, private. It wouldn't have been right at any other time than now.

They undress each other. Arlo unbuttons Petra's cardigan, eases it away from her shoulders, feels her skin so warm and smooth to his touch. The swell of her modest breasts cupped by a plain black bra. He moves his fingertips over the soft flesh, glides his palms over their perfect fit. More than a handful's a waste. These are ideal. He hooks his little fingers under each bra strap and looks at Petra before he starts to ease them down. Her eyes are wide with expectation and liquid with desire, her lips are moist and parted and he has to stop what he's doing just to kiss her again. And then his gaze drops, he lifts the black straps away from her skin and two perky nipples spring out as if winking at him. And now she's unclasping the bra for him and as she does so her breasts jut forward as the garment falls away. Arlo catches his breath as he hovers his hand and Petra takes his wrist and guides him to her skin. And she gasps as her nipple is caught and squeezed between his fingers and they look at each other again.

He draws her against him. He's anticipated how she'd feel in the flesh, these last couple of nights—fantasized about it, wanked over it—but the reality gloriously transcends all of that. There's something about feeling her body against him, her skin kept one step removed from his by his own clothing. It's fantastic, it's maddening.

Petra feels strangely, pleasantly, vulnerable;

253

semi-naked yet enveloped and enclosed. The things his hands and fingers are doing to her body. The sound of his quickened breathing. She tugs his T-shirt from his jeans, eases it up and as he stretches to take it off she finds her face at his chest and all she wants to do is kiss and stroke and immerse herself in this expanse of his manliness. She kisses and she licks and she sweeps her face millimetres over him so as to feel the soft smattering of chest hair brush like a whisper against her skin. She runs her hands down his back, from his shoulder blades to the waist of his jeans, and he's doing precisely that to her. Running her hand along the bulge and stiffness behind his denim, her sex quivers and she parts her legs a little so that his thigh slips in between and she rocks her hips to increase the pleasure.

They lie on the bed, limbs locked, lips locked, hands free to roam, their groins gyrating.

He crouches over her and her hands travel up over his arms, more muscular than she's imagined, more beautiful. He lifts locks and individual strands of her hair away from her face, strokes her cheeks, her forehead, stoops to kiss her nose, her chin.

'May I?' he whispers and he's smiling and he looks really thrilled.

'You may,' Petra whispers back. And as he unbuckles her belt and unzips her jeans and hoicks up her hips so he can pull her trousers down, she closes her eyes and sinks into the feeling of being truly made love to. He's left her knickers on and he's kissing her stomach, low low down, where the elastic meets her skin. Lower down now, where the elastic meets her inner thigh and he doesn't need to ask if he may because she's spreading her legs for him to press his mouth against the gusset of her panties and she's wriggling and writhing because she wants him to rip them off. But he doesn't. He's straddling her, undoing his own belt, unbuttoning his jeans and she's lifting herself up, pushing his hands away so she can undress him, reveal him. She's at once shy and yet inquisitive about his cock. It's holding the cotton of his boxers aloft but what will it look like? She runs her fingers up and down its length, can sense it twitch, even leap; it's hot. Gently she pushes him down onto the bed and she places her kisses in one long, slow line from his nose over his lips, his chin, his neck, his chest, his stomach. And she kisses along the waist of his underwear too because she wants him to know how good that felt. Through the gap in his boxers she can see a thatch of dark curls, pheromones wafting through, the smell of sex. She takes his shorts down and his cock springs impressively to attention. His hands are around her upper arms and he's pulled her against him and they're rolling over the bed, kissing and caressing; his cock is pressing at her waist, her stomach, and she's opening her legs but getting only his thigh. Now his fingers. It feels like her sex is kissing his fingers. His fingers aren't enough. Her hand is grasping his cock. Their mouths are glued together and their tongues dance deep.

Their eyes are closed. Their eyes open. Locking into each other's gaze they stop kissing, they stop moving and they just look. They look and look and slowly they move again. And they don't take their eyes off each other when some force in her sex guides his cock smoothly, easily, ecstatically into her. And they don't stop watching each other as they move and move; they see the pleasure they are feeling registered on the other's face. Is this as beautiful for you as it is for me? Yes, it is. They're not fucking urgently, their bodies are fusing and the pace is instinctively luxurious. The momentum is increasing but it's still tantalizingly slow enough for them to acknowledge every flush of pleasure in the glaze of each other's eyes, the reddening of their cheeks, the hastening of their breathing. And it's so blissful and so erotic and Petra knows she's never felt it so good and Arlo knows he's never had a fit so perfect and without drama they're coming, they're coming, seamlessly synchronized, they're coming. There's no shouting or yelping or affected panting; there's actually no need for sound. They're speechless anyway. They don't need to be told. There isn't a word for it. To ride together the vivid crest of physical pleasure, to share such a cerebral high of complete emotion. And the spurts from Arlo subside into a last few tired jolts. And the spasms from Petra ease into a woozy wetness.

They grin at each other, a little triumph, a lot of happiness. He slips out of her, lies beside her, strokes her hair, tucks it behind her ear. Their faces are very close. Blue eyes and brown. Nose tips almost touching. The poetry of the orgasm has ebbed into the sunny ordinariness of the afternoon in hand.

But Petra bites her lips and she says, Shit, we didn't, you know, use anything. *Shit.*

And Arlo stops grinning. He looks very serious.

But Petra, he says, it's irrelevant—there's no precaution necessary. We don't need to guard against a single thing any more.

'You and me.'
'And me and you.'


## CHAPTER THIRTY-FOUR

'I want to show you something.'

Arlo, who hadn't really been asleep but had sensed Petra gazing at him intently and was enjoying the feeling, slowly opened his eyes and raised an eyebrow. 'If it's that thing you do with your hips when you're on top, then yes, please.'

Petra laughed—she didn't really know what the hip-thing was, though she was glad he liked it. Languorously she trailed her hand over Arlo's chest. What a perfect afternoon. Sod the glorious day happily going on outside, no doubt a landscape bathed in early summer sunshine, a sky scattered with Gainsborough clouds and air so fresh you could taste its sweetness—what better place to be than in bed?

They had made love a second time, then dozed. They'd had mugs of hot chocolate, sitting up in bed, side by side, sipping and chatting like an old couple. Kissed a lot. She clattered about the kitchen, brought hot buttered toast to bed. Dozed again. Crumbs in the sheets.

'You can touch your nose with your tongue,' Arlo said.

'What?'

'Or go cross-eyed? I don't know—what is it then? Show me.'

'It's this,' said Petra and she twisted half off the bed, delving around under the mattress. Arlo was

257

far more intrigued by the sinuous undulations of her torso, the sheen on her skin. He placed his hand at the dip of her waist, kissed the bank of muscle running smoothly along her back. He wanted to make love to her again, this way, from behind, press himself against her, kiss her and feel her from this angle.

'Down, boy!' she said and he rolled onto his back laughing, saying, Fucking hell, Petra Flint, what are you *doing* to me?

'I want to show you *this*.' She passed him a large jewel. He took it from her. Transparent yet heavy with colour, in fact saturated with colours: navy, lilac, midnight, violet, plum, lavender. Faceted so that it both captured the light and spun it out simultaneously. He held it between thumb and forefinger. Petra straightened his hand and placed the gem on top, along the line between his index and middle fingers. The light, the colour, appeared even more brilliant.

'Blimey,' Arlo said, 'what is it? A sapphire?'

Petra smiled. She'd had this conversation herself, with Lillian McNeil. 'It's the colour that sapphire wishes it could be,' she quoted dramatically. 'It's tanzanite.'

'Tanzanite.'

'And I don't know what to do with it.'

'Is it yours?'

'Yes, it's mine.'

\*       \*       \*

Two months after Lillian McNeil died, the school year ended. During the long summer that followed, Arlo received his A level results in music, English

258

and history and packed his bags for Bristol University. Petra and her mother moved again, this time to a small, dull flat in a nondescript area where the fingers of Cricklewood poke into the outer reaches of West Hampstead. Petra returned to school that September with eight O levels under her belt but no Mrs McNeil for lunch-times and no more Arlo at all. She tucked her head down and worked diligently. Just after the autumn half-term, she was summoned to Miss Lorimar's office again, though this time she wasn't called from her class. Instead it came as a discreet request from her art teacher at the end of class and the beginning of break.

Miss Lorimar seemed not to notice Petra's arrival though Petra had knocked and been told to enter. The headmistress was doing the *Times* crossword. Petra watched her pen scuttle over the across clues, falter once or twice and dive on a down clue or two. The headmistress looked up. 'Good morning, Petra—do take a seat. Wretched thing.' Petra wasn't sure who or what was wretched but she decided it was the crossword and not herself or the blue leatherette chair.

Her headmistress put down the biro as if it was hot. She tipped her head to one side and regarded her pupil a little quizzically. 'Did you have a nice half-term?'

'Yes, thank you, Miss Lorimar.'

'Refreshed? Ready to storm headlong into your A levels?'

'I am trying,' said Petra, 'very hard.'

'Good good,' Miss Lorimar said. She tapped a brown paper parcel in front of her. 'This is for you. It came to the school with a covering letter from

Messrs William & Brandt.'

Petra did not recognize the name and couldn't fathom why she was receiving mail at school. After all, despite it being a soulless hinterland, postmen did visit the cusp of Cricklewood. William or Brandt. Never heard of them.

'They are solicitors,' Miss Lorimar told her. 'They acted for your friend, Lillian McNeil. And in her will, she left this to you.'

Petra felt her soul leap. 'For me?' She looked at the parcel. She looked at Miss Lorimar and beamed. 'I know what it is!'

'You do?'

'It's the painting I loved—of Kilimanjaro. In Tanzania.'

'I know where Kilimanjaro is, dear.'

'It's the one her husband painted. Hector. It's abstract—a little like Clyfford Still.'

'Open it and see.'

'There's *two*! Oh wow. This is the one her husband painted. And this is the watercolour. Mrs McNeil loved it out there, in Tanzania. She had so many stories of her travels—and she told me many Masai legends too.'

'There's something else, Petra. See? In the paper—the velvet purse.'

The shock of seeing that black velvet pouch swept Petra's smile away and she quickly sat on her hands. 'I know what that is too,' she said quietly, regarding it a little shyly.

'Aren't you going to open it?'

'It can't be for me.'

'Yes, it can. In black and white, or at least black velvet, care of Messrs William & Brandt. Come on!' and Miss Lorimar's eyes sparkled like a child at Christmas—a bizarre sight indeed for one of her underlings to behold.

Petra took the pouch to her lap, untied the cord, tipped the contents quickly into the palm of one hand and cupped her other hand over the top. She thought she saw Miss Lorimar actually bounce on her chair in anticipation. Slowly she opened her hands, like a clam revealing its treasure.

'Good God!'

Headmistresses oughtn't to blaspheme, surely.

But Petra knew that Miss Lorimar had been helpless not to. It was a natural reaction on first seeing a 39.43 carat tanzanite.

*     *     *

It had been Arlo's reaction too.

'And this is it?' Arlo asked, taking the gem between his fingers.

'Yes,' said Petra.

'Shouldn't it be in a bank vault—not under a mattress?'

'That,' said Petra, 'would be a tragedy. You can't lock something this beautiful away.'

'You can't plonk something this valuable under your mattress, though.'

'I almost didn't have it at all. My mother said I could keep the pictures but that I wasn't allowed the gemstone. She said it wasn't right. I had to knock on Miss Lorimar's door the following day and say, I'm sorry but my mother says I can't have this because she says it isn't right.'

'But you do have it.'

'She was a dark horse, Miss Lorimar,' Petra laughed. 'Just after I took my A levels, just before I left school, I was summoned to my headmistress one final time. She took down a reproduction Ming vase from on top of a shelf and tipped out the black velvet purse. She handed it to me and said that now I was eighteen I didn't need to ask my mother's permission.'

'She'd kept it for you?'

'Yes. In a fake Ming vase high up on a shelf. It was so strange—it was all so covert and yet so charmingly conspiratorial. She said to me, "When your mother said it wasn't right—I have a feeling she meant it wasn't right for you to have been the adored focus of someone else's world. I think your mother felt guilty, Petra. I don't think she wanted you to have a token of a friendship that eased a very dark time for you." And really, that was the last conversation I had with my headmistress.'

'From a Ming to a mattress,' Arlo said. 'It's a bit ignominious.'

'But I don't know what to do with it,' Petra said. 'It's my writer's block. It goads me and yet it sustains me too. It's what motivated me to apply to Central St Martins. I know, I just know, that an essential part of my creativity is locked within this gem. But I can't access it. It's frustrating beyond belief. How can I do this beautiful stone justice? And what can I possibly create that would be testimony enough to the wonderful Lillian McNeil?'

'Is that why you're here, Petra?'

She looked at him.

'It is now.'

She'd left herself bare, yet she'd done so on purpose. Arlo's tipped head said, Tell me more. Petra raised her eyebrows at herself and looked a little sheepish. 'Initially—when I first came up here before Easter—it was because I'd split up with a bloke.'

'Nursing a broken heart by brooding all over the moors?' Arlo said. 'Very Brontë.'

'It was not a broken heart,' Petra said, quiet but decisive. 'More of a bruised ego.'

'"Fallen in love with someone you shouldn't have fallen in love with",' Arlo said but he wasn't looking at Petra.

'The Buzzcocks,' Petra said. The fact that she'd recognized the lyrics pulled Arlo back to her.

'I'm impressed.'

'But look,' said Petra and she pulled back the sheet, stretched herself out, pointing her toes, arms stretched above her head, 'no bruises. None on the outside, none on the inside.' She thought it the best way to show him she had history but no baggage; that she had history and a sense of humour.

Arlo's eyes swept along her curves. He ran the tanzanite gently over her body, plopped it down on her stomach. 'Good enough to eat.'

'I have licked it, you know,' Petra said and she giggled.

'Putting your mouth where the money is,' Arlo mused. 'How much is this thing worth?'

'Loose like this? A lot. Thousands. Because of its size, its clarity and colour, it's internally flawless. Made up into something—a lot more.'

'And yet you struggle to make ends meet, living in a rented flat in North Frigging Finchley? By the way, I wasn't talking about the tanzanite being good enough to eat.' And Arlo lay a cloth of light kisses over her body to emphasize the point. 'Who was this bloke?' he said casually, between mouthfuls.

'Rob,' said Petra. 'Not my type.' And she stroked Arlo's head, the velvety sensation of his closely cropped hair feeling lovely on her palm.

'Did you show him—Rob—the secrets of your mattress?'

'He wasn't particularly interested.'

Arlo brought his face up from Petra's stomach. He grinned. 'Of course, I'd love you if there was dust under your mattress rather than thousands of pounds' worth of jewels.'

He just said he loves me.

'The thing is Arlo, when I do—finally—make something for this tanzanite, who on earth will I allow to buy it?'

\*       \*       \*

Compared to chips from the paper, supper was a grand affair, with the table set, side-plates with folded napkins, candles lit, a bottle of wine. The food Petra had bought from the deli was perfect. They were ravenous.

'I'll bet people back in London think you are eking a frugal existence out in the sticks,' Arlo said. 'My mum took some persuading that one could even get a cappuccino, never mind a bloody good one, up here. She couldn't quite believe it when she saw rocket pesto on one menu in Stokesley and saffron couscous on another in Helmsley, and Jerusalem artichoke on a menu in Yarm.'

'I must admit, I thought it'd be mostly ham and eggs, or pies pies pies.'

'Shame on you, Miss Flint. It's a wonderful area—it really is. I don't think I'd live anywhere else now. The villages are great, the landscape is stunning and there's the bonus of being so near the coast.'

'I haven't been. Yet.'

'Well, that's a date, then,' said Arlo and they laughed. 'Another one. There's loads of places I must take you. Down to Runswick Bay. Up to Roseberry Topping. Bilsdale and Raisdale. We'll take the North York Moors Railway from Grosmont to Pickering. We'll walk the Cleveland Way, we'll go a way along the Lyke Wake Walk. The pier at Saltburn. The Wainstones, the Hanging Stone, a stick of rock from Scarborough. We'll fine dine at the Tontine. Have Sunday lunch at the Star in Harome. Fresh dressed crab from Whitby. We'll cross over the Transporter Bridge one way and the Newport Bridge the other. We'll go and see the Angel of the North, the goths at Whitby, the bikers at Helmsley.'

'I'd like to see the ruined abbeys.'

'Rievaulx. Fountains. Byland. Guisborough. St Hilda's. I'll take you there.'

'All these dates, Arlo—they'll eat up all your weekends.'

He shrugged. 'I don't mind. It'll be half-term soon enough. Summer holidays six weeks after that.'

'Do you not go home?'

'This is home, Petra—for me.'

Petra nodded and knitted the frisee with her fork. She'd never considered that home could be anywhere other than where you'd been brought up. Even if you didn't particularly like it. She never thought that home is where the heart is could be more than a saying, more than a song.

\*    \*    \*

'Why are *you* here, Arlo?' she asks, as they snuggle into bed past midnight, having chatted the evening away.

'Oh,' he says blithely, 'I'm just here for the pussy.'

Petra punches him lightly and then bashes him with her pillow. 'Pillock,' she says. 'Not *here*, here. I meant—'

'I know,' Arlo says, 'I know. A bit like you really—something went awry for me back in London, a few years ago, and an opportunity arose here which I took without a backward glance.'

'What happened, what went awry, Arlo?'

He turns and lies on his back. 'I knew you'd ask me that.' And then he says 'idiot' at himself, under his breath, which Petra wasn't meant to hear, but they both know she has.

Petra tells herself to stop prying, it's late, don't push—not now. Don't spoil what's been so perfect by digging too deep just yet. 'Tell me.' Shut up!

'Oh—it's long and complicated and boring, Petra. My career was at a crossroads. I broke up with someone I'd been with for a while. You know—one of those life-defining intersections that tend to epitomize one's late twenties.'

'What happened—with your career?' Petra gives herself full marks for manipulating the divulgence into less contentious territory.

'I changed my tune,' Arlo says.

'Stop being so enigmatic!'

266

'Seriously—I'd always been in bands, from school through university and beyond. I worked in the music industry, but I knew that while my music had a market, I didn't. I wasn't cool enough, or young enough—certainly not good-looking enough.'

'The Magic Numbers are no oil painting.'

'Perhaps not—but they're marketable enough for that very reason. The industry needs the whole package. But anyway, if I'm truthful, over and above losing my nerve performing—I dreaded it, I hated it—I also lost my love of songwriting.'

'I loved it when you sang to me.'

'But I wasn't performing, Petra—I was just singing.'

'Your songs were great.'

'Other people seem to think so. I was fairly successful as a songwriter—as the continuing royalties show. Bizarre.'

'Doesn't it rankle? Hearing some other voice work your music? Isn't it like seeing another man with your ex-girlfriend or something?'

'Not really,' says Arlo. 'While I write a song, I'm inextricably bound to it. The moment it's finished, it becomes separate, autonomous.'

And Petra thinks to herself, Quick! Lead nicely on—pick up on the ex-girlfriend strand now. 'Oh,' she says. 'Yes, I can see that. And. Then. So you broke up with someone around that time too?'

'Yes. It was all miserably synchronized.'

'Oh. Poor you. What was she—'

'Helen. We'd been together a few years. You know how it is—you either go for it, big time, or you let it go.'

'Do you keep in touch?'

267

'No.'

The tone of his voice surprises Petra. It's unequivocal. It bars further access to the subject. She had wanted to ask—to double-check—was there anyone at the moment, had there been anyone up here. But she can't. She thinks to herself, Perhaps he's just really really tired. We've spent the best part of twelve hours getting to know each other intimately—making love and talking, sharing.

'Night, Arlo,' she says and she kisses his shoulder because he has turned away from her. She tells herself to let him sleep. She has a feeling he's very much awake.

*    *    *

Petra wakes up very cold. It is dawn. She is slumped against a kitchen unit, she is sitting in a puddle of wee. She is mortified. What on earth has she to sleepwalk about? More to the point, had Arlo seen? She wipes the floor clean. As quietly as the creaky taps let her, she soaks a tea towel and washes herself down. She tiptoes back to the bedroom, sneaks back into bed. Arlo turns towards her, spoons against her, enclosing her in his arms. Why on earth would she have tried to walk away from Arlo?

Just a bad dream.

Everything's OK. See—you're in his arms.

Go back to sleep.

# CHAPTER THIRTY-FIVE

She did go back to sleep. She woke at gone ten, by which time Arlo had been awake for an hour. He had been watching her for the best part of half an hour. The worst part of half an hour had been on waking, when a sense of dread had swept over him in a dark wave. He had lain beside Petra, not daring to turn or look. He'd kept his eyes fixed on the ceiling which, in the Old Stables, provided ample dinks and cracks conducive to ruminating. As much as his heart surged, his stomach plummeted. For every thundering beat of his heart proclaiming love and lots of it, his conscience hammered back that Love could only mean one thing. And just in case Arlo feigned not to know the meaning of love, his memory charged in to remind him.

But all it had taken was a tiny sleep-sigh from Petra. Despite the noise of the conflict raging inside him, one perfectly timed little whisper of her breath had lured him around. He turned to her, gazed at her, and for the best part of half an hour he fed upon the peace and loveliness from her repose until the emptiness and negativity had been washed away and a full tank of hope and happiness replaced it. When Arlo had seen Petra for that first time, just before Easter, it had been like revisiting the feelings she'd instilled in him seventeen years ago. Remember me? Yes, of course I remember you—how could I ever forget? And for a while it had been those memories of a halcyon time when life was simple and so much felt good, which had seduced him. But as Arlo looked at her in the here and now, on a quiet Sunday morning in late May, it was unequivocally the Petra of the present, not the past, who soothed his soul and charged his heart even while she was asleep.

'Good morning, Miss Flint.'
'What time is it?'
'Gone ten.'
'Have you been awake long?'
'The best part of half an hour.'
'Did you sleep?'
'Eventually. As per usual.'
'Are you OK?'
'I'm fine. I'm used to it.'

*    *    *

Arlo felt if he held on tight to the present and went forward fast, then his past wouldn't catch up with him. It would be left behind to fade; to dissolve into less than a memory, something so nebulous and distant it would have no impact on the horizon of his future. Helen had hated walking but Petra said she loved it so they cycled to Great Ayton and hiked to Roseberry Topping from the Gribdale Gate approach. Arlo didn't let go of her hand, not even up the arduous and narrow stepped path though this caused them both to stumble. Petra thought it was fantastically romantic, even though she had to tug him occasionally and say, Slow down, it's not a race. It was a magnificent day and by the time they'd made it to the summit of the oddly shaped hill, they were down to T-shirts. The view was 360 degrees; Arlo could look all around, and in whichever direction he looked, whatever was behind him, Petra was at his side.

'My first lesson isn't until eleven tomorrow—I could stay tonight, if you like.'

'I like,' said Petra, beaming.

*       *       *

What she didn't like, though, was bumping into a colleague of Arlo's that afternoon in the ice-cream queue.

'Savidge!'

'Garton.'

For a split second, but not short enough for Petra not to notice, Arlo looked panicked.

'This is Jenn! Jenn, this is Arlo Savidge—the music maestro at school.'

'Hi, Arlo, I've heard a lot about you.'

'Hullo, Jenn—you're a brave woman taking on Garton.'

'Actually, it's been my pleasure.'

All eyes were on Petra who wasn't yet sure whether Garton was a Christian name or a surname.

'Hi, I'm Nige Garton.'

'Hullo, I'm Petra Flint.'

'This is my girlfriend, Jenn.'

'Nice to meet you, Jenn.'

'And you.'

All eyes burned at Arlo.

'She's an old friend of mine,' he said without fidget or mumble or any intention of quantifying this. 'We've just done Roseberry Topping.'

And then Arlo turned down Nige and Jenn's invitation to join them, ushering away his old friend Petra Flint before she could even ask for a

Flake in her cornet.

*     *     *

She licked her ice cream without really tasting it, thinking to herself how dumb she felt, and lonely; despite sitting next to Arlo, beside a picturesque weir which tumbled and plunged as if it was a display put on just for them.

'Petra?' Arlo nudged her. 'Your ice cream's dripping.'

She licked the vanilla trail oozing over her fingers, then regarded the cone. 'I don't really want it.'

He nudged her again and put something on her knee. It was a penny. 'For your thoughts,' he said.

'They seemed nice,' she shrugged. Arlo looked puzzled. 'Nige—and Jenn.'

'Nige is a great bloke,' said Arlo, then he regarded Petra. 'Will ten pence do it? Go on. A quid, then?'

Petra failed to maintain a sullen expression as she fiddled with the coins. 'Sorry, I'm just being—sensitive.'

Arlo nudged her again.

What the hell. 'Am I just an *old friend*, then?'

Arlo tossed the coins from her knee one by one into the river while pondering his tone of voice before he spoke. 'You haven't been to school for a long long time, Petra,' he said gently. 'If I'd said, "This is Petra, my new girlfriend," the school grapevine will have twisted itself silly by the time I arrive back.'

Petra gladly felt livid with herself for being such an idiot.

'The thing is, I'm famous for *not* having girlfriends, Petra. In all the time I've been in Yorkshire, for all the time I've been at Roseberry Hall—there hasn't been anyone. At all. No one. Not a sniff. They've teased me, over the years, as you'd expect. Not the boys so much—my colleagues.'

'But *am* I more than just an old friend?'

'You're my mad and gorgeous attention-seeking new girlfriend,' he said, 'whom I happen to have known for years.'

Petra looked at him. He raised his eyebrows and gave her a kiss.

'Finally, I can enjoy my ice cream,' she said, kissing him back first.

*          *          *

If the previous day their lovemaking had been woven with poetry and awe, today it was more down to earth, boisterous even. When they returned to the Old Stables, they stripped each other enthusiastically, eager to try it this way and that. They laughed a lot, giggled too. Petra did an involuntary fanny fart but before she could be mortified, Arlo said a deadpan, Bless you.

He fingered her in such a way, an infuriating but intentional fraction of an inch off orgasm, that she writhed and cursed and slapped him and then gave him a blow-job that left him hollering for mercy. This time, hot and sweaty and about to come, Arlo did concede that OK, perhaps they ought to use something. And after a frantic and blaspheming struggle with the cellophane of a brand new box, he was fully cloaked for safe sex.

Lolling over each other in post-coital languor, Petra propped herself up on one arm, her already flushed face now squashed too.

'You're very good at it,' she told him. 'At sex.'

'Thank you. I usually charge by the hour but it's two for the price of one on Sundays.'

He flipped her onto her back, propped himself up, squashing his own features. 'You're not too bad yourself.'

'So I've been told, many a time.'

'Tart.'

'Thank you.'

'Do you mean I'm not your first, Miss Flint?'

They laughed and lay side by side. 'Arlo—you said there hasn't been anyone, since you've been here?'

'Yes?'

'But isn't that ages?'

'Yes, but it's like riding a bike—you don't forget how to do it.'

'But you're a hot-blooded male.'

'Yes, but you can choose not to put the heating on.'

'Proverbial cold showers? But for *years*?'

'I made a conscious decision, Petra. Call it cclibacy, whatever—but without the martyrish sense of abstinence. It's been no big deal.'

'Year in, year out?'

'It wasn't difficult. It's like flicking a switch. Until it became a habit, just part of me.'

'But why?'

He fell very silent. Petra brought her face in

274

front of his, gave him a searching little look, kissed his cheek. 'Why?'

'I couldn't be doing with women, Petra.'

'Post-Helen?'

'If you like.'

'Tell me?'

'No—it's in the past.'

Tell me tell me!

'But then I came along?'

'You did, Petra. You came, out of the blue, and turned my life right around.'

And Petra Flint was happy with that and she drifted off to sleep feeling less curious now, and more than a little proud of herself.

*       *       *

In the early hours, as Arlo lay wide awake, he knew why he hadn't told Petra about Helen but he wondered why he hadn't told her about Miranda. He wouldn't be telling her more about Helen—he felt totally justified on that count. Nothing to be gained there, no point. But he didn't know why he'd shied away from telling her about Miranda. Moreover, why had he laboured the point of having been celibate instead? It would have been easier if he had been honest from the start. Recently, I shagged a colleague a couple of times—when I thought you weren't going to show. After all, Arlo didn't like to lie. Telling Nige that Petra was an old friend wasn't a lie. It wasn't even untrue—it just wasn't the whole truth. But why hadn't he qualified her status to Nige? Was it solely to avoid gossip—and was this only for Miranda's sake? Or was it that he himself needed to acclimatize to his change in personal circumstance?

However, telling Petra that he hadn't slept with anyone for years had been an outright lie. His mother had always said you're more likely to get into far deeper trouble if you don't tell the truth. That little adage had got him through life very well. Tonight, though, sleepless and confused, it seemed easier said than done.

Sleep. Why can't I bloody *sleep*.

\*      \*      \*

Bugger it. It would be half-term soon enough, summer holidays not long after. And then Miranda would leave, after which he'd issue a public announcement about Petra and then everyone could know and everything would be fine. Arlo thought he'd probably just try to avoid telling further lies until then, rather than making a point to confess the truth.

He was just drifting off to sleep when Petra flung back the sheets and sat up.

'Sod it, I forgot about that, didn't I?'

'Forgot about what?'

She didn't answer.

Arlo touched her back. 'Petra? You OK?'

But she slipped from the covers without responding. She walked right around the bed to the window and put her shoes on the sill, toe to toe. Then she turned and appeared to look straight at Arlo.

'Petra?'

She mumbled something.

'Pardon?' He put on the light. She was now

276

crashing around in the cupboard. 'Petra!' He slipped out of bed and went to her side. Gently he touched her elbow, her cheek. Called her name again. Nothing. She left the bedroom wearing a coat and he followed a few steps behind, slightly unnerved, a little intrigued, not sure whether to wake her or just watch. She went through to the kitchen, put out all the mugs in a long line and added a large, long squirt of washing-up liquid in their general direction.

'I'd rather have sugar than Fairy,' Arlo said, but still she didn't react. She took the small cyclamen from the kitchen sill and put it in the fridge. 'I agree,' said Arlo, 'definitely at their best when chilled.' Still no response. But it was watching her walk hard into the sharp corner of the kitchen worktop which made him really want to intervene. Yet though she winced, the sound was discombobulated and she continued on her shuffle away from the kitchen without a fuss. She stood in the centre of the living room. From behind, it looked to Arlo as though she was regarding something intently. Quietly, he came alongside her. Her expression was vacant, her eyes glazed. Hadn't he read somewhere that if you wake a sleepwalker, they die of shock? Well, perhaps not drop down dead exactly, but isn't it widespread knowledge that you are not meant to wake them?

So he didn't. This wasn't for his amusement, this was about her safety. So he didn't set tests for her by calling her name or asking her questions. He followed her very closely, gently changing her course if she was heading for furniture, for a wall. She went to the bathroom, began to squat nowhere near the toilet so he guided her over and held up the coat for her because she made no attempt to. After that, she stood stock-still in the bathroom for a while, then took the toothpaste and put it in the coat pocket, made a careful tower out of four toilet rolls. With a nudge from Arlo, she walked back to the bedroom, carefully sat on the side of the bed, kicked off imaginary shoes then lay down and returned to sleep. When he was quite sure she was out for the count, he gently took off the coat and hung it up, took the toothpaste from the pocket and put it back in the bathroom, dismantling the loo-roll tower. In the kitchen, he took the cyclamen from the fridge and returned it to the window sill, rinsed out the mugs and put them away. Finally, in the bedroom, he put her shoes back on the floor. But he couldn't do anything about the bruise on her hip from the edge of the worktop. He could only give that a quiet kiss before enveloping her for the rest of the night.

Finally he felt sleepy and appeased. He thought how if he had left the loo rolls and the mugs as she'd arranged them, had he not returned the toothpaste or the shoes, perhaps it would have elicited a revelation, a disclosure of a private side to Petra, intimate details. Didn't he want to know everything about her? Of course he did, passionately. And yet, he'd chosen to safeguard her privacy. He'd actively destroyed all her evidence by returning everything to normal. This wasn't so much to save Petra any humiliation (*I stopped you wetting yourself* is not the thing to say to a brand-new lover) but that, by affording her her own secrets, he could keep hold of a couple of his. Even if not secrets, per se, surely everyone is entitled to have things they'd rather not talk about.

Things you keep to yourself. No harm done. Things which, if left unspoken, don't in any way lessen the love.

## CHAPTER THIRTY-SIX

As Arlo buttered toast and hunted for jam in the staff common room, he had to laugh at himself. Though he had anticipated fending off a barrage of insinuations and merciless probing from Nige, it never came. Nige hadn't even told the others, Hey, I came across Arlo with a fit bird but she's just an old friend. Nor had he taken Arlo to one side to say, Your mate Petra's pretty, isn't she? Nige hadn't asked him a thing, hadn't mentioned it all. And it was now midway through the week. But what caused Arlo to laugh at himself most was that he was strangely put out, rather than relieved. Isn't it written all over my face then? Does it not illuminate me like an aura? Does everyone truly have me written off?

'Nige says hi, by the way,' he told Petra over the phone. And then he wondered why he'd lied to her again, no matter how anodyne it was.

'Say hi back,' said Petra and he cringed.

\*       \*       \*

Petra was having a wonderful week. A fat cheque arrived from Charlton and two of her clients commissioned work direct. With her London rent helped by a friend of Eric's desperate for a place for a week or so, and with Charlton's blessing to

279

stay on in Stokesley for May and June at least, she was able to pay off her tab with her gem merchant and still have a pleasing balance in her bank account. The more she acknowledged her good fortune, the more seemed to come her way; it appeared one wasn't remunerated for simply counting one's blessings, one had to appreciate them sincerely. And Petra certainly did. She had started to feel very, very lucky. And high. Day-to-day life was good enough—but that each day began and ended with lengthy phone calls from Roseberry Hall, each one seminal in some way, had Petra positively floating.

She loved to hear all the anecdotes from Arlo's day at school and he loved to listen to her enthuse about her work and they still loved to regularly marvel at the fact that they had found one another again. It had to be way more than a coincidence, there had to be forces at play! Time and distance couldn't keep us apart! We were meant to be! I feel good—don't you? They also rediscovered forgotten events and people over which to reminisce and neither of them were shy about revealing just how much they were looking forward to the coming weekend and the weekend after that, then half-term. And then more. There was no game-playing, no playing hard to get; there was no point whatsoever in doing that. There was simply affection and hope.

They could have snatched half an hour together, mid-week, if Petra had cycled over to the school, but they were both quite enamoured with the old-fashioned aspect of a courtship.

'It's like having a boyfriend at the fancy boarding school down the road.'

'It's like having a bit of totty in the village.'

'Sod off!'

'I'll phone you first thing tomorrow—sweet dreams, Petra, sleep well.'

Arlo always said, 'Sleep well,' he always asked her how she'd slept. She loved that. She thought him most intuitive.

'You're not a normal bloke, Arlo. Normal blokes don't usually do chatting by phone—they mostly grunt, in my experience.'

'Am I abnormal, then?'

'No. No. Actually—you're lovely, Arlo, really lovely. In my experience.'

'You're not so bad yourself, honeychild.'

*     *     *

At first Kitty, Eric and Gina had kept Petra's bench clean and empty, as if she might walk into the studio at any moment and pick up her tools. But there again, she'd taken her tools with her and though they certainly would not entertain working at her bench, it did quite quickly become a useful extra surface. Initially, Petra had been a daily topic of conversation, talked about if she had been in touch, worried about if she hadn't. But their growing sense of Petra being quite able to look after herself came directly from Yorkshire, from the type and frequency of her contact. Strangely, it was that she phoned and texted less and less that helped them miss her less and less. Now, when she phoned them it was like Lucy phoning her—a friend who lives far away, always a pleasure to hear from them, to catch up and chat. Petra hadn't inundated them with the ins and outs of her first weekend with Arlo—that was for her texts to Hong Kong. But Petra had sent a text to Gina, Eric and Kitty straight after, saying bingo! me happy bunny! ;–) Pxxxx

Hurrah! Gina replied.

Gory details required . . . Eric texted back.

If he hurts u I'll kill him sent Kitty.

Petra loved her mobile phone. Life was good when one could stroll around miles from home with a pocketful of friends.

Fone u 15 mins Lxxx beamed through to Petra's phone when she was in the queue at the Co-op, giving her just enough time to finish her shopping and return home, make a cup of tea, before her phone rang.

'Hong Kong calling,' Lucy said, sounding as though she was around the corner.

'Stokesley answering,' said Petra, feeling as though she might as well be in Hong Kong.

'How are things? How's *the boyf*?'

'Wonderful—it's all wonderful.'

'You have to sneak a photo of him—you said he's a techno-phobe so just point your moby at him and pretend you're looking for a signal or something but take a picture. He won't know. But I need visual evidence. I need it!'

'OK, I'll try. He's lovely, Lucy. He really is. Am I mad for saying that out loud? Will I jinx it if I do?'

'How lovely? Lovely for the moment? Lovely for the time being? Lovely after Rob—though anyone would seem lovely after *that*?'

'I think he may well be lovely in a for ever kind of way,' Petra said quietly. Lucy heard it the first time but pretended she hadn't and made her repeat it.

282

'Petra!' And the way Lucy cooed her name, with such affection and joy, made Petra surge.

'It *is* love,' Petra said, 'and I'm really happy, Luce.' And she told her old friend about holding hands on a three-hour walk, about kissing in a moonlit garden, about candlelight and hot chocolate, about phone calls first and last thing, about sitting by a river while the weir tumbled and the ducks chattered.

'Sex, Petra—you have to tell me that there's been lots of good squelchy sex alongside all this romantic guff.'

Petra paused. 'Not just lots of it, *lashings* of it.'

'Thank Christ for that. And you have to tell me that you don't permanently wax lyrical in purple prose and only make love by candlelight. Is it real? Do you talk and walk and joke and jest and hump and shag?'

'Well—it's early days. But we're certainly on that path. And we spend ages nattering about bollocks. And of course we walk—this is North Yorkshire.'

'Has he introduced you to the headmaster?'

'Don't be daft.'

'His friends?'

'Give him a chance.'

'His mother?'

'Sod off! Anyway, she's down south.'

'Down south! *Down south?* Listen to you, Yorkshire lass!'

'Oh, but I love it here, Luce.'

'That's because it's all a bit of a fairy-tale honeymoon at the moment—you need to do a winter, Petra. You need to see Arlo when he's in a strop, you have to allow yourself to get on his nerves—you need to weather a few down times,

283

even bad times, before you can truly say that.'

'Don't pop my bubble, Lucy.'

'I'm not—honestly, I'm not. I'm so happy for you—I have a really good vibe, too. But I know how you can be easily swept along so it's my duty, as your friend, to be a voice of reason.'

'OK. OK. I hear you. I do.'

'Good. Now tell me everything, and not about the ducks and the moors and the hand-holding—I want the other stuff, girl. The rude bits. In glorious Technicolor. With sound effects.'

'I so want you to meet him.'

'Have a great big wedding then—I'll be your bridesmaid.'

And Lucy thought that her friend would probably take this as a sign to spend the rest of the afternoon daydreaming about such an event. If she knew Petra, she wouldn't be practising her signature with Arlo's surname replacing hers, she'd be in the studio designing her wedding ring. But there again, from what Lucy deduced, maybe it wasn't so far-fetched after all.

Actually, Petra didn't daydream the afternoon away. She didn't practise *Petra Savidge* and she didn't design any ring. Not because she feared she might jinx anything, but because Arlo was simply so real. He really was. He wasn't an idea. She didn't have to dream up scenarios or imagine his personality for him. She felt she knew him pretty well already and, day by day, she was enjoying coming to know him even better.

\*　　　\*　　　\*

Arlo was due to spend the weekend with Petra as

284

soon as his duties were done on Friday evening. Petra worked productively from the crack of dawn so that she could pack up by lunch-time and prepare. Fresh chicken. Veg. Flowers and fancy bubble bath. Nice cheese. Her list was long and she was fairly confident she'd be able to find everything in Stokesley. It was truly T-shirt weather at last, which just served to increase her good mood.

'Hiya!'

Petra was just about to go into the homewares boutique, telling herself that she wouldn't linger, let alone buy anything else, if they didn't have fancy bath oil. She turned at the greeting. At first, she didn't recognize the woman. About her own age, smart in a great suit, killer heels, blonde hair slicked back into a classy chignon.

'Hiya!' the woman approached. 'Imagine jeans and a T-shirt and a pony-tail? But I'm not shaking my hair out—I'll never get it back.'

Petra clicked. It was the girlfriend of Arlo's colleague. Jenn. Last seen, and briefly at that, in the ice-cream queue, in jeans, T-shirt and a pony-tail. 'Hullo.'

'Thought I recognized you—Petra, isn't it?'

'Yes. Great to see you—Jenn. You look fantastic.'

'Thank you—I like to think I scrub up well. Do you work around here, then?'

'I do—in a studio,' said Petra, moving away from the steps of the shop.

'I like the sound of that—are you an artist?'

'A jeweller.'

'Oh my God, I like the sound of that even more—you can be my new best friend! Oh—as long as we're talking proper jewellery and not hippy beads or friendship bracelets?'

'Fine jewellery,' Petra laughed. 'Platinum, gold, silver—precious gems.'

'Oh. My. God.' Jenn clasped her hands to her heart. 'Am I *loving* you.'

Petra laughed. She sensed she was going to like Jenn a lot.

'Did you make this?' and Jenn touched Petra's necklace. Petra nodded. 'It's gorgeous.'

'Thank you. Do you work here, then, too?'

'I do—over there.' Jenn chucked her thumb towards a Georgian townhouse as if she was hitchhiking. A florist on street level, a solicitors occupying the two storeys above, the firm's name in staid gold lettering on the windows. 'Now you're thinking to yourself, Does she arrange flowers or does she press the law?'

'I am,' Petra laughed, 'but I think I can guess by how soil-free your manicure is.'

'Yeah, I'm the florist,' Jenn said, then she grinned, 'or I would be if I could tell a lily from a lisianthus. I'm a boring old lawyer, I'm afraid.'

Petra regarded Jenn, thought for a split second before she spoke. 'Are you just popping out—I mean—if you are, shall we get a quick coffee? You know—if you've time. If not, another day, perhaps?'

'Bugger coffee, love,' Jenn laughed, 'I'm off for my dinner—come and join me.'

Petra forgot about fancy bubble bath and her shopping list in general and eagerly joined Jenn at the Deli where soon enough they dared each other to say yes to sharing a bottle of wine.

'I shouldn't, I have clients this afternoon.'

'I shouldn't—I have a hot date this evening.'

'Do you now! The chappy Nige and I saw you with?'

'Yes,' Petra said, 'Arlo.'

'These poncey teachers,' Jenn rolled her eyes. 'Arlo! Nigel! Mind you, it's nothing compared to the kids' names—poor sods. Troy! Lars! What happened to Tom Brown's schooldays? I knew you and he were an item. I knew it! You were both radiating that first flush. But Nige wouldn't have it—he said you were just old friends because that's what Arlo had said.'

'Well, we are old friends too,' Petra said, more to defend Arlo than Nigel.

'And new lovers?' Jenn came in close, filled up their glasses, gave Petra a conspiratorial wink. She reminded Petra a little of Lucy in her larkiness, her ability to chatter nineteen to the dozen yet be keen to listen, a boisterousness underscored with warmth.

'Yes,' Petra said, 'we are.'

'Tremendous. Here's to you—to a night of passion tonight and to a long and healthy happy-ever-after. Cheers.'

'Cheers, and here's to you—and to Nige obeying the law.'

Jenn giggled and soon set Petra off. They sat together for a decadently long lunch (according to Petra) or dinner (according to Jenn). Telling each other all about themselves in between sips of wine, revealing all sorts of secrets in between mouthfuls, discovering various similarities and shared empathies while helping themselves to forkfuls from each other's plates.

'Shit. I'm pissed. What will Arlo think?'

287

'Don't give him the chance to think, love—if I were you I'd lay myself out on the couch wearing nothing but a feather boa.'

'Where on earth am I going to find a feather boa on a Friday afternoon?' Petra said, quite liking Jenn's idea.

'I bet Boyes will have one. For about a quid,' said Jenn, eager to help.

Ten minutes later, the two of them were giggling their way across the street and browsing the old-fashioned store. They didn't find a feather boa, but by the time they said goodbye to each other, with a kiss on the cheek and the swapping of mobile numbers, they'd each found a new friend.

## CHAPTER THIRTY-SEVEN

Telling Petra about Miranda had been uppermost on Arlo's mind. Because he'd reasoned that if he told her, if he admitted to something that, in the grand scheme of things, was just a piffling matter anyway, then he would feel exonerated for not telling her about the other. About Helen.

But when he arrived and found Petra gloriously woozy, naked on the sofa apart from a stripy woollen scarf strategically draped, he swiftly forgot all about confessions and serious stuff. And as they lay in each other's arms, Petra rabbiting on about her lunch with Nige's Jenn, Arlo considered that Petra was so vividly his here-and-now, that to hark back to something of so little consequence to him personally or to them as a couple seemed really quite ridiculous. Storms in teacups over mountains

288

and molehills sprang to mind. Much Ado About Nothing. He thought, I'll bet Miranda hasn't given any of it a second thought anyway. Modern girl that she is; sex for the sake of sex. He doubted whether she'd spent a single moment deliberating the finer points of morality in the modern age before she'd taken her hand to his flies.

It would be best all round when she left, though.

And he'd be asking Nigel to keep schtum for the time being, happy as he was for Petra to have befriended Jenn.

He did ask himself in a faint voice whether the fact that he had now chosen not to discuss Miranda thus meant he really ought to at least mention Helen.

But then Petra's voice pulled him from his darkened past into his glowing present.

'Come on, Big Boy—this sofa is a bit prickly, let's go to bed.'

*       *       *

Soon enough, half-term came around and with it the opportunity to spend normal time together, away from the confines of school timetables, the chance for Arlo to play host, the chance for Petra to dip into his world albeit a quieter, unpopulated version. He'd held off specifying which day she should come until he'd ascertained when most of the staff, Miranda included, were leaving. Saturday evening, it seemed. So Sunday morning would be perfect.

And it was.

A misty dawn, at the crack of which Arlo had started spring cleaning his folly, soon lifted to present a day sparkling with the true arrival of summer. A cloudless sky, the land verdant and lush, the sound of summer all around: buds bursting into flower, the hum and drone of busy insects, an arpeggio of birdsong. It was as if active preparations were afoot in nature with which to welcome the tourists during the next couple of months.

Petra no longer felt like a tourist and her hope was to be classed an honorary local. But as she cycled up the drive to Roseberry Hall she wasn't sure quite how to introduce herself to the disembodied voice coming through the intercom. Visitor? Guest? Friend? Old friend? Girlfriend?

'Oh. Hi. I've an arrangement with Arlo Savidge?'

This was good enough for the voice in the intercom; the gates swung open and Petra cycled on, a little more slowly. Was she to report to reception? Present herself to the headmaster? Where would she find Arlo? Look straight ahead, Petra. Over there. See, he's waving at you like a madman.

'I've signed you in,' he said, taking her bike and pushing it, his other arm relaxed around her shoulder, 'and it'll be me who signs you out— whenever I decide that shall be.'

'Detention again, sir?'

'Detained at my pleasure, Flint.'

The lawns undulated in deep green velvet wafts, rolling towards the brighter hued playing fields which plotted and pieced the land until the distant moors claimed it back. With the sunlight eliciting the cream in the stone at the expense of the grey, the fine buildings sat stately and sedate while a network of pathways snaked circumfluous routes this way and that.

'God, it's spectacular. You are a lucky bunch. We can pretend we have some huge private estate to ourselves.' Petra stopped and took it all in.

'Not quite to ourselves,' said Arlo. 'A few odds and sods will be lingering, a few odd sods lurking.'

'A strange humpback guarding the tower? Quasimodo ringing the bells?'

'No—that'll be the Walley Brothers.'

'The Who?'

'I can't explain.'

'I can see for miles,' Petra said, standing still and gazing about her.

'Come on—this is me. This is my folly.'

'Folly. Walley,' Petra said, more to herself than to Arlo. 'I'm going to love it here.'

Arlo let Petra enter first. He sat, quietly following her round with his eyes. It was something of a novelty; having a house guest, being a host. Having a girlfriend at all, really. Nothing too weird about any of it. Just new. Nice, actually.

Petra's circumnavigation of Arlo's abode was methodical and slow. She ran her fingers lightly along the furniture, the door frames, the spines of his books; glanced in the mirror and then changed her focus to give him a quick, shy smile. She looked up and she looked down, she looked into corners and crannies. She lingered in front of his record collection, vinyl and CD, slightly in awe, a little intimidated. Haven't heard of half of these—do I say I actually quite like Robbie Williams or is that naff?

She touched a string of Arlo's guitar, wondering if he'd play for her again. She was charmed by the tiny, well-appointed kitchenette and was pleased by the bedroom, surprised that the bathroom was sparkling, that the loo seat was down. Time will tell, she thought to herself, whether this is in my honour or indeed another string to this man's bow.

'Small, but perfectly formed,' Arlo said suddenly, too shy to say, And the same can be said about you.

'It's very nice,' said Petra. An understatement—she thought there was something sublime about the place. 'You have some interesting stuff.'

'Choose some music,' Arlo invited her.

'No, no,' she said, a little flustered, 'you choose.'

'Bob Seger? Steve Earle?'

She shrugged—hoping it looked like nonchalance rather than ignorance. He chose. She wasn't quite sure whom but she intended to find out because the music was amazing. Arlo came over to her, cupped her face in his hands. He was so pleased that she was here, in his place, filling his space, at his invitation. He kissed her. 'I don't know whether to take you to bed right now or give you the guided tour of the school or just get going and go out. It's a beautiful day. It's your call.'

Petra pretended to deliberate. 'We could have a quickie and then make tracks?'

Arlo laughed. 'Saucy minx.'

Petra feigned to look put out but couldn't maintain it. She watched Arlo's face change as he started to kiss her, to caress her. She put her hands flat against his chest and gave him a little shove. 'On second thoughts, there's plenty of time for indoor sport. But as you say—look at this glorious day.'

'You can't leave me in this—' he paused and

glanced down at the protuberance holding aloft the crotch of his trousers, '—at this angle.'

'I'm not leaving you,' Petra said, 'I'm just putting you on pause for a couple of hours.'

He shrugged. He'd kind of just done the same thing to Bob Seger.

\*      \*      \*

'We have wheels,' he told her as they strolled out, his hands in his pockets, her arm linked through his.

'Of course we have wheels,' Petra laughed. 'My bike is now like an extra limb.'

'Two wheels good, four wheels better,' he said and he led the way along the path towards the main buildings of the school. 'Stay here a mo'.' He went in, came out swinging a set of keys. 'Your carriage awaits.'

'La di da,' Petra said.

Then she burst out laughing.

'It's a minibus!' Petra exclaimed.

'It's a spanking new Mercedes-Benz Sprinter,' Arlo objected after a surreptitious glance to see what it actually was.

'It's still a minibus.'

'Get in, woman,' Arlo said in a tone of voice that implied if she didn't behave, he'd send her to sit at the back on her own.

\*      \*      \*

Nustled between two soaring cliffs, at the foot of a demanding hill with a broad sweeping horseshoe bay looking out easterly across the North Sea, the

293

old and tiny fishing village of Runswick Bay was postcard perfect whatever the weather but on a sunny day it was truly idyllic. Petra loved it in an instant. The vertiginous approach, the meandering narrow streets, the magnificent setting, the poetic divergence in scale between nature and man. Like barnacles clasped to the side of a whale, Runswick's brave little fisherman cottages with their rosy red roofs appeared to cling on determined, while the land dropped in a fast twist down to the sea. The thatched coastguard's building, the lifeboat station with its causeway, the tiny chapel, all standing proud and brave—like little beacons of faith for the men of yore who had taken their chances with the ominous grey swell of the North Sea.

She turned to Arlo, her eyes sparkling.

'I want to live here!'

'You'd need to see it with a bit of winter first,' he laughed and he took her hand and led her to the beach.

'But I'd *love* to see it all stormy and bleak—thundering waves roaring up at the cliffs! Spume smarting the buildings! Lightning spearing the sea! Cliffs crowned with snow! Me—a tiny speck in the midst of it all!'

'You're a shameless romantic, aren't you?' Arlo said, picking up a small clay rock and bashing it down to split it. Trying another. And another. 'Look—fossils,' he said finally. 'Only don't ask me what of.'

'I know I am,' Petra said quietly.

'Sorry?' Arlo was busy with his palaeontology.

'A romantic.' Petra shrugged and smiled, feeling strangely emboldened by her surroundings.

'Absolutely.' In the face of such natural beauty, what in the world was there not to be honest about? Arlo looked at her quizzically; a rock in each hand as if he was balancing some great metaphysical equation. 'I *am* a romantic,' Petra reiterated. She turned to the sea. 'It's got me into trouble in the past,' she said over her shoulder, 'but I wouldn't be any other way.'

Arlo came to stand alongside her, put down his fossils so he could slip his arm around her waist. 'And did you want to be a princess when you grew up?'

'Not exactly,' Petra said, happy to be teased, 'though hoping for a handsome prince has certainly thrown a slimy toad or two my way, but that's not to say it's damaged my belief in happy-ever-after. It would be plain silly not to believe in happy-ever-after.'

Arlo looked out to sea as he considered what she'd said. Kissed her gently on the cheek. 'It's one of the qualities I love most about you.' He stopped; she was all eyes, all ears, even the curls of her hair which had spun loose from her pony-tail seemed to bounce with expectation. His smile was broad. 'And yes, Petra, I did just say that I love you.'

She was grinning and then frowned and fidgeted. 'But now you'll think I'm just being polite if I say that I love you too.'

Arlo shrugged.

'Fuck shit bollock wank,' she laughed and stuck two fingers at him. 'I love you, Arlo Savidge.'

'She's *certainly* not being polite—so she really must love me,' Arlo proclaimed to a dog who had bounded up to sniff around his legs before belting off again. Arlo took her hand and they walked to

295

the seashore. 'Blimey—aren't we getting deep and meaningful,' he said rather brightly.

'Deep and meaningful is good,' she said at length.

Arlo nudged her, then slipped his arm through hers. 'I know it is.'

'And actually, I'm quite proud of myself,' she told him, 'because you know, I grew up amidst all that crap and unpleasantness where love had been lost—but it never made me cynical and I emerged relatively unscathed.'

'Odd, isn't it—my folks set an example I've aspired to follow. Yours set one which has made you crave the polar opposite but we're both on the same track,' he said carefully. 'It's strange, Petra. But we're peas in a pod, really, you and I. From two very different sources.'

'Non-identical twins.'

Arlo laughed. 'Not quite sure about the incestuous connotations there.'

Petra laughed. 'Me neither.' Then she paused. 'Are you like me in feeling that cruel blows from past love don't dent your belief in future love?' Helen Helen Helen won't you *please* tell me a little more about Helen?

'Mostly,' he said and then he kissed her so tenderly that the ambiguity of his answer, the tinge of hesitancy in his voice, were swiftly swept out to sea.

*'Rivers flow into the sea*
*yet even the sea's not so full of me,'*

Arlo sang.
Petra looked at him. 'I love your voice.'

*'There's a hole in my heart
that can only be filled by you.'*

'I love you,' she said, walking on, winking gratefully at the sea as if it had empowered her to reveal her feelings.

Arlo stood for a moment, looking far out to the horizon.

*'And this hole in my heart
Can't be filled with the things I do.'*

For a moment, he couldn't see a thing.

*       *       *

Bed-time loomed. And the closer it came, the more of an issue it became for Petra. She knew from humiliating experience how her sleepwalking was often at its worst when she stayed in a new place. While Arlo washed up coffee cups, she slipped away to the bedroom and assessed it carefully. She lay on the bed, flung out her arm to see where it reached. Nothing. It would be better if there was something. Something to clonk against or tumble over or to trip her up and wake her. Next, she counted the steps from the bed to the window, to the wall, to the door; she gauged what furniture jutted out, whether there were any rucks in the carpet. As quietly as she could, she closed the door. She wanted to see how easily it opened and, as she closed her fingers around the handle, she prayed it would be tricky—surely the door of a folly would be a little warped, stick in the frame, need a lot of pulling at some idiosyncratic angle. It opened soundlessly, however, and with ease. She closed it again, turning the handle slowly and fully until she heard an encouraging click, then she pushed her weight against the door to ensure it was shut tight. She went back to the bed and walked over again, put her hand around the knob. She didn't even know how much force she exerted when sleepwalking, or whether twisting a handle this way and that came instinctively. She'd had no trouble pushing aside a sturdy old armchair she'd wedged up against the door at Eric's parents' house even though she'd loaded it with the *Encyclopaedia Britannica*. She'd then gone into his brother's room and got into bed. With him in it.

But there was no armchair in Arlo's bedroom. Nor were there any sturdy books. Just LPs, thousands of LPs stacked together like a long, rectangular caterpillar. Petra tried the door. Again, it opened easily. She closed it again. Took off her shoes, placed them in the path she thought she might walk. This time she closed her eyes, hoping to best emulate the way she walked when asleep. Shoe. Ouch, corner of bed. Shoe. Where is the door? Where is the sodding door? She opened her eyes. The door was open and Arlo was standing there, staring at her.

'What are you doing?'

Petra was mortified. 'Oh! Nothing. Nothing. I'm just—tired. I kicked off my shoes and practically fell asleep on your bed in an instant! So I was coming to say I'm going to bed. I can hardly keep my eyes open! Actually, maybe I have something in my eyes—perhaps that's why they feel so tired.'

From the way Arlo was looking at her, it was obvious that either he didn't believe her, or else he thought she was nuts. But she just didn't want to tell him about it. Her sleepwalking had irritated Rob supremely, frustrated her parents, amused her friends. No one really took it seriously, that was for sure. Petra just didn't want Arlo to know. At least not yet. Not when love had so recently taken wing, as fragile in its newness as a butterfly just unfurled from its chrysalis. On a deeper level, Petra felt embarrassed: she didn't know why she sleepwalked and she had no idea how to stop it. Nobody did. All she wanted was a good night's sleep in Arlo's arms; night after night safe in bed with him. Surely the more of those she had, then the bad spell would be broken at last? Just then she thought she was going about it the best way she could.

'I'm just tired. Just about to put my shoes away.'

'Oh,' he said, still looking puzzled. 'OK, well, I'll join you in a minute or two.'

'OK!' she said with an oversized grin, giving him a quick, unnecessary thumbs-up which she regretted instantly. Stop it! Act normal. It's Arlo. It's Arlo. It's love. Don't worry.

*     *     *

But of course she walked. Arlo was still awake—as was so often his wont in the small hours—when Petra sat up quickly and left the bed. She banged into the corner of it, made her odd, stilted passage to the door regardless, opened it easily, went through to the sitting room. Arlo followed her. She was standing very still. He walked right in front of her.

'Earth to Planet Petra,' he said, with a little wave in front of her eyes. She pushed his arm down with surprising force and shuffled a few steps forward. He stayed in front of her. 'Arlo to Petra,' he said gently, 'come back to bed, sweetheart.' As gently as he could, he turned her shoulders, letting her do the walking while he did the guiding. Back to bed. Snuggled up close. Holding her against him. Don't go. Don't leave. Stay.

'Where is it that you go, Petra?'

She said something. In a flat monotone mumble.

'I go looking,' he thought she said.


## CHAPTER THIRTY-EIGHT

'How did you sleep?' Arlo asked casually from a muffle of pillow, waking at the scent of breakfast in bed which Petra had just brought in. Hot buttered toast. Sod the crumbs.

'Oh fine, fine,' Petra said. 'You?'

'Terrible.' He noted that she looked momentarily panicked.

'Why? Oh God, do I snore?'

'No,' he laughed. 'It's just I don't sleep very well. Haven't done so for a few years. A sort of insomnia, I suppose. No matter how tired I am, I lie awake and stare at the ceiling. Sometimes for hours.'

'Perhaps you should paint sheep on your ceiling to count?'

'Believe me, I've thought of that.'

'Things on your mind?'

'Not really—that's the problem. If there were things on my mind I could try and work through them. But I just lie there, not sleeping, with

300

adrenalin caught at the base of my throat—sometimes my heart races. Do you remember that feeling when you had an exam the next morning? That mixture of doom and excitement? Anticipation and dread? It's like that.'

'Arlo, that's terrible. You know, I read somewhere that if you're lying in bed and you can't sleep, then you should leave the room.' Petra leant over and took a sizeable bite of Arlo's toast, having finished two slices of her own. 'You should only associate the bedroom with being a sanctuary of sleep. If you're not getting any—then go to another room for a while. If it's really bad, perhaps consider a course of cognitive behavioural therapy—it's meant to be brilliant for insomniacs.'

'I'll take your advice,' Arlo said, though he was tempted to say, You're a fine one to talk, just to see how she'd react. However, he'd sensed that, wherever it was she went while she slept, it was private territory and if he barged in just now, he'd be trespassing.

*       *       *

They went to Whitby that morning, by minibus again. Petra was transfixed by the ruined Abbey. Then as they meandered through the town, Arlo had her in stitches with lurid tales of Dracula, pulling her into doorways here and there to kiss her dramatically along her neck. As they browsed the jet and marvelled at the goths, she told him all about Kitty and how much she'd love Whitby. Why don't you invite her up for a weekend, Arlo suggested. I might just do that, Petra mused. On their journey home, they interviewed each other

301

for their Desert Island Discs. Arlo just about allowed her to take Robbie Williams. And Petra let Arlo take Marcy Playground, wherever that was or whoever they were. Petra chose *Jane Eyre* as her book ('I'd never have guessed—I had you down as a sci-fi girl,' Arlo said drily, laughing when she bashed him) and her tools as her luxury, having first ascertained that her island would be replete with natural reserves of precious metals and gemstones. Arlo chose a razor as his luxury, not that he minded growing a beard (he'd had some success with a goatee in his twenties) but because he confided to Petra that he was relatively obsessed with keeping his hair closely cropped. 'You vain poof,' Petra laughed but she affectionately stroked his head all the same.

*　　　*　　　*

The first Arlo knew about it was the scream. A desperate scream of glass-shattering purity. It jerked him out of his sleep with the force of an electric shock and he sat bolt upright, noticed in a glance that Petra was missing, and knew instinctively it was she who had screamed. But now there was only silence. It was eerily quiet as if the scream had come out of the night and had been instantly swallowed up by it. It was now so quiet that momentarily Arlo wondered if he'd imagined the sound. Sometimes, he dreamed musically—the images and emotions described to his subconscious in bizarre terms of notes and rhythm that always made sense at the time and that sometimes he jotted down on awaking. But Petra was gone from his bed and it was she who had screamed and as

302

Arlo scrambled into his clothes, he called her name. She was not in the bathroom. Nor was she in the sitting area. She wasn't in the kitchen. No sign of her at all, no evidence of her having even been there, apart from the ominously open door. 3.02 a.m. He cursed himself for having actually been asleep.

'Petra?'

\*     \*     \*

Arlo shuddered. In the thin air of the small hours, the trees loomed a little menacingly, ominous silhouettes clawing at the night sky. The silence was thick and oppressive but Arlo didn't dare break it with audible footfalls, for fear of damping out any further sound from Petra. He tiptoed across the path to the safer surface of the grass. Called her name, over and again.

\*     \*     \*

Nothing. Arlo shivered. It was surprisingly brisk. Though the paths were lit well enough for errant schoolboys to be caught sneaking out for a crafty fag after lights-out, they were not lit well enough for somnambulant females to be found.

'Is anyone there?'

There was a rustling. During numerous insomniac sorties of his own, Arlo had become well acquainted with the wealth of wildlife which claimed the school grounds as their own at night. But right now he didn't care for badgers and owls, he just wanted to see Petra.

'Petra. Petra Flint?'

303

'Arlo?'

It was her. Somewhere. Her voice, thin and desperate and fogged by tears.

'She's here.'

Who the fuck is that? A male voice. That direction.

'Where's *here*?' Arlo called out.

'Here.'

No, this direction.

He ran, calling her name, calling hullo, calling that he was coming. Petra, I'm coming.

*     *     *

There she is. Sweet Jesus. Buck naked. Arms closed defensively around her body. Head downcast with shame. Knees buckling a little with fear. Or with cold. She is flanked by two men. There's a Walley Brother on each side. Christ, thinks Arlo, foxes would be better than them.

'She yours, then?' asks one Walley with a leer at Petra, a sneer at Arlo.

'Yes,' Arlo says, striding up close while pulling his top over his head, drawing Petra close against him, wrapping his sweatshirt around as much as he can. 'She's mine.' He kisses her head gently, holds her body very tightly, whispers, 'You're fine, Petra, you're fine.'

'We found her,' Walley Two is saying, 'asleep in the grass. We didn't know what she was at first, did we? Walk around like that often, does she? In her birthday suit? All hours?'

304

Petra buries her face deeper in Arlo's chest.

'Had to prod her to wake her.'

'Couldn't wake her. Had to turn her over to see if she was dead.'

'Wasn't. Could see her breathing.'

'Could see a bit too much. You never heard of a nightgown, miss?'

'Pyjamas, miss?'

'Lucky it was us, really. You ought to count your lucky stars. Don't want the boys coming across this. A sight for their sore little eyes.'

'Their sordid little eyes and filthy little minds.'

'Thank you, Mr Walley, thank you, Mr Walley,' Arlo says. 'I'm grateful you were around. We both are. She's fine. You're fine, Petra. Everything is OK. You can leave her with me. You can leave—now.' Arlo knows you have to spell things out for the Walley Brothers. They may claim to be simple folk but they're sly enough to twist what they find and scatter seeds of malevolence across the school grounds. Like when Head of Maths Mrs Goode's son turned up from Cambridge University halfway through term. Kicked out, came the word from the Walleys. Glandular fever was the truth. And when Mr Henderson crashed his car. Drunk as a skunk, said the Walleys. Minor stroke, said the hospital. And when Simeon de Vries failed every GCSE the Walleys rolled it out that it was down to the kid smoking too much wacky baccy. Not so, said the doctor, diagnosing ME soon after.

'She was asleep,' Arlo tells them clearly. 'She doesn't know she does it. She sleepwalks. She cannot help it.' He feels Petra pull back a little, he can sense her staring at him, then he feels her think better of it as she sinks back into the safety of

305

his arms. 'It's an affliction,' he says. 'It's a serious condition and it is not, I repeat *not*, gossip.'

The Walleys look a little put out. You don't want to get on the wrong side of them. Creepy and in the background they might be, but you don't want to give them voice.

'I can't thank you enough,' Arlo suddenly says. 'Thank you so much—both of you. No—really. Thank God it was *you* who found her. Poor Petra. *We're* so pleased it was you, Mr and Mr Walley. Can you imagine if it was someone else? Someone who didn't understand these things—someone who isn't as discreet as you two, nor as wise? We are *so* grateful.' Arlo is making a mental note to buy them a bottle of whisky, each, the very next day.

'Well, all right then,' says Walley One, a bit miffed to be praised rather than insulted.

'As you say, good job it was us,' growls Walley Two.

'Lock your door,' Walley One says as he mooches off into the dark.

'Keep the girl dressed,' says Walley Two as he follows his brother into the murkiness of their night.

Petra is shaking. Arlo eases his sweatshirt onto her properly. 'Come on, you,' he says. 'Cup of tea. Let's get you back inside. Let's get you warmed up. I have chocolate too. Come on, Petra, chocolate tastes especially good in the middle of the night. I should know.'

\*       \*       \*

She sips. Arlo has added lots of sugar, muttering something about sweet tea being good for shock.

He has placed small chunks of milk chocolate on her knees which he replenishes each time she eats one, breaking them off from a very large slab. If she talks, she talks, he quietly decides, sipping a mug of highly sweetened tea himself.

'Thank you,' Petra says and she looks sheepish. 'I'm so sorry.'

'That's OK—but are you OK?'

She shrugs. 'I'm—appalled.' She casts her eyes downward. Her feet are dirty. She tries to tuck them in to each other. 'It's toe-curlingly embarrassing,' she says. Literally—she and Arlo both think.

'You sleepwalk,' Arlo says and it is not a question.

She darts her gaze up at him, and then away. 'Well—sometimes.'

'More than sometimes. I've watched you—you do it at the Stables, you do it here. You build towers out of loo rolls. You put houseplants in the fridge. You put shoes on the window sill. You bash into things yet you don't wake up.'

Petra buries her face in her hands.

'You go walkabout, starkers, through the grounds of one of the UK's leading public boys' schools.' Arlo says it so sensitively that he almost manages to raise the corners of Petra's mouth. But her shoulders droop and she looks absolutely defeated by it all. 'It must be bloody awful for you, Petra. Christ, it must be a strain.' And he really, truly means it. Petra can hear his utter commiseration in the timbre of his voice.

'It is,' she nods. No eye contact, as yet. 'I didn't know you knew.'

'I do know.'

'You didn't say?'

'I didn't think you'd want me to see.'

'I don't.'

They sit in silence. They eat more chocolate because it gives them something nice to share, something to do other than talk.

'Have you always done it? The sleepwalking? Is there anything you can do? That I can do? That can be done for you?' Arlo puts his mug down and walks to the kitchen. Comes back with the washing-up bowl full of warm water, brimming with soap suds. He kneels down, places her feet in the bowl, a towel across his lap. He can look up at her downcast face, catch her eyes, at this angle. He holds her gaze for a moment. Then, gently, he bathes her feet. Each toe in turn. This little piggy went to market, he says. This little piggy stayed home. This little piggy went sleepwalking squeak squeak squeak out into the big unknown. A teardrop falls to Petra's knee. Arlo puts his finger over it, as if it's an ant that is to go no further. 'Don't cry,' he tells her. 'You're safe with me.' He sits beside her, draws her feet onto his lap and rubs them tenderly, turbans a towel around them.

'I started when I was about eight,' she tells him. 'I've sleepwalked ever since. In some periods of my life more often than in others. I went deaf in one ear for five weeks when I fell down some stairs. I've found myself nakcd, locked out on the fire escape of a country hotel at my friend's wedding. I have wet myself countless times. I peed on a pile of toys belonging to a friend's kid sister. On my ex's armchair. I've walked right out of my flat and been picked up by the police. Clothed, thank Christ. I've had black eyes, grazed knees, bruised shins, sprained wrists, swollen jaw, split lip.' She pauses. She toys with a piece of chocolate until Arlo picks it up and places it in her mouth. 'I hate going to bed because I never know where sleep will take me.'

'Can't anything be done?' he asks. 'Can't anyone help?'

'I went for trials at the world-famous sleep centre at Loughborough University,' Petra says, 'and for more tests at the renowned sleep clinic in Harley Street. They monitored me, night after night. They glued electrodes onto my scalp, onto my body—a polysomnogram which monitors brainwave activity, heartbeat, breathing. There was a CCTV which showed me ripping the pads off—and I was really tugging hard. I had little bald patches after that.'

'I don't have the excuse of electrodes,' Arlo teases gently and Petra smiles.

'I've tried sedatives—Valium and Xanax—but they made me feel dreadful, drugged almost. I've tried internal alarms and buzzers on my doors and motion sensors in the room—but I never wake up.' She shrugs. 'Just one of those things, I suppose.' She pauses.

'Have you tried going to bed early?'

'Doesn't help.'

'Staying up very late?'

'Makes no difference.'

'Therapy?' Arlo asks. 'Might it not be linked to some childhood trauma?'

'But I was only eight years old—what does an eight-year-old have to worry about?'

'Your parents?'

'They were fine then. They didn't split up until I

was fourteen.'

'Sorry—I didn't mean to—'

'No one understands,' she says. 'My mum used to get quite cross. My ex would get so impatient with me—as if I did it on purpose. And then he'd use the details for dinner-party conversation. My friends tease me mercilessly. As if I do it for their entertainment. For God's sake, would I truly choose to humiliate myself to this extent? Eric has always been very caring, Kitty and Gina worry for me—Lucy too—but no one can really help because I can't help it.'

'But Petra, why do *you* think you do it?'

Petra thinks long and hard but her expression says she's nowhere near an answer.

'Do you fear dreams? Nightmares? Are you afraid of the dark? Of silence?'

She shrugs. 'I don't think so. My dreams are mostly very boring—usually just me returning to my childhood home and walking about. What I'd love most of all is simply to wake from having a really good night's sleep.'

'Me too,' says Arlo and Petra touches his cheek. 'What can I do?' he asks her. 'For you? What can I do to help? There must be something that can be done.'

'No one can do a sodding thing,' Petra says and she's petulant and fed up because she's starting to feel very very tired and more than a little sorry for herself. 'I'll always do it,' she confesses. 'I've resigned myself to the fact. There is no sodding cure.'

'I could put a lock on the bedroom door?'

'I'd go through the window.'

'I could lock that too.'

'I don't want to live in a prison. My dad put a lock on the outside of my bedroom door for a while. I hated it. It terrified me. I couldn't even get to sleep in the first place, knowing it was there. Say I needed to get out? Perhaps I *need* to get out, perhaps that's what it's all about.'

'But you don't want to spend too many nights being ogled by the Walley Brothers.'

'God, tonight was particularly awful,' Petra says. 'One of the worst. To be so out of control. That's what a specialist told me—it's about brain activity. It happens within the first three hours of sleep—the deep, dreamless, slow-wave sleep. It happens when the brain doesn't move from one sleep state to the next—the cortex of the brain, responsible for consciousness, stays asleep, but the area controlling the sensory system and movement is awake. The conscious part may be sparko but the subconscious is up for action. It's called a hyper-arousal state, apparently. I've given up on a cure.'

'Lobotomy!' Arlo says it with relish, he wants to lift her mood, he wants to change the subject; he doesn't like to see her so despondent and dark.

Petra looks at him, very straight before softening. 'Thank you. And I am sorry. And if you get involved with me, you may have sleepless nights.'

'I *am* involved with you and I already *had* sleepless nights anyway. It'll be a nice change, having something other than the cracks in the ceiling to watch.'

'Listen.'

They listen. Birdsong.

'It's dawn.'

Outside the window, the thin light of the new

311

day is slipping through the dark like the tail of smoke from a spent match.

'We could go to bed?'

'It's beautiful.'

'Then let's get dressed, Petra. I know where I'm going to take you.'

'Where?'

'*Everywhere peace, everywhere serenity, and a marvellous freedom from the tumult of the world*—as my friend St Aelred said.'

## CHAPTER THIRTY-NINE

Arlo's friend St Aelred turned out to be the third Abbot of Rievaulx Abbey and it was to these elegiac Gothic ruins that Arlo took Petra. They headed out on the Helmsley Road. Ahead of them Ingleby Bank, Clay Bank, the Wainstoncs and Carlton loomed through the dawn like benevolent mammalian masses. The drive through Bilsdale was stunning in itself, the moors shrouded by the early-morning mist like an ephemeral duvet blanketing the land while regular folk still slept. Because of the lie of the land from this approach, the Abbey was kept secret in a hidden valley. Then, two miles from Helmsley and eighteen miles from Stokesley, Arlo turned off the moor road and suddenly they were driving down a steep and twisting lane until they came to the village of Rievaulx. Like a small flock protected by a mighty, divine shepherd the little rustic cottages on their grassy knolls were positioned at the foot of the magnificent ruins. The Abbey itself stood silent and proud, as if patiently waiting for kindred spirits to share its secrets, its beauty, in the fitting privacy of a time not controlled by English Heritage.

'We'll leave a donation later,' Arlo said, vaulting the wooden five-bar gate. 'I bring the boys here when I do devotional music with them. Helps it all make sense. I've often thought that in its ruined state Rievaulx is probably far more rousing and spiritual than if Henry VIII hadn't sacked it.'

'Sing hey nonny nonny for the dissolution of the monasteries,' Petra laughed and they walked through the grounds in silence. The magnificent run of arches: aisle, gallery, clerestory. Monumental stone, some columns soaring high, some reduced to little more than stumps. Some stone blackened from time, some stone pale and creamy. Petra touched her way around, feeling the lichen and beneath it the stone, hand-hewn. All for the love of God. 'There's a sadness here—don't you think? A haunting beautiful sadness. A poetic melancholy. As if the ravages of war and of time have served only to strip the place back to its very core. Truly a heart of stone.'

They continued to walk, round and through, over and again.

'Look how the landscape is central to the impact of the place, as if the buildings have been absorbed into nature and yet the architecture captures the views, the land—containing it,' Petra marvelled. 'Isn't it amazing how something so solid like these hulking great pillars, these arches spanning God knows how many feet, in the context of the landscape, the air, actually seem so light, delicate almost.'

313

'We'll have to make a trip to Fountains Abbey next,' Arlo said. He paused. 'And Bylands. In fact, why not give up your day job and come and teach architecture at the school?'

Petra reddened. But for a secret moment, she did consider it. She walked on a step or two behind Arlo. Something caught her eye. A lone, late bluebell, growing strong and determined in the shadow of the transept. She fell to her knees so she could see its flowerheads up close. She glanced over to Arlo, but he was preoccupied, craning his neck in the refectory, lost in his own world here.

\*     \*     \*

And suddenly she's back at school and it's double English with her favourite teacher Mrs Balcombe and it's Gerard Manley Hopkins who Petra loves. Then it'll be lunch and Walnut Whips and tales of Africa with Mrs McNeil. Followed by an afternoon at the boys' school for pottery. Perhaps Arlo will be there, shyly serenading her. Perhaps he'll just sit with her, strumming his guitar and humming to himself while she works the cold wet clay through her hands. They'll smile, now and then, without saying all that much.

\*     \*     \*

Back in the dawn of a new day, at Rievaulx Abbey, very much in the here and now, Petra cupped the bluebell flowers in her hands, gazed at them intently—their sentient little faces—and she thought again of Hopkins. *There lives the dearest freshness deep down things.* And in an instant, she

314

knows she won't be teaching architecture at Arlo's school because she loves her day job far too much. And all of a sudden she knows what to do with her tanzanite; what it wants to be. She'd just been afforded a dazzling glimpse of how the finished piece might look. And the process of making it had belted across her mind like a film reel on fast forward.

At this stage, that was all she needed to see; all her best works have germinated just like this. She knows that it is now stored, logged in her creative lobe, to be accessed whenever she wants, analysed frame by frame. She had caught sight of the end result and it's thrilling. Best of all, she knows she has the tools, the trade, the skill. Talent is Petra's greatest gift and she treasures it. The tanzanite was Mrs McNeil's great gift to Petra. And as Petra stood in the grounds of the beautiful Cistercian monastery, knowing just how she can do justice both to the stone and to Mrs McNeil's memory, her heart soared alongside the pillars of Rievaulx.

'Can we go?' she called to Arlo. She was so fired with the desire to work that she forgot all about her total lack of sleep.

*     *     *

By three in the afternoon, Petra was feeling all sketched out. Arlo had worked well alongside her, planning lessons and plundering his music collection for the purpose, listening to drifts and rifts with his headphones on. Every now and then, Petra picked up tinny hints filtering out and she'd think, Oh! I know that song.

She closed her sketchbook and put it face down

on the floor. Arlo was sitting cross-legged, his back to her, his shoulders swaying to whatever it was he was listening to. She padded over to him on her hands and knees. He turned and smiled, patted her head, then ran her pony-tail through his hand as if it was a cat's tail. She laid her head against him, kissed his shoulder. She pressed her ear against the headphone. I know this! I know this! It's Neil Young! It's 'Heart of Gold'! She brought her face in front of Arlo's, her eyes alight, and sang the song at the top of her voice. He laughed, pulled the earphones down around his neck like a DJ. Still she sang and jigged and he gave her a round of applause.

'All-time favourite Neil Young song?' he asked her.

' "Cinnamon Girl",' she replied, not having to think. 'You?'

' "Needle and the Damage Done".'

Arlo yawned. He was starting to feel hazy from lack of sleep. 'God, I haven't felt this way for years,' he said. 'It's like doing coke, when you just do not sleep. Then you feel slightly delirious at precisely this time in the afternoon.' He looked at Petra who was looking slightly aghast.

'Coke?' she asked, rather wide-eyed. 'As in *caine* rather than *a-cola*?'

Arlo laughed. 'Not even sixteen cans of Coca-Cola could keep me going all night. Yes, Petra, the naughty coke.'

'I've never tried it. I'm a bit square,' she told him, looking a bit sheepish.

'I did loads of it. I was a twat in the music business, remember,' he said, looking a bit sheepish too.

Petra yawned.

'Am I boring you?' Arlo teased.

She laughed and shook her head. The whites of her eyes were a little bloodshot, dark circles underneath them, her skin pale. Arlo thought she looked beautiful. 'I'm tired,' she apologized.

'Let's pop out for *ours teas*—as they say round here. Actually, I'm starving—I'll take you to Yarm for a slap-up supper. Then we'll have an early night.'

'Or we could just have hot buttered toast in bed. Sod the crumbs,' Petra said. 'Anyway, I thought teachers were meant to be poor?'

'As a teacher, I am poor,' Arlo said, 'but I also receive those healthy royalties from my music.'

'A most eligible bachelor,' Petra said. Then she blushed and looked away but not before she noticed that Arlo had reddened too.

*       *       *

Later on, home from Yarm, Petra and Arlo found their second wind and, over mugs of tea and a lot of Neil Young, they talked until it was really a quite respectable time to go to bed.

'Are you worried?' Arlo asked her. 'About going walkabout?'

'A bit,' Petra replied, pumping the pillow and pulling the duvet up to her nose.

He turned on his side to look at her. 'You sound worried.'

'It's not just that—I take it as a given that most nights I'm off.' She paused. Plumped the pillow again. Pressed her hand gently against his chest. 'I don't know, Arlo—you know so much about me

317

now. All my naked truths. You've seen me, literally, laid bare.'

'I know you inside out,' Arlo said and to prove his point, his fingers made a rather smug journey up between Petra's legs while he raised an eyebrow cockily.

'Stop it—I'm being serious.' She tried not to laugh, pushed his arm away. 'My sleepwalking. My crappy parents. My disastrous relationship. My weak points.'

'Your sense of humour, your beauty, your sweet sweet nature. Your prodigious talent. Your strength,' Arlo countered, softly. 'Your courage.'

'So why do I feel a little vulnerable?'

'Because you're entrusting me with you at your most private,' Arlo said, 'plus you're also very, very tired.'

'But will you tell me your secrets?' Petra asked. 'Reveal the chinks in your armour?'

'Are you saying I'm your knight in shining armour?'

'Oh, you are my verray, parfit, gentil knight,' Petra said. 'But will you? Tell me? Show me—let me see?'

'Not now,' Arlo said, with a glance at the clock revealing midnight wasn't that far off.

'But some time?' Petra persisted. 'Soon?'

'I don't have secrets,' Arlo said abruptly. 'Not really. Nor do you—just your quirks, just your experiences that make you you.'

'But what's made you *you?*'

'You women—you do pick the oddest moments for heart-to-hearts.'

But what do you mean by *you women*, Arlo? Who specifically? Tell me about who's made you

318

the man that you are.

'There's nothing much to say,' he brushed the concept away. He lifted curlicue slicks of her hair away from her face, placed them over her shoulder to reveal the flow of her neck. 'I'm just like you. I've had my fuck-ups. Learned a few lessons. I'm older and wiser and find myself in love with the girl I was very first in love with.'

Petra decided that she ought to be content with this, for the time being at least, and she kissed him slowly, softly, to tell him so.

'Will you wake?' she asked, just as he was reaching for the bedside lamp. 'If I—you know?'

'I promise—even if I'm asleep.'

*'I have spread my dreams under your feet, tread softly because you tread on my dreams.'* She smiled. 'My all-time favourite poem.'

'Funnily enough I set it to music when I was seventeen or eighteen,' he smiled. 'Sweet dreams, Miss Flint.' He turned off the light, cuddled up close, nuzzled the nape of her neck. 'Beautiful day.'

They spooned for a while. Then they turned to lie on their backs, side by side, shoulders, hips and ankles just touching. Arlo encircled Petra's wrist with his fingers, like a loving handcuff, and she drifted off to a dreamless sleep feeling madly exhausted, happy and secure.

## CHAPTER FORTY

Late the next morning, Arlo was in the shower, singing his teenage soft-rock version of 'He Wishes for the Cloths of Heaven', alternating between gravely bass and surprisingly sweet falsetto. Petra sat up in his bed, her knees under her chin, grinning to herself as she listened to him. If music be the food of love—and all that jazz, she thought to herself. Play on. And on and on.

There was knocking at the folly door. Arlo was belting out his anthemic chorus. 'Tread softly! Tread softly! You tread upon my dreams, oh baby. Oh yeah. Yeah yeah! Don't go treadin' 'pon my dreams, baby.'

So it was up to Petra to tread softly to open the door.

And have Miranda Oates hurl her dreams into a nightmare.

*     *     *

'Who are you?'

'I'm Petra.'

'But who *are* you?'

'Oh! I'm Arlo's girlfriend. Can I help you?'

Petra watched as the woman on the threshold looked momentarily baffled before an expression of utter disdain replaced it. The woman laughed and, for the first time in her life, Petra truly knew what it was like to have someone laugh in her face. It was a sound that felt like being spat at.

'Arlo Savidge has a *girlfriend*?' the woman ridiculed. 'Since when!'

Petra felt affronted, so much so that she added extra time for good measure. 'Three months or so.'

'Well, I'm Miranda Oates,' the woman said, proffering her hand like royalty which Petra automatically took and shook. 'I teach here too.

320

And I've been gamely fucking your so-called boyfriend.'

Petra started silently screaming at herself; a desperate and deafening scramble of instructions: Don't believe her! Don't show you're upset! She's lying! He hasn't! Wake up!

'I don't think so,' Petra said at length.

'*I* rather do,' Miranda countered. '*Girl*friend? Don't you know, Arlo doesn't *do* girlfriends. Fuck-buddies maybe—but not girlfriends. Hasn't he told you? Commitment is a Savidge anathema.'

'No, it's not,' Petra protested. 'Anyway, he's told me he loves me.'

Miranda made much of being unable to suppress a patronizing giggle. 'You're deluding yourself!'

Petra felt panic starting to rise like bile. 'Look, what do you want?'

Miranda sighed breezily. 'Oh, I came back to school early—so I was just calling by on the off chance of a shag.' She looked Petra up and down. 'Busy boy. I didn't think he'd have company. I didn't think I'd have to queue.'

Petra wanted to yell, Fuck off. She had a strong urge to scratch Miranda. But while she dug her nails hard into the palms of her hands she also had a perverse desire to hear more.

Miranda twitched her lips. 'Did he spin out his celibacy yarn? Is that how he got into your pants? Did he make you melt with tales of his broken heart? His self-imposed exile from the joys of the flesh? Years and years of abstinence and then wow! along came you? I wouldn't get too excited about the "love" thing,' Miranda mocked, 'Arlo doesn't believe in love.'

321

'Yes, he *does*,' Petra said. 'He has told me, unprompted, that he is in love with me.'

'Drunk.'

'Sober.'

'And let me guess—you then sucked his cock, you were so delighted.'

Petra found herself silently racking her memory as to whether a blow-job had followed Arlo's declaration.

'Look, just tell him I'm back,' Miranda said, as if she was suddenly bored. Then she gave Petra a patronizing wave with her fingers as if she was taking leave of a child.

Petra closed the door. Beneath the thundering beat of her flailing heart, she could just about hear Arlo still singing his heart out about cloths of heaven. You tread upon my dreams.

You've stamped mine out.

\*          \*          \*

'Hey! Sleepyhead,' he was calling, 'fancy getting all soapy? Come and join me.'

You must be bloody joking, Petra thought as she scrambled into her clothes. Then she left. Cycling fast down the drive, watched by Miranda, unseen. Dog in a manger.

## CHAPTER FORTY-ONE

All Petra wanted to do was run away. As she pedalled for all she was worth back to Stokesley, chanting, Bastard, bastard, bastard, to maintain

322

rhythm and scramble for power, she worked out that she could pack up the Old Stables, blow some money on a taxi to Northallerton and be back at King's Cross by tea-time. Proper tea-time—biscuit-and-cuppa Southern tea-time—not Yorkshire tea-time of having one's sodding supper at six o'sodding clock. Sod Yorkshire. Sod bloody Arlo. Bloody men. They're all the sodding same. What an idiot for thinking that Arlo was any different. For fooling herself that, for the first time, she was truly in love with a very real person and not some ideal she was hoping to create. She'd done it again. Idiot girl.

Fuck-buddy. Do all men have one then?

Celibacy. Not such a bad idea. She might try it.

Savidge. Savage.

*     *     *

Safely inside the Old Stables, Petra tried not to stop to look around or think: immersing herself in packing, tidying and cleaning instead. And she was on her hands and knees, scrubbing the hearth with a bristle brush and scalding hot water, when the doorbell sounded.

Sod off, she said under her breath without looking up.

The knocking continued.

'Sod off.'

'Petra? It's me, it's Arlo.'

I bet it bloody is. 'Sod. *Off.*'

Silence.

Knocking. Slower.

Petra stomped to the door, opened it a fraction and said, Sod off. Closed it. But not before Arlo

323

had pushed his foot through to stop this.

'What on earth is this all about?' He seemed genuinely incredulous. 'I come out of the shower, the place looks like a bomb has hit it and you're nowhere. You'd gone.' He tried to push the door, but Petra pushed back. 'You left your phone. Here. Petra, what's going on?'

She looked at him. That beautiful, handsome face, those eyes, these lips that have kissed her and spoken false promises. Desperate sadness engulfed her.

'Petra?' So softly. That lovely lovely voice. 'What is it? What happened?'

She looked at him, her tear oozing oily and hot. 'Ask your fuck-buddy Miranda what happened.' And, from the sudden pallor hijacking his face, Petra read guilt writ large and she knew unequivocally that he had lied to her. It was irrelevant how much was true, he had lied to her. He needn't say a word, really. As pale as he was, the blood draining from his face, so Petra pledged to herself that he'd pale into insignificance in her life. He let her push the door shut. He let her lock him out.

*     *     *

There was more knocking at the door an hour later, just as Petra was doing her double-checking.

'Oh, will you just fuck off!'

Silence. Then: 'What kind of talk is that, you stroppy cow! I've called by to see if you fancy lunch.'

It was Jenn. Suddenly, the proximity of a hug from a girlfriend was enough to have Petra open

324

the door wide. Jenn took one look at her. 'What's he done? I'll kill him.' She sounded a bit like Kitty, and Petra loved her for it. She told Jenn who pondered the facts.

'The thing is, you're telling me what this Miranda Oates told you,' Jenn said, 'and I have met her—she's a bit of an old slink, if you ask me. But Petra, you're not telling me what Arlo actually *did*—because you've not given him the chance to speak for himself.'

This didn't work for Petra. All the manic cleaning and packing—she didn't want to stand still and think about it all. She had a train to catch, she didn't have the time or the inclination to workshop.

'She's jealous, I'll bet,' Jenn steamed on, 'wants to wind you up. You've got what she wants. *She* wants him—he wants *you*. Hell hath no fury like a woman scorned, and all that. She's probably made half of it up—including the timing.'

Petra shook her head, her face flinching at a reflux of acid scorching her throat.

'There's often an overlap—at our age, in relationships,' Jenn said evenly. She raised her hand. 'I'm guilty—but don't tell Nige. He's probably guilty too, the stud. But I don't want to know—it's enough for me to know that it's me who he wants, who he loves.'

'But that's the point, you *don't* know about any so-called overlap,' Petra stresses, 'and you wouldn't want to, would you? But I can't rewind Miranda's words. I can't erase them from my memory.'

'If it feels like you can't forget—do you think you can forgive?'

'No!'

Jenn was visibly shocked at Petra's vehemence.

'It's happened to me before, remember?' Petra said. 'Once bitten, twice shy.'

'You can't tar Arlo with the same brush,' Jenn said.

'Anyway, I think the lying is actually a far greater crime than the overlap. He *lied*, Jenn. He seduced me with a big fat lie. That's no basis for lasting love. What else has he lied about?'

Jenn looked crestfallen. She glanced around the Old Stables. 'Is that it then? You're all packed up? Back off home with you?'

Petra shrugged. 'I can't see how I can stay.'

'But you love it here—you're always telling me so. Won't you stay anyway? Forget His Nibs, we'll get you a nice Boro Boy—dear God.' Jenn laughed and raised a smile from Petra. Jenn took her hands in hers. 'I'll miss you, pet. You're my friend. My fab new friend.'

'Well, stay in touch.'

'But I love having you close by.'

'I liked being here. It was—wonderful.'

'Can I just say—don't be too rash to use the past tense. Promise me?' Jenn put her hands on Petra's shoulders. 'So go down to London—let it all settle. See the wood for the trees. But if he comes hammering at your door, hammering at your heart, please let him in.'

Petra shrugged. She didn't want to tell Jenn, He doesn't actually know where I live, thank God.

'I'd best be letting you get on, then.'

Petra nodded.

'Can't tempt you to lunch at the Deli—my shout? Drown your sorrows with a bottle of their finest vino?'

Petra shook her head.

'A lift to the station?'

Petra smiled but declined.

'Give us a hug, love,' Jenn said, audibly choked.

*       *       *

All packed up and ready to go. Cab should be here any second.

A knock at the door.

Here it is.

No, it's not. It's Arlo.

'There was a cab waiting,' he says, 'to take a Miss Flint to Northallerton Station. I've sent him away.'

'Arlo!' Petra looks livid.

'For fuck's sake, Petra—am I not allowed my version of events?'

'What does it matter,' Petra says. 'It happened.'

Arlo sighs. 'Look, can I just come in. Let me speak. Listen or don't listen—just let me talk.'

Petra looks at her watch as if she is giving him five minutes. Then she folds her arms and focuses on his collar bone because eye contact is not an option.

'I did sleep with Miranda.'

It cuts Petra to the quick far more harshly than when Miranda had said the same. 'You fucking lied!'

'I'm not lying now.'

'All that bullshit about not having had sex for so long.'

'Sex is one thing. Making love is something else.'

'Bollocks. It's fucking semantics. Or should that

be semantics of fucking.'

'Christ, you don't half swear when you're angry,' Arlo says softly, loving her even more. 'I've never heard you say anything more abrasive than "sod" and "sodding".'

Petra jabs her finger at his chest. 'You made me believe you. I don't want to be involved with someone who has fuck-buddies. Someone who lies. I know your type and you're not *my* type.'

'Petra—this is complicated.' Arlo is fidgeting for words. Trying to use his hands. He can't think what to say or how to say it. 'We met each other, out of the blue, you and me, after years and years. It was magical. Then you disappeared. And all the while Miranda had been coming on to me. And I didn't make a play for her. I just let her. Perhaps it was weak. But after so long—to suddenly feel what I was feeling for you. I don't know—it freaked me out. It was unnerving. I'd got used to the idea of not having anyone in my life. It had felt safe that way. Then Petra's back. The girl who, it occurred to me, had always been *there.*' He touched his heart for emphasis. 'I didn't know what to do with the feelings. OK—and my body was in overdrive.'

'So you fucked Miranda? Doesn't that make me feel special.'

'It's not even about Miranda—it's about the feelings that flooded me when I saw you again. They were massive. And I chose not to tell you about Miranda Oates—firstly because it was of so little consequence to me, personally. And secondly, because I didn't want anything to complicate this immense purity of what we have.'

'Well, it's all nice and sullied now.'

Arlo bites his tongue because he wants to say,

328

Christ, Petra, will you stop all this aggression. 'There must be something I can do.'

'There isn't. I'm going back to London. I'm going to forget all about you. We didn't even have much in the first place—way back when. Sitting in a school playground every now and then, saying not that much? All we've done is look back on those days as some halcyon fairy tale. It was stupid. Nothing happened anyway. We've reinvented the past.'

'No, we have not. We may not have said much, we may not have seen each other all that often, but what we said and the time we shared was absolutely enough because I remember the feelings vividly. More vividly than I remember your Dunlop Green Flash and your mad bouncy bob—and they're pretty clear in my mind too.'

She wishes he'd stop talking because she's getting flashes of seventeen-year-old Arlo in her mind's eye and how she felt and it's all crystal clear and in bright colour.

'Petra, I've never felt this way before.'

'Cliché.'

'It's true.'

'It's bollocks.'

'It isn't.'

'And what about Helen? The great mystery that is Helen? The very reason for your self-prescribed so-called bullshit celibacy? You and Cliff bloody Richard.'

She sees Arlo flinch. 'I don't want to talk about Helen.'

'Well, I want to hear about Helen.'

'I'm telling you, Petra, you really don't.' Arlo chews his lip. He squares his shoulders. He comes up very close, cups Petra's face in his hands. A tear films over his left eye. It sounds as though shards of glass have spiked his throat, lacerated his voice. 'I love you, Petra Flint. God, I love you. Like I've never loved another.'

'But how can you expect me to skip hand in hand into our future when your past is so full of secrets and lies?' Petra is definite. 'Little by little I find stuff out and it stinks. If Miranda was a fuck-buddy, what was Helen? Your wife? The First Mrs Rochester—is she mad in some attic somewhere? Who *is* she? Your undoing? Your true love?'

'I *can't* talk about it.'

'I *need* to know.'

As he shakes his head, Petra thinks she sees shame rather than secrecy crumple him.

Whether he can't speak, or whether he has chosen not to say another word, is unclear. He leaves the Old Stables and walks away, trampling his dreams underfoot. Petra stands, shocked and immobile, for a few minutes more. But no one comes knocking. She calls for another cab. She catches a later train to London. She is back in North Finchley at way past supper-time. With nowt for our tea.

## CHAPTER FORTY-TWO

Her Studio Three took one look at Petra and swung into action. While Eric boiled the kettle and Kitty put her arms around Petra, Gina quickly tidied away all the stuff that had gathered on Petra's workbench.

'I'm fine,' Petra told them, a steeliness to her voice. 'We broke up,' she said, bolstered by a good glug of tea, 'but I'm fine. I'm back.'

'For good?' Eric asked.

'*Good* might be a bit strong. For better or for worse, I am back. Time will tell.'

'I'm so sorry,' Gina said. 'Sounded like you were living your Brontë dream.'

'The Brontës didn't shy away from some bloody dark passages,' Kitty said to Gina.

'Turned out my tale was more Stokesley Lows than Wuthering Heights anyway,' Petra told them, managing a sorry smile.

'I was looking forward to whirlwind, windswept summer nuptials,' Gina said. Eric and Kitty shot daggers at her. 'Sorry—but I was.'

Petra just shrugged. She looked at Eric. 'Are you going to say told-you-so? You can. You were right.'

'No, I'm not, missy,' he said, 'and I was wrong. For however long it lasted, you were a happy bunny up there—so I stand corrected. But I hope you've still brought some of the good back down with you.'

'I tell you what I have brought with me—my tanzanite.' Relieved for a seamless change of subject, Petra took the gem out of her bag and its beauty spun colour and light and silence around the studio. 'I know what it's going to be. After all these years, it's as clear as—tanzanite! Wait till you see.'

It was only then that Petra realized her sketchbook was still face down on Arlo's floor. Half under the sofa. Though her mind's eye still contained a detailed image of the finished product, that sketchbook, filled on one of the happiest days

331

of her life, had been her roadmap of how to achieve it.

*    *    *

The four of them stood and stared at the jewel.

'You know, Garrison Keillor finished *Lake Wobegon Days* and left the entire manuscript on a station platform, never to be seen again,' Eric told Petra. 'He had to rewrite the whole bloody thing. And look how brilliant Wobegon mark two is.'

'Perhaps this is a sign I shouldn't make anything with it,' Petra said. 'Perhaps I should place it in a bank vault and sell it in twenty years' time—when there's no more tanzanite left in the whole world.'

'Perhaps I should go back to being a natural blonde, take out my piercings, have laser treatment on my tattoos and become a nun,' Kitty said drily. 'Don't be daft, Petra—that tanzanite defines you. It's your destiny. You put it in a bank vault, you may as well bugger off and become a recluse.'

'Kitty's right,' Gina said. 'You need each other, you and that stone.'

'Perhaps he'll post the sketchbook back down to you,' Eric said.

'He doesn't know my address,' Petra said.

'Well, when he next sends you a late-night or drunken text you could text back send me my book you fucker,' said Kitty.

'He doesn't have a mobile phone.'

'Weirdo,' said Eric but from Petra's reaction he knew this was the wrong sentiment to have expressed just then.

'He may phone you anyway,' said Gina.

'He hasn't so far,' said Petra.

332

*     *     *

Of course he hasn't.

There's two days left of half-term and he's taken himself off to the tiny cottage Helen's family own on the west coast of Scotland.

He hasn't just been hiding from Miranda.

He has been hiding from himself.

*     *     *

Petra soon tired of being so systematically inundated with advice and concern. Lucy urged her not to be hasty. Told her not to be so stuck on unattainable romance in the face of the messiness of regular life. Suggested Petra listen to Arlo and then talk to him. Lucy said that lies are sometimes kindnesses in a strange guise and told her to feel flattered that Arlo had been so utterly mad with love for her that he'd resorted to shagging some whore.

'She's not a whore, she's Head of English or something. She's just a bit of an old slink.'

'Slink?'

'Isn't that a fantastic word for trollop? Jenn uses it.'

'New-Best-Friend Jenn?'

'You'd love her, Luce.'

Petra missed Jenn. She missed her too much to dare phone her. Jenn would only say, Come back, you daft cow. She'd tell Petra to come on, forgive, move on, move back. But surely hearing Jenn's voice would only remind Petra of how far apart they now lived.

333

Her Studio Three watched her like silent hawks. Eric turned up at her flat, unannounced, to stay the night on her sofa. Which was a good job as he managed to prevent her sleepwalking out into the night in her gumboots again. Kitty took Petra for a drunken night out to a goths' dive in Soho where a slender man with black lipstick tried to persuade her that amyl nitrate was the answer to life itself. But all Petra came away with was a cracking hangover and Gary Numan on her brain for days after. Gina invited Petra for dinner with her family but had so drummed into her daughters 'Don't-mention-the-boyfriend' that Harry and Henry were able to talk of little else.

'Are you a spinster now?' Harry gasped.

'There are loads of fish in the sea, you know,' Henry said.

'You'll be OK,' Gina told Petra, handing her fresh fat towels and a little bar of tissue-wrapped gardenia guest soap. 'It's him we have to pity—losing you. Sleep tight. We'll go to Harvey Nicks tomorrow—buy shoes. It's far easier to walk through troubled times in a gorgeous pair of new heels.'

The next morning, Petra woke up on the floor of Henry's bedroom, being stared at. 'What are you doing here?' the child asked. 'What's wrong with our spare room?'

'I must have sleepwalked,' Petra said, surreptitiously patting the carpet, relieved to find it dry. 'I sleepwalk.'

'That's just *so* cool,' said Henry.

'Not really,' said Petra. 'It's a pain in the arse.'

'You said arse!' Henry said. 'Did it get on your boyfriend's nerves, then?'

Petra skipped over the memory of Arlo rescuing her from the Walley Brothers, of talking until dawn; she put her hands behind her back to stop herself remembering the feel of him gently holding her wrist as she fell asleep. Instead, she thought of Rob. 'Yup,' she said, 'it did.'

'He's a twit,' said Henry and Petra loved Gina for the vocabulary she'd passed on to her children.

*      *      *

Taking various buses back to North Finchley from Chelsea, Petra thought how tiring it was to have so much love, attention and worry directed her way. If it was soothing at first, now it left her feeling drained and somehow exposed too. Being the object of everyone's concern was onerous, and their affection was starting to cloy. Yet Petra did not want to be on her own either, because that was when the exquisite sadness hit hardest. What she needed was to be among people for whom she held little significance. People who didn't care much for details, who knew little of her past, less of her present and were not particularly interested in her future. She phoned her mother from the top deck of the number 13 bus. And she phoned her father soon after. She spent Sunday in Watford, entertaining her step-siblings while her father played golf and her stepmother wafted around just beyond the perimeter of conversation. Then Petra went down to Kent on Monday and stayed the night with her mother whose cottage smelt of chicken shit and who talked mostly drivel until Petra left her on Tuesday afternoon.

# CHAPTER FORTY-THREE

There were ten minutes to go before assembly. Arlo couldn't avoid the staff room; not least because he'd run out of coffee, could not function without it and was well aware that it would be percolating enticingly—a full complement of digestives, ginger nuts and fig rolls by the side of the machine—in the staff room. He had not yet seen Miranda but it was clear that the umbrage she'd taken from his absence in the Highlands had led her to reveal the details of their couplings to anyone over school age who would listen. And as he walked across the grounds towards the promise of caffeine, his colleagues either wolf-whistled, slapped him on the back or else looked at him in bewilderment. He met Nigel Garton on his way to the staff room.

'I know about Miranda,' Nige said under his breath, a backdrop of Fifth Year artwork—mostly phallic cacti in Conté crayons—seeming to taunt Arlo as they climbed the stairs, 'but I also know about Petra.' He didn't give Arlo time to comment. They walked on alongside a stretch of wall thankfully unadorned. 'Jenn saw her before she left.' Just before they went into the staff room, Nige turned to Arlo. 'I hope that's OK—for Jenn to have told me. I'm—we're—engaged. I did the whole bended-knee malarkey over half-term. I'm—we're—well, we're hoping you make a go of it with Petra. We like her. And I like what she's done for you.'

Arlo felt quite moved though the surroundings

somewhat compromised his willingness to show it. 'Congratulations, mate,' he said, 'and I like what Jenn's done for you too. No mean feat. But as for me, I'm afraid it seems I've sown too many wild Oates.'

Nigel physically brushed this away, as if it was an obstacle no greater than a pesky fly. 'Talk to her.'

'I'm going to have to,' Arlo said, 'until the end of term.'

'Not Wild Oates—*Petra*.'

Arlo stiffened. 'Do you think I haven't tried? She wouldn't listen. Anyway, she's gone. As well you know.'

'Don't be like that.'

'Like what, Nige?'

'Defeatist. That's not you.'

'Shall I say it in capital letters? I TRIED. SHE WOULDN'T LISTEN. SHE'S GONE.'

'So—*make* her hear,' said Nigel, holding the staff-room door open for Arlo. 'Go and bloody *find* her. Jeez. It may be difficult—but it's not rocket science.'

\*   \*   \*

Arlo announced to his GCSE class that their double period would be short but sweet.

'And that doesn't mean I'm going to let you bunk off early, Tobias—so put your books back on the desk, please.' He stopped. This was one of his favourite lessons—he enjoyed delivering it each year. But he didn't want to say the next sentence.

'Sometimes, something can be of such profound beauty that its time is, by definition, limited.' He paused. 'If it lasted longer, it wouldn't be so good.'

That can't be true, he thought. He lost his words. All eyes were on him. He cleared his throat, told himself to focus, for fuck's sake. 'A single sublime melody may not survive in a more lengthy or convoluted form. Classical or contemporary. Sometimes, it's just not possible—in fact, it makes no sense—to expand on something which is already perfect in itself.' No sense? Nonsense! Nothing's impossible. Nothing's impossible. Focus!

'It is the musician's prerogative to know when the staff should be left bare.' Staff. *Staff.* Bloody Oates laid bare. 'If a piece of music is stretched beyond its limit, its impact lessens and the sound wanes.' That's better.

'Now, I'm going to play Schubert. Don't confuse him with Schumann, please. This is the *Quartettsatz in C Minor*—a single movement of an unfinished quartet for strings. Unlike many musical historians, I'm happy to think that the artist felt the work quite complete, that perhaps he changed his mind about the need for three more movements, that the melody he created here can carry an entire work in its own right. It is self-contained and exquisite.'

The class listened. They liked it.

'Bach,' Arlo continued, changing the CD quickly. 'Again—the first movement of the *Cello Suite in G*. I don't much give a toss for what follows. This does it for me. It's divine, autonomous, really.'

Arlo was tempted to play it through a second time. He resisted.

'Who can tell me anything about Jethro Tull?'

Up shot Willem's hand. 'Eighteenth century. Pioneer of the English agricultural revolution.'

338

'Well, yes,' Arlo said slowly, 'if this was your history lesson, I'd give you an A+. But the subtle difference is that this is a music appreciation lesson. Anyone? No? Chap who can play the flute standing on one leg—quite literally?'

The class shuffled a little. They prided themselves on knowing the bands Mr Savidge alluded to. When they didn't, it was a harsh blow to their eager pursuit of musical credibility.

'You're forgiven,' Arlo told them, 'but you'd also be mistaken to pass them off as just a bunch of weirdy-beardy prog-rockers. Their seminal 1971 album, *Aqualung,* is like an aural version of Hogarth's *Conversation Pieces*—reproductions of which adorn the art studio so ask Mr Hunter to talk you through them, to *walk* you through. I want you to listen to this. Seventy-eight seconds of utterly transcendent melody.' The song was 'Cheap Day Return', acoustic and gentle despite the searingly prosaic lyrics. Arlo played it very loud. Then he let the class sit in silence for a further seventy-eight seconds. 'What would happen if Ian Anderson had drawn that out? Made it last, say, a hundred seconds? Or two minutes? An entire album's length?'

'He'd have sort of lost it,' said Tobias. 'I mean, he'd've sort of lost the centre of the song?'

'Very good—the impact would be compromised, the melody diluted by too much time and over-involvement. What does it remind you of? Willem—yes?'

'The hippy shit my dad plays.'

'Rarely is published music *shit*, Willem,' Mr Savidge said pointedly. 'Anyone else?'

'An Elizabethan ditty?' Lucas said. 'Not in the

tune specifically but in its—I dunno—well, it's *pretty*, isn't it? It's intimate in that Elizabethan way.'

'Excellent, Lucas. Excellent. Let's think about *Greensleeves*,' Arlo said, picking up his guitar and playing, 'one of the most perfect melodies ever written, extremely short and succinct. Then Vaughan Williams decided to make a large portion of sickly syrup from it. Something heavenly diluted into something that is just—nice.' The boys laughed, thinking that they knew what Mr Savidge meant. After listening to Vaughan Williams, they did.

'There is beauty in brevity—I can't impress this on you enough, gentlemen. To maintain that beauty, to respect it, is to ensure its enduring impact.'

Arlo felt suddenly winded. As he fumbled with a CD he thought to himself, But that's not right, that can't be so, that can only be right in terms of music. Not life. Not me and Petra. The beauty between us cannot be that we died young. I don't want brevity. I want *years* with her. I want evermore.

'I want to grow old with her.'

'Sorry, sir?' Willem was confused.

'Mr Savidge, sir?' Tobias, likewise.

'What?' So was Arlo.

'What did that mean?' Lucas asked. 'What you just said about growing old?'

'Who's *her*, sir?' asked Willem.

'Pardon?' Arlo hid his embarrassment with a look at his class that suggested they were either hearing things or else just plain dim. 'This is Mozart,' he said with a swift change of subject. 'We

340

are going to finish with the *Serenade for Thirteen Wind Instruments*. I want your arms on your desks, guys. I want to see your skin. If any student of mine is without goose bumps after the Adagio, they will not be welcome back to my class.'

*        *        *

Arlo was filing the CDs back, muttering under his breath that his goose-bump test was genius, possibly his greatest contribution to the teaching profession. He congratulated himself for being able to go seamlessly from Viennese chamber music to British prog rock. Jethro bloody Tull, hey! He glanced at the track listing on the CD and, against his better judgement, took out the disc and selected 'Wond'ring Aloud'. OK, he hadn't heard it for ages; yes, on one level it was another beautiful melody perhaps worthy of inclusion in next year's lesson, at little over one hundred seconds long. But he chose it for another level entirely: for the resonance of the lyrics. *Wond'ring aloud/will the years treat us well?* At any other time in his life, he'd have found the song pleasant enough, cathartic even, sentimental perhaps. Today, though, he sensed it could send him spinning to the edge of sanity and he knew this was a place he needed to be. He needed to feel himself clinging there until he sensed he had the strength to haul himself up. Then he'd have the answers.

*Wond'ring aloud*
*will the years treat us well?*
*As she floats in the kitchen,*
*I'm tasting the smell*

*of toast as the butter runs.*
*Then she comes, spilling crumbs on the bed*
*and I shake my head.*

*And it's only the giving*
*that makes you what you are.*

The goose bumps from Jethro Tull lasted longer than from Mozart. Arlo wasn't quite sure on whom this looked worse, himself or Mozart. Of all the music ever written, it was Jethro bloody Tull cutting him to the quick. He returned to his folly. Stood with his eyes closed, conjuring the smell of hot buttered toast. Petra's favourite. An image of her bringing a plateful back to bed. The divine juxtaposition between crumbs in the sheets and her sweet soft skin. Arlo slumped onto his living-room floor, staring into nothingness. Then his focus shifted and he caught sight of Petra's sketchbook, half under his sofa, waiting to be found.

*       *       *

A man with a mission. First, Arlo went to the computer room, surfed the Net, scribbled down details on a scrap of paper. Then he made two phone calls before discoursing on Arnold Schoenberg and the emancipation of dissonance to his A level group. After this he went to his headmaster. After that he made further phone calls. At lunch-time, he found Nige.

'I'm going to find her, Nige,' he said. 'There's no way that I'm letting her go.'

'Good man,' Nige said.

'So I'm going to London.'

342

'Oh yes? When's that, then?'

'Day after tomorrow?'

'Bloody hell, mate!' Have you passed it with Pinder?'

'Pinder—and a dozen others. No red tape is going to trip me up.'

Arlo had thrown himself into the arrangements, checked and double-checked all the details, packed and repacked a holdall, but the night before he was due to leave, something felt greatly amiss. As if something was missing, something he'd forgotten and though he went through his bag once again, scrutinized the paperwork, he was stumped. The Who, playing in the background, provided the answer. Look behind your own blue eyes, Arlo Savidge, to find out why you're the sad man, the bad man.

*But my dreams*
*They aren't as empty*
*As my conscience seems to be*

\*       \*       \*

Of course. Miranda.

\*       \*       \*

He'd been so preoccupied, he'd hardly given her a moment's thought. It occurred to him that if he'd been too busy to actively steer clear of her, then it was obvious that actually she'd been keeping herself out of his way. And as much as 'Wondrin' Aloud' was his song with Petra, so 'Behind Blue Eyes' was his song with Miranda. And however

343

much he'd rather avoid her, Arlo knew he could not leave for London, he could not leave the school and he could not hope to truly find Petra until he'd sought out Miranda, to sort it out.

It was late. But as Arlo walked to her folly, he thought how it was never too late. He hadn't prepared a speech, he wasn't actually sure if it was forgiveness he sought or an apology. Whether it was an explanation he had to give, or whether he'd get a slap around the face. Or whether he would feel entitled to say, Who the fuck do you think you are talking to my girlfriend like that.

He knocked. Waited. She opened the door. They glanced away from each other's eyes to each other's feet. Hers were bare, her toenails now without varnish.

'Hi.'

'Hi.'

They looked at each other, their eyes darting to a point over each other's shoulders.

'You're off to London? It's the talk of the staff room.'

'Yes, tomorrow.'

'So you've come to take your leave?'

'Actually, I've come to clear the air.'

In one glimpse, Arlo saw both gratitude and annoyance in Miranda's eyes. 'Come in,' she said.

He chose not to sit. In what order should they apologize? Ladies first? After you? Age before beauty? Shit before shovel? Whose crime was the greater? As Miranda opened her mouth, Arlo spoke first.

'Miranda, for my part—I'm sorry. I didn't mean to lead you on. I should have been straighter with you. I should have thought with my conscience, not

344

my dick.'

She nodded.

'I know in these situations blokes say, "Hey babe, it's not you, it's me." But for me, it's not you—it's Petra. I really did think I was done with love. Then Petra came along—but then she disappeared. And then I thought that maybe a good old-fashioned zipless fuck would be the answer.'

'It's OK, Arlo,' Miranda interrupted, because though she appreciated Arlo's candour and though she knew she had an apology of her own to give, she really could do without hearing too much about St Petra. If she wasn't going to be Arlo's fuck-buddy, she certainly didn't want to be his confidante. 'I'm—I behaved,' she sighed. 'I was a total cow, Arlo. No, worse, I was a bitch.'

Arlo shrugged.

'You'd been so clear about not wanting a girlfriend, per se. But then you said that if things ever changed, I ticked all your boxes.' She looked a little forlorn. 'That's flattering to a girl—even if she says she's only after a little bit of fun.'

Arlo nodded. 'I misled you. I didn't want to be tactless. It was all so—complicated.'

'You'd've been kinder if you'd've been a little crueller,' Miranda said.

'My head was saying one thing, my heart another, yet my body wasn't taking a blind bit of notice of either. Pathetic, really.'

Miranda smiled for the first time. 'Can I take that as a compliment, then?'

'You certainly can.'

'The madness of it is, I was actually feeling totally fine. We'd had our thing, you'd told me the score, I was cool. But then I came back to school early, came across the Walleys and asked them who was around and they said you and your lady friend. I was intrigued, infuriated. And then I saw her and immediately I saw why I'm not your type—because she's, well, she's just so *you*. There's me, all brazen about casual shagging—but actually I was suddenly jealous.' She paused, looked at Arlo, shrugged. 'Actually, I was evil, Arlo. I couldn't stop myself. Have I fucked things up for you?'

'We'll see.'

'Is that why you're off to London, then? Is there anything I can do? I could tell the truth, say sorry to her, tell a lie and pretend nothing happened between us? Ever. I don't know. Anything. As much to ease my conscience as to play Cupid.'

'Thanks. It's down to me now. And her.'

'It's late—you'd better go.'

'Yes. Early start.'

'Good luck, Arlo—you may need it.'

'Thanks. I can hear the Walleys on their rounds. Lock your door. Goodnight, Oatcake.'

## CHAPTER FORTY-FOUR

At a motorway services on the M1, over halfway to London, Arlo sat in Burger King, wolfed down a burger without tasting it, picked at the fries and fiddled with the straw in his drink. In his other hand, tucked tight, was the scrap of paper with Petra's mobile number written on it. Eleven numbers should not have been difficult for Arlo to commit to memory—especially as Petra's had a certain flow to them. After all, he could play great tracts of music off by heart and knew the dates of most of the hit singles since charts began. And the record labels. And the songwriters, too. But he hadn't been able to learn Petra's number by rote. He thought perhaps one had to own a mobile phone for such a sequence to stick. Maybe he just liked unfolding the paper and reading off her handwriting. He scrunched up the burger wrapper, pulverizing leftover bun and a few soft chips with it. Then he went in search of a pay phone. He inserted money, read Petra's number, hovered his finger above the keypad—but returned the handset to the cradle. He hadn't pressed follow-on-call and he stood there, unfeasibly pissed off that he'd lost his money along with losing his nerve. He told himself to get a grip or get on with the journey. Then he thought it was probably best to call her once he'd arrived, anyway. He considered phoning his mum. But decided against it, despite feeling guilty about this. She didn't know he was coming down, she needn't know. Time was going to be tight.

\*        \*        \*

Once in London, unpacked and bolstered by a really good cup of coffee from yet another new chain of high-street coffee shops which had apparently sprung up since his last visit, Arlo studied the phone number again. There were two phone booths right in front of him. The proximity of Petra, just at the other end of the line, was tormenting. What would he say? Hi—can we talk? But how might she respond? No—sod off? Might she not answer at all—then what kind of message should he leave? It wasn't as if he could say, Give me a call on the moby. And say he did get through and got beyond the greetings, what then? I'm in London—can I see you? And what if she simply said, No, you can't?

'Bloody stupid idea of mine,' Arlo said under his breath. He fiddled with the paper, folding and unfolding it, turning it over. And then he stopped. He'd been so focused on her writing, her number, he hadn't bothered to notice that she hadn't written on the front at all. She'd written on the back—scribbled down her number on the back of an invoice. Bellore. Her suppliers. Their address, phone number, fax, email. Hatton Garden. It was a treasure map! It led directly to Petra's stamping ground. I'm looking for a jeweller named Petra Flint, he could say, Do you know where I might find her? Did he look like a client? A friend? Convincing? He had to look like one of the three. Or did he look like a lovelorn stalker from the sticks? He caught sight of his reflection in shop windows as he marched with purpose to the nearest tube station. He looked positive, that was the main thing.

\*        \*        \*

This was Arlo's first visit to Hatton Garden. The swell of nerves at the tangible closeness of the woman he loved caused him to take his time with his route, to find inordinate interest in the shopfronts, in the buildings, the destinations of the red double-deckers which passed. But then he came across the intersection with Greville Street without having to ask for directions. Initially, though, he turned right and found soon enough that this was the wrong way. He then read great significance into the fact that the wrong way had taken him to Bleeding Heart Yard: there must be a message in that. He retraced his steps with a sense of urgency—as if he might just miss her if he didn't now hurry.

Bellore's premises was right at the end of Greville Street, practically on the corner of Leather Lane, opposite a rather insalubrious modern pub, and Arlo made a mental note to drown his sorrows there if it all went horribly wrong. The shopfront, though small, was chic and inviting compared to some of the supplier merchants he'd passed. It looked more like a boutique and was most certainly open to the public. Strings of semi-precious stones trickled down the walls, cords of brightly coloured leather too. Central display cases presented the glint and sparkle of more expensive gems and precious metals. Towards the back of the shop, the walls were dominated by racks of tiny transparent drawers containing a myriad of silver and gold findings—clasps and fastenings and rods and hooks and all manner of fascinating gubbins. A large squat safe sat intriguingly in the corner. In the centre of the floor space, a sturdy measuring and cutting table, armed at one side by an alarming guillotine.

The shop was crowded. Arlo went downstairs where it was no less busy with customers poring over drill bits and rasps and tools that wouldn't look amiss in a dental surgery or torture chamber (which, from Arlo's childhood memory, were one

349

and the same). But there was no Petra downstairs. He went back up to the main shop floor. No Petra up there either, not that he had really expected such an extreme coincidence. He'd come to Bellore because it was the most logical starting point, the most promising source for where to go next; it was a step in the right direction. She works around the corner, sir. I'm sure she's in the studio today—she came in to buy some silver just this morning, sir. You ring the bell, sir, as clients often do. She'll be glad to see you, sir. Lovely Petra Flint.

But who to ask? Arlo observed the busy staff and their absorbed clientele—all as varied and colourful as the merchandise in the shop. Older ladies with strong thin fingers that had possibly seen a lifetime of creativity. Jewellery graduates with chipped nail varnish scrounging for under a fiver's worth of bits and pieces. Well-heeled women of independent means, indulging their hobby with sizeable orders. Secretaries in their lunch-break wanting to rustle up a necklace for tonight's hot date. And people who looked like Petra—active jewellers popping in from studios in the environs for essential supplies for works in progress. Arlo observed the staff, mainly young and eminently approachable—but all of them occupied. He looked at his watch and reckoned a couple more minutes would be fine. Suddenly, there was the lull that Arlo needed. One woman with a long wish list and a member of staff assisting her, a couple of students dipping into the drawers at the back as if they were children in a toy shop choosing marbles, and a goth—quite a pretty one—inspecting tourmaline. A male sales assistant at the till was taking quick sips from a large

Arsenal mug.

'Excuse me,' said Arlo, trying to swallow a butterfly stuck in his throat, 'I'm looking for Petra Flint.'

'Petra?' the sales assistant asked, his familiarity with her name bolstering Arlo.

'Yes—I don't know where her studio is. I'm a friend. Fleeting visit from Yorkshire.'

Though Arlo could sense that someone was staring hard at the side of his face, he was utterly focused on the sales assistant, hoping to come across as warm and affable and convincing. The sales assistant suddenly looked over Arlo's shoulder, raised an eyebrow, gave a nod. 'She's the one you want,' he told him. Arlo turned. It was the goth.

'Oh no, no!' Arlo laughed quickly, returning his attention to the sales assistant. Should he talk about Arsenal for a bit? Would that open the door? But Arlo was a Spurs supporter and even in extremis, he could not countenance such betrayal. 'Petra *Flint*?' he stressed. 'She's about so high— just normal looking. Well, very pretty actually. Long dark curly hair.' He was starting to fluster. 'She's a jeweller of some repute, I believe? Works for Charlton Whatsit. Big into tanzanite.'

The sales assistant drained his mug and then motioned it towards the goth again, nodding as he swallowed. He cleared his throat. 'Yeah, we all know Petra—but as I say, this lady will help you.'

'First time I've been called a lady, Dan,' the goth said with a flattered growl. 'I could get used to it.' Then she turned to Arlo who was suddenly transfixed by the bizarrely delicate pink gold chain running from the hoop in her nose to one of the many hoops in her ear. 'I'm Kitty,' she said. 'Don't tell me you're bloody Arlo.'

*     *     *

They sized each other up for a moment. 'Yes,' he said, offering his hand, 'I'm bloody Arlo.'

It raised a smile and she no longer looked as though she might bite. 'About bloody time,' she said. 'What kept you?'

'Logistics,' Arlo said. 'And the headmaster.' He looked at her squarely. 'And nerves.'

She nodded. She took the scrap of Bellore invoice from his hand, observed Petra's handwriting on the other side. She nodded again. 'Come on, Sherlock,' she said, 'I'll take you to her.'

*     *     *

They left the shop and Kitty set off at a fast walk.

'Hold on,' Arlo called after her, 'you'll have to wait up a minute. I'm not quite ready.'

She stopped, turned, took a long look in Arlo's direction, couldn't quite believe what she was seeing and burst out laughing, which eventually lessened into a surprisingly feminine giggle. It softened her face, as if giving voice to the natural prettiness beneath the hair dye and the Halloween make-up and the piercings.

Arlo shrugged as he approached. 'What could I do?' he said to her. 'It's the middle of term. I *am* a bloody teacher.'

*     *     *

He was told to wait on the pavement but as Kitty disappeared into the building, she cast a fleeting wink over her shoulder, which Arlo caught gratefully. The door shut. It was a shabby door painted in flaking undercoat, a variety of locks which had obviously been changed a number of times, a small pane of glass so dusty it was opaque, a rusting metal grille behind it. That damned butterfly was caught in Arlo's throat again. He thought about *The Silence of the Lambs,* remembered something about butterflies in victims' throats. Incongruous—but it kept his mind off the fact that Petra was just inside the building and he had no idea what was going to happen next.

\*       \*       \*

Inside:
'Petra—someone downstairs for you.'
'Ta, Kitty.'
Nothing unusual in that. The Studio Four often had deliveries to be personally signed for.
As Petra descended the stairs, she wondered if she just heard Gina say, Good God; and did Eric just say, Fucking hell? But her conclusion was, Oh Kitty, not another tattoo.

\*       \*       \*

Petra is wondering, What have I ordered? Didn't I tell Dan I'd come into Bellore early next week for the platinum? I won't be able to pay him until then, anyway.
And Arlo is wondering, What the hell was it that I was going to say? I had it all planned. My mind's
353

gone blank.

*      *      *

The door is opening.

*      *      *

Out into the bright light of a summer's day.

*      *      *

'Hullo, you.'

*      *      *

She can't answer. She can only stand and stare.

*      *      *

He can't say another word. All he can do is gaze back.

*      *      *

So they stand and they gawp in the middle of the pavement and they are tutted at, knocked into, by people bustling between Leather Lane and Hatton Garden. Life is going on. It's just a Thursday afternoon in June. It's only Petra and Arlo who feel that they are standing at the still point of the turning world.

    'What are you—?'

    '—so I could see you.'

*       *       *

He gives her the sketchbook. But it is the enormity of Arlo's complete gesture, that he is *here*, which is the immediate salve, and in itself it has more resonance than any soliloquy. Whatever he says, wherever this goes, the point is he came. He found her.

'You sod,' she says, 'I can't hit you now, can I? Not after you've come all this way.'

'If it makes you feel better, then you can.'

'I've been getting on with my life, buoyed by the thought that if ever I saw you again, I'd give you a good old-fashioned whack across the chops.'

'Petra, no one but you could say "whack across the chops".'

'I have a mean left hook.'

'I'm sure you do. But I've come down from Yorkshire to see if you'd rather just kiss me.'

After a moment's deliberation, she steps towards him and Arlo wonders which it is to be. A kiss or a slap.

She comes in close, lifts her face to his and places her hands gently on his arms. A kiss. Yet he steps away. He looks flustered, a little flushed. 'Not here. Not now,' he murmurs. She frowns, backs off. The urge to belt him is back.

'Boys,' Arlo says over his shoulder. 'Guys—this is Petra Flint.'

*       *       *

Her field of vision widens. There are four schoolboys—tall ones, Sixth Formers perhaps, loitering a respectful distance behind Arlo. In their

355

uniforms. Eyes agog.

'Felix Sutcliffe, Callum Jones, Thomas Allsop, Alexander McLeod. And there would have been two more only I couldn't track down their parents in time to process all the paperwork.'

One by one, the boys step forward to shake hands with Petra who hasn't a clue what to say or what today is all about or what will happen or what she's meant to be feeling.

'Hi,' she says.

'Hullo, miss,' they say. They look as confused as she feels.

'We're off to a gig tonight,' Arlo says brightly, 'at the Forum in Kentish Town. Then tomorrow we are going to a lunch-time concert at Wigmore Hall. In the morning, an old friend of mine, Michael Smith, is showing the boys around Columbia Records. Tomorrow evening we're going to the Troubadour. We leave Saturday morning.'

Petra pauses. 'Oh.'

Arlo nods. 'Fleeting visit. Packed schedule. Should be fun.'

She pauses again. 'Yes.'

'We came down in the minibus.' Arlo is floundering. 'We're staying at quite a nice B&B in Swiss Cottage. With off-street parking.' With each mundane detail, the previous poetry of the caught moment diminishes. He and Petra are no longer at the still point of the turning world, they are standing awkwardly in the middle of the pavement, getting in people's way.

'Mr Savidge—aren't we meant to be at Ronnie Scott's now?'

Arlo looks at his watch. 'Shit. Ronnie Scott's too. I clean forgot. And Ronnie Scott's was basically the key selling point to the headmaster. Thanks, Felix.' He fiddles with his watch. 'They said three, three thirty. You don't turn up at jazz clubs early. We're having a little tour of the club,' he tells Petra. 'I organized it. The boys can see the sound check—which is a contradiction in terms but I'm sure you know what I mean.'

She doesn't really, but she nods anyway.

'You could come too,' he says, 'to Ronnie Scott's—to the gig later. You could come everywhere with us.' She looks a little wary. She also looks a little reluctant.

'I can't, really,' she says.

'Mr Savidge, are we going by tube?' Felix is presenting him with a map of the underground.

'Shall I call you later anyway?' he asks Petra.

'OK,' she says, suddenly wondering what any of this is about. Has there been any meaning in the last few minutes? Over and above the return of her sketchbook?

'We'd better go.'

'OK,' she says.

\*         \*         \*

Petra watches Arlo and his little posse cross the street. He turns and gives a wave that changes into a shrug; she raises the sketchbook for a moment and then heads back into her building. She's not far up the staircase when there's a flurry of knocks at the door she's just closed and Arlo is calling her name. She retraces her steps. Opens the door. In a blink, he's inside. His hands are in her hair and his lips are all over her face. And it's now that she wants to cry and hit him and hold him tight and tell

357

him to go away.

'The only way I could get time off school was to bring my students with me,' he tells her. 'The only way we could do London was if, musically, I could prove it would be worth the boys' while and worth the school's funds.' He kisses her again. 'But my guiding ulterior motive was purely that I had to see you, Petra. Sod the meters of red tape and myriad permission slips and miles of motorway—I had to see you. Because I need to tell you that we're going to be OK, you know. You and me. We're going to be more than OK.'

Petra's lip twitches and it isn't a kiss that's causing it, it's a But. 'But Arlo,' she says, 'you may be here—but it was me who left. And I left because you lied. And because of the Miranda situation.'

Arlo has been expecting this, of course he has, but still he's nervous now the moment has finally come to plead his point. 'But Petra, I am here because I won't let you go. Because really, truly, there was no situation with Miranda.'

'But you slept with her!'

'I don't sleep.'

'You know what I mean. And you did lie.'

'Will you listen, will you believe me, when I say I'm just a stupid fuck who deludedly thought I could avoid hurting you by retaining certain details? An idiot who didn't want to complicate something so new and so full of promise?' Arlo looks at Petra. 'It's the truth, Miss Flint. It may seem flimsy. But actually, it's all I can give you.'

'But the timing—me, us, Miranda?'

'No overlap whatsoever.'

'You sure?'

'I promise.'

Though the upper part of Petra's face is creased into a frown, slowly the lower part breaks into a small smile. 'Why do I feel I still want to whack you across the chops?'

Arlo shrugs, allows a little laugh out loud. 'Please go ahead, if you need to. Though I'd rather you kissed me.'

Petra steps forward and again he's not quite sure which it will be until the gentle press of her lips against his leaves him in no doubt.

'We're going to be OK, you know,' he repeats, this time in a whisper. 'You and me, we're going to be more than OK.'

\*       \*       \*

Someone is coming down the stairs. It is Eric.

'Oh hullo,' he says and his voice is camp and slightly withering and his surprise is meant to be so obviously feigned. 'Cappuccino, anyone? Or are you just leaving?'

'Eric,' Petra says with a swift, cautioning look, 'this is Arlo, say hullo.'

'Hullo.'

'I have to go,' Arlo says. 'Hi, Eric.' He turns to Petra. 'I have to go.' He takes his fingertips to her cheek, strokes down to her jaw until she rests her face gently in his hand. 'I really have to go. Which is the best way to the tube?'

'I'll show you,' Eric says, holding open the door. 'Cappuccino is it, Petra?' he calls over his shoulder.

She's not speaking. Eric and Arlo turn. She's just standing there, nodding. She looks absolutely poleaxed.

# CHAPTER FORTY-FIVE

'Has she said a word?' Eric asked, coming back with coffees all round; Petra was so lost in thought at her bench that he felt he could talk about her as if she wasn't there at all.

He went and stood in a huddle nearby with Gina and Kitty, the three of them assessing Petra like doctors conferring on a most unusual case.

'No,' Gina said, 'she's just been sitting there, with a rather inane grin on her face.'

'It's not an inane grin,' Kitty objected, 'it's more a beatific smile.'

Eric peered in closer and gently prodded Petra. 'I'd say the girl's in shock.'

Petra looked at them as if they were all hopelessly myopic. 'He's come all this way. To see me.' They nodded as if she was just out of a coma and thus anything she said was OK by them. 'And he's brought his class with him.' She giggled. They continued to nod. 'And he doesn't really have a spare moment.' They shook their heads. 'So he's either been driven slightly mad by love or else he's driven all this way because he is madly in love. With me.' Kitty nodded vigorously. Gina looked more reserved. Eric rolled his eyes. 'Do you think I should go to Ronnie Scott's—rush there right now?'

'Too late,' said Eric, 'and a bit too keen.'

'Shall I go to the Forum with them, tonight then?'

'You go, girlfriend,' Kitty said, suddenly American.

360

'Oughtn't you to wait for him to call?' Gina asked.

'Shut the fuck up, Mom,' Kitty growled in a surprisingly authentic Hicksville accent.

Gina looked as though she was going to send Kitty to the Naughty Step.

Petra hid her face in her hands. 'God. I am meant to be *working*, the sod.'

'Ditto,' said Gina, going off to hammer.

'Me too,' said Eric, returning to his bench. His mother had taught him that if he had nothing nice to say, he was to say nothing. He felt the same was true for giving advice.

Kitty loitered by Petra. 'Will you show me?'

Petra let Kitty pore over the sketches, handed her a clutch of photographs of the ruined abbeys she'd visited. 'There's something so romantic about these great Gothic edifices,' Petra said. 'In their current, ruinous state they are beautiful, so dramatic—but there's a sort of poetic melancholy about them which perhaps comes from their history too. And yet they continue to stand in the landscape, regal and proud. The vistas they create actually seem to enhance the natural scenery. There's also this amazing physical dichotomy—they look like delicate lacework, yet they are made of stone centuries old. But what time and historical events have not compromised is how the hearts of these places still beat so strongly.'

'And so?' Kitty prompted, eyeing the brown box on which Petra's hand rested.

'And so—this.' She opened the box and carefully lifted out her preparatory work. 'Think platinum,' she told Kitty, 'with my tanzanite in the centre.'

Kitty took the piece from Petra. A bracelet—but

361

unlike anything she'd ever seen. Just wire, plain old craft wire. Strands of different thicknesses worked into a graceful armature of delicate arches and columns, some perfect, others pointedly truncated. Caught within this intricate framework, a purple boiled sweet.

Petra took it from her. 'That's what I'm trying to work out,' she explained, prodding the sweet with her little finger. 'How I can have my tanzanite as the heart of the work but not in a clasp, not in a static setting, not restricted to one view, one angle only. The heart of the work must be visible from all sides so that the colour and light of the stone pulsates.'

The piece transcended being merely a bracelet or cuff, it was the closest thing to wearable sculpture. Petra's genius was her ability to attain such startling grace in something so sizeable.

'Initially I thought of a ring, or a brooch or a pendant—but my tanzanite wouldn't really suit a ring. The setting would compromise the beauty of the cut. It must be seen in the round. And I decided against a pendant because what I want is for the wearer to be able to really see the piece whilst it's on. No point having almost 40 carats of eye-clean vBE tanzanite around your neck if you can't bloody see it. And brooches are too static. So that's why I thought something for the wrist. Near a pulse point. And I want it to move—I don't want a front and back. I want it to be kinetic. Somehow.'

Kitty took the work off Petra again, contemplated it. 'Think: hinges,' she said at length. She looked at Petra, flushed with her idea. 'Hinge all around the stone—then the wearer can twist it and turn it and the jewel will always be in the

362

round.'

Petra and Kitty twisted and turned the piece, the boiled sweet knocking this way and that. 'Tanzanite isn't as hard as diamond or sapphire,' Petra said. 'I have to secure it but I want to do so with no visible means of support. And I need to protect the surfaces.'

'You've got your work cut out for you,' Kitty warned her, 'but it'll be your magnum opus. The idea is incredible and I can already see the finished work. Go and talk to Charlton—remember his early work, when he first hit the scene? That was based on hinges and intricate engineering.' She paused. 'Christ, Petra—this really could be your thing. Once you've resolved the mechanics, you could do similar pieces with other gems. I *love* it.' She stopped. 'You could charge the *earth*. You'll have to—the materials in themselves will cost a fortune.'

'I know,' Petra groaned.

'But it will be self-perpetuating. Make one or two and they'll be snapped up and then you'll be commissioned in advance. Fuck it—you could even sell them on the strength of designs just like this, in wire and boiled sweets.' She peered into the box. There were two more boiled sweets, still in cellophane twists. One green. One red. 'There you go—emerald and ruby. Where is your tanzanite?'

'At home,' Petra told her, taking the sweets off Kitty and holding them up to the light.

'Under your mattress?'

Petra nodded.

'Have you considered what it will be like for you when this piece is finished? When it's on someone's wrist and there's no more tanzanite in your bed? How will you feel?' Kitty looked suddenly alarmed. 'Christ, Petra—the princess couldn't sleep with a pea *under* her mattress—but how are you going to sleep *without* your tanzanite there?'

\*     \*     \*

'Oh, the girl will be fine, Kitty,' said Eric, eavesdropping shamelessly, 'because she'll be sleeping soundly in the arms of Prince bloody Charming.' He paused for dramatic effect. 'Or, rather, Mr bloody Chips.'

Petra reddened. With a jolt, she was back from gold abbeys and tanzanite and platinum cloisters and her potential fame and fortune.

'Go to Ronnie Scott's,' Kitty told her sagely, 'or the Forum—wherever he asks you, you must go.' She tossed her head and took a long, lupine sniff at the air. 'This is your time, Petra, this is your time.' She closed her eyes. 'It's given.'

\*     \*     \*

'Was that your girlfriend, then, Mr Savidge?'

'I hope so.'

'You hope so? Lovers' tiff, was it, Mr S?'

'Not really. More like a cataclysmic impasse.'

'Is that why we're here in London, then?'

'Well—OK—sort of. Are you complaining, guys?'

'No, Mr S!'

'God, no.'

'Not at all.'

'No way!'

*　　　*　　　*

Arlo was currently guiding his flock through Soho. Dragging them, really. The plethora of sex shops and adult-video stores decelerating the Lower Sixth's pace to a lusty shuffle.

'Mr S—this is much better than school.'

'And if you want to have some—you know— *quality time with your lady*, well, me and the guys will be fine, Mr Savidge.'

'In your dreams, Callum Jones. In your mucky dreams.' Arlo laughed. He marched them along Wardour Street and herded them into Frith Street. 'Right, here we are. Ronnie Scott's.'

'Can we smoke, Mr S?'

'No, you bloody well cannot.'

*　　　*　　　*

Two hours later, after a lot of jazz, zero cigarettes and a quick shower and change of clothing back at the B&B, Arlo was seating his class at Pizza Express in Kentish Town.

'Can I borrow someone's mobile phone?' he asked from behind the menu. Felix offered his teacher his. 'Thanks,' said Mr Savidge. 'Mine's an American Hot, with extra mushrooms. I won't be a mo'.'

He loitered on the corner of Prince of Wales Road. Petra's number was now on the screen of Felix's phone. All Arlo had to do was press Call. He clocked the time. If she did want to come along, he was only giving her an hour and a half, and counting. He pressed the button and cleared his throat of the persistent butterfly.

'Hullo?'

'It's Arlo.'

'Oh my! You have a mobile phone?'

'No—it's one of my pupil's.'

'I see.'

'Yes.'

No time for pauses.

'Petra—would you like to come along tonight? It should be good. Quite raw. The bloke used to be in 3 Colours Red—the band, not the film. Do you remember "Sixty Mile Smile"? No? "This is My Time", perhaps? Well—will you come anyway? Say you will.'

'Yes, Arlo, I'll come.' But then Petra would have said yes even if it had been Keith Harris and Orville. This is my time, she told herself. This is my time.

*       *       *

It was daft really. She arrived late and yet when they trooped in, they were practically the only people there—the main act not due on for a further hour and the support act having no obvious supporters. Petra had been late because she'd turned the contents of her wardrobe over in search of something suitably rock-and-roll to wear. She tried the grunge look but reckoned she looked like a mad old bag lady. She changed into jeans and a T-shirt but worried that she looked as though she'd made no effort. She dared to squeeze into her one mini-skirt but decried her legs as too pasty—tried black tights but they looked ridiculous for this time of year. She woke up Lucy, who said sleepily that a vintage ball-gown's always a winner. But Petra had nothing remotely close and nothing she could readily adapt. She phoned Kitty who considered the venue, the band and then said leather and hair loose. But though Petra could oblige with the hair, she owned no leather.

'Perhaps I shouldn't go,' she said.

'Don't be so stupid,' Kitty said. 'It's a bloody gig—it'll be dark and noisy and you'll be covered in crap beer by the end of it anyway. And Arlo probably won't give a damn what you wear—he just wants you to be there.'

Petra opted for a shortish skirt in a retro print, a white T-shirt, black trainers and a denim jacket because it meant she had pockets for phone, money and keys and didn't have to be encumbered by a bag. She tied her hair back because the last thing she wanted was for sweat to transform her ringlets to resembling snakes on acid, however rock-and-roll that look might be.

*     *     *

It was still a funny sight to see Arlo chaperoning four hulking Sixth Formers and yet they seemed reluctant to leave his side, even when they went inside. They were also polite to the point of shyness with Petra and though she could hardly hear herself think, let alone speak, she persisted in yelling interesting questions at them above the din, about schools and hobbies and other things that made her sound like their mums' friends. It amused Arlo. Petra sensed it amused him and she was desperate to nudge him, to poke her tongue out, to swear at him, hug him. But she daren't. It

367

felt less of a date and more that she was gatecrashing one of his classes. However, they did manage to exchange glances every now and then, which said, God almighty, this is a *gig*! We should be necking in some sticky sweaty corner! We should be getting pissed on vodka tonics in plastic beakers! We should be jumping around in the mosh like loonies!

The main act was superb, if thunderously loud, and his devoted followers leapt and pogoed and punched at the air. Petra had drunk two vodkas in plastic beakers, fast, and it made her believe she had springs in her legs and could pogo with the best of them. So she gamely did. Arlo delighted in the sight, even more so because his boys were gobsmacked.

'Come on!' they could see her mouth move at them. 'Come on!' She bounced over to take Alex and Thomas by the hand and haul them into the throng with her. Then she did the same to Felix and Callum. And then, once they were leaping about, she made her way over to Arlo.

'No way!' he gesticulated. 'No fucking way.'

'Yes way!' she shrieked. 'Come *on*!'

But when she then danced away from him, grinning a sixty-mile, one-hundred-watt smile, he shrugged and bounded into the crowd with her.

It was exhausting, exhilarating. It was deafening and pretty dangerous—the floor wct with a slippery cocktail of beer and spirits, the amps cranked to maximum output, the lighting trippy, the crowd boisterous. Petra felt hoarse and sweaty and a bit drunk and very hot and her feet had been stamped upon and she'd been shoved and jolted and someone's cigarette had come perilously close to her cheek. But she was dancing with Arlo and she felt energized, high and happy.

'I'm so glad I came.'

'What?' He couldn't hear her.

'I'm so glad you came.'

'Sorry?' He could see that she was saying something or other.

She gave up and grinned, snuck a kiss to his lips, and Arlo fondled her bottom and they both knew that his students had very probably seen.

*     *     *

Gig over. Out into the night. Ears ringing, sweat chilling. Make-up a bit smudged. White T-shirt stained. Beer sticky on the legs. The soles of their shoes clogged and tacky with God knows what. The boys begging Arlo to let them queue for a kebab.

'We didn't smoke, sir.'

'I think there's probably more harm in a dodgy kebab than in a ciggie, Thomas.'

'Can I have a fag instead of a kebab then, Mr S?'

'No, you bloody well can't!'

'If we queue for a kebab, it gives you and Miss Petra some, you know, *time*?'

Arlo and Petra glanced at each other, then they looked at Felix as if he was a genius. So the boys queued and Arlo and Petra stood, out of earshot but in view.

'So,' he said.

'So!' she said.

'Did you enjoy that?'

'Did I! That Chris McCormack is a rock *god*!'

'Are you drunk, Flint?'

369

'I think I am rather! Do I look like the wild woman of Borneo?'

'You look lovely. Tomorrow.'

'Do I look lovely—tonight?'

'No. I mean yes. I mean you look lovely. And what I mean is *tomorrow*. Can I see you?'

'Aren't you tied to your flock?'

'I can leave them in the capable hands of a shepherd at Columbia Records.'

'Your friend?'

'My friend Mike Smith.'

'Good old Mike Smith.'

'He's a lovely bloke—you'd like his wife too. I'll introduce you one day.'

'Talking of wives, did you hear about Jenn and your Nige?'

'Of course.'

'I miss Jenn.'

'Come back.'

'I don't know, Arlo. I—'

'Look, I need you to meet me tomorrow, Watford Junction. I'll escort the boys to Columbia Records first thing—then make my way over.'

'Watford? Why *Watford*?'

'I have an errand. I need you there. There's something I have to do. Something I have to tell you. Somewhere I have to go. Something you need to know.'


CHAPTER FORTY-SIX

There was a shoe in the fridge when Petra went there for the milk for her morning coffee. But she removed the shoe as if it was nothing unusual, nothing more sinister than a yoghurt past its sell-by date. Something that shouldn't be there—but no big deal. Very privately, she was frustrated at the indisputable evidence of her somnambulism because actually, she had awoken feeling well rested and eager to have the day under way. Oh, most auspicious day! A trip to Watford. A mystery! Why Watford? Why, why? She went back into her bedroom and sat on the edge of her bed contemplating the mug of coffee, blowing on it measuredly like a flautist, sending glinting concentric circles rippling across the surface, sipping demurely as if the Nescafé was Noilly Prat.

'Why Watford?' she wondered out loud. But she didn't dare answer herself out loud too. Nothing must tempt fate. She let two thoughts scuttle across her mind:

*Watford is where my father lives.*
*Is Arlo all set to do the honourable thing?*

A surge of adrenalin coursed through her. A sense that this was to be one of the defining days of her life.

Little did she know it was to be one of the defining days of Arlo's life, too. But he was acutely aware of the fact. It had prevented him from sleeping a wink.

\*　　\*　　\*

It did cross Petra's mind that Watford underground station would be more convenient than Watford Junction mainline—it was a pleasant walk to her father's house from there. But of course there was no way she could alert Arlo to this; nothing should compromise the magnitude of the gesture she was willing him to make. She did wonder if Arlo had actually been in touch with her father and if so, how had he come by his number? And if he hadn't, then might it be a wasted trip— because it was unlikely her father would be at home on a Friday morning. And then she thought that her daydreaming was veering off on a ridiculous tangent. Perhaps this trip had nothing at all to do with her family. But it would be amazing if it did have to do with the other. With betrothal. Perhaps there was some idyllic spot, which happened to be nearer Watford Junction, that Petra didn't know. Or perhaps they were going to meet someone. Arlo's mum, maybe? How far was Potters Bar? Could Watford be her suggestion? Is there a stately home near there with a nice place for lunch or something? Where's Hatfield House? Petra was hoping to meet her; Arlo spoke so fondly of her. And, being someone whose parents showed little interest in her, Petra had long been on the lookout for surrogates: subconsciously or otherwise. Was today really going to be that mystical day when she was going to be invited into a family? Whatever, Watford was fine by Petra.

Here we are.

Where's Arlo?

There he is.

Christ, he looks dreadful.

\*       \*       \*

Petra was aware that Arlo had seen her but that he

372

had chosen to look away. He was a hunched figure, deathly pale. His hands plunged deep into the pockets of his jeans, his shoulders hunched up against his ears, as if he was trapped in a micro-climate; that it was winter in his world and that he was freezing cold. Actually, it was T-shirt weather; cropped jeans and sandals for Petra.

'Hullo?' she said, cocking her head to peer up into his downcast face.

'Hi,' he said, darting away from eye contact as if it hurt. 'Hi.' He ushered her into a taxi, mumbling something to the driver.

She gave him a long, tender kiss on his cheek. He pecked her back. His eyes bloodshot, so dark around the sockets that it looked as though he'd been daubed with coal dust. He had that haunted look about him—like those photographs of miners who'd been trapped in some hell-hole deep beneath the surface of everyday life. Waiting to be rescued.

'Are you OK?'

'Didn't sleep.' He looked up at Petra and she wasn't sure whether his expression was so much beseeching as one of terror. The journey continued in silence. 'Here's fine,' he suddenly said, repeating himself when the cabbie said, 'But—' He took Petra's hand, dragging her. 'Come on,' he said and he set off; a sense of dread about the manner of his walk, as if his body was resigned to going in one direction but his soul was trying desperately to pull him in the other.

I don't think we are going to my father's, Petra thought. And I don't think Arlo is going to propose to me today.

So where is he taking me? And why has he

asked me to join him on a journey that he so obviously does not want to make?

*      *      *

His pace falters and then picks up and then falters again. As if positive thoughts are in constant battle with negative.

'You OK?' Petra had asked him a couple of streets ago.

'Fine,' he had said, unconvincingly.

'Where are we going?' Petra just asked him, deciding to be bright and cheery.

'Not far now,' he answered, his voice like paper being torn, floating away in the rush of traffic on the A41.

Petra thinks perhaps she ought not to talk until they've arrived at wherever it is that they are going. His hands are still in his pockets, but she links her arm through his and she thinks it's a good idea to smile for the both of them.

*      *      *

They are walking now alongside a cemetery.

Approaching the gates.

And this is where Arlo stops.

He turns to Petra.

*      *      *

'I—' His voice is choked by tears. Petra can see him visibly bite down hard on his bottom lip. He has his back to the gates. He is swaying, just perceptibly, from foot to foot—whether it's to

374

keep his balance, or whether he is losing it, is unclear.

'Arlo?' Petra says gently, touching his forearm with her fingertips. He takes a step back. Won't look at Petra. 'She's in there,' he says, with a quick look over his left shoulder.

*     *     *

Petra is standing in front of Arlo so she has to move a little to one side, to peer in the direction to which he alluded. She can't see anyone. Well, she can see an old boy, with his wheelbarrow. But she can't see a 'she'.

'Who is?' she asks.

'Helen is,' Arlo says.

'Helen's in there?'

'Yes.'

He's still not looking at her.

'Where?' Petra is flummoxed.

'In *there*,' Arlo says.

'She's in there right now?' Petra asks.

'Yes, she's in there,' Arlo says. He is shaking. 'She's dead.'

*     *     *

Petra is so physically winded by this that she staggers a step backwards. She is shocked, horrified and she's clasped her hands to her mouth—gobsmacked, literally. 'Helen *died*?'

Arlo is staring at his feet, his shoulders are starting to heave. Petra knows that he is crying and momentarily she is not quite sure the best way to react, for Arlo's sake. She's never seen a man cry.

375

Should she leave him alone or crowd him with the surges of love and sympathy she's feeling? She takes a step closer. Another. His hands are in his pockets. Occasionally, his voice breaks through the mostly silent, racking sobs. She slips her arms around his waist and lays her head against his chest. His heavy heavy heart. Her whirling, whirring mind. What should I say? How do I feel? Christ, she's *dead*.

Petra is relieved to feel, finally, Arlo's arms around her. He's not so much holding her tight, but clinging to her. And he's crying; his voice light, like a boy's. And Petra is OK with this. So she tells him so.

'It's OK, it's OK.'

And when he is quieting down a little she gently, very gently, says, 'What happened?'

And he says to her, in a voice as clear as the skies above them, 'I killed her.'


## CHAPTER FORTY-SEVEN

It does cross Petra's mind that the bench she and Arlo have limped to, and have sat on in long, long silence, is probably reserved for the elderly. It's dedicated to the memory of Alfred Harold and his dates show that he departed this world at a ripe old age. The bench is outside the cemetery, but huddled close to the wall. Arlo is slumped with the effort of his revelation. Petra is sitting bolt upright with the shock of it. It's as if it has left his body and speared hers.

'What happened?' she asks.

376

'I drove her to it,' Arlo says, 'literally.'

Petra isn't sure what she feels. Is she to run from him? Or is she here to save his soul? It feels as if her world is on the verge of demolition. Does she have time to stay and listen? Just so that she knows? But she is wary of what she's about to hear. Yet he's brought her this far. Haven't they both come this far? And that's big. She rests her back against Alfred Harold's bench and she and Arlo are shoulder to shoulder, touching.

'Ten years ago,' Arlo starts and then stops. Petra looks at him because she's sensed he's stopped breathing. He's staring hard and she knows he's a decade away. He exhales. 'Ten years ago, I met Helen. She was four years older than me. Very attractive. Very—well—sorted, in a way. I was songwriting. She was forging ahead in management—worked for a company that consulted at the record label I wrote for. I really really liked her. I know this sounds stupid—but I liked the fact that she was so driven, ambitious, tailored. She was a proper woman, I suppose. She was unlike anyone I'd been with—who up until then were mostly younger than me and in the music business. Archetypal rock chicks. It's difficult to paint you a picture. It's irrelevant in some ways. I was seduced by the whole yin-yang aspect—me the musician, strumming and strolling through life, working when I wanted, how I wanted, wearing what I felt like, living it up into the small hours, sleeping until the afternoon. Helen was this motivated, vibrant woman who was up with the lark and first in the office and wore expensive suits and killer heels. Initially, I got off on being her bit of rough—though actually, our backgrounds and families were very similar.

'I liked the way she bossed me around and organized my life. Everything felt so easy. I didn't have to think. We had good food, good wine, good sex, good prospects, good friends. So when she proposed to me a couple of years later—on a leap-year Valentine's Day—I didn't really think about saying no. I said yes. I thought, Why not? Everyone was delighted, of course. My mother was thrilled. Helen bossed her around too, in the nicest possible way—took her clothes shopping, tea at the Ritz, organized for the house to be redecorated, invited my mum over to her parents'. Organized her parents to involve my mum in all sorts. My mum was game. She'd been widowed, remember.

'And so my life bowled on. The wedding soon became everything. Helen chose the ring and I sent a cheque because she'd even thought to arrange for the invoice to be sent to me. She showed me pictures of our wedding venue, details of where we'd honeymoon, particulars of houses she thought would be suitable. And on and on it went. Was I happy? I wasn't unhappy. I was happy trotting at her high heels. I didn't have to think.

'Then Rox wanted a song and they didn't much care for my new stuff. And I wrote something specifically with them in mind—with their singer's voice in my ears—and they didn't like that either. And they said, How about a ballad? I hadn't really done ballads in a long while. I told them so and they said, Well, what did you do a while ago, and I laughed and strummed a few chords of "Among the Flowers" very fast and their jaws dropped and they said, We love, we love it. I said, Are you mad—I wrote that when I was a teenager.

'Anyway, I had to stand there and perform it for them and their manager, having not even thought about that song, let alone sung it, for years and years. But something swept over me, engulfed me, while I sang it. I'd love to say it was a vision of you, Petra—especially as look at us now, the full circle that we've come—but it wasn't like that. However, what the song did do, was transport me back to a time of such idealism, a time when my wishes and hopes were so pure, a time when I wrote songs like that because I believed absolutely that love made the world go round, that love was the greatest thing to which one should aspire, love was what songs were meant to be about, love was life's driving force.

'Deluded, maybe—I was only sixteen, seventeen, when I wrote "Among the Flowers".

'But singing it again made me experience anew all those dormant feelings. Those sky-reaching hopes and the freshness that had once defined me, that had inspired me to write that song, flooded back. And while I knew that I had over-romanticized love—because, back when I wrote it, I didn't really know anything about it, of course—I did know that there had to be more. Between me and Helen. There had to be more. Marriage—however old-fashioned—remains the apotheosis of love. And even though my early twenties had hardened some of the softness of my teenage dreams, I still knew that if you are to marry a woman you ought to really, really love her.

'And giving my love song to Rox was like relinquishing a little bit of me. When I looked to see what was left I saw a man about to fuck up his life and the life of another. I didn't want to be that man. And actually, I couldn't do that to my mum. She'd loved my dad so. I couldn't throw away that gold-edged leaf from their book which they'd so lovingly written.

'I had to call it off. For everyone's sake. For my sanity.

'I was a coward. I dithered and dallied and turned deaf ears to my conscience. And the wedding was getting closer and closer and the plans were being refined and the details were becoming even more ornate and expensive and with one week to go I thought to myself, If I don't say something now, I will be walking up that aisle in seven days' time and the rest of our lives, the lives of so many, will be my fault.

'But still I was a coward. And I was awful—I was sullen and cold, I suppose hoping to give Helen reason to call it off first. But she just laughed and patted me—I really remember that: she patted me—and she said, Don't you go getting cold feet now, the deposits are non-refundable. And Petra, I don't even know if she was joking. When I think back to it, Helen was so meticulous and organized, of course she'd have ensured money-back clauses where possible. She was brilliant at stuff like that. But it made me feel shit and I thought I'd better just shut up and put up.

'It was making me ill. I couldn't keep any food down. I couldn't work. All I could do was sleep. I'd sleep for great tracts of the day. Maybe it was a form of narcolepsy, I don't know—perhaps I slept to block it all out, to have time out from worrying about how to do what I knew I had to do. I could be anywhere—home, bus, work, eating, reading, talking—and sleep would just envelop me like a heavy black cloak of sublime nothingness.

'Helen was worried. Helen organized a doctor's appointment. Helen thought I had a virus, or a reaction to the jabs we'd had for our honeymoon. I didn't go to the doctor. I was asleep. I wouldn't have gone anyway. That night, when Helen came home from her last day at work—two days before the wedding—she was white as a sheet. And I just about managed to tear myself away from the TV to say, Are you OK, babe? And she said, You don't love me, Arlo, do you? And my pause was all the information she needed. And she said, Shit. And I said, I'm sorry. And she said, Do you really not love me? And I said, I really really like you— you're an amazing woman. And she said, Did I think I could still marry an amazing woman that I really really liked? And there was no pause before I said, No, I didn't think I could. And Helen yelled, Are you telling me that I'm to call off my wedding? And I yelled, It's my wedding too. And she screamed, It was never your fucking wedding, Arlo.

'And that's the last thing she said to me.

'She drove off in a fury. I don't know where she was going. No one does. To her parents, I suppose. But there was a crash.'

*     *     *

'You didn't kill her,' Petra weeps, turning to Arlo urgently.

*     *     *

'I did,' Arlo says before Petra can continue. 'She was on life support. Her parents thought I should

381

be the one to turn the machine off. On our wedding day. They thought it would be symbolic. They thought it would help me heal. They thought it was what Helen would have wanted. So you see, I did kill her, Petra. I broke her heart. I broke her body. And then I turned the fucking machine off and that was that.'

His breath is coming fast and shallow.

'And they all still think I'm some kind of saint for whom tragedy struck at such a young age. And I haven't corrected them. Everyone loves me, everyone cares about me, everyone feels so desperate for me. I've never told anyone the truth, Petra. I've been living a lie. I've never told anyone any of this. No one knows. No one knows. Just you. My lovely lovely you.'

Petra's fingers go fast to Arlo's lips and she stares at him intensely. 'That's enough,' she says. He's had enough pain. She doesn't think she can absorb any further details. She can't believe there possibly can be any more.

Gently, he pulls her fingers away, kisses the palm of her hand while he closes his eyes against the pain of the past and what he presumes to be his lost future—who is sitting on the bench next to him, staring him lovingly in the face.

'For the last five years, I've been getting all this love which I just don't deserve. I'm seen as victim, not perpetrator. People want only for my happiness. They all think I deserve happiness, that I deserve to find love again. Hence me running away from everything I knew. Becoming a teacher. Making the North York Moors my home. Hence the celibacy. And then you. Into my life came you.'

382

*      *      *

'But Arlo—?'

*      *      *

Again he silences her. 'No. Do you know something, Petra, when you left me over the Miranda stuff, I desperately needed some space to myself—so do you know what I did? I rang Helen's parents and said, Hullo, how are you, can I use your little place in Scotland and they said, Arlo, Arlo, how lovely to hear from you, of course you can. How are you, Arlo? How are you? Will you come and see us soon?'

Tear-stained and tired, he turns to Petra.

'That's me,' he shrugs. 'Nice, aren't I?'

*      *      *

Petra daren't speak. She just hopes that her own tears, and her slow shake of her head will be read in the spirit they are meant: Don't say such things, Arlo. You poor poor man of mine.

*      *      *

He turns his head and stares along the cemetery wall.

'I haven't been back, Petra. I haven't been here. I haven't been in there. Not since the funeral.'

Petra follows his gaze. She puts her arm around him, a slow and gentle embrace, like an adult soothing a child.

'I've never said sorry.'

383

'It's never too late,' Petra tells him. 'It's never too late. You're here now. Go. Go to Helen. Go now, Arlo. Take your time. I'll wait. I'll be here for you. I promise.'

*     *     *

He looks at Petra as if she's an angel. He looks at Petra as if she's insane. He looks along the wall towards the entrance and whilst he's looking there, he starts to nod. And then he leaves the bench and walks away.

*     *     *

Petra waits. Almost fifty minutes she waits. And while she waits she concentrates hard on things like the configuration of paving stones. She searches for tessellations in the cemetery wall. She tries to find a sequence in the colours of the cars that hurtle past her. She counts between lorries. Anything, anything. She'll think about anything else.

*     *     *

Arlo is walking back to her. He looks desperately tired.

He pulls her to her feet and holds her against him, kisses and kisses the top of her head.

'I have to go,' he says. 'I have to go right now. I have to collect the boys from Columbia Records. Then on to Wigmore Hall. Then we have to pack. We leave at the crack of dawn.'

He whispers thank you, and sorry, over and over

384

again. He leaves her. Jaywalks over the A41. Disappears from view.

Petra is left, sitting on Alfred Harold's bench, trying to digest but far too full to ruminate.

Eventually, she decides she should make a move. She wonders whether to phone her father and say, Dad, can you come and collect me, I'm a bit stuck. But Petra has never turned to her father in all the times she's been stuck. And he'll be at work anyway. It's just a regular Friday morning in June. So Petra heads off down the A41 because she knows there are two huge supermarkets further on. And at ASDA, she takes a cab back to Watford Junction.


## CHAPTER FORTY-EIGHT

Petra did toy with the idea of phoning Felix's mobile and asking to speak to his teacher. She'd gone directly from Euston to the studio, staying long enough only to assure the others what a wonderful time she'd had the night before and to force an enigmatic smile to explain away her late arrival. She was unsure whether Watford was to be the making of Arlo and her, or whether it was the death knell which rang in her ears alongside Arlo's words. She did know she did not want to talk about it just yet. Politely declining her Studio Three's suggestion of Friday evening drinks, Petra left to spend the last part of the afternoon with Charlton discussing hinges and links and pivots. It was only later, sitting in her dank little flat passing her mobile from hand to hand, that she had an overwhelming desire to reach out to Arlo. The enormity of what he'd been through, the repercussion for the rest of his life, began to sink in. She knew he was somewhere in Swiss Cottage until dawn. But she also knew that a student's phone did not provide the best route. The tragedy was immense. She hadn't experienced anything which came even close. What on earth could she say? But she saved the boy's number anyway.

Her phone rang almost immediately. She jumped. Felix? No, Lucy. Petra was strangely disappointed.

'Hi, Luce.'

'Well?'

'Well what?'

'*Well what*, she says! Petra! Come on—I'm all ears. How was the concert?'

It hit Petra that, despite Lucy being her oldest, closest friend, she couldn't, she wouldn't, betray Arlo's confidence. It was the strangest feeling. It no longer mattered that, historically, Petra told Lucy everything; that sometimes she felt unable to make decisions without Lucy's guidance, that she had so often depended on her friend to know what to do, to tell her what to say, to decide what was good for Petra, what was not. Though Petra mightn't know how it would all pan out with Arlo in the long run, just then she did know that she deeply respected him and felt his torment acutely. She didn't feel the shame he so obviously endured, nor was she embarrassed by the facts. They distressed her, of course they did, but for her at least their impact was positive. So, though it was Lucy on the phone—her beloved, trusted, revered friend phoning all the way from Hong Kong at two

386

in the morning her time—just then Petra loved Arlo the most. In fact, she loved him with every fibre of her being. It was a feeling she had certainly not experienced thus far in her life. She felt exhilarated and exhausted.

'Petra? God, come on, girl—it's like getting blood out of a stone. Oh! Ah! Hang on—he's there with you *now*, isn't he? That's why you can't talk—you dark, dark horse, you!'

'Shall we speak soon?'

Lucy laughed with delight.

'Give the teacher an apple for me,' Lucy laughed.

'Bye, Luce. Speak soon.'

\*     \*     \*

Soon after she'd finished speaking to Lucy, Petra dialled Arlo's folly. She knew that he wouldn't be there, but just the ringing was affirming. She could picture the place so clearly. She wanted to be back there soon. She'd speak to Charlton first thing Monday.

\*     \*     \*

'Is that for me?'

Arlo glanced in the rear-view mirror of the minibus at the sound of Felix's mobile phone. So far, on the journey, the boys' phones had rung often enough for Arlo to be able to now differentiate between their various ring tones. Felix had already had a couple of calls.

'No, sir, sorry, sir—it's my,' Felix mumbled, 'it's my mum.'

387

The other boys sniggered for a moment. Felix didn't take the call. The A1 was closed and they were being sent on a detour through the Fens; the flat landscape dull in places, desolate in others, exuding an overall loneliness, a solitariness which echoed how Arlo felt. He felt very flat. London seemed far away. If he couldn't be in London—and he really couldn't be in London—then he wanted to be way beyond the Fens. He craved the landscape to roll and clamber, to herald Yorkshire. To be back within the confines of school, where he was safe, where he didn't have to think, where life wasn't complicated and there were no reminders of how complicated his life had been. He put his foot down.

'You've been flashed, Mr S.'

'Flashed?'

'Speed camera, Mr Savidge.'

'Fuck it.'

The boys grinned at each other. Even the Lower Sixth loved it when a teacher swore.

'Guys, could you put your phones on silent, please—I find it distracting.'

'Can we listen to some music, then?'

'Yes, Mr S!'

'Of course.' Arlo ferreted around in his bag. 'This is a compilation I've done. I call it "Reverse Blasphemy"—it's songs by the great and godly which, in my opinion, were actually done justice in cover versions. However, be careful in whose company you say you prefer the Byrds' version of "Mr Tambourine Man" to Bob Dylan's, or St Etienne's version of "Only Love Will Break Your Heart" to Neil Young's—though it's probably very cool to prefer Johnny Cash's "One" to U2's. Ditto

388

Ugly Kid Joe's take on Harry Chapin's "Cat's in the Cradle". Or Jeff Buckley's "Hallelujah" rather than Leonard Cohen's. To me, Dylan is God, but I have to concede that Guns n' Roses do "Knockin' on Heaven's Door" better. And it's a fact universally acknowledged that Joe Cocker's "With a Little Help from My Friends" is far better than the Beatles' but that nobody will ever do Hendrix better than Jimi himself. Anyway, have a listen. And there's a competition for you to tell me who did the originals.'

'What's the prize, Mr Savidge?'

'A copy of this compilation, Thomas.'

'Cool.'

And suddenly Arlo felt that all might be well in his world after all. This is what he did best, wasn't it: music, teach. Not love, not London.

And see—the landscape is climbing now they have passed the Vale of York.

With home tangibly close at last, Arlo switched off part of his heart.


CHAPTER FORTY-NINE

It was four days since Arlo had left London and though Petra was concerned not to have heard from him, an overriding sense of relief stopped her feeling too fraught and kept her spirit strong. However, she knew not to tempt fate by asking Charlton for the keys to the Old Stables just yet. She thought to herself, If ever someone needed a little unhurried time to themselves, it's now and that person is Arlo. Her response to her Studio

389

Three's probing was to be non-committal in a carefully employed upbeat manner—so that suspicions were not aroused and she was spared further questioning. She was the same with Lucy. There was a part of her wishing she could say out loud to them all, See! I'm dealing with this by myself—something huge but I can cope—aren't you proud of me? But that would defeat the object somewhat. It was true; she was deep into an extreme situation yet she felt no need to consult anyone but herself. If she had confided in those to whom she was so close, she would have had to reveal her sense of relief. And though the feeling of it was good and encouraging, the source of it was slightly troubling.

Would I be feeling this fine about things if Helen were still alive?

It's always easier if an ex is no longer on the scene. Helen was certainly out of the picture but did this really mean Petra was relieved she was dead? Petra felt a surge of guilt and shuddered at such a heinous thought. The enormity of the situation, of Arlo's past, had enabled her to rate Miranda as inconsequential, to judge Miranda's venomous reaction to her as actually quite flattering. She didn't doubt the hierarchy in Arlo's affections, nor the strength of his feelings for her. In a warped sort of way, women—whether living or dead—were mad for a man who had eyes only for her. So, though she was itching to see him, to hold him, make love to him, to tell him everything was going to be all right from now on, she felt prepared to allow him time. He needed to be the one to say, I'm OK, I'm ready, I miss you, come.

Though she told herself to be patient, to give him space, by the Thursday she rapidly justified that Arlo might appreciate a nudge in the right direction. She reasoned that though she hadn't heard from him, nor had he heard from her. And it was this thought that compelled her to dart from the studio, find a quiet doorway and phone Arlo. There was no reply from the folly. Of course not, he'd be teaching.

*     *     *

Home from the studio, Petra was all set to grab the phone and dial Yorkshire again when, in her mind, she heard Mrs McNeil's vivid voice warning her against doing anything on an empty stomach. So Petra took a long look in the fridge, a pointless exercise considering how little was in it, heated the remainder of the carton of Covent Garden soup she'd had for her supper yesterday and poured it into a mug. She'd intended to buy a nice baguette but in her urgency to be home she'd forgotten. There was some pitta in the fridge too, slightly hard, but she sprinkled a little water over it and toasted it. She pricked the pitta with a fork and added butter just as an artist might use a palette knife to smear oil paint onto canvas or a bricklayer load cement onto a run of wall.

'I like a bit of pitta with my butter,' she trilled to herself as she took her supper through to the living room. She sipped soup, licked an ooze of melted butter trickling to her wrist and thought about what she'd say to Arlo, the tone in which she'd say

391

it.

Hullo, you.

How's you?

Hey, you.

Hey.

Oh, will you just stop bloody clomping around up there—I can't hear myself think!

Her neighbours appeared to be dancing in clogs directly above her and, as Petra frowned up to the ceiling, she could have sworn she could see it bulge and bow as the family galumphed around. She took her mobile into her bedroom, muttering to Mrs McNeil that she'd finish the soup later. The clog dance was only slightly more muffled in her bedroom. But she dialled. And waited. Perhaps he didn't hear the phone. She dialled again. Still no answer. Demoralized, she returned to her soup.

*     *     *

She tried Arlo's number again, an hour later.

He's answering!

'Hullo?'

'Arlo! Hey you hullo it's me how's you!'

Had she just imagined he'd answered?

'Hullo? Arlo? Are you there? It's Petra!'

She could hear him clear his throat. Maybe he'd been eating his supper too!

'Hi.'

'Hey!'

An unnervingly long pause. Blether blithely on, Petra told herself. 'I thought I'd give you a call. I've been thinking about you—all the time. As you can imagine. And I just wanted to say I miss you, Arlo. So I thought I'd jump on a train tomorrow

392

afternoon—be with you early evening. Even if you have Saturday morning school—I don't mind. I just want to—you know. Be with you. Again.' Honest yet effervescent. Good. 'Arlo?'

There was silence. She thought of Helen. Miranda. 'Arlo,' she soothed, 'I love you. Everything's going to be OK.' But the silence was even thicker. 'Arlo?'

'Petra—'

'It's OK, Arlo, everything will be all right. I'm here.'

'Petra—I. This isn't going to work. I'm sorry.'

Now the silence was Petra's. She couldn't have said a word anyway, not with soup creeping back up her gullet.

'I'm sorry,' he was saying, his voice sounding distant in comparison to the heartbeat thundering in her ears. 'It's me. I can't do this. I'm sorry.'

She sensed if she didn't say something, he'd hang up.

'But Arlo—'

'I'm sorry, Petra,' he said. 'It's better this way. Believe me.'

'Are you going to hang up on me?'

'Goodbye, Petra.'

And she said, But I love you, to the dialling tone.

\*     \*     \*

If I'd phoned him on Monday or Tuesday or Wednesday—if I was up in Yorkshire by now—could I have prevented this?

\*     \*     \*

393

Petra had felt quite happy allowing Arlo all the time she assumed he needed. But it had never crossed her mind that when she finally spoke to him, he'd say, Sorry, goodbye.

He was meant to say, Will you come, will you be here, I need you.

*       *       *

Those sodding bloody elephants clodhopping about upstairs. How can a girl think.

*       *       *

She couldn't sleep. At least that meant she wouldn't sleepwalk. And her insomnia made her feel closer to Arlo. What's he thinking? she wondered. What's he thinking right now? What's he feeling?

And then it hit her that Arlo probably didn't know what to think because he hadn't visited Helen's grave since he buried her and the day he buried Helen he also buried all thoughts of her. Celibacy. Insomnia. Anything to keep thoughts and memories at bay. For five long years.

Oh my God, oh Christ. A young life violently extinguished. Arlo believing he is to blame. How can I have been so glib as to think my future with Arlo could be the rosier, easier, for Helen's death? It will mark Arlo's life for ever. It makes everything far more complex. What can I do? I have to do something.

How can I soothe?

Can I save?

I'm sure I can.

*     *     *

A single voice started to filter through the whirr in Petra's mind. It was Mrs McNeil's, with one of her favourite dictums.

*Pursue your dreams—especially when you think they're getting away from you.*

Petra felt sleepy at last.

I will soothe. I will save.

*     *     *

But she awoke very early feeling dispirited. Women always think they can save men—it's our greatest failing. These weren't Mrs McNeil's words, they were Petra's. She showered for a long time. What can I do? Perhaps the only thing I can do is just try to accept the magnitude of what happened to Arlo. See if I can simply help, rather than save. Because I do so love him. And he's hurting and I want to soothe.

She packed a holdall and set off for Hatton Garden. She didn't go to the studio, she went directly to the Charlton Squire Gallery only to curse Charlton in his absence for being so successful that he didn't need to open until ten bloody thirty. So she went to the studio and filled two hours working intently on the system of hinges and pivots that were not far off enabling a purple boiled sweet to rotate in any direction. When Gina and Kitty and Eric arrived, Petra said as casually as she could manage that she was just popping over to Charlton's and did anyone need anything. She wished she hadn't added that last part as she was given a long list of coffee particulars from the others.

*      *      *

'Hullo, darling,' said Charlton. 'How's it hingeing?'

*      *      *

'Brilliant,' Petra said, adding to herself that an awful lot hinged on Charlton too. 'Charlton—I don't suppose I could use the Stables this weekend—spur of the moment, I know, but I have my ticket and my bag is packed.'

'Oh darling, I am sorry. Friends are up there for the next week or so,' Charlton said. Petra looked crestfallen. 'It's free for most of July though,' he added because July was only a fortnight away. Petra just about managed to muster a thank-you before she fled the gallery.

She looked about her and suddenly hated London, felt trapped. Ignored Mrs McNeil when she heard her voice saying, *Everything happens for a reason*.

I can't pursue my dreams if I'm stuck here in sodding London.

And then she thought, Who needs Charlton when I have Jenn?

*      *      *

'Of course you can come!' Jenn said. 'That's bloody marvellous, that is. Nige is doing Saturday morning tomorrow and some poncey school thing

396

tonight so you and I can paint the town red, girl. Or we can have a takeaway washed down with plonk and do our nails and watch crap TV. But there again, it's karaoke night at Chapters and I am not known as the Dancing Queen for nothing, you know. When does your train arrive? I'll collect you from Northallerton—I'm visiting a client in York anyway, so I'll be passing.'

When Jenn finally paused for breath, Petra managed to slip in that Arlo didn't know she was coming.

'Will you be wanting to see him tonight, then?' Jenn sounded bereft already.

'He doesn't want to see me at all,' Petra told her.

Although it lasted just a second or two, Petra could feel how thoughtful Jenn's pause was. 'Oh.' She paused again. 'Can I help?'

'Yes,' said Petra, 'I think you very possibly can.'

\*       \*       \*

It was on seeing Jenn that all the fighting spirit Petra had experienced on the train crumbled into the need for a long hug and a short, sharp sob.

'Come on, chuck, let's get you home,' Jenn said. 'Plenty of tea and sympathy. Or, if you prefer, wine and a whine.'

\*       \*       \*

Petra had been to Jenn's house in Yarm a couple of times before. It was small, but stylishly done, with white walls and knocked-through rooms giving a sense of space and calm; expensive scented

397

candles, silk scatter cushions, luxurious cream tufted rugs and framed Joe Cornish photographs giving the atmosphere of a boutique hotel. Petra compared it to her own flat. Yorkshire pounds obviously went much further than London pounds. But what was the point mulling over such a fact when Petra couldn't afford to buy in London nor, it seemed now, was there any reason for her to be even thinking of property up here.

'I need to phone the office, pet—you run yourself a bath and have a good old soak. Have yourself a glass of wine. Go on! It's Friday night. I am.'

There were two bedrooms upstairs. The master double looked out to the front and had its own door to the bathroom. The spare bedroom looked out over the back-to-back courtyards, Jenn's having a table, four chairs and a bright pink parasol squeezed amongst pots of flowering annuals. After her bath, Petra lounged on the bed, running her hand over the crisp white linen, admiring all Jenn's touches: soft voile panels, creamy velvet curtains, little girly knick-knacks, limed oak furniture, everything spick and span. Petra had to admit that actually this was preferable to the Old Stables. She knew that too much navel-gazing was not good for a person and that while Jenn would happily navel-gaze alongside her for a while, she'd probably end up suggesting Petra pierce hers and offer to do it for her after another six glasses of wine. No. The Old Stables would be a step backwards. This trip up north was to be about finding ways to move forwards.

*     *     *

They didn't go to Stokesley. They didn't go out at all. Jenn had crept upstairs to find Petra asleep and had let her rest until 9 p.m. when she woke her with a Hurry up, love, ours teas are getting cold.

Clearing away the takeaway cartons—with Jenn decanting leftovers onto a plate and shamelessly admitting it would be her breakfast the next morning—they took their wine into the front room and flopped, replete, onto the sofa. Jenn burped under her breath. Petra matched it with a belch of her own at which Jenn clinked their glasses and said, That's my girl.

'Do you want to tell me the nitty gritty?'

Petra shrugged. 'There was someone else,' she said, wondering how she could be ambivalent without either hurting Jenn's feelings, doing a disservice to Helen, compromising Arlo's confidence or making him seem like a sod.

'Not that old slink at the school? She's leaving anyway.'

'No, not Miranda,' Petra said. 'Someone else—a long time ago.'

'Oh God, the ghost of first love?'

'I think she made things very difficult for Arlo,' Petra said carefully, 'because she really wanted things to last.'

'Silly cow.'

'Well, not really. I mean, they were actually engaged. But he called it off. Please don't tell Nigel. Ever. Whatever happens.'

Jenn marked an 'X' over her heart with her index finger. 'Is she still on the scene?'

Petra looked at Jenn and thought, What do I say now. If I say no, that's true enough but is it enough truth? 'No.'

'Is she a bunny boiler?'

Petra had to smile. And then it vanished. My new best friend. It's so much worse. 'She died.'

'Bloody hell, bloody bloody hell.' Jenn thought about this as she replenished their glasses. 'It's a commitment issue,' she announced. 'He'll be thinking, Oh God, I love this woman but look what happened last time. So he's doing what all little boys do best—running away and hiding in a flipping tree with his hands over his flaming eyes. Daft bastard.' Jenn paused, her eyes glinted, she lowered her voice theatrically. 'He may even be worrying that you'll die.'

Petra's face told Jenn that she hadn't considered this.

'You did the right thing belting up here, pet,' Jenn said, chinking their glasses. 'You know, in my vast and colourful experience, I have come to the conclusion that all boys are daft bastards. It's actually down to us to tell them how they're feeling. Bless them—they wouldn't know otherwise. They wouldn't have a flaming clue.'

\*     \*     \*

The next morning, Petra borrowed Jenn's bike and promised she'd update her by text or a phone call at the earliest opportunity. Jenn had managed to subtly find out from Nigel which teachers were on Saturday morning school. Arlo's name was not mentioned and Petra wanted to intercept before he made headway into any plans he had for the day. The first part of the route, from Yarm to the school, was unfamiliar and was thus easier, somehow, for Petra to ride. The latter part was the same as from Stokesley, and though the road was straight and relatively flat, pedalling felt arduous. Petra's body seemed to be putting more energy into adrenalin production than into powering her legs or her lungs.

The gate. The intercom. She knew her way around it. In the distance, a Walley Brother, skulking around with a wheelbarrow heaped with God knows what under a tarpaulin flapping about like a dead bird's wing. Boys washing the minibus. Boys playing cricket. Howzat! I don't know, I don't know at all, I don't know what I'm meant to say or what he's going to say when he sees me. I don't know how it's going to go.

She knocks at the folly.

'It's open,' comes the reply.

In she goes. She closes the door. She's alone in the sitting area. She loves this place. Don't look— not just yet. Don't tempt fate. Don't muck this up.

Arlo comes through from the bathroom, bare-chested, a towel around his waist, another towel in his hands, wiping his face dry though he's inadvertently missed a glob of shaving foam on his jaw. He continues to wipe his face as if he's unsure what expression will alight there if he stops. He's wet, little rivulets coursing a crooked path between the hairs on his legs.

'Hullo,' says Petra and she gives a shy wave, for emphasis.

'What are you—?'

Petra shrugs. Turns her head to look through to the kitchen because she can't quite look him in the eye and she fears he might not be looking back at her anyway. The light glances off her face. 'Well,'

401

she says. 'I don't know.' And she shrugs her shoulders and says, I don't know again. Then she stops thinking, releases her lips from her teeth and looks bluntly at Arlo. 'I came because you're not getting rid of me that easily, mister.' He's stopped wiping his face; the shaving cream remains. 'I feel how much you love me—and I know you know how much I love you. And it would be very very bad—and also pretty dumb—to let such a good thing go to waste.'

Arlo slings the towel over his shoulder, he strokes his head pensively. In a week, his hair has grown, it looks nice so fuzzy. 'Petra—I. You deserve more.'

'Maybe so,' Petra says, 'but I'll be the judge of that, thank you very much. I'm a stubborn old thing and all I want is you.'

'This isn't about you,' Arlo attempts to say.

'I know,' says Petra, 'I agree. It's about *you*.'

He comes over towards her but veers left to flop onto the sofa. He turns his head and looks through to the kitchen and the light catches his face.

'Arlo—nothing that you told me makes me feel any the less for you. If anything, it's made me love you more. To be party to your pain is a privilege.'

He raises his eyebrows but won't meet her eyes.

She sits next to him, turns her body towards him though he continues to look straight ahead, or straight into the nub of the matter.

'All these years, Arlo,' she says, 'all these years you've felt that you're keeping this dreadful secret but actually I think that secret's been keeping you.'

His brow furrows, but she sees that it does so in grief not disagreement.

'And it's not a dreadful secret, Arlo—what

402

happened *was* terrible. Almost unfathomably so. But it was a terrible accident. It was not your fault. You don't need to do penance. You don't need to be celibate. You don't need to punish yourself any more. You're a good man, Arlo. Otherwise you wouldn't have felt it to the depth that you have.'

The knot between his eyebrows remains. Petra takes her thumb and gently tries to iron out the crease. 'You didn't kill Helen, Arlo,' she whispers. 'She died. She just died. A horrific accident. A very real tragedy. But if she hadn't died, you still wouldn't have married her. You did the right thing. Her death was not punishment. It was a tragedy, it was an accident. It was not your fault.'

'I've been living a lie,' he says. 'I'm a coward. I don't even have the courage to tell the truth.'

Petra feels a little cross with him. 'This is not cowardice, Arlo Savidge,' she says sternly, 'it's utter selflessness. The truth, in this situation, would have added unnecessary hurt to so many who were suffering so much. I think you're amazing. You did the right thing—by everyone, at the expense of yourself. Do you hear that? You've done the right thing. You're that kind of man. That's why I love you. You know what's the right thing to do.'

She puts her hand over Arlo's and slumps a little. She doesn't know what else she can say, really. Even if he truly does not want to continue his relationship with her, she's still glad to have been able to tell him that he's OK, that what he did was right, that he must stop blaming himself and punishing himself.

'Is leaving you the right thing to do?' he asks. As he turns to her, his eyes swim into hers. 'Tell me that's not cowardice.'

Petra waits for her moment. 'It *is* utter cowardice, you silly sod,' she says softly. Then she pokes him on the arm. 'Tell me you don't really need me to tell you that leaving me was the *wrong* thing to do.'

'Well—perhaps you could just tell me instead what's the *right* thing to do?'

Petra thinks she can tell that he does know the answer but that he needs to hear it from her. 'Let me love you with all that I am, Arlo—and I'll let you love me right back.' It's not enough, she can see that. 'Let me in—and let yourself out, just little by little. You've incarcerated yourself for these long five years. I am telling you that you can now begin to come out.'

He is silent. Distant. 'That's a tall order, Petra. And it's easier said by you than done by me. I've become accustomed to the grief and the guilt. They've shaped my life.'

'I'm sure,' she says. 'But will you let me be here for you?'

'*Amor vincit omnia*?'

She considers this. 'I don't know if love does conquer all, Arlo. But it certainly provides us with the blanket to comfort our woe and the armour to face our battles.' Oh, lovely man. She lays her arm gently around his shoulders. 'It's OK,' she tells him.

'But it hasn't been OK for such a long time.' And his face crumples as he cries.

Petra can blot his tears, kiss them away, whisper hope into his heart, but finally she acknowledges that she can't make it all better in a single day. It will take time. The road ahead might be rocky in places but it stretches way beyond the horizon to the future. And, from the way Arlo has finally let himself sink into her embrace, she knows they're in this together.

*　　*　　*

'I should get dressed,' he says. He smiles at her. His blotchy eyes and snotty nose. 'Are you busy today?'

'Nope,' she says, scooping that glob of shaving foam from his jaw and tapping it onto her nose.

It makes him smile and behind their redness his eyes do shine. 'Shall we go for a walk then? A long one?'

'Yes. Let's.'

## CHAPTER FIFTY

What made Petra's return to London all right wasn't merely the tangibility of Arlo's planned visit the coming weekend, it was the knowledge that there was no urgency to the future, the future didn't have to be in one place or the other, it was now located firmly between the two of them. The train journey back south was thus easy to make—though she very nearly did an about-turn back to King's Cross station when she came across the unbelievable mess at her flat.

The ceiling had fallen in.

Upstairs's floor was in her front room, on top of all the furniture and her possessions.

Sodding bloody clodhopping elephants, thought

Petra.

Bloody leak, said her neighbours, We're surprised you didn't notice any bulge in your ceiling.

*       *       *

Eric came to the rescue. Petra was packed and ready for him.

'Is that all?' he said, looking at her one suitcase and two carrier bags.

'My clothes, my tanzanite and the food from my fridge,' she said.

'Come on, the cab's waiting.'

Though he gazed out of the window as if fascinated by the scenery of Finchley, Eric listened thoughtfully while Petra rabbited to Arlo on her phone. There was no plea for sympathy, no dramatizing of the situation, no little-girl-lost working the heart-strings of her beau. What Eric heard was his friend Petra chattering away. And it made him laugh hearing her tell Arlo to sod off after some obviously snide comment in response to all her Robbie Williams CDs being ruined.

'She can listen to mine,' Eric eavesdropped in.

'Tell Eric to fuck off,' he could hear Arlo laugh.

Eric liked it that Petra giggled, liked to see her eyes sparkle as she listened. He liked to see her so happy that she was really relaxed and truly herself. He'd never seen her that way when she'd been with someone in the past, he'd only ever seen her that way in the periods in between. This Arlo, Eric thought, He's all right. This Arlo has brought out the best in Petra and he's making her very happy.

Kitty was slightly miffed that Petra had turned in the first instance to Eric and not to her.

'You won't find Dannii Minogue posters in *my* flat, and it's a Shirley Bassey-free zone,' she said. 'My spare bed has an orthopaedic mattress and I have every candle in the Diptyque range.'

'But you're in *New Cross*,' Petra explained, 'and my passport is under the rubble. At least the Brondesbury postcode starts with an "N".'

'God—you and all things North,' Kitty said. 'Soon you'll be telling me there's no "R" in bath or laugh.'

*      *      *

Actually, Eric was a very good host. He and Petra had lived together as students and he'd kept the shared house ordered and clean back then. His own flat now was in a quiet street, near the park. Decorated not by the Minogue sisters but with framed black-and-white photos on neutral-coloured walls. Two voluminous sofas placed perfectly for the plasma television, his vast DVD collection (without a single Marlene Dietrich film) concealed behind flat matt touch-spring cupboard doors. He had a fair few Diptyque candles of his own. His kitchen was small but high-tech and the plentiful fresh produce in his fridge was all but colour coordinated. His spare bed may not have been officially orthopaedic in the mattress stakes compared to Kitty's, but it was very comfortable and if Petra was to sleepwalk, she'd have to creak over the bare floorboards past Eric's bedroom first and he'd wake up and find her. Just like he used to do ten years ago. He really was as close as Petra would ever come to having a protective older brother.

*       *       *

She did sleepwalk. On the second night. But Eric heard her fiddling with the chain on the door. He found her wearing his dressing gown—she must have been into his bedroom to get it—and she'd stuffed the pockets with fruit and the remote control.

'It's very important that we get there in good time,' she told him while he guided her back to bed and told her, Yes, that's right, of course we will, don't you worry, come this way, Eric's here, Eric's here.

'I wonder where I was going,' she said the next morning while Eric brought her a glass of melon-and-pomegranate juice, freshly made by one of his shiny gadgets.

'God knows,' Eric said. 'Do you ever know where you are going?'

'I can never remember a thing. Although occasionally I *think* I think I'm in my childhood home. But there again, maybe that's in dreams. I don't know.'

'But I wonder why you'd imagine yourself back there? It was years ago for a start—and a place about which you feel indifferent at best.'

Petra shrugged. Eric shrugged back.

'Who knows,' she said. 'Not I.'

'One of life's great mysteries,' Eric said, 'your late-night sorties. What does Arlo think?'

408

Petra thought about this. 'He's like you, Eric. He wakes up for me and makes sure I'm OK.'

\* \* \*

Eric did tell Petra that Arlo was more than welcome to stay at the flat that weekend and initially Petra accepted on his behalf. But then Arlo told her that his mother had invited the two of them to stay with her and when Eric saw Petra as excited as if she was going to Buckingham Palace for the weekend, he decided not to be insulted that his offer had been rejected.

\* \* \*

'Love suits her,' Gina said to Kitty as they admired Petra's advanced mock-up of the tanzanite piece. 'It's obviously fanning her creative flame. Golly, she's worked fast.'

'It's stunning,' Kitty said.

They took it in turns to try it on, moving the boiled sweet this way and that.

'Has she decided on platinum? I think she should. She'll be able to charge thousands—tens of thousands.'

'She'll be able to retire,' Gina laughed.

'Up to North bloody Yorkshire.'

'Actually, she'll never retire, Kitty.'

'Maybe so—but once she's sold this she'll be able to afford a house up there *plus* kit out a state-of-the-art studio.'

On the Friday lunch-time, Petra had finished the design. She felt euphoric, triumphant, and she lapped up the praise and wonderment from her

Studio Three. She took the bracelet straight to Charlton who considered it in silence for an inordinate amount of time.

'Do you have your tanzanite on you?'

'Yes, of course—you don't think I'd leave it under Eric's spare-room mattress, do you? He has a cleaner twice a week.' Petra took the velvet pouch from her bag and tipped the stone into Charlton's hand.

'You could just sell me the stone, you know.'

'Charlton—how many times?'

'I know, love, I know.' He looked at his watch. 'Can you stick around, Pet? There's a certain someone due in, any time now. Someone you should meet. Someone who's going to like this very, very much.' His mobile phone rang which he answered briefly before making his way to the back entrance.

Petra prayed she didn't blush when Charlton brought his client through. A British actress married to an American actor, the pair of them never far from the covers of the glossiest magazines. The woman was gracious and, Petra noticed, had the most beautiful forearms. Clever old Charlton. Petra's jewellery would be perfect.

'This is Petra Flint,' he introduced and Petra feared she'd just curtseyed unintentionally. 'Have a look at this,' Charlton said to his client. 'May I?'

Petra handed over the cardboard box. The actress lifted the lid and it was as if a light was concealed within it—her face was immediately illuminated with delight. She took out the bracelet and her smile spread to prodigious proportions. 'How do you—?'

'Here,' Petra said to her, 'let me show you.' She

410

popped the subtly hidden clasp and wrapped the bracelet around the woman's wrist. Then she turned the section with the sweet. 'You have a go.'

The woman twisted it and turned it and held her wrist up to the light and let it swing down by her side. She walked about the gallery, glancing at her wrist in the mirrors, in the reflection from the display cabinets. She walked back to Petra and Charlton. 'It's the most stunning thing I've ever seen. I *have* to have it.'

Petra beamed at Charlton who was cleverly wearing his nonchalant salesman's face.

'But,' the actress faltered, 'what is this exactly? Is it white gold?'

'No, it's metal.'

'Oh, I see.' The actress looked a little confused. 'And is this a *real* sweet?'

'Yes,' said Petra. 'The Assay Office would grade it with a run of E-numbers.'

The actress laughed extravagantly. 'Well, I love it anyway. Can I take it today?'

'You dizzy bimbo,' Charlton stepped in. Petra baulked until she saw that the actress had taken this as flattery. 'This is the working model, darling. Petra was thinking platinum for the real thing. Platinum—and *this*.' He clicked his fingers and Petra passed over the velvet pouch as if it was a move they'd rehearsed in honour of the actress's visit. Charlton tipped the tanzanite into the actress's hand.

She sat down breathless, as if the sheer beauty of the stone was felt as weight. Petra was pleased to see that she placed the stone along the line between her fingers, examining it methodically. 'This must be 35 carats?'

411

'39.43 carats,' Charlton said, without needing to look at Petra for confirmation. 'It's incredibly rare. A vBE EC—violetish blue exceptional, eye-clean. A beautiful pear cut of ideal proportions—50 per cent table width, crown height 1/3, pavilion depth 2/3.'

'Oh. My. God. Oh my God oh my God!' The actress looked up at Charlton and Petra with tears in her eyes. 'I always thought myself a ruby kind of girl—but this is stunning. *Stunning.* I have to have it. Christ almighty. It's out of this world!' She put the tanzanite into the palm of her hand, folded her fingers around it and clutched her fist to her heart. She addressed Petra. 'I want it in platinum—or white gold. Actually, I don't care, really—I'll leave that part to you. But can I have it soon? I *need* it.'

'It'll cost you,' Charlton laughed.

She brushed the air dismissively with her other hand. 'Darling, I'm going to be fifty this autumn. Mr B said he'd buy me the world. I told him I'd happily settle for a yacht. But what I want now is *this.*'

'You're mad,' Charlton said. 'A yacht costs far more. Get Mr B to buy you the yacht for your birthday. You can buy this for yourself with the change from your latest movie.'

'You're right!' she said. 'All girls should treat themselves every now and then.' She turned to Petra, gave her back the velvet pouch with a look of theatrical reluctance. 'You are a genius,' she said in the tone she probably used for her plastic surgeon too. She came up close and put her hand on Petra's cheek. 'You are blessed,' she whispered, 'and I'm honoured to have met you.' She kissed her and Petra wondered whether her burning cheeks had scalded the woman's mouth. No, that was probably just the sumptuous colour of her meticulously applied lipstick. And perhaps a little Restylane too.

'Champagne, darling?' Charlton interrupted. 'Petra? You too?'

'Oh no thanks,' Petra said. 'I think I'll just—I'll just.' What she wanted to say was, I think I'll just race back to the studio and tell my Three all about this.

'Her beau is coming down from Yorkshire,' Charlton told the actress.

'How romantic,' the actress murmured, whilst clocking the brand of Charlton's champagne with approval.

'Come on, your highness,' Charlton said to her, 'come through to my office. I need to take a hefty deposit from you.'

'Thank you, my darling girl, thank you.'

'Goodbye,' said Petra, 'and thank you.'

The actress blew her a kiss. Charlton winked at her and made a telephone gesture with his hand.

*     *     *

The Studio Three had not expected to see Petra back that afternoon. Nor had they ever seen her looking so red and shiny.

'What's happened?' Gina asked.

'Have you taken drugs?' Kitty asked.

'Is everything OK?' Eric asked.

'OK?' Petra could only squeak. '*OK*? I've only just gone and sold the piece!' Out tumbled the story. By the end of it, the Studio Three were as flushed as she.

# CHAPTER FIFTY-ONE

Esther Savidge wasn't sure quite what to expect. It had been surprise enough to have her son phone, mid-term, and announce he'd be in London the coming weekend. But it had been something of an outright shock when he'd declined to stay at home because he'd be staying with his girlfriend.

'Girlfriend? You don't have a girlfriend, darling. Do you?'

'Yes, Mum, I do. I told you about her at Easter.'

'The schoolgirl? I mean, the girl you knew from school?'

'Yes. Petra.'

'That's Greek for "rock".'

'That's quite interesting, actually. Her surname is Flint.'

'What does she do, darling? This Petra Flint of yours?'

'She's a jeweller, Mum. Amazing.'

'Well, with a name like that, she couldn't find a better vocation.'

'But shall we come and visit you, anyway?'

'You want me to meet her? Already?'

'It's not "already", Mum. It's been going on some time.'

'Since Easter?'

'Yes, give or take seventeen years or so. But anyway, Mum, the point is—I want her to meet *you*.'

*       *       *

Then Arlo had phoned the next day saying he wasn't sure if he was coming down to London because Petra's ceiling had fallen in. And it was only natural for Esther to say, But darling, why don't you both come and stay here. And it warmed her heart when her son so readily accepted.

So now, on Friday afternoon, Esther was pottering around the house plumping cushions and straightening pictures. She always left the framed photos until last because they took the longest. It was impossible to dust them, to place them, without lengthy contemplation. He's bringing a girl home, Esther told a photo of her late husband. I wonder what she's like, Esther asked a photograph of Arlo at twenty-one. And what do we do with you? she asked a photograph of Helen. We'll never pretend that you don't exist.

She flicked the duster across the mirror, caught sight of herself, touched her earrings—small diamonds simply set—twirled her plain gold wedding band around her finger. A jeweller—this girl of Arlo's, she thought to herself. Well, isn't that something.

*     *     *

Any nerves Petra had had during the week at the thought of not simply meeting Arlo's mother for the first time but also staying in his family home, were quickly dissolved by the glut of excitement from her afternoon with Charlton. Meeting Arlo at King's Cross station, she gabbled fifty to the dozen as they changed platforms for Potters Bar.

'I hope you're not all talked out,' Arlo said to her as they alighted and Petra became anomalously quiet. 'My mum's a great one for a chinwag.'

Petra stopped. She looked suddenly perplexed.

'What's up?'

'Will she like me?'

'She'll love you, Miss Flint.'

'You're lucky to have a mum with whom you have such closeness.'

'I know I am,' said Arlo. 'She's the best. You'll see.' With that, he took her hand and they walked up a neatly tended path to the front door of Arlo's home.

*     *     *

The first thing Petra noticed was the smell. It was gorgeous and it proved to her how she'd become inured to the smell of chicken shit in her own mother's home. Her father's house just smelt, oddly, of nothing. Esther watched, initially baffled then touched, as Petra stood in the front room inhaling thoughtfully.

'What a beautiful scent,' she said.

'It's Jo Malone,' Esther said, turning in the direction of the candle.

'Oh, I love Jo Malone,' Petra said. 'My friend Eric buys me their bath oil each Christmas and I try and make it last the year through.'

'Do you succeed?' Esther laughed.

'I fail—spectacularly. It's all gone by Easter.'

'Cup of tea?'

'Yes, please. Oh, I bought you these.' Petra gave Esther a tin of fancy chocolate biscuits. 'Your son mentioned you like your chocolate.'

'Isn't that how you met—or re-met, I believe? Choosing Easter eggs?'

416

Petra blushed and nodded. 'I paid for his.'

'And then he gave it to me!' Esther exclaimed, hands on her hips. 'Cheeky monkey—has he reimbursed you?'

Petra had to think about it. Easter seemed such a long time ago. 'Do you know—he hasn't.'

Arlo reappeared from upstairs. His mother and his girlfriend were looking at him accusatorily. 'What?' he asked.

'Nothing,' they both said with a conspiratorial glance at each other.

*     *     *

Arlo showed Petra around.

'It's such a lovely, peaceful home,' she said, 'with such a welcoming smell about the place.'

'That'll be Mum and her candles,' Arlo said.

'No—it's something else. It's warmth—that's what it is.'

'This is my room,' Arlo said, 'and I'm sorry, Petra, but unless you can cope with sharing a single bed, you'll have to sleep in the spare room.'

Petra looked at him as if he was joking, but he was very serious. 'It's my *room*,' he said. 'I can't come home and *not* sleep here.' Petra looked put out. 'Much as I'm desperate to ravish your body,' he whispered, coming close to her, kissing her and making a lusty grab at her bottom.

'I suppose I could sneak into your bed, let you do the ravishing, then sneak out again and get a good night's sleep in the spare room?' Petra said, between kisses.

'Sounds like a good idea to me.'

'What will your mum think?'

417

'About?'

'Well, what'll she think if we *don't* sleep in the same room?'

'Oh, my mum's quite used to my foibles.'

'What if I sleepwalk?'

'The floorboards in the hallway are creaky—I'll hear you.'

Petra looked at Arlo's bed. It was most certainly just a regular single bed. With a Tottenham Hotspur duvet cover. 'Anyway, I can't sleep under *that*,' Petra declared. 'I'm an Arsenal girl.'

\*        \*        \*

While Arlo took a shower, Petra went back downstairs and asked Esther if she could help. Esther gave her cheese to grate and as they prepared supper, they gamely chatted.

'I don't mind telling you I felt a bit anxious when Arlo told me you were a jeweller,' Esther said. 'I don't really know much about jewellery. In fact, I'm pretty much wearing all that I own.'

'But why would you be anxious?'

'Well, I suppose I'd feel the same if you were a fashion designer—I'd suddenly feel rather frumpy. Or if you were a chef—what would I do for supper?'

'You don't need to drip with diamonds to get into my good books,' Petra said. 'I'm a tanzanite girl anyway.'

'Tanzanite?'

'The rarest gem on earth. In a few years' time, it'll all be gone. There will be no more tanzanite at all.'

'Really?'

418

'Yes.'

'Tell me more. Here—grate these.'

'Tanzanite is only found in one location in the whole world—in a three-mile area in the foothills of Kilimanjaro. Not only that, it's only found in a specific part of the rock. Look!' Petra grabbed a tea towel, not noticing that Arlo had reappeared. She pleated the fabric so it resembled a ruff. She pointed to the centre of the looped sections. 'Tanzanite is only found in what is called the *boudins* of the rock. It's all to do with the Pan African event 585 million years ago and a freak geological phenomenon. It's thought that in a decade or so, it'll all be gone. Finished.'

'What's it like? I don't think I'd know tanzanite if a great lump of it fell onto my lap.'

'Well, part of its uniqueness, why its beauty is so exclusive, is that it's trichroic—it has a different pure colour on each of its axes. Predominantly blue tanzanite is the rarest as the blue axis is oriented along the width of the crystal not the length—so there's more wastage, therefore, to cut for this. It's easier to cut along the violet axis. Do you see?' She paused, wondered if she was babbling, but her audience seemed captivated. 'Geologically speaking, it's a blue zoisite. But Henry B. Platt—grandson of Louis Comfort Tiffany of Tiffany's, New York—chose to market the gem as tanzanite. It was 1967 and he claimed there were only two places on earth you could find tanzanite—Tanzania and Tiffany. He worried that "zoisite" sounded a bit like "suicide"!'

Esther tried the word out loud and laughed.

'It was only discovered in 1967—and there's only one generation's mining. But over and above

419

the amazing facts of its creation and its discovery—and its imminent disappearance—is the pure romance of the gem. It's wrapped with beautiful Masai legend. They say a magical fire struck Kilimanjaro and when the embers died down, the hill sparkled with vivid blue–violet stones amidst the ash. Masai women are given tanzanite on the birth of their children. Blue is a very sacred colour to them—the women only wear it once they've borne children. The Masai believe the stone has healing powers. It's also the birthstone for December. And that's when my birthday is.'

Esther was just about to suggest they eat when Petra sallied forth again. 'You know something else—and this is fundamentally important when one considers the atrocities of conflict diamonds, blood diamonds—but tanzanite is the most ethically mined gemstone. It's carefully governed and a percentage of the profit is put back into the Masai community.'

'This is fascinating, Petra,' Esther said. 'Was this part of your degree?'

Petra smiled and shook her head. 'It's part of my childhood.' She paused. 'The stories—and the passion—were passed down to me. It pretty much dictated what I'd do with my life.'

'Are your parents jewellers too? Gemmologists?' Esther stopped herself. She remembered what Arlo had said about Petra's childhood.

But Petra's laugh put her at her ease. 'Hardly,' she said and then she told Esther all about Mrs McNeil.

*     *     *

420

When she'd finished, Arlo interjected: 'That's how we came to know each other, Mum. Petra would come to my school and do pottery after visiting the famous Mrs McNeil.'

'Did you ever meet her, darling?'

Arlo shook his head.

'What a pity,' Esther said. 'Her generation had so much to impart. Our lives have had a paucity in comparison.' She poured wine for the three of them and raised her glass. 'To Mrs McNeil, then.'

Petra surged with emotion.

*     *     *

After supper, Petra showed Esther the bracelet. She didn't tell her about the actress and the commission because actually, the thought of who would buy the piece and at what price had been so far from the work's conception and creation as to seem strangely irrelevant. Petra put the bracelet on an awe-struck Esther. It was the first time that Arlo had seen it and he swelled with pride. As Petra bolted upstairs to find the tanzanite, Esther turned to Arlo.

'She's not just a pretty face,' she said with a wink.

'She's so much more, Mum,' he said, 'so much more.'

Esther looked at her son quizzically. There was something different since she'd seen him last. 'You seem—darling, you look *exhausted*. But you seem—content, actually you seem happy?'

Arlo scanned the framed photographs and looked around the room. He turned to his mother and shrugged, smiled. 'I'm doing good, Mum.

421

Petra—she's. Well—she's changed things for me. I've changed because of her. I didn't realize how much I'd been bottling up. I didn't realize how destructive it was to do that. And I never knew that sharing could be so liberating.' His eyes focused on the picture of Helen. They stayed there a long while. His mother thought how he hadn't looked Helen in the face since she'd been in that frame. Which actually predated her death by some time.

'Five years, darling,' she said gently. 'It's long been time to let go.'

Arlo looked at her. 'With Petra, for the first time, I've wanted to talk, to remember, I've been able to grieve, to regret.' His mother nodded. 'That's good, isn't it?' His mother nodded again. 'I think it would be important for me to see Helen's folks. I feel I need to explain to them too. To ask their forgiveness—'

Esther raised her hand to block the end of his sentence. 'Arlo, no,' she said firmly. 'It's been five years, darling.'

'But it's only just recently that I've—you know—*accessed* what I've kept locked so deep. I've literally let those great perimeter walls of the school surround me—keeping me in, keeping people out. But now it feels like I've opened my own Pandora's Box and spread the contents before myself and I see that some of them belong to Helen's family.'

Esther looked concerned. 'Visit by all means—but not to make yourself feel better. I think you'd be wiser to let Petra bring *you* back to the joys of life. And love. Visit by all means—but as yourself as you are *now*, Arlo, five years on. Don't dredge up Helen's death. They will need peace as much as you.'

'But I want to explain. I feel I've been such a loathsome coward—'

Esther took her finger to her lips to sternly silence Arlo. 'Don't you say that about yourself, my boy. You had the shock of your life. It was desperately traumatic. Look how it's reverberated all these years. But you're dealing with it. And they're dealing with it. And perhaps Petra is dealing with it too.'

Arlo looked a little unsettled. 'Well,' he said, 'perhaps. But I think I'll phone them anyway.'

'If you do, promise me you will take their lead.'

'Life is worth little without honesty,' Arlo said.

'I'm glad you know that now,' said his mother.

\*     \*     \*

Petra didn't dare take her chances with the creaky floorboards, nor would she countenance Arlo expertly dodging them to sneak into the spare room for a furtive quickie. So she and Arlo gave each other a chaste kiss goodnight at the bathroom door and went to their respective rooms. Actually, Arlo was exhausted. Only a week ago he had contemplated life without love. Now love filled his life and it was a very, very big deal.

\*     \*     \*

He woke up promptly at seven in the morning and then smiled at the thought of no Saturday school today, no school whatsoever and a whole weekend with the girl he loved. He lay in bed for a few minutes longer but was eager to look in on Petra.

The spare-room bed, however, was empty. He went downstairs to join Petra for a cup of tea. But she wasn't there. With a thudding sense of dread, he checked the front and back doors and was relieved to find both still double-locked. So where was she? Where had she got to? He went upstairs again, checked the bathroom. Oh God, not Dad's study. No, it seemed not; his father's study was pretty much as it always was. The periphery of the room still walled with his books and journals and files; the central floor space prosaically purloined by his mother for the ironing board and clothes airers. But if Petra wasn't here either, it left only one room. His mother's.

He knocked cautiously. There was no sound. He opened the door slowly. There was his mother, propped up in bed with a cup of tea, her reading glasses on, the Rosie Thomas novel he'd bought her in hardback, open. She was sitting up on his father's side of the bed. This was almost as peculiar a sight as that of Petra, soundly asleep, on his mother's side of the bed.

'It was the strangest thing,' Esther said softly with a glance at Petra as if she was a stray cat who'd chosen to stay. 'At some ungodly hour my door opened—and there she stood. I thought she wanted the loo or something. But she came right in, sat down on the edge of the bed and muttered something about nothing. I kept saying her name but it made no difference. Then she stood up and said that she was sleepy; pulled back my covers and in she got. I don't know if she would have laid down right on top of me if I hadn't shifted out of the way.'

'She sleepwalks. I didn't think to mention it.

Sorry.'

'Does she do it often?'

Arlo nodded, came in and sat by his mother on his father's side of the bed. 'Most of her life, apparently.'

'What an affliction,' Esther said.

'She's hurt herself quite badly on occasions.'

'Poor love,' Esther said and she gently stroked through a ringlet of Petra's hair.

'She hates it,' Arlo said. 'She'll be mortified when she wakes.'

'I read somewhere that it can be linked to trauma—you know, in childhood.'

'She's had every test under the sun,' Arlo said. 'Sleep clinics, electrodes, CCTV, drugs.'

'What a thing,' Esther shook her head.

'Perhaps she just wanted to snuggle up with you, Mum,' Arlo said, standing and heading back to the door. 'I don't think she ever really got to do that.'

\*       \*       \*

Petra stirred, turned, opened her eyes and, with her field of vision filled by Esther's nightgown, closed them tightly again. She turned onto her other side, opened her eyes again only to clock Arlo's legs. She scrunched her eyes shut and groaned.

'Oh God. Oh no.'

Gently, Esther rested her hand on Petra's bare shoulder. 'Don't you worry, my darling. I was very glad of the company and you don't snore like my previous bedmate did.' Arlo grinned gratitude at his mum and she gave him an affectionate nod. Still Petra had her face buried in her hands. 'Arlo, darling,' Esther said, 'can you pass Petra my dressing gown. It's on the back of the door.' Then she changed her touch to a lively pat on Petra's back. 'I'm going to make breakfast. Who's for a full English?'

'Me, please,' said Arlo.

'And me,' muffled Petra.

*      *      *

After breakfast, Arlo went to the corner shop to buy the Saturday papers and Petra took her cup of coffee through to the lounge. She was gazing at the family photos on the mantelpiece when Esther came downstairs, dressed.

'That's how I remember Arlo,' Petra told her, when she'd come to stand alongside. 'That hair— like Jim Morrison from the Doors.'

Esther laughed. 'I like this one,' she said. It was a photograph of a picnic, with Arlo all toothsome at ten, standing alongside his father, both bare-chested, posing like bodybuilders. She took Petra along the mantelpiece, revealing the who and the when and the where of each picture.

'What a happy collection,' Petra remarked, wondering sadly to herself where the photos of her childhood were, whether they still existed. Had her parents fought over who would have them? Or had they been turfed out with the rest of the bones of contention? A photograph on the bookshelf caught her eye. A girl. She went for a closer look. Arlo had told her nothing of how Helen looked but Petra knew in an instant that this was her. How beautiful she had been. 'Helen?' she asked.

'Yes,' said Esther, 'that's Helen.'

426

'Wow,' said Petra because the look of the girl warranted such a response.

Esther took the picture from Petra, looked at it, smiled. 'You know,' she said, 'Helen did love Arlo. And he really, *really* loves you.'

Petra stood alongside her and they looked at Helen together. 'He's doing OK,' Petra said and Esther wondered whether she spoke to the picture or to her. Petra turned to her. 'He's doing OK,' she said again. 'It's been a tough old time for him. I think meeting me brought it all to the fore.'

'Meeting you has been an excellent thing.'

Petra blushed. Then she glanced at Helen again. 'He blames himself,' she said quietly, as if aware that she was exposing something of a secret.

Esther smiled kindly. 'I know he does,' she told Petra. 'It's been a desperate burden for him. But you know, I also knew that he wasn't happy during the period leading up to the accident. And it *was* an accident, whatever Arlo might think to the contrary, however much he has tortured himself otherwise.'

Petra fell quiet, as if deliberating how much more of Arlo's confidence to reveal. 'He's been talking about visiting Helen's parents,' she said at length. 'He feels he ought to—I don't know—open his heart to them. Ask their forgiveness. Assuage his remorse, I suppose.' And when she turned to Esther, she did so for guidance.

'I know,' said Esther. 'We talked about this yesterday. If you can add anything to what I've said, feel free.' She put Helen back on the bookcase. 'He listens to you, Petra. And that's a wonderful thing for his old mum to see.'

'You're not old,' Petra laughed.

And Arlo arrived back and said, What's so funny? and his mother and his girlfriend said, Oh, nothing.

It was time for elevenses. They could all do with a nice cup of tea.

\*　　　\*　　　\*

The weekend was lovely though it ended too soon with Arlo needing to take a lunch-time train to counteract the infernal works on the line and still be back at school at a civilized time. Esther told Petra she needn't rush off but Petra said that she had something she needed to do. However, before she left, after Esther had taken both her hands and kissed each cheek, Petra invited her to come into town, to meet her for lunch, to see the studio, to meet the Studio Three.

'I'd love to,' Esther said. 'Let me give you my mobile number.'

'You have a mobile?' Petra said, amazed.

'Oh Lord, you didn't think my son being a Luddite was genetic, did you?'

\*　　　\*　　　\*

Petra had not realized until that very morning that there was something she really did need to do. Having accompanied Arlo back to King's Cross and spun him a white lie about feeding Eric's neighbour's cat, she left him, covered in kisses, waiting for his delayed train. She changed stations and headed for Watford. She bought anemones, their stems succulent and twisting, their sooty black faces framed by vibrant crowns of richly hued

428

petals.

She didn't know what she was going to say, really. And she couldn't anticipate how she'd feel. But she knew she had to go there. To make her introduction. And then, to take her leave.

The grounds were peaceful by definition and seemed all the more serene for the presence of many great graceful trees standing tall and benevolent. There were lots of visitors, all keen to reciprocate kindly glances of empathy. Petra had to ask for directions to Helen and, as she approached the grave, she felt tears prickling. She read the inscription on the stone carefully. It was very simple, beautifully carved. Just her name, her dates and how much she had been loved. More tragic than anything Petra had personally known. Horrifically, desperately tragic.

We wish you had not died.

Petra laid the flowers down, stood still and silent for a while. Then she knelt and bowed her head and said over and over, Dear Helen dear Helen dear Helen—I hope you're OK with this, it's important to us that you are.

\*       \*       \*

Arlo did visit Helen's family quite soon after.

In bed with Petra a week or so later, Petra gamely chatting about this and that, he suddenly interrupted her, hushing her with his fingers to her lips.

'They were happy for me, Petra,' he said, 'when I told them about you. Helen's folks. They were genuinely happy for me.'

And from the ease with which Arlo recounted

this, as well as from his unfurrowed brow, Petra deduced that during the visit, he'd done everyone proud. His mother. Petra. Himself. And Helen.

## CHAPTER FIFTY-TWO

The last few weeks of term galloped along for all concerned. The GCSE and A level boys at Roseberry Hall willed their last exams to come around finally and they were then duly rewarded with long summer days to lounge around, play sport and simply take stock of all they'd achieved. The rest of the pupils summoned bursts of energy to complete any outstanding work—and some of the work was quite outstanding indeed—to ensure favourable send-offs from this year's form tutors and an auspicious start to the next school year. For the teachers, the summer holidays seemed all the more tangible once they'd written the boys' end-of-year reports. An official farewell barbeque was organized for Miranda Oates and the following weekend those colleagues who were also friends organized a more raucous send-off with a pub crawl through Great Broughton. Arlo was invited—but he couldn't attend as it was a weekend he was spending in London. Miranda said she understood. And she did. She did understand. Which wasn't to say she wasn't slightly hurt. But she kept that to herself. Almost the end of term. Out with the old. A long, hot summer. Then in with the new.

In London, Petra's landlords did not charge her rent and their insurers gave her an allowance; of which, after some pressure, Eric accepted half. Petra put the remainder into a kitty that enabled them to have their weekly shop delivered by Ocado and M&S. She really enjoyed living with Eric and though she still went walkabout at night, the sorties were definitely less frequent. Arlo and Eric rubbed along just fine and Petra and Arlo also spent another weekend with Esther, whom Petra had seen a few times in between visits too. Esther had been intrigued by the way the Studio Four worked—together as a studio as well as individually as jewellers. She'd spent a peaceful afternoon, sitting quietly in the corner of their hive of creativity, watching Petra buzz around and Eric act like queen bee. Charlton had charmed her and Petra continued to delight her.

'Are you and Arlo going to go somewhere nice this summer?' Esther had ventured as they took a stroll to St Paul's one lunch-time.

'Well, we did talk about it—but I have to work. I really want to have the tanzanite piece finished. And one of the actress's friends wants a similar piece but with emerald so I've made a start on that.'

'Also an actress?'

Petra nodded.

' "A" list?'

Petra nodded again.

'Jeweller to the Stars!' Esther had clapped and a couple of tourists had turned to stare.

'I don't think Sean Leane or Stephen Webster or Theo Fennell need watch their backs just yet,' a very red Petra had mumbled.

*     *     *

In early July, the school year came to a close at Roseberry Hall with just the Walley Brothers mooching about, tending the grounds and terrifying any moles or foxes off the property. Only the rabbits remained; their long cocky ears looking like the equivalent of sticking two fingers up at the Walleys. Most summers, Arlo came and went from his folly but this year, Jenn had invited him to avail himself of her spare room—with Petra most welcome too. And though it was more convenient for Arlo and Petra to use London as their headquarters over the summer, their friendship with Nige and Jenn was now such that spending time together was actively planned.

Nige and Jenn were to be married in the New Year.

'And then I'll be moving into married digs at Roseberry,' Jenn exclaimed.

'They're hardly *digs*,' Nigel protested. 'Boardman House is one of the most sought after. It's beautiful,' he said to Petra. 'Rooms and rooms.'

'I know,' Petra winked at him, 'I've seen it.'

'Rooms and rooms and boys and boys. Apparently, I have to dispense TLC in times of homesickness,' Jenn said with mock despair. 'Anyway, from January I'll be looking to rent out this place. I'll not be selling it. Just renting it out.' She looked at Arlo. 'Know anyone, do you, Arlo?' Before he could respond, Jenn turned to Petra. 'And you—would you know anyone, Petra? Might you know someone who's looking for somewhere to live up this way, perhaps?'

*       *       *

At the end of the month, on a weekend in London, Arlo looked up a couple of his old friends.

'Do you remember Jonny Noble?' Arlo asked. Petra thought hard but shook her head. 'Of course you do,' Arlo laughed. 'He was the world-class rhythm guitarist with the Noble Savages.'

Petra thought back to that distant lunch-time one spring when Arlo's band had played at her school. 'Vaguely,' she said. 'I can see you all up on our stage—but I can't make out his face, really. I just see you—you and your curls and your school shirt rolled up to your elbows. Are you blushing, Mr Savidge?'

'No, I'm mourning my curls.'

Petra laughed. 'Anyway, what of this noble Jonny boy?'

'I gave him a call. I thought we'd meet up later. He was intrigued to hear about you. And you'd love him—he's just the same.'

Petra was game. 'What does he do now?'

'He's an estate agent,' Arlo laughed, 'but I think he still picks up his guitar every once in a while.'

*       *       *

Petra didn't recognize Jonny though with his thick dark hair and slim physique he probably looked closer to his schoolboy self than Arlo did. However, his affection towards Arlo and his geniality towards Petra made her feel as though he was indeed an old pal. He and Arlo spent the first half-hour joshing with each other, enlivened with a few slaps on the back and ruffling of each other's heads. They had a prime table, outside the legendary Flask pub in Highgate.

'It's a toupee, you know,' Arlo told Petra, patting Jonny's hair.

'I won't even rise to this, Savidge,' Jonny said, 'you bald git. Has he told you he thinks he looks like Bruce Willis, Petra?'

'Oh yes, Jonny,' Petra said straight, 'but I think he looks more like Phil from *Location Location Location*.'

Jonny roared with laughter. 'Where do you live now, Petra?'

'Oh, well sort of in North Finchley—only the ceiling fell down so I'm staying with a friend in Brondesbury.'

'Very nice area,' Jonny nodded sagely. 'Where did you grow up? Where were you living when we were all at school?'

'Well, my teenage years were spent in a flat on the poor man's side of West Hampstead.'

'Very des-res now,' Jonny remarked.

'But up until then, my family home was in that odd area between Hendon and Cricklewood.'

'It's not so odd now,' Jonny said.

'Randoline Avenue.'

'Randoline Avenue?'

'You won't know it.'

'I very do, my dear, I very do. I have currently two or three properties for sale there.'

'Well, we lived at number 43.'

'Number 43 is currently for sale,' Jonny said, having not stopped nodding.

'Yeah right!' Petra laughed.

'On those last hairs on Arlo's head do I swear that I have number forty-three Randoline Avenue,

434

London, North-west two, on my books for sale. It is a three-bed, 1930s semi, with off-street parking. It came on the market a couple of months ago. We are sole agents.'

'Bloody bloody hell!' Petra marvelled.

'Fifty-foot rear garden facing south-east, sizeable conservatory.'

'Oh, can't be the same place—we didn't have a conservatory.'

'The vendors put it in a couple of years ago.'

'Did they? That's rather grandiose.'

'It's added thirty grand to the price. I'll take you round if you like,' Jonny said. 'Nothing like a trip down Memory Lane.'

\*     \*     \*

Curiosity saw Petra taking up Jonny's offer on Monday lunch-time. Arlo accompanied them.

'There it is!' she said excitedly. 'Fancy new drive. We had the front door red, not black.'

But as Jonny's key went into the lock, Petra felt suddenly a little shy of the place. It had been almost twenty years. What memories could she possibly have, really? And what would be the point of unearthing new ones?

\*     \*     \*

Although she didn't recognize the smell of the place, the way the light bathed the entrance hallway from the tall window as the stairs climbed was immediately evocative. Arlo caught Jonny's arm swiftly, raised an eyebrow, and the men allowed Petra to take the lead. All the doors were shut. They had been stripped back to the bare wood though Petra distinctly remembered them as white gloss. Opening each was odd, in a Lewis Carroll way. With her hand on the doorknob, how the room used to look flashed across her mind's eye. When she pushed the door open, however, the interior was of course totally different. But seeing someone else's brown leather suite didn't cancel out the memory of her family's beige velvet one. And she could easily carpet over the current laminate flooring with an image of the rather pub-like blue-and-gold patterned wool mix of her childhood.

'The kitchen's twice the size,' she marvelled. 'Blimey—and look at the conservatory.' Everything was rather echoey. She turned to Jonny. 'They don't have much stuff.'

'Oh,' he said, 'they've already moved out. I just always suggest my clients part-furnish—or *dress*—the properties if they are empty. All this furniture is just hired while the house is on the market.'

Petra led the way upstairs. All the doors were closed up there too. They were still the gloss white of her childhood and not stripped like those downstairs. 'This was my bedroom,' Petra said quietly, opening the door slowly and peeping through before stepping in. There was a single bed, in the same position hers had been. It appeared from the curtains and the wallpaper border that a boy had most recently had this room. The airing cupboard still jutted into the room from one corner and Petra wondered if it was the same hot water tank inside it, portly in its big red Puffa jacket. Did it still sigh and creak—as if to say that providing hot water for a family was so very onerous?

Jonny and Arlo stood well back to allow Petra to continue her tour. Spare bedroom. Petra found her hand faltered. She moved on instead to the next room—the bathroom, now with corner bath freeing up space for a walk-in shower. At the front, her parents' room. Again, she felt herself waver before opening the door and going in. The same fitted bedroom furniture, which had been the height of Scandinavian curvilinear chic twenty-odd years ago. How bizarre to keep that, yet build such a fancy conservatory. She walked over to the window. Same old view, though the road seemed narrower these days. Perhaps because every house now had two cars. One in the drive. One on the street.

Giving Jonny and Arlo a quick smile, Petra went back along the hallway, peered into the bathroom again, and shut the door. Went back into her bedroom for a few more minutes. Then shut that door too. Lastly, she did look into the spare room briefly but she didn't step inside and she left that door open before she went back downstairs, stood by the front door and said, Thanks, Jonny, that was—bizarre. Let's go.

\*       \*       \*

Petra was quiet and reflective for the rest of the afternoon.

'There's so much I do remember,' she said to Arlo, 'and so much I sense I don't.'

\*       \*       \*

Later that evening, Petra went to bed early leaving Arlo and Eric to enjoy a beer and a rerun of *The Office* on TV.

'Can I make a phone call, Eric?'

'Sure.'

'Thanks.' Arlo dialled Jonny.

'Hullo, mate! Please don't tell me you're going to put in an offer on Randoline Avenue, for old times' sake?'

'No, but I am going to ask you for a massive favour,' Arlo said to Johnny, 'and I don't even know if it's legal.'


## CHAPTER FIFTY-THREE

'Where are we going?'

'It's a surprise.'

'I hate surprises, Arlo! Tell me where we're going?'

'What kind of girl hates surprises?'

'Well, it's not as if you are carrying a Tiffany bag, is it? *That's* a Tesco bag. What's in it? And don't say surprise.'

'Supper.'

'A picnic?'

'Sort of.'

'Oh good! Tell me where we're going.'

'Dear God, will you just shut up, woman.'

\*     \*     \*

The winsome, petulant pout that Petra fixed to her face was soon wiped off and the stroppy wiggle

438

she'd adopted fell to a snail's pace when she realized Arlo was taking her back to Randoline Avenue.

'Why?' Petra asked.

'I'm not entirely sure,' Arlo said. 'It's a hunch.'

'You have *keys*?'

'I know the estate agent,' Arlo said. He opened the door. 'Jonny said to be discreet. No lights blazing, no rock-and-roll.'

'But what's your hunch, Arlo?' Petra stopped on the doorstep, caught his arm. Her face was criss-crossed with anxiety which, in itself, suggested to Arlo that he was doing the right thing.

He put his hand on the back of her neck. 'Look, this may sound simplistic—I just thought that perhaps if you came back here, stayed here, well, maybe you *would* remember stuff. Perhaps you might sleepwalk—you know, back in *time*? See if it was anything here which set you off in the first place?'

Petra stared at him. 'But I never know where I'm going and I never remember where I've been,' she whispered. 'All this feels—odd.'

'But you see, when you were little, there wasn't really anyone here for you. Now you're returning as a grown-up—and you have me.'

He put the key into the lock and then stopped. 'We can go, Petra. We can go right now. You have only to say. I won't mind. I don't want to force you. It's probably a stupid idea of mine.'

There was a moment's heavy silence. 'It's OK, Arlo.' The frown had gone from her brow. 'Let's do it. It's crazy. But why not. If the sleep clinics in Harley Street and Papworth Hospital could find no reason, then there's no harm in trying an alternative angle. But I think you're mad, Arlo—mad as a fish.'

*      *      *

They spent the evening downstairs sipping red wine out of plastic cups, dipping pitta bread into a variety of dips and spooning Ben and Jerry's ice cream into each other's mouths. They didn't talk about the house in terms of her childhood but Arlo sensed that Petra was putting off going to bed. However, though he'd got her this far, he certainly was not going to force her upstairs to bed. Eventually, she could not stifle a yawn though she blamed the red wine. Arlo yawned too.

'Did you know, yawning is the most contagious thing on earth?' Petra told him. 'It's the same yawn—just going round and round the world. I'll bet you someone next door is now yawning and so it will continue, down this street, off into Cricklewood and on and on. The good folk of Yorkshire will catch it in a few hours. I did an experiment once—I yawned at my friend's dog and lo, it yawned too!'

Arlo gave her a tender gaze that said, I know you're waffling, Petra, because you don't want to go to bed and let the night unfold. He went upstairs to use the toilet and suddenly Petra didn't want to be downstairs, by herself. He came out of the bathroom to find her there. She looked as though she'd lost a few inches in height.

'You OK?' he asked, lifting her chin to kiss her.

She nodded. 'I suppose I'm tired now.'

They squeezed into the single bed in Petra's old bedroom and lay there, pretending to be perfectly

440

comfortable. After an hour or so, Arlo made his apologies and moved onto the floor. It wasn't particularly comfortable there either but tonight was not about getting a good night's sleep.

*　　　*　　　*

But Petra does sleep. And then, at three in the morning, she rises. Arlo has only dozed. Now he lies stock-still, sensing her sitting bolt upright.

'What's that noise?'

'Petra?'

No answer. She is not awake. Quickly, he moves out of her way as she steps down from the bed. She's scratching her head and muttering about what that blinking noise is. There is no noise. The house is utterly silent. She pads across the room and Arlo follows. Out into the corridor.

'Hullo?' she says but there's no one to answer her. She's hovering outside the spare-room door, stepping lightly from foot to foot as if she's a child needing the toilet. She opens the door a little and peers in.

'Uncle Jeff?' She stops. Looks in a little further. 'Uncle Jeff?' She backs out, and continues along towards the master bedroom. She stays by the closed door. Then opens it a fraction.

'Dad?'

She appears to be rooted to the spot. 'Dad?'

Suddenly, she spins and runs on her tiptoes, fast back to her bedroom. Shuts the door in Arlo's face. When he goes in, he finds her in bed, way down deep under the covers, shaking.

He sits on the edge of the bed and lays his arm gently over the mound of her.

441

'Where did you go, my beautiful girl, what did you see?'

*　　　*　　　*

What's that noise? I heard something. I definitely heard a noise. I think it's the middle of the night. I must go and see. I'm a bit scared, I am. But I'm sure I heard a strange noise. I'll just tiptoe out onto the landing and see what I can hear.

'Hullo?'

There it is again. It's a funny sound—like a bear or something. It's coming from the spare room.

Listen.

I'd better look inside.

Oh. It's Uncle Jeff.

'Uncle Jeff?'

Why are you sideways on the bed, Uncle Jeff? Why don't you have any of your clothes on? Why are you crawling all over my mum, making those strange noises? It sounds like she can't breathe. Why are you wearing ladies' shoes, Uncle Jeff? You look silly. And you have a big fat hairy bum.

'Uncle Jeff?'

Why's no one answering me?

I'd better go and find my dad.

'Dad?'

There's funny noises coming from that room too.

Something's not right. What are the grown-ups *doing*? I didn't even know Uncle Jeff was staying the night. I thought he'd just come for supper. Him and Auntie Mags. And Auntie Anne too.

The door isn't quite closed so I will look through the gap. Auntie Anne is kneeling on my

442

mum and dad's bed. I see her red hair, pouring down her back. She has a baggy bottom and really yuk red pants. What is Auntie Mags doing and what is she wearing *that* for? That's not a bra, her bosoms are poking out.

Is *that* my Dad?

Why is Auntie Mags tying him up?

They're all laughing and talking in funny voices. I can't hear what they're saying. If I open the door a bit more, maybe I will.

'Dad?'

Why aren't they wearing many clothes? This is not right. It's a silly game and I wish they would all stop playing it.

Auntie Mags is turning around.

I don't want her to see me. I don't want anyone to see me. I must go back to my room. Quick quick quick quick quick.

*      *      *

Petra was lying in bed, staring at the ceiling, when Arlo woke up.

'Good morning up there,' he said, chilled and stiff on the floor.

'Do you remember those luminous stickers made for bedroom ceilings?' Petra asked him. 'I never had any of those. I always wanted them.'

'I tried them once, a couple of years ago, when I was fed up counting sheep.'

'Did they help you sleep?'

'Far from it—I'd start faffing around in the God-forsaken small hours, trying to replicate the specifics of the northern hemisphere night sky.'

'Oh.'

Arlo rose from the floor. Petra turned to look at him. 'Looks like you have cellulite,' she said and Arlo inspected the puckering of his skin from a night on the carpet. He sidled into bed next to her. She nustled into his chest and he stroked her hair thoughtfully.

'Who's Uncle Jeff?' he asked quietly.

'He was a friend of my parents,' Petra said and her tone of voice tells Arlo that where she went last night, what she saw, was still vivid. 'He was married to Maggie—Auntie Mags. God knows what happened to them.' She turned to Arlo. 'There was also Auntie Anne. I don't think she had a partner. They weren't real aunts and uncle—they were friends of my parents. They often came over. All of them.'

'Last night—' Arlo started.

'I know,' said Petra. A fat tear squeezed out from her eye and oozed down her cheek.

'What did you see last night?' Arlo whispered. 'Was it what you saw when you were little?'

'I saw them all at it,' said Petra, covering her face.

'Oh.'

'I think my parents must have been—you know, swingers. How fucked up is that?'

'Christ, Petra. How old were you? Can you remember?'

'I must have been about eight, I suppose.'

'Was that when you started sleepwalking?'

'Yes.'

\*     \*     \*

After a breakfast of croissants and apple juice

444

drunk straight from the carton, Arlo looked at Petra intently.

'You need to make your peace here, you know, with all of that, before we leave here. God, the whole swinging thing, it must have been bewildering, disturbing, for a child to come across—but as an adult looking back, try to see it as bemusing or even amusing or just downright ridiculous. We're going to leave all of that rubbish here in the house. Closure without opening the door to your childhood memories any wider. Closure when we close this old front door of yours.'

Petra shrugged.

Arlo held her shoulders steady and looked at her sternly. 'It's about putting the past to bed, Petra. In my case and in yours. You've shown me that. Look what you've done for me.'

'They probably have no idea that I saw,' she told him. 'I wonder what they'd say if I told them.'

'And I wonder what Helen's parents would have said if I *had* told them. Look what you've taught me about there being a time for silence.' He cupped her face in his hands. 'You can't cancel the past but if you lay it down gently enough, you can put the past to bed. Let it rest. Find your peace. Sleep well.'

Petra looked at him and her expression said, Help me, then, help me if you can.

'Do you know that Philip Larkin poem? Do you remember the Noble Savages singing it? Actually, we weren't allowed to sing it at your school. That poem—about your parents fucking you up?' Petra nodded. 'Well, Mr Larkin would have done well to have met someone like you, Petra—though anthologies of modern poetry might have ended up the poorer. I know you regret not having a close relationship with your parents. And Christ, what you saw when you were eight years old, what you experienced when they split up when you were a teenager, the kind of indifference you've faced from them ever since—it's a wonder you're *not* cynical, fucked up and bitter. But look at you, Petra. Look at what I see. I see this beautiful, beautiful woman who's so talented and so caring and so brave and so strong. And who, most important of all, knows how to love. You truly know how to love. It's a natural instinct for you.'

Petra's head dropped. Arlo put his arm around her.

'It doesn't matter what you saw,' he told her quietly but emphatically, 'because what you found makes no difference to the life that you're leading so well. You don't need to go looking any more, Petra. You don't need to go looking ever again.'

## CHAPTER FIFTY-FOUR

It was early August when Petra announced that they really ought to go and visit her mother.

'Has she phoned?' Arlo asked.

'No,' Petra hesitated. 'But there again, she never does,' she said with a new equanimity.

Melinda said she'd be delighted to see her daughter though she hoped this new beau didn't have a gas-guzzling car like that other bloke. When Petra told her mother that Arlo didn't even have a mobile phone, let alone a car, she heard her mother applauding down the phone.

'She probably won't be in,' Petra warned Arlo as the minicab from the station dropped them in sight of her mother's cottage. 'Oh, and ask for your tea black.'

But Melinda was in, as were half her hens, and they all seemed to squawk at Petra and Arlo when they entered. Arlo asked Melinda so many questions that she didn't have the inclination to talk much more about herself once she'd answered him. They'd talked about eggs and feng shui and carbon footprints and vegetarian shoes. So they sat and sipped their herbal tea and looked at each other. And Melinda thought she'd ask her daughter how her summer had been.

'Interesting,' Petra told her. 'Interesting.' She paused. She could feel Arlo glance urgently at her. 'An old friend of Arlo's is an estate agent. Guess which house is on his books?' Her mother shook her head. 'Randoline Avenue.'

'Good gracious me.'

'I went and had a poke around.'

'Whatever did you do that for?' Melinda baulked. 'It was a ghastly house.' She shuddered.

'It has a fancy conservatory now.'

'It was ghastly because of what happened there.'

'Happened?' Petra again felt Arlo's concerned glance bore into her.

'Me and your father divorcing,' Melinda frowned.

Suddenly, Petra no longer needed to make her mother think back. 'I know, Mum. I just was curious to see what I remembered.'

'Did you remember much?'

'Not really,' Petra said and she could sense

Arlo's stare soften. 'I remembered the water tank with the red padding.'

'You used to call the water tank Bertie,' Melinda said softly.

'I don't remember that,' said Petra.

'I do.'

Melinda busied herself replenishing the rock cakes, which had to be slid carefully onto the plates so as not to break the crockery.

'Your daughter is about to make her fortune— did you know that?' Arlo said.

'Oh yes?'

'Do you remember Mrs McNeil?' Petra glinted. 'From when I was at school?'

Melinda looked a little uncomfortable and she glanced at Arlo rather than at Petra. 'Yes, I do.'

'The stone? The tanzanite? Well, I've sold it— I'm making it into a platinum bracelet.'

'Clever you. Clever you,' Melinda said, staring at her rock cake. Then she paused and looked directly at Petra. 'Odd, though, that you wouldn't want simply to keep it.'

*       *       *

It followed that, if they'd been to see Petra's mother, then a trip to her father was in order too.

He wasn't in when they arrived but the children made Petra and Arlo the centre of attention and dragged them through to the garden which enabled Mary to disappear inside the house for a while. When John Flint returned, Arlo strode over with his hand extended.

'How do you do, Mr Flint, I'm Arlo Savidge.'

John glanced at Petra whilst continuing to shake

Arlo's hand. 'Nice to meet you,' he said. 'Did you come all this way to see us? Can you stay for lunch or are you just passing?'

'That was the idea, Dad,' Petra said, 'if it's not too much trouble.'

'Right, right. Well, I'll go and change then.'

And he took a very long time to reappear.

As they sat in the garden waiting for something to happen—lunch or Mary or John—Arlo put his arm around Petra. 'There's no golden rule that you have to be close to your parents, you know,' he said. 'You don't even have to like the people that they are.'

'I know,' Petra said, 'I do know.'

'It would be far worse if you all fell out,' he said, 'and weren't speaking at all. In your case, a full-on soul-baring confrontation may not be worth the effort in the long run. You have two parents and they fucked up but they must have done something right because your outlook on love and marriage is so utterly positive.'

While Petra considered Arlo's words, she swung her legs absent-mindedly, catching her foot each time on a plastic pirate ship run aground on the grass.

'What hampers you from accepting your relationship with your folks for what it is, is that *you* know too much,' Arlo said, 'but *they* don't know that. And they mightn't be the most warm or loving of parents—but I bet you anything they'd be horrified if they knew that you knew. Remember— that wasn't their intention. It's an age-old thing, isn't it—cringing at the thought of one's parents making love. But actually seeing one's parents having group sex—well, that's off the bloody radar.

449

What they got up to—it wasn't depraved, but there again it wasn't particularly wholesome. It was, however, private and consensual.' He gave Petra time to consider this, waited for her to nod. 'But in the long run, it wreaked havoc with their lives. And the cause—and the effect—have been with you practically your whole life, Petra.'

'It may have been what split them up, you know,' Petra said. 'I've read articles about similar situations—wife-swapping and threesomes usually come to grief.'

Arlo looked at her. 'Damn,' he said, 'and Nige and I were talking just the other day about whether you and Jenn would be up for it.' Petra glared at him for a split second before a mischievous grin sliced the gorgeous dimples into his cheeks. She thumped him. And he hugged her.

'What's going on out here?' John asked, coming into the garden with hastily made sandwiches.

'Did you know that your daughter is the buzz-word in contemporary jewellery design, from Hatton Garden to Hollywood, Mr Flint?'

'No,' said John, who hadn't yet said to Arlo, Call me John.

'She's in demand by the great and godly of stage, screen and beyond.'

'Really?'

Petra didn't think she'd mention Mrs McNeil to her father because she couldn't remember whether or not he knew about her at the time. She thought he probably did not. Instead, she rifled through her bag and brought out one of the final sketches for the tanzanite bangle. She'd slipped it in this morning. Just in case the opportunity arose.

John looked at it. 'This is marvellous,' he said

and he looked at Petra and she saw that actually, he looked rather proud.

*　　　*　　　*

Although Petra couldn't quite commit to leaving London completely by the start of term a month later, she did give up her flat. It wasn't much of a sacrifice; she never felt particularly emotionally attached to it. And anyway, Eric had gone to great lengths to assure her that she was more than welcome to lodge with him. Similarly, in Yarm, Jenn had given Petra a set of keys to her flat with a pink satin ribbon attached. Come and go as you please, they both told her.

So it was back to school in September. Petra missed Arlo inordinately that first week; their reunion at the weekend was sweet and intense. And though she was tempted to stay the following week with Jenn, she had so much work on that she was compelled to return to London. Charlton would be taking a reasonable cut for himself for the first two bracelets he had secured for her—yet it had been his suggestion that she set up her own website and Gina's husband was helping her do so.

'We'll make this your virtual gallery,' he told her and the concept did get her mind ticking. Orders for her earrings, the hair slides and crocheted necklaces soon started to trickle through. And one day, after a lengthy period spent on spreadsheets, Petra typed in 'jewellers studios workshops Yorkshire' into an Internet search engine and was quite surprised by what came up. She was suddenly aware that Eric was looking over her shoulder. She fumbled around trying to minimize the page but

Eric stilled his hand over hers, over the mouse.

'It's OK, Petra,' he said and he smiled. 'All of it is OK.'

And she knew Eric was right. She thought to herself how lucky she was. From London to Hong Kong via Yorkshire, the world wasn't such a big place really, not when it was one so full of friends.

\*     \*     \*

The bracelet was finished. It was all Petra had hoped it would be. She felt euphoric. She had it professionally photographed from every angle. Kitty and Eric heaped their praises on her and Gina brought in champagne.

Charlton informed her that the actress would be coming in a fortnight.

'Now it's full steam ahead with the emerald one,' Petra laughed.

\*     \*     \*

Once Petra knew that the money was in transit, something inside her changed. It was subtle at first. She went from looking at the work a few times a day to having a glance only every now and then, to not taking it out of the box at all. Everyone sensed there was something troubling her but she didn't let anyone probe because she wasn't entirely sure herself what it was that irked her so.

Up in Yorkshire for the weekend, she rose from her sleep. She walked away from Arlo's bedroom and through the lounge into the kitchenette. She didn't switch the lights on; fumbling with the lid of the kettle in the dark, filling it with water which

452

splashed everywhere. She set it to boil. Took a mug, a tea bag, poured milk without spilling a drop.

She sat, in the dark, on Arlo's sofa.

'I don't think this is what you'd want,' she said quietly. And she said it over and over again.

Petra wasn't sleepwalking. She was wide awake.

She wasn't sure how long she'd sat there for but when she returned to the bedroom with cold feet and the start of a headache, she clocked the time was nearing half four. She put on a pair of Arlo's socks and slid into bed, cuddled up against his back.

'Are you awake?'

He wasn't.

'Are you awake?' she said a little louder, nudging his body. 'Are you awake?'

'I am now,' he said groggily.

'I can't do it,' she said and her voice shook.

He turned towards her. Her eyes accustomed to the dark, she could see his focusing intently on her. 'Can't what, Miss Flint. What can't you do?'

'I can't do it, Arlo,' she said. 'I can't let Mrs McNeil's tanzanite go. Not in that bracelet. Not to the United States.'

*     *     *

She dreaded telling Charlton. The actress was flying in on Friday. When Petra's feet finally dragged her from the studio to the Charlton Squire Gallery late on the Monday afternoon, she felt ill.

'You look peaky, darling,' Charlton said. 'Everything OK?'

'No,' Petra whispered, 'it isn't.' Charlton seemed

huge today, top to toe in black, a diamond-encrusted skull and crossbones dangling from a choker around his neck.

She clambered over her words, leaving sentences hanging vertiginously. Charlton listened intently and then, after a nauseating silence during which her head started spinning, he began to laugh.

'I was wondering when you were going to say that,' he said. 'I'm amazed it took until now.'

'Sorry?' Petra's head stopped spinning but she couldn't keep her eyes still; they were scouring Charlton's face in confusion.

'Darling, as soon as I saw your design on paper—let alone in metal with that fucking sweet—I started rearguard action.'

'What?'

'Plan B, Pet, Plan B.' He paused. 'It's Monday. I need to make a call. Excuse me for a moment.'

He disappeared into his office leaving Petra to man the shop and by the time Charlton came back, she'd sold a pair of her own earrings and one of Charlton's belt buckles.

'You need to meet me at Oxford Circus tube station, ten o'clock tomorrow morning,' he told her. 'And bring the bracelet.'

\*       \*       \*


Neither Arlo nor any of the Studio Three could help Petra work out what was at Oxford Circus tube station.

\*       \*       \*

454

Charlton led Petra a little way down Regent Street before turning down a side-street. He rang the top bell of a small office. He and Petra were buzzed through and climbed steeply to the top floor. The office space was cramped because most of the room was taken up by a large cage, in which were a number of safes. Two young women sat sharing a desk.

'Hi, Charlton,' they said.

'This is Petra Flint,' he introduced. He turned to Petra. 'This lady represents one of the few companies left mining for tanzanite. And this lady is from the foundation which ensures ethical mining and fair-trade initiatives.'

'We hear you have something to show us,' she said, eyeing Petra's bag.

'Charlton told us it'll blow our brains,' said the other.

Not quite knowing what any of this was about, Petra took the box from her bag and let the women inspect her bracelet. 'It's a beauty!' 'Stunning!' It didn't take Petra long to realize their primary focus was on the stone and not the whole.

'Can you match it?' Charlton asked.

'Don't be ridiculous, Charlton,' said the first woman. 'It's tanzanite. Of course we can't match it. But we'll have something comparable.' She unlocked the cage, opened a safe and brought out a few white leather purses. Each contained a sizeable stone. 'But you may have to go for a different cut,' she told Petra, almost apologetically. 'And of course you'll also need to rework the housing to accommodate a new stone. We can find a similar weight—but the colour of yours, it's truly exceptional. We won't have anything that blue. Tell me more about it—how did you come by it? Have you had it graded?'

'I've had it for over sixteen years. It was bequeathed to me by a lady whose husband was a prospector in Tanzania in the 1960s—he was looking for rubies at the time because of course no one knew of the existence of tanzanite. So, no one else has had this stone. I believe it's vBE, eye-clean. 39.43 carats.'

'Wow.'

'Double wow,' said the other woman. She grinned at Petra. 'And it's definitely not for sale?'

Petra laughed and shook her head. 'Nope. Never.'

*    *    *

So Petra didn't make her fortune from that first bracelet because she had to balance the profit against the purchase of a new stone. In the end, the actress came away with just over 40 carats of tanzanite which in her reckoning was preferable to just under. Even if the cut was not as mesmerizing as Petra's and the new stone was a touch more violet than blue. It was still dazzling. Just not quite the colour of dreams.

# EPILOGUE

Did Petra Flint sleepwalk again? Occasionally, but Arlo would watch her leave the bed and mostly she would just hover by the bedroom door before retracing her steps and coming back to sleep.

And did Arlo Savidge's insomnia disappear? Not entirely, certainly not overnight, but it subsided significantly. And if there were nights when he couldn't sleep, he found that gazing at his girlfriend was far more soothing than staring at marks on the paintwork. There was nothing specific keeping him awake any more, just a hard habit he was slowly learning to break. And if things go bump in the night then he wakes up and guides her back to bed.

He kept her secret and she kept his and they found in each other a place of such safekeeping that they knew any future issues or grievances, on whatever scale, could be dealt with together. Custodians of each other's hearts.

*          *          *

'Ah, the return of the native,' Kitty greeted Petra after a fortnight's absence up north.

'How are you, Kitty,' Petra gave her a fond hug.

'One of these days I'm going to surprise you, Petra. I'm going to jump on a train and spring a visit. All this talk of looking for a studio and finding inspiration in the landscape. I bet I'd find you sprawled on Jenn's sofa watching daytime TV.'

Petra laughed. And then she thought about it.

'Why don't you come up and visit, Kitty? I'll take you to Whitby. You'd love it. Goths and amazing jet and fantastic chips too. Please come.'

Kitty returned to her bench but the look on her face told Petra she was actively considering the invitation. 'Maybe.'

'Name your date!' Petra laughed, excited.

'Next month perhaps? Otherwise it'll have to wait until after Christmas.'

'Oh Kitty, please come.'

'How long are you down for this time?' Gina asked, bringing over a cup of coffee.

'A couple of weeks, actually. I need to get cracking on the bracelet with the three rubies. Where's Eric?'

'Said he'd be in by lunch-time.'

Petra's mobile phone bleeped through a message. 'That'll be him now, probably.'

Mum says pls come 4 xmas

Petra looked at the message and frowned. Who on earth was this? She didn't recognize the number. Was it Tinks, her mother's barking friend? It couldn't be her father, that would make no sense at all. She sent a message back.

Who is this?

There was no reply. Must be the text equivalent of a crossed line, Petra thought to herself. She deleted the message and thought no more of it until her phone bleeped again over an hour later.

It's me

For Christ's sake.

Who's me?

Another interminable wait. Petra was starting to feel irritated.

Arlo u mad woman—who did u think it was?

Petra's fingers felt all thumbs as she tried to scroll through the options on the message to have the number called back instead of replied to by text.

'Hullo?' said Arlo's voice as if he didn't have a clue who'd be ringing him at this time. He was walking between lessons and was eager not to let the boys see him practising what the school preached against during school hours.

'Arlo? It's me. Whose phone is this?'

'It's mine.' He sounded quite put out.

'But you don't have a mobile phone.'

'I do. As of today.'

'But why did you get one?'

There was a pause.

'Because I miss you.' He paused again. 'I miss you when you're not here.'

Petra was in too much of a swoon to be able to answer him.

'Anyway, Mum wanted to know if you'd like to come for Christmas?'

'I'd love to,' said Petra.

'Shall I text her or will you?' Arlo asked.

'You do it,' Petra laughed. 'She'll be amazed.'

*     *     *

A couple of weeks before Christmas, not long after Kitty's visit, Arlo and Petra were down in London again, sitting on Eric's sofa reading the Sunday papers. Or rather Arlo was trying to read the papers while Petra fidgeted.

He peered over the top of one of the supplements and gave her a stern look.

'Are you reading that?' she asked.

459

'I'd like to be,' he said.

She crawled across the sofa and scrunched the paper away from him. 'Can I put something by you?'

'Can I read the papers afterwards undisturbed?'

'Promise,' said Petra. Arlo watched as she drew breath. 'It's just—well, I know what I want to do.' She paused. 'With my tanzanite.'

'I've heard that one before,' Arlo laughed, looking down to the pile of papers, about to retrieve one.

'No—I mean, for good. And it really is for *good*. Remember when Charlton took me to buy the new stone for the original bracelet? And I met those two lovely women in the mad tiny office with the huge cage? Well, one of the women is the administrator for the foundation which ensures all mining is ethical and that a percentage of the industry's annual profits are directed back to the Masai community.'

Arlo wasn't sure where this could possibly be leading.

'There's a small museum,' Petra said, 'near one of the empty mines.' She stopped. Her eyes sparkled. 'I'm going to give them my tanzanite. To put in their museum. That way, Mrs McNeil can return to Tanzania. I've told them they can have it on the condition that it's on permanent display and that it becomes known as the Lillian McNeil Tanzanite.'

\*       \*       \*

Esther Savidge wasn't sure what sort of Christmas Petra was used to or what she'd like so she decided

460

the best thing to do was simply to invite her to partake of a Savidge Christmas. Which probably differed very little to many other Christmases happening across the world. In Potters Bar. Or North Finchley. Or Yarm. Or Brondesbury. Stokesley. New Cross. Hong Kong. Chelsea. Hatton Garden. Even in Watford. Or Kent.

'We usually have goose—is that OK?' she'd said on the phone to Petra.

'It's very OK,' Petra had said.

And it was. It was delicious.

The only aspect Petra hadn't been sure about was the opening of the presents. Traditionally, she liked to rip open her parcels and packages at the crack of dawn. The Savidges, it transpired, opened theirs after lunch. In a calm, controlled manner. Each person opening just one parcel in turn.

A cashmere scarf. Hardbacked novels she'd had her eye on but had been waiting for in paperback. Jo Malone bath oil. A calendar sumptuously illustrated with Joe Cornish photographs of North Yorkshire. A pair of running shoes, because Arlo said she was always going on about getting fit. And an envelope with a 'P' on the front.

She would open that last. Just vouchers or something.

\*        \*        \*

'Is this from you?' she asks Arlo when there's nothing left but the envelope.

He nods.

She slips her finger under the seal and jags it open. She pulls out the contents. A page of A4 paper headed 'ITINERARY'. And two plane tickets.

Destination: Kilimanjaro International Airport. Date: 17 February.

She stares at Arlo.

'It's half-term,' he shrugs nonchalantly as if it's on a par with a weekend away in the Cotswolds. 'I thought we ought to accompany the Lillian McNeil Tanzanite home.'

She throws her arms around his neck while Esther claps her hands in delight.

Petra glances down the itinerary again, absorbing more information this time. There's a six-day trek to Kilimanjaro, to watch dawn break from the peak on 23 February.

Tears are in her eyes. It's all so unbelievable. But actually, it's very real because it says so in black and white on the A4 paper in her hand.

Arlo has one final surprise in store for Petra, though she claims not to like surprises. But this one is a question he's intending to pop when they've reached the summit of Kilimanjaro, that mountain of Petra's daydreams. And though Arlo knows how Petra will answer, he can't wait to ask her anyway.

# AUTHOR'S NOTE AND ACKNOWLEDGEMENTS

Tanzanite is one of the world's most sought-after gemstones. In contrast to the horror and lawlessness in the trade of 'conflict' or 'blood' diamonds, protocols have been established to ensure that all tanzanite is traded through legitimate and transparent channels by licensed dealers. Tanzanite is the only gemstone to be given an official 'clean bill of health' (at the International Gem Convention in Tucson, 2003). To champion tanzanite's heritage and safeguard its integrity, the Tanzanite Foundation was established as a non-profit, industry-supported organization.

The Tanzanite Foundation carefully monitors methods of practice and conduct and works to maintain the integrity of tanzanite's route-to-market while highlighting the importance of social consciousness and ethical methods of operation. Committed to making a real difference to the lives of the local community at tanzanite's source, the foundation funds social and economic upliftment. Initiatives are meaningful and sustainable and, to date, include a medi-clinic, a community centre, the Nasinyai Primary School and a new secondary school, infrastructural upgrades to the roads, the Small Mines Assistance Programme, and fresh water supply to 2,000 villagers and 4,500 head of cattle.

I am indebted to Alex Duxbury and Gabriella Endlin at the Tanzanite Foundation for letting me spend many an absorbing hour in their company, for providing me with fascinating research material and for allowing me sit in 'the cage' surrounded by stunning tanzanites. Thank you so much.

\*      \*      \*

From Hatton Garden to Runswick Bay, researching *Pillow Talk* was a real treat—a true perk of my job. I'm so grateful to Dan and the staff at Bellore (39 Greville Street, London EC1N 8PJ, www.bellore.co.uk); also to Louise Fennell, Sean Leane, Ana de Costa, Andrew Howe at Wright & Teague, Kate Reardon, Petra Bishai and her students at Kensington and Chelsea College— thank you all for letting me natter and/or loiter.

Special thanks to Sam Barbic for so generously opening the door to her somnambulant world and allowing me to peep inside and poke around. Here's to a good night's sleep.

To Nigel and Jennifer Garton—thank you for the loan of your names and your fantastic hospitality Up North.

\*      \*      \*

When I was at school, the teachers often complained about my propensity for day-dreaming. Nowadays, part of my job requires me to do just that! However, my words would be stuck in the clouds, or confined to my laptop at the very least, were it not for the expert collaboration of the skilled team supporting me.

My heartfelt gratitude to everyone at my publishers, HarperCollins—particularly to Lynne

Drew my brilliant editor and pal, Claire Bord and Victoria Hughes-Williams; to Amanda Ridout; to Lee Motley; to Damon Greeney, Karen Davies and Sylvia May; to Elspeth Dougall, Wendy Neale and Clive Kintoff; to Leisa Nugent and Lucy Upton; to Marie Goldie and the Glasgow crew.

However, were it not for my wise and wonderful agent, I'd be stuck for a publisher—I am thus indebted to Jonathan Lloyd a.k.a J.Llo, at Curtis Brown Ltd, and to Alice Lutyens and Camilla Goslett who summon Mr Lloyd from Very Important Meetings and Very Long Lunches when I want to speak to him. Mary Chamberlain, my diligent copy-editor, and Sophie Ransom, my industrious publicist, complete Team North.

My thanks to all of you, for the support, the fun—and the success.

\*       \*       \*

To Haringey Library Services, particularly Susan, Hilary, Germaine and Lai-Ming, thank you for my magical space and those much appreciated cups of coffee.

Thank you, Jonny Zucker, for the Fabs and Minstrels and office goss.

Behind the scenes and after office hours, my warmest thanks to the Cohens, the Sutcliffes and Jerney de Vries. Also to the Earls Farm savvy club, especially Souki, Sue and Sarah.

\*       \*       \*

Finally, to Jo and Luce and Kirsty and Sarah (again), to Kle and Jeanette and Cousin Kate and

Melanie and Karen. When it comes to friendship, you are priceless gems and I love you.

*     *     *

www.cancerresearchuk.org (in memory of my beautiful friend Liz Berney, 1968–2005)

*     *     *

www.rhysdanielstrust.org